# enduring
## Light

# enduring
# Light

*a novel*

# CARLA
# KELLY

bonneville books
an imprint of cedar fort, inc.
springville, utah

ISBN 13: 978-1-59955-984-1

Published by Bonneville Books, an imprint of Cedar Fort, Inc.
2373 W. 700 S., Springville, UT, 84663
Distributed by Cedar Fort, Inc., www.cedarfort.com

LIBRARY OF CONGRESS CATALOGING-IN-PUBLICATION DATA

Kelly, Carla, author.
  Enduring light / Carla Kelly.
     pages cm
  Includes bibliographical references and index.
  Summary: A newlywed couple struggles with the hardships of maintaining a ranch in Wyoming in the early 1900s.
  ISBN 978-1-59955-984-1 (alk. paper)
  1. Mormons--Wyoming--Fiction. 2. Ranching--Wyoming--Fiction. 3. Domestic fiction. I. Title.
  PS3561.E3928E53 2012
  813'.54--dc23
                                    2011040691

Cover design by Angela D. Olsen
Cover design © 2012 by Lyle Mortimer
Edited and typeset by Melissa J. Caldwell

Printed in the United States of America

10 9 8 7 6 5 4 3 2 1

*To Laura Lee Wilkinson*

who loves a cowboy, ranching, and Wyoming

❦✎❦

*W*hat will give a man joy?
That which will give him peace.

—*Brigham Young*

# Part One

## Salt Lake City

❧ ⨯ ❧

*We have endured many things . . .*

—*13th Article of Faith*

# Prologue

Julia Darling decided after one week at home in Salt Lake City that she preferred her newspaper-covered walls on the Double Tipi. That first night—after the neighbors, the bishop, and the doctor had finally left her in peace—she had closed her eyes in utter exhaustion and wished herself back on the ranch, or even in Cheyenne, just holding Paul Otto's hand.

The reality that he was far away and the ranch house burned to ashes only made her weep. She tried to be quiet, but her tears brought Papa to her side, who sat on her bed and asked so gently, "Where does it hurt, honey?"

*It's my heart*, she wanted to tell him. *It's breaking because Paul is so far away.* All she could do was turn away and make herself as small as she could, almost as though she were trying to crowd herself back into the puny protection of the cut bank, where she had prayed so hard and waited out the firestorm. She stared at her calendar: September 22, 1910. Had the fire only been one week ago? Why did she feel so old?

Mama understood. She came in the room next and knelt beside her bed. "It's not your shoulder, is it?" Mama had said.

"I need Paul," was all Julia could say.

She started to cough, and Mama carefully wiped away the ash that the doctor had said Julia would be coughing up for a few more days. She heard her parents whispering together, and then Papa left the room. Mama climbed in

3

bed with her, much as Julia had comforted her last Christmas, after Iris's death.

"I know you need him," she agreed. "I would too if I were you."

Julia's hand went to her closely cropped hair. "Except I'm a freak."

She felt Mama's chuckle rather than heard it. "That's a bit dramatic, my dearest! The rest of your hair was just too burned and brittle, or I wouldn't have cut it so close. It'll grow back, sooner than you think."

Julia felt the pressure of Mama's arms, gentle around her shoulder. "We nearly lost you." Mama's voice faltered. "I can't bring myself to think about it." She kissed her. "Just rest now. You're home and safe. Paul will keep."

Mama stayed with Julia until she pretended to sleep, then kissed her again, and left the room. When Julia heard her footsteps fade down the hall, she turned onto her back, gritting her teeth from the dull throb in her shoulder. She touched her fingers to her neck, wincing at the pain from the burn. Her hand moved lower to her breast and then to her ribs, where the burn finally stopped. Too bad she couldn't have crowded her whole body into the cut bank. She closed her eyes against the memory of the flaming branch crashing on her.

She sighed and opened her eyes to stare at the ceiling. "Paul, what must you think of me now?" she asked herself.

She forced herself to breathe steadily and slowly, as the doctor recommended. All she could do then was what she had done through that horrible summer on the Double Tipi, even when she had so foolishly thought, at first, that Heavenly Father wasn't listening.

"Father, this is hard," she prayed, barely moving her lips. "Comfort me, Jesus," she whispered. "Paul too."

The house was quiet. As she lay there in complete misery, she gradually relaxed. Her eyes began to close. She thought she heard singing from far away, low but reassuring, a passable baritone.

"Dear Evalina, sweet Evalina, my love for thee will never, never die."

# One

*J*ulia thought she was prepared for her first long look. For a month, she had avoided looking in the mirror, not ready to face a ruin. It was amazing how she could avoid looking in the bathroom mirror. The floor-length mirror in her bedroom was easy to ignore, since she had tilted it down and pushed it away with her foot. The scars on her chest were mostly covered because she had always been a modest dresser. She just hadn't been ready to stare into a mirror.

Her greatest relief came the day in late October when Doctor Evans unwound the bandage holding her arm to her side and lifted it from the sling. On his approval, she cautiously flexed her arm.

"Be wary, Julia," he told her. "If it happens once, a dislocation can happen easier the next time, and this was a bad one. Your doctor in Wyoming did some rough and ready work, but I can't fault him at all. Still, it was a tough dislocation."

She even managed a joke. "You should see Doc McKeel with livestock."

"Talented fellow."

Julia took a deep breath. "What about my scars?"

He had trouble meeting her eyes and took a long moment, as though considering what she wanted to hear.

*Just the truth, doctor*, she thought, her eyes on his. "Tell me."

"They're yours to keep," he said at last. "They'll fade more, but that's all."

She nodded. "My hair?"

He smiled. "Coming in curly, my dear. That happens sometimes. Maybe you'll start a trend."

"Unlikely," she replied, thinking of her lovely long hair, so easy to sweep up into an elegant pompadour. "I look like someone's little brother."

Drat if he didn't keep smiling. *That's what happens when your doctor is also your uncle*, Julia thought sourly.

Decidedly unprofessional, he kissed her cheek. "Jules, you'll do. I'm happy to report that you are completely sound and just have to get used to a few scars." He shook his finger at her, but his eyes were kind. "What's this about not going to church all these weeks? Time to get outside, Jules. That's my prescription."

He was right; she knew it. After Uncle Evans left, Julia went to the window, looking down with a half smile. She sat in her window seat, enjoying the new freedom of pulling her knees to her chin and wrapping both arms around her legs, now that the sling was gone.

Her smile left as she watched two neighbor girls across the street. They were returning from the stake academy, their hats wide and fashionable—just the kind that Paul always said scared horses—and their hair abundant underneath. She fingered her little curls, supremely dissatisfied.

"Now or never, Julia," she said as she stood up and pulled her mirror away from the wall. Still not looking, she tipped up the glass and stepped back. She knew what she looked like, but there was something so honest about a mirror, which reflected what others—Paul, in particular—would see.

She couldn't help her gasp. *When did I get so thin?* she thought, then reminded herself how Mama had been coaxing her to eat.

That was nothing compared with her hair, growing in wildly curly. Her eyes wide and shocked, she thought of when she was five and determined to follow her older brothers everywhere, even though they called her the Wild Woman of Borneo. Now she was exactly that.

Her curls paled into nothing when she saw her neck, with its red crisscross of scars from that burning branch. She stared, then slowly unbuttoned her shirtwaist, letting it fall to the floor. She undid her chemise and removed it.

A sob escaped as she scrutinized her left breast, where, after her shoulder, the branch had struck the hardest before it glanced off her rib cage. Her other breast was completely normal, which made the scarred one even more grotesque to her horrified eyes. She raised her left arm, careful not to move quickly. Her shoulder felt tight, but there was no real pain. She turned sideways, watching the burns continue their webbed way toward her back.

Grim, Julia faced the mirror again, looking at herself. She pulled on her chemise and picked up her shirtwaist, buttoning it slowly, her eyes on the scars on her neck, but her mind on the scars below. Only Paul would see those after they were married. If they married. There, she had thought the unthinkable.

*I can't do this to you*, she thought, *not when you have been through so much. I can't. After all the sorrow and regret of Katherine, you deserve better than scars and silly hair.*

Julia sat down at her desk and waited for her mind to settle. When she was calm, she pulled out a sheet of stationery. She dabbed at the tears, blowing the stationery until it dried. She picked up her fountain pen, took a deep breath, and started to write.

She knew from experience how long it took a letter to get from Salt Lake City to Gun Barrel, Wyoming, but she also knew how long it could sit in the post office until someone from the Double Tipi took the time to ride so far for mail. She didn't really expect an answer; she had made herself perfectly plain that it was best he forget about her. With all his worry over finding his scattered stock, dealing with a complicated fall roundup, building another house, and preparing for winter, she was just one more aggravation. She would understand if he didn't reply.

A week after she had mailed the letter to Paul, Julia managed church for the first time since her return to Salt Lake. Mama had found a perfectly darling bonnet at Auerbach's that helped her spirits, even if it did nothing to hide her mass of little curls. A new dress, a lovely deep green, had been a pleasure to pull over her head, even if she had to ask Papa to bore another hole in the belt to make up for the weight she had lost. Her friends and neighbors seemed glad to see her. No one had stared, and not even the little boys giggled.

She would have felt more at peace, but there was Ezra Quayle, her former fiancé, with his new wife, obviously in the later stages of pregnancy. Her own heart parched, Julia watched as he kept his arm so protectively around her and wondered why he had not been so demonstrative when he was engaged to her and not that little snip from Murray.

The thought came to her after the sacrament that quite possibly Ezra had been just as relieved to quit their engagement as she was, but was too much of a gentleman to do so. This idea earned a wry smile from her. *We would never in a thousand years have suited each other*, Julia thought.

Papa had a meeting after church, so she walked home arm in arm with Mama, almost content.

Almost.

She had managed that first Sunday meeting. She was almost cured of standing in the parlor and facing northeast, toward Wyoming. Now she had to stop staring at her scars in the mirror each night before pulling up her nightgown. Maybe this was a good time to visit her brothers in St. George, she pondered a week later, after she had indulged in her nightly tears, prayed for Paul, and got up off her knees.

Tonight's reading in the Book of Mormon had been especially difficult. She had been reading steadily and was now on her second visit to Mosiah. She had thought about avoiding chapter eighteen, but she knew if she was ever going to be content, she had to read it. She could try not to remind herself about "mourning with those that mourn, and comforting those that stand in need of comfort," even if it had been the verse that brought Paul to her last Christmas after Iris died and she needed him even more than she knew. Better just read it, get it over with, and remember that people read it every day without remorse or the wish—almost overwhelming some days—that Paul would come now, when her need was even greater.

"It's been two weeks, almost three now. He must have seen the sense in what you wrote," Julia whispered to herself that night. "You know it's what you want."

She turned onto her side, curling up in the little ball that she couldn't seem to avoid, after that harrowing time in the cut bank. She wondered if Blue Corn had showed up yet in the tack shed, signaling winter in Wyoming. She thought about the men eating out of cans again and turned her face into the pillow.

In all the time since her return, she had not cooked anything. Mama had found another copy of the *Boston Cooking-School Cook Book* to tempt her and had bought more measuring cups and spoons. Maybe a visit to St. George *would* help.

*I have my memories*, she told herself. *That will do*. She closed her eyes to force sleep, but all that did was burn Paul's image in her mind: Paul sitting so straight on Chief; Paul's brown eyes, infinitely more interesting that her blue ones, even if they could bore a hole through someone he didn't like; Paul's black hair, enviably straight, with just a hint of reddish brown; his elegant handlebar moustache he had probably cultivated years ago to make him look older, but which served as a pleasant contrast to high cheekbones. Most of all, she thought of the little wrinkles around his eyes, the wrinkles of a man who spent his working days outdoors, facing into Wyoming wind and sun. Funny how they softened when he smiled at her. And who would have ever suspected that thin, slightly turned down lips were attractive? Probably only all her Scots ancestors. From somewhere in paradise, they must be enjoying every minute of Paul Otto.

*Stop it, Julia*, she told herself wearily. *Just turn over and go to sleep.* She wanted to turn over, but her shoulder still hurt too much. *Please let this pass*, she thought.

She opened her eyes to stare at the ceiling, imagining Paul's hands on her head this time, hearing his blessing beside the river. Only then could she let go of the terror and sleep as the reality of that desperate blessing continued to give her peace.

Julia woke up late. She put her hands behind her head—she enjoyed doing that again, without so much pain—and let the day come peacefully. A slight smile on her face, she listened to Papa whistling in the bathroom as he shaved. Mama must already be downstairs, because the smell of bacon drifted up to her room. She sniffed appreciatively, surprised that her mouth was watering. Maybe she would get up the nerve soon to make cecils in tomato sauce for her father. He had asked for them several times but stopped because his request made her cry.

A few minutes later, she heard Papa's usual knock on

her door and knew he was passing by on his way downstairs. She smiled again at his "Up you get, Julie Jules," a mainstay from her childhood.

Julia sat up in bed. It was time for Mama to take the broom from the closet and tap on the kitchen ceiling, always the signal for her and Iris to get out of bed and hurry downstairs. With a sudden pang, she remembered her brothers groaning in the next bedroom—long unoccupied now—and dragging themselves downstairs. *I do need to see them*, she thought, getting out of bed.

Mama didn't bang on the ceiling. Julia got up anyway, hurrying through the usual bathroom rituals and putting on her robe, the one that mercifully tied at the neck and hid nearly everything. She was looking under her bed for her slippers when she heard someone taking the stairs two at a time. She stood up, frowning, and wondered what had happened belowstairs to upset the usual routine.

Julia gasped when her door banged open and Paul Otto stood there. Her hand to her mouth, she stared at him.

His eyes started at her head, which made him smile. She felt her breath coming in little pants, her eyes on his as they traveled the length of her. In complete silence, he came closer to her. She saw how poorly he was dressed and knew he hadn't had a moment to think about new clothes. Everything he owned had burned up in the fire. He had at least a two-day growth of beard, and his hair was long around his ears. She wondered what the other passengers on the Overland Express must have thought about sharing their railroad car with a Wild Man from Borneo.

She held her breath when he slowly undid her robe and let it drop from her shoulders. She tried to cover her nightgown front with her hands, but he gently lowered them to her sides and unbuttoned her nightgown. As she watched, transfixed, he carefully pulled the fabric back from her scarred shoulder.

He spoke then, and his voice sounded rusty, as though he were the one just waking up and not her. "My love, did you honestly think I would love you less?"

With a sob, Julia threw herself into his arms. He laughed and staggered, then plopped down with her on the bed. She didn't even try to stop him from kissing her then, because that would have been pointless. It would have been equally pointless not to kiss him back, because she had never wanted to kiss someone so much in her life as Paul Otto.

She clung to him, gathering as much of him as she could hold and discovered that he was doing that precise thing too, only more gentle about it as he tried not to hurt her shoulder.

"I do not feel comfortable or satisfied or remotely content unless you are right beside me," he said at last, holding her off a little and then pulling her close again. "Even if you hadn't sent that blamed letter, every single hand on the Double Tipi—and I include the always-forgiving James—would have tossed me on that train anyway."

It was her turn to pull back. "I am a mess and a ruin."

He hugged her. "Yeah, I know. Then why on earth can't I keep my hands off you?"

"You're a lunatic?"

"Nope. I am of sound mind and way-too-sound body. Face it, Darling: I love you."

He kissed her again, then took his hand off her hip. "Oops," he said. "I'd better slow down. There's no line shack anymore."

Julia unwound herself from the man she couldn't manage without and sat beside him on her bed. She opened her mouth, and Paul put his fingers over it.

"Don't try to reason with me or think there is

anything that will make me love you less."

"My hair? I don't know what to do. It's so curly."

He grinned and rubbed his hand in her hair. "It sure is. I'm having a hard time keeping my hands out of it, but maybe that's a better idea than on your hip, eh?"

"My neck, my shoulder. They're so . . ."

He nuzzled her neck. "I've been wanting to do that for months and months. Tell me when to stop."

Julia pulled away, unable to help her tears.

"Hey now," Paul said, serious. "Two days ago, Doc and I were in Gun Barrel with the team to pick up a load of lumber for the house—our house. There was your letter. I read it and got on the train, all in the space of about fifteen minutes, so you have to take me as I am too. Julia, I love you."

She couldn't help from leaning against him. "Paul, you don't know the extent of my scars. They go . . ."

"All the way to your waist," he said simply. "Darling, you wouldn't let go of my hand on that train ride to Cheyenne. You clamped on like rigor mortis when we took you to the Gillespies'. Who do you think got you out of your burned clothing? Emma and I—because you wouldn't let go! I know exactly how extensive those burns are. Funny how it doesn't make any difference to me."

Her face fiery red, Julia closed her eyes. Paul kissed the top of her head. "I didn't want to tell you, because I knew you'd be embarrassed. Now you know. Julia, those scars don't matter to me. Only to you, I think." He chuckled. "Quit worrying about them."

Paul tightened his arm around her and put his lips close to her ear. "'Way down in the valley where the lily first glows,'" he sang softly. "'Where the wind from the mountain ne'er ruffles the rose, lives sweet Evalina, the dear little dove, the child of the valley, the girl that I love.'"

He was starting the chorus when Julia kissed him.

"Either that's my reward, or you wanted to stop the flow," he said in her ear when he could speak.

"You know," she said, her voice quiet.

They sat together in silence for a long time. Julia finally gave a shuddering sigh and turned her face into Paul's sleeve. "I won't write another letter like that. I promise."

"I'm relieved," he said and kissed her curls again. He sniffed the air. "I like bacon, but I'm putting in a request for cecils in tomato sauce this morning. Your mother said you haven't felt like cooking, but I want cecils."

Julia pushed the little bundles of meat and onion around in the frying pan. She had tried to convince him to let her get dressed first, but he had merely helped her into her robe again and took her arm as they went downstairs together. She did send him back upstairs for her slippers, while Papa hid behind the *Deseret News* and tried not to laugh.

"Paul wants cecils. It's high time I started cooking again," Julia said to the wall. "Don't you dare laugh, Papa."

Paul ate his way steadily through her outpouring of cecils, concluding with a discreet belch. Julia sat beside him and watched him eat, which made him smile. "She does that, you know," he said to her mother, who nodded.

"How bad is the food on the Double Tipi now?" Julia asked.

"Could be worse," Paul said as he chased the last bit of cecil with a piece of toast. "My cousin Charlotte from the Fort Washakie Rez is cooking for us." He caught her skeptical glance. "No fears. She learned to cook at an Indian school in Kansas, and *not* from Little River."

"But where is she . . ."

". . . living? In a corner of the new tack room." He smiled. "Blue Corn is already in residence in the old tack room, which means . . ."

". . . winter is here," Julia finished, a frown on her face. "It's . . ."

". . . early," Paul said.

"Impressive," Jed Darling said, pushing back from the kitchen table. "You finish each other's sentences already. It took your mother and me ten years to start doing that. Better marry him, Jules."

"I think I will, since he probably won't let me do anything else."

"Dead on." Paul looked at Mama. "After I take a bath in your wonderful indoor bathroom with hot running water on demand, do you think I could persuade your lovely daughter to take me to—what is that alphabet place?—for some clothes?"

"Oh, but . . . ." Julia began, feeling the familiar fear in her stomach again.

"I also need to at least order an impress-Julia suit, since mine burned up," he said, still looking at her mother. His voice faltered then. "After all, I lost everything in that fire except my Darling."

They all sat there, silent. Her eyes brimming again, Julia looked around the table at the people dearest to her in all the world: her mother and father, who went through worse last year with Iris's death; and Mr. Otto, who had dropped everything and came to put the heart back into her, because he was not inclined to forget Mosiah Eighteen. She took Paul's hand.

"It's ZCMI, and yes, I'll . . . I'll take you there."

The hardest part was getting on the trolley. Church hadn't been this hard, mainly because she knew everyone in the ward, and they knew what had happened to her. The trolley was filled with strangers.

She tried to hang back. Without breaking his stride, Paul put his hands on her waist and lifted her onto the trolley platform. His only comment when they sat down was that she was cutting off the circulation to his fingers.

She knew it wasn't proper, but she leaned close so she could speak in his ear. "They're all staring at me," she whispered.

"You're wrong," he whispered back. "I look like a wild man because my hair's too long, and Doc's clothes never did fit. They're wondering what on earth such a pretty lady, neat as a pin, is doing with a Genuine Article."

She looked out the window. "You're a no hoper."

"That's supposed to be a revelation?" he asked, which only made her shake her head and loosen her grip a little.

First stop was Papa's barbershop next to ZCMI. "Thank goodness," Paul said as he sat down. "Now I can read those back issues of *The Police Gazette* that you banned from the ranch house."

Julia laughed and pointed to the magazine pile. "You're out of luck, cowboy. Just a stack of *Improvement Eras* and *Juvenile Instructors*! This is Utah."

"I call that free agency and how to enforce it," he muttered.

He wasn't deceiving her. *And I thought I couldn't love you any more than I loved you before breakfast*, she thought as she took a deep breath and released his hand. "Tough. I'll be next door in Housewares. It's at the back of the store. Look for all the ladies."

"I swore I'd never go in Housewares again, after that department store in Denver," he told her, rising as a barber pointed to an empty chair.

"I guess you'll have to force yourself," she replied. She grinned at him. "Do you think that barber drew the short straw and got you?"

She left the barber shop smiling.

Tidy, shorn, well-groomed, and making Julia's stomach flutter even in Housewares, Paul hesitated at the department entrance, then plunged in with that same resolution she had seen on his face when he shod horses. She put him out of his misery and took his arm, leading him toward Men's Ready-to-Wear.

"You're on your own here, cowboy," she said. "I know you can't buy a ready-made suit, but you can get everything else. You'll find me in Millinery." She kissed his cheek when he sighed. "Be brave."

He was, coming toward her in Millinery an hour later. She waited just outside the department, feeling charitable enough to spare him more hats and ladies. He was dressed in a new shirt, a tie as dignified as one of her father's, wool trousers, and a vest. "I threw away everything except my boots and hat," he told her. "The suit—it's black—won't be ready for two weeks, so save it for me for Christmas." He looked over her shoulder at the hats, and his eyes narrowed in a familiar, determined way. "Now *that's* what I like. Julia, I'm going in there. Don't try to prevent me. I insist."

Not sure whether to laugh or gape, she followed him into Millinery, stopping with him in front of a little feathery hat in handsome bronze tones, perfect for fall.

"That one," he told her and nodded to the clerk. "You won't scare a single horse, and it'll show off your pretty eyes. That's the one. I can't see your face under that big brimmed thing."

She hardly breathed as he took off her big hat, the one that hid her wild curls. He gave it a backhanded toss toward Ladies Foundations and set the little hat on her head, tipping it at a rakish angle. "Perfect," he said, stepping back. "You are the loveliest lady."

Julia swallowed and pressed her lips tightly together. *I must have been an utter angel in the premortal existence, to deserve this man*, she told herself. *And I thought I couldn't love him any more than I just did in the barbershop*. She took a deep breath and stood still while he whisked out a new handkerchief and dabbed at her eyes.

They had lunch with Papa at his favorite café, then Paul left her to guard all his purchases while he spent a few minutes with her father in his office in Zions Bank. *I am so vain*, she thought as she sidled toward a teller's booth where she could see her reflection in the glass and the new hat. She turned this way and that, admiring herself.

"I thought you were supposed to guard my jeans, shirts, and drawers over there," Paul said, coming up quietly behind her. He looked at her reflection too. "And here you are, peacocking in a bank." His hand went to her waist. "Nice," was all he said, but it was enough.

She started toward the trolley stop when they left the bank, but Paul took her hand. "One more store, Darling," he told her. "I know you're starting to droop, but I'm only going to be here three days, and this won't wait."

Her breath started to come in gasps when he stopped in front of a red brick building with Daynes and Sons Jewelry in gold scrollwork above the entrance. "Paul, you're not going to . . ."

"I am." He tightened his grip on her arm when she drew back.

"The fire! Your cattle! A house to build!" Julia exclaimed. "Two Bits!"

He laughed out loud and tugged down the little brim of her hat until she had to hang onto it with both hands. "What the Sam Hill does our tailless cat have to do with a jewelry store? Darling, you will never cease to amaze me." He gave her a little push in the small of her back toward the entrance. "Ah. Two Bits. I forgot to tell you. I retrieved him from the Marlowes, and he is now king of all he surveys in the bunkhouse." He kept steering her. "He mopes around, looking in dark corners for you and whining. Doc says I do much the same thing."

Julia couldn't help laughing, then made another attempt to be stern with her man. "Mr. Otto! Do be serious! You can't afford to waste money on a ring. It couldn't have been a good roundup this fall."

"I've had better cow gathers," he agreed. *Mr. Otto?* Before getting on the train to Cheyenne, Mr. Otto swooped down on the First National Bank of Gun Barrel and robbed it."

"Do be serious!"

"I am! Trust me. The banker was only too happy—you know how he likes me—to write out a whopping cashier's check, which now resides in Zions Bank." His expression changed then, when hers didn't. He put his hands gently on her shoulders. "I can see that you're going to be surprised in a few months when you are Mrs. Otto and discover you're married to a pretty juicy stockman. Darling, I'm good for it, and I didn't rob the First National."

He held the door open and gave her a final push. She watched, astounded, as two sales clerks made a beeline toward Paul Otto, reminding her of her first day in Gun Barrel, when everyone deferred to him. She looked at Paul, wondering for the umpteenth time what force he exerted in restaurants, banks, and shops. He strode purposefully toward the display cases.

"What shall we show the little lady?" said the clerk who beat his colleague in a dignified dash.

"Whatever she wants." Paul smiled at Julia. "Give her a big choice. That's all she ever wanted in an engagement ring."

"You remembered," she whispered.

His lips were close to her ear. "I'm a whole lot brighter than Ezra Quayle."

## Two

$\mathcal{P}$aul was far better looking, but Julia already knew that. Still, it was nice to stand at the Majestic next morning, keeping an eye on the French toast Paul had requested and another eye on him. There hadn't been anything wrong with her former fiancé's appearance, but Ezra had never made her look twice and then look again.

There he sat, leaning back in his chair, smiling at her with that twinkle in his eye that made the heat rise from somewhere in her stomach to turn her face rosy—and she knew she couldn't blame the cooking range. She looked away, thinking of the times he hadn't looked so self-assured, and then looked back. He winked a slow wink that made her wish for their wedding day to come quickly.

"I think it's done, Jules," Mama said. Julia returned her attention to the French toast.

Everyone had their slices, and Papa had just finished the blessing when the doorbell rang. Mama excused herself. When she returned, she had a little box, which she handed to Paul.

"They were quick," he said, opening the package and taking out a little box.

Julia held her breath, thinking one last time of all the reasons why none of this was reasonable, and rejected every one. If she had foolishly wanted to be forever beautiful for the man she loved, she knew, looking into his eyes, that she already was. And if Paul, with his own doubts and remorse for things in the past, felt for one second that he should not move ahead, she would have seen it in his eyes. All she saw was love, and it calmed her as nothing else could. It must have been a powerful look she gave Paul, because Papa stood up and took Mama's hand. "Maude, I think we need to take a little walk to the end of the block. Let's see if the houses on the next street are still standing," he said.

"Let's do that, Jed," Mama said. "I've been worried about those houses."

Papa clapped Paul on the shoulder and gave him a little shake. "Someday, you'll have to tell me how you got J. Fred Daynes—I know him well—to set a stone on such short notice. What did you say?"

Paul shrugged. "I just asked. Nothing special."

"He has a way, Papa," Julia said, surprised at how feeble her voice sounded just then. "I've decided to accept it."

"A ring or my way?" Paul teased.

"Both, to spare you any possible disappointment," she replied calmly. "Please pass the maple syrup. I want it to be good and soaked in."

He smiled that slow, edgy smile and handed over the maple syrup. His hand was rock steady, but hers was already shaking. With a chuckle, he helped her pour on the maple syrup, then set it down and took her hand. "Sticky," he said, then licked her finger, which did nothing to calm the jitters in her stomach.

Then she was in his arms. "I would have done this without a ring, you know," she said as her hands went to his face.

He kissed the palms of her hands. "Still sticky. I know. You'd have done it if I had lost every cow, the ranch, and if the bank blew up. And I'd still have asked you."

"Better get about it then," she said, her voice soft. "Don't bother to kneel, please. I think that's silly."

With another smile that made her heart stand still, he opened the little box and took out her ruby ring. "Marry me, Julia," he said, and there was no question. "Marry me forever."

"I will, Paul. Forever might be long enough." She leaned her forehead against his chest and gathered him close. "We'll have to wait and see, I guess."

"Actually, I need your hand right now," he told her.

She obliged, holding her left hand close. He slid on the beautiful ring. "Definitely rubies," he said. "You have excellent taste in men and jewelry."

He kissed her then, his hand gentle on her wounded neck, and then he just held her. She let him, her arms tight around him too.

There was nothing to fear in church this time, not with Paul beside her in the pew. She wore her stylish little hat and held her head high, unconcerned about her short hair. She didn't think about her scars until they started to itch and there was no discreet way to scratch them.

She couldn't avoid looking at Ezra Quayle and his wife sitting two pews closer to the front. Funny she hadn't noticed last week that he was getting pudgy. Julia glanced at Paul's lean stomach and smiled to herself. She knew she had a prettier engagement ring than Sister Quayle (even Mama couldn't remember her first name. "She's just not memorable," Mama had told her), because she had worn that same ring a year ago.

She liked the way Paul just rested his arm across the back of the pew behind her shoulders, barely touching her, unlike Ezra, who had a real grip on his wife. *Maybe he's afraid she'll bolt the room if he lets go*, Julia thought. *He always was a bit of a manager.* Julia noticed her father's amused glance as he sat next to her and decided she had better concentrate on the bishop's talk. She wouldn't put it past Papa to quiz her about the talk, once they had returned home as he used to do when she was ten and not paying attention.

But maybe Papa wasn't going to scold. He whispered, "Happy, Jules?"

She nodded.

He leaned closer. "Then pay attention!"

She couldn't help it that her shoulders started shaking. She pressed her lips together. Paul leaned closer from her other side and whispered to them both "Do I have to sit between you two?"—which made Papa's shoulder's start to shake. Mama glared at them all.

Dinner was Welsh rarebit and duchess potatoes, with a tomato aspic, and loaf cake with opera caramel crème frosting to round out the meal—all of Paul's favorite things packed into one sitting, because he was leaving early the next morning. Fannie Farmer would never have approved of that mealtime combination, but Miss Farmer wasn't in love, Julia reasoned.

*Maybe if we eat slower, it will drag out the hours*, Julia thought, dreading tomorrow. She and Papa would have to wave good-bye at the depot, when she wanted to leap on the train and go home to the Double Tipi.

After the last bite, Paul stood up and held out his hand for her. "Dear Darlings, I have a house call to make with my fiancée," he told her parents. "I probably should have paid this call sooner, but I think my time was better spent right here."

Julia looked at him, a question in her eyes, but put her hand in his.

"There was a letter from my Uncle Albert Hickman, along with that letter from you, which we will promptly forget," he said. "He's visiting his son Thomas—that makes Thomas my cousin—who lives only three blocks over. I think he plans to winter there, and he wanted me to know about it."

"Thomas Hickman," Papa said and shook his head. "Oh, the irony of life. I've known Ed—he goes by his middle name—for years. He's in the nearest ward to the east. Right there, all this time."

Paul nodded. "I thought Julia and I would pay a call. Walk with me, Darling."

The familiar fear returned, and he saw it in her eyes. "Hey, now. Uncle Albert saw you when you looked pretty finely drawn, a few months ago."

"I suppose he did," she said. "I don't remember him."

"I doubt you remember anything about that ride on the Overland Express," Papa said, his eyes kind too.

"It's like this, Julia," Paul said as they strolled the three blocks to Ed Hickman's home. "I'm hoping you will visit with Uncle Albert between now and Christmas. Your choice, though. I can't say I recall too much about my first meeting with him, either, mainly because I was so worried about you." He stopped. "Still, there was something in his eyes that I can't get out of my mind. I think he has a lot of regrets about what happened all those years ago."

"Maybe you should have stopped by sooner," Julia chided.

"I did, or sort of. I dropped in on them before I invaded your house three days ago." He clapped his arm around her shoulder. "I said hello, told him I had to see my gal, and said I'd be back Sunday afternoon." He shook his head. "I know I startled them by showing up out of the blue, and so early in the morning. Cousin Ed said something about one of the Three Nephites as I left. Any idea what he meant?"

Julia patted his chest. "I'll explain it to you later!"

She remembered Albert Hickman vaguely as one of the heads that seemed to be perched on stalks, looming far above the bed in the Gillespies' house, the morning Papa arrived to take her home. It was good to see him now as a dignified man with a full head of white hair and a smile that reminded her a little of Paul's smile.

"It's nice to see you upright and conscious, Sister Darling," the old gentleman told her as he shook her hand.

"It's nice to be that way, sir," she replied, shy. She reached behind her and took Paul's hand. "I apologize that we have to be reintroduced, but I don't recall much about our first meeting."

"Just as well," he said and showed them into the parlor. "If you don't mind some plain-speaking, fish bait looked better than you did."

Julia burst out laughing and glanced at Paul, who was grinning. "You're kind, my love, but Brother Hickman, *you're* honest!"

The old man took her other hand. "Those are Hickman traits: kindness and honesty. Hopefully your future husband inherited both."

"He did, Brother Hickman." *My future husband*, she thought, transfixed. No one had actually said that before now. Hearing it made the matter somehow official in her mind.

"But please, I'm Uncle Al to you," he was saying. He looked at his son. "Ed tells me that the soon-to-be Darling branch of our family will give us amazing respectability in Utah circles."

"Respectable?" she teased in turn. "Papa would assure you that the Darlings have their share of road agents and irrigation water cheats."

Uncle Al had the most wonderful combination of British Isles brogue and southern Utah twang, Julia decided. *I could listen to you for hours*, she told herself as they sat in the parlor and she let the talk between uncle and long-lost nephew swirl around her.

Julia observed the Hickman men in the room, looking for more resemblance than just a smile. Maybe it was the thin lips, she decided, and certainly the elegant length of their fingers. She had first noticed Paul's hands back when he was still Mr. Otto. Each man was tall and lean, as well.

She spoke up during a lull in the conversation. "Uncle Al, do you have a picture or maybe a tintype of Mary Anne?"

If she had known the old man's blue eyes would suddenly tear up, she never would have said anything. "Sir, I'm sorry to mention her."

"No, no, my dear," he was quick to say. "I've been doing the same thing: looking for a resemblance to my sister. I have a daguerreotype taken before we left Plymouth. We were from Devonshire. Such a lovely place." His voice turned wistful. "So green. And here we are in a desert. Ah, well." He made a visible effort. "May I call you Julia?"

"Certainly."

"Julia, I'll have my daughter in Koosharem send the image to me here, and you can see for yourself." He looked at his nephew. "Paul, you can see it when you return." He bowed his head. "I have so many regrets . . ."

Paul took his hand. "Discard this regret, Uncle: your older sister had a very good life in Wyoming. We all wish it had been longer, but she and my father were happy. You'll have to meet her Shoshone family some day. You'll like them. I know I do."

After a long pause, Uncle Al nodded. "That's something."

"It's everything," Paul said firmly. "I, for one, am glad the way things happened. I wouldn't be here if they hadn't." He touched Julia's cheek. "Maybe you and Julia can get together this fall. Might you tell her what you remember about my mother?"

Julia nodded. "I'll visit." She felt suddenly shy. "If you want me to, Uncle Al."

"More than anything," he said.

They strolled home in the gathering dusk, Paul saying nothing until they were climbing the steps to her front porch. He took her hand and steered her toward the porch swing. Papa had been meaning to put it away for the winter, but it was still there, moving slowly in the slight breeze that had come up.

He tucked her close to him, his arm around her good shoulder, and just pushed the swing with his foot, saying nothing. He didn't have to; she knew what he was thinking.

"It'll pass quickly enough," she told him, when she had noticed him swallow several times. "You'll be back for Christmas. Please bring James too."

He nodded, still unable to speak.

"Relatives do that to me too, sometimes," she said, her hand resting inside his vest, just over his heart.

"There's some real sadness in him," Paul said, his hand over hers. "Find out what you can, Darling." He kissed her. "I'll be counting the days until I see you again. Maybe I can find a respectable calendar somewhere in Wyoming. I doubt it, though."

"I'll send you one!" she said, trying to lighten the mood, even as she wished time would stand still. They sat in the swing until the streetlights came on. Papa came out finally, looked at his watch, and harrumphed a few times.

"I know, I know," Paul said as he stopped the swing. "I'm a desperate rancher, and you're not going to let a desperate rancher stay out too late with your daughter."

"You read my mind, son. Don't forget to put out the cat and lock the door when you come in, Julia."

"Papa, we have never had a cat."

She could still hear her father laughing as he climbed the stairs.

"*We* have a cat," Paul said, amused. "And a burned house, and a pile of lumber now." He sighed. "Julia, when I get home, I'll saddle up and keep hunting for my cattle. I'm going north through Niobrara County this time. My neighbors and I are all taking different directions."

She knew what he was trying to say. "If there's only a one-room house in March—"

"Friday, March 17," Paul interrupted.

"—I don't mind. I draw the line at moving into the bunkhouse, however."

"Horrors," he said. "I'll evict Blue Corn from the tack room, if I have to."

"You won't. One room's enough."

An hour later, she locked the front door, after looking around elaborately for the cat. Paul laughed when she called, "Here, Kitty, Kitty." That only led to another kiss on the stairs and then a long moment holding him.

"That's for stuffing the heart back in my chest," she said finally. "I'll try not to get discouraged."

He kissed her forehead. "If you do, just read the Book of Ether. There are 151 places where it says, 'And it came to pass.' I started counting them, along about Rock Springs."

Julia couldn't sleep that night, but at least in the morning she could report to Paul over bacon and eggs that there were really 152 places. He only grinned and held out his plate for more eggs.

"Charlotte hasn't quite figured out the nuance of fried eggs softer than moccasins, so I need to store up the memory of these little beauties until Christmas," he said, by way of explanation. "Before I leave, tell me, is there any trick to oatmeal I should know about?"

"Nuance?" Papa asked, raising his eyebrows. "Funny,

that isn't a word I probably would ever associate with either Wyoming or the Double Tipi."

"It's pretty slow in the bunkhouse, and I'm a lousy cribbage player," Paul replied. "Doc has a dictionary, and I am up to the N's now."

Julia's oatmeal demonstration, when her folks had wisely left the room, was less than successful, what with Paul looking over her shoulder, then resting his chin on the top of her head, with his hands generally on her waist. "Slow down, cowboy," she said reluctantly.

"Basically I just stir it until it looks like lava?" he asked her neck.

"Mr. Otto, you are incorrigible," she whispered, unable to concentrate on oatmeal.

"Just curious."

"About me or the oatmeal?" she asked.

*If you're trying to distract me from your coming departure, you're doing an excellent job*, Julia thought. She stepped back from the range and fanned herself with her apron when Paul went upstairs for the portmanteau he had purchased at ZCMI to hold his new clothes.

It was snowing when they left the house, the first storm of the season. Papa drove carefully to the depot. Her hand in Paul's, Julia watched the snow drift down on trees still bearing their leaves. She felt his upcoming departure settle around her shoulders like mortar.

Even Paul couldn't work miracles at the train depot. After he shook hands with Papa, who waited in his automobile, and walked with her toward the waiting train, Julia felt herself begin to droop. She envied the couples who were hugging and kissing relatives and getting on the train together.

"It's our turn in March," Paul said, following the direction of her gaze. "I'll turn up like a bad penny a few days before Christmas. With James."

She didn't mean to cry, but it was too much. He held her close as she whispered, "I just don't feel easy with you out of my sight. I wake up every night, thinking about that cut bank and how shallow the water was, and wondering if you had heard the shots I fired. And then I can't sleep again. I can barely breathe." It came tumbling out of her as she sobbed and his grip tightened.

"I didn't know it was that bad, Darling," he said. "I wish you had told me."

"I just couldn't." She shook her head, embarrassed and wondering where her courage was. "What good would it do?" She lowered her voice, not wanting anyone to overhear. "I'm still alone at night, and I'm still afraid."

"We can't speed up the process. You know it's the temple or nothing."

Julia could barely look at him, thinking of all the trouble she was and how little time he had to accomplish so much: find his cattle, build a house, go to church when he could, and get through what was shaping up to be a tough winter. "I know," she said. "I just have to endure."

"*We* have to endure," he said, his voice firm. "Still . . ." He glanced at the conductor, who was pulling out his watch and frowning at them. "Let's see if that Mr. Otto hasn't lost all his charm. Say a prayer, sport."

Julia said her all-purpose, three-word prayer, amending it to "Comfort *us*, Jesus." She watched Paul walk to the conductor, give him that patented, measuring stare she was intimately acquainted with, and hold up five fingers. She couldn't help her smile as the conductor—supreme potentate on the Union Pacific—nodded and pointed to a door slightly ajar. Paul held out his hand for her.

In a moment they were in what looked like an over-grown broom closet.

"What . . . ?"

Paul sat her on a stool next to a wall of janitorial

supplies. "Your middle name's Amanda, isn't it? I didn't bother with the finer points when I did this last summer."

She nodded, already feeling a lift to her spirits. She closed her eyes as Paul took off her hat, the feathery thing he had bought three days ago, put it in her lap, and placed his hands firmly on her curly hair.

"Julia Amanda Darling, by the power of the Holy Melchizedek Priesthood, I give you a blessing of comfort."

His words were quietly spoken, calm and firm, as he blessed her with peace of mind and freedom from fear, and the courage to endure the pain of their separation. He admonished her to think more of others and less of herself. Maybe his words should have stung a little, but they didn't. What he said, what he pronounced on her head, was precisely what she needed. She could only add her prayers to his and draw strength from his resolve, as he had so obviously intended.

When he finished, Paul kissed the top of her head, fingered her curls as though he wanted to imprint that memory in his senses, and rested his hands briefly on her shoulders.

"You okay, sport?" he asked.

She turned around to look him square in the eyes. "Never better."

"I have to catch a train then."

The conductor was still waiting by the passenger compartment. He nodded to Paul. "One minute left," he said, with another nod to Julia and a decided twinkle in his eye.

Paul kissed her. "I'm serious about your curly hair," he whispered. "I really like it short. I'm thinking . . . When ZCMI delivers my suit, just . . . just keep it at the foot of your bed. I'd leave my Stetson too, but the other one burned up. A stockman is *naked* in Wyoming without his lid."

With one last tug at her hair, he got on the train and did not look back. *That's better*, Julia thought. She squared her shoulders, turned around, and left the train depot without a backward glance.

The ride home with Papa was a quiet one. "He gave me a blessing, Papa," was all she said, and maybe all she needed to say. When she got home, she went upstairs into the bedroom across the hall where Paul had stayed. Thank goodness Mama hadn't stripped the sheets from the bed yet. She grabbed the pillow on his bed and pressed her face to it, sighing in relief to breathe in the fragrance of bay rum. She put his pillow on her bed, pressed her face into it, and slept soundly for the first time in weeks. When she woke up, she went to the kitchen and looked around for the replacement cookbook Mama had bought, and which Julia had not the heart to open. She smiled when she found it and flipped to the chapter on cakes.

"Now, what would you like, Uncle Albert?" she asked out loud, turning the pages. She stopped on Lemon Queens, and her mouth started to water. "*I want this, Uncle Albert*," she murmured. "I'll try it on you, and make it for Paul in December . . ." She wavered a moment, because suddenly Christmas seemed almost as far away to her as when she was a little girl, and waiting impatiently for something wonderful under the tree. *I suppose I have not changed much*, she thought next, and her face grew rosy. *I'm still anticipating something wonderful.*

Her resolve returned. Paul had told her to think of others and not of herself. She smiled again. *I'll think of you, Uncle Albert, and maybe only a little of myself, because I want Lemon Queens.*

The Lemon Queens took two days. When she finished the first batch, Julia and her parents ate so many that a gift of Lemon Queens would have looked sadly wanting, even if she had put them on a very small plate.

They were eating those Lemon Queens when the doorbell rang, and Papa answered it, returning with a telegram. "For you, Jules," he said, and there was no disguising the worry on his face. "I hope it's not bad news."

She thought of the telegram announcing Iris's death and nearly handed it back to Papa. She didn't; hadn't Paul admonished her to be a little braver? She reached in her hair for a hairpin to slit open the telegram, before remembering her hair was too short to need them now. Mama handed her one.

The frown left Julia's face as she read the telegram and laughed. "I am marrying a funnier man than I realized." She popped another Lemon Queen in her mouth.

"Read it," her parents demanded.

*Dearest Darling. Stop. I love you. Stop. If I can't find my cattle, we'll hock the ring. Stop. Love, Mr. Otto.* She checked the telegram's place of origin. "Hah! Rock Springs. He's always inspired in Rock Springs!"

They finished that batch of Lemon Queens in relief. She made the next batch in the morning after Papa had left for Zions Bank and Mama had taken the streetcar four blocks over to her usual Wednesday brunch and bridge game. "I'd walk, but look at all this snow!" she had declared as she stuck a hatpin in her new winter hat. She paused, one glove on, her eyes full of sudden anxiety. "Jules, you'll be all right if I leave?"

Until then, Julia hadn't been aware that neither of her parents had left her alone since her return to Salt Lake City. "I'll be fine, Mama," she replied, taking out the hatpin, and setting Mama's hat back on her head at a more jaunty angle. "I'm going to make Lemon Queens for Uncle Albert. You go play bridge and try not to cheat."

It was snowing harder when she set out for the Hickman house, the Lemon Queens secure in Mama's food tote that had seen considerable action at Relief Society bazaars and church socials.

Ed Hickman's wife answered the doorbell. "Sister Darling, we were hoping you would visit again."

"Here I am," she said, holding out the tote. "Lemon Queens."

Sister Hickman took them as Julia removed her coat and shook the snow off it outside on the porch. She hung it on the coat rack, along with her hat, and jumped in surprise when Sister Hickman took her by the arm.

"Miss Darling, I didn't mean to startle you, but I'm relieved to see you here. Since your visit, Father Hickman has been saying how much he wants to return to Koosharem."

"I don't understand," Julia said, puzzled.

Sister Hickman stepped closer and lowered her voice. "He says that, and then he says how much he wants to see you again. We don't know what's troubling him."

"He's probably irritated that Paul and I paid such a short visit on Sunday," Julia said. "Maybe he wants to know about Paul's life on the Double Tipi. I have plenty of stories!"

Sister Hickman ushered her into the parlor, where the old man sat, his feet propped on an ottoman and hands crossed over his stomach. He was frowning at the far wall.

Quietly, she came closer and touched Uncle Albert's arm. "Sir? I thought I'd visit."

She wanted to think his expression was welcoming, but she wasn't certain. He made a visible effort to welcome her and tried to rise.

"Never mind, sir," Julia said. "You look too comfortable to have to get up. Shall I sit here?"

"Do that." He smiled then, and the bleakness left his

eyes. He seemed disinclined to speak, so Julia plunged in.

"Before he left, Paul told me how sorry he was that he couldn't spend more time with you when you came to Cheyenne with my father."

She stopped. Uncle Albert was crying. She reached out her hand. "I know you must have wanted to spend time with your sister's son, but there was so much turmoil then. Is . . . is that it?"

"It goes back a bit farther," he told her. "That letter from your father to me, telling me about Paul's existence, stirred up considerable emotion, as you can well imagine."

"I can."

He was silent again. *What do I say?* Julia asked herself, unsure. She sat back, thinking of Paul's blessing at the train depot. *Others. Think of others and less of myself.*

"Uncle Albert, how about this? Let me tell you about Paul's life on the Double Tipi. I don't want to wear you out, of course, but you might find it interesting. And then maybe on another day, you can tell me about Mary Anne. Paul has told me that she never wanted to talk about—"

"I'm positive she didn't," he interrupted, his British brogue decidedly pronounced. His expression softened then, when he realized he had startled her. "Yes, let's do that, Julia. Tell me about Paul."

"I haven't a more favorite subject," she said, relieved. "Let me start with the advertisement in the *Deseret News* from 'Rancher Desperate.'"

Julia walked home slowly, late that afternoon. The elementary school in the next block was out for the day, so she went to one of the swings on the playground and dusted off the snow. She sat there, turning her face up to the still falling snow, and breathed deeply of the cold air. The Hickman's parlor was too warm, or maybe she had a powerful longing to be sitting on her horse, Paul at her side, riding to the ranch. It was hard to take a deep breath in Salt Lake City, with low clouds that settled in every winter.

Julia thought over what she had told him, remembering how interested he had been when she mentioned James, the little boy who had wandered onto the Double Tipi four years ago during winter. His interest had deepened as she told Uncle Albert how Paul finally deduced that James had been part of a Polish family of homesteaders, burned out of their holdings by stockmen greedy for more land.

She frowned then, recalling how Uncle Albert had almost recoiled when she suggested a comparison between James and Mary Anne Hickman, lost and looking for the handcart company again. Uncle Albert had little to say after that. She had put his silence down to exhaustion at an afternoon of talk and memory, but maybe it was more.

"I told him everything I knew about Paul," she told her parents over leftover Boston baked beans, potatoes en surprise, and Brussels sprouts that evening. "It felt good."

"Did he enjoy hearing about his long-lost nephew's life?" Mama asked as she took Julia's Swiss pudding from the icebox.

"I'm not sure," Julia said, gathering up the dishes. "I hoped he'd want to tell me about his sister's life in England, but he seemed to be almost stalling, because he didn't want to talk."

"It may be a harder subject than we know, Jules," Papa said, after some thought. "Go easy there."

"Why?"

He moved aside the pudding and leaned forward, elbows on the table. "When I was a little boy, we lived a little higher on the avenues. I was home sick one day, and my mother had gone visiting teaching. I wrapped myself in a blanket and sat in my room, looking down on the houses on the other side of the street."

"I've done that," Julia said.

"I knew the people in each house. I knew all about them, or I thought I did." His expression turned faraway. "It had been a tough year in the ward—after all, the ward was my boundary, when I was little. People had died, babies had been born, two families lost their homes to bankruptcy, and one of the widows in the ward committed suicide." He looked at her. "You don't know where I'm going with this, do you?"

Julia shook her head.

"Julia, I stood in the window, looked at the houses, and realized I had no idea what really went on inside them. People can hide big secrets, and we are none the wiser. Go easy."

# Three

Julia went upstairs slowly, thinking about what Papa had said. She opened the door to her room when Mama called up the stairs:

"Jules, Paul's suit came just before you got home. I hung it in the closet in your brothers' room."

Julia went into the room that Paul had used. The new suit hung in the closet, black and totally elegant. She took the suit, hanger and all, and carried it to her room, laying it across the foot of her bed, just as Paul had said. She sat there, her hand on the sleeve, until the room grew dark.

She would have visited Uncle Albert the next day, but it was Relief Society, and Mama had put her on the planning committee for the Christmas bazaar. On Friday, Sister Hickman called to say that her father-in-law was indisposed. Saturday was spent getting ready for Sunday dinner, now that she was cooking again, and Sunday was Sunday.

On Monday morning, Julia took a loaf cake with Paul's favorite opera crème frosting to the Hickmans. She knocked on the door, waited, and knocked again, when no one answered. She had turned to leave when Uncle Albert opened the door.

He looked more cheerful than when she had seen him last. "I made you a cake," she said. "I iced it with Paul's favorite frosting."

"You're going to spoil that boy, you know," he said as he ushered her inside.

"I know. I can't wait."

He laughed, and she relaxed. He pointed to the chair she had occupied on her last visit and took the cake into the kitchen. When he returned, he had herb tea for both of them. "Even after all these years, it's a poor substitute for Earl Grey tea. My dear, once an Englishman, always an Englishman, but rules are rules."

She smiled and accepted the cup and saucer. They sipped in companionable silence, and then Albert put down the cup with a click.

"You would like me to tell you about my sister Mary Anne, would you not?"

"I would. I'm also interested in what it was like to be part of the Willie and Martin handcart companies." She reached in her bag. "If you don't mind, I'd like to take notes. I'm certain Paul wants to hear everything you have to say."

"I will tell you then, but it may surprise you," he said. "I've been thinking about this since our last meeting. I put you off even, and avoided you, because part of this narrative is painful."

"I imagine it is," she said softly.

"Painful in ways you *can't* imagine, believe me," he said. He looked at her. "Are you entirely ready for the truth?"

She hadn't expected that. "Well, yes. Everyone knows how valiant the Willie-Martin handcart pioneers were."

Uncle Albert sighed. "My very dear Julia, can you imagine how hard it is to be the Church's good example of what it is to endure?"

He had her there. "Hmm," was all that came to mind on short notice.

"Let me suggest this: Once begun on some enterprise, whether it is a handcart journey to Zion"—he leaned closer to look into her eyes—"a terrifying time crouched in a cut bank, or childbirth, as my dear wife once pointed out to me, you are compelled to see that enterprise through to the end. Would you agree, Julia?"

"I would," she said, feeling her face grow hot as she remembered, and wondered why he was doing this to her.

"Let me suggest something else. Whether you are lost in the snow"—he stopped for a deep breath—"or about to die in a blaze, you have no agency in the matter beyond this: *how* you endure that trial. Breathe slowly, Julia. It makes it easier. Believe me, I know."

She did as he said. Without even realizing it, she found her hand held tightly in Uncle Albert's grasp.

"I fear that future generations will make us hand-cart survivors into noble icons of suffering. Believe me, Julia, we did complain!" He said that with a twinkle in his eyes that reminded her forcefully of his nephew. "We complained about everything, but there was a certain zeal I would have a hard time explaining to you of this generation." He released her hand and stood up, as though the idea was too big to contain. "We were headed to Zion, and we knew the Lord would help us. In our minds, we were descendants of Moses' Camp of Israel, make no mistake."

"Heavenly Father did help you," Julia said. She stood up and helped him back to his chair, when he appeared to wobble. "I know He did."

"I agree completely. But should we have set out in August, when wiser people told us to wait and travel the next season? Certainly not, but once enterprises begin, they create a life of their own."

He took her hand again as though he needed the comfort this time. "Once the whole thing began to unravel, all we could do was endure."

*I know how that feels*, she thought suddenly.

"Was that how you felt in the cut bank?"

She nodded, and it was a long moment before she

could speak. "I hung on, said my last prayers, and trusted God."

"There it is, the lesson. You turned it over to the Lord."

The room was silent, except for their breathing. "I don't think anyone really understands that, do they?"

He shook his head. "Not until it happens to them, my dear Julia. Some people never learn. Or some people learn and then forget, and that is the danger."

Julia looked down at the tablet in her lap. The page was blank. She couldn't speak, so she wrote, *You endured*.

He shook his head and motioned for the tablet. With a firm stroke, he crossed out the *You* and wrote *We*.

Stunned, she sat back, staring at the sentence. *We endured*. When she spoke, she tried to keep her voice calm. "Uncle Albert, I am *not* on the same level as you in the Willie and Martin companies."

"That's where you're dead wrong, child. You endured."

She couldn't even hear herself breathing now. The only sound in the room was the clock ticking. "I've been such a complainer! My hair is coming in like a wild mop, and my scars are ugly." Julia blushed and was almost afraid to look at Paul's uncle. "I'm used to being the pretty girl. But now . . ."

"You're still the pretty girl." He took her hand. "Paul sees you that way. It's in his eyes when he looks at you. Julia, you and I are survivors. We know more than most, and we have a real stewardship, you and I."

As she sat in the quiet parlor, it became quite clear to her. "What we learned isn't worth much if we don't remember what we learned."

It was her turn to leap to her feet and walk to the window, to look out of it at the snow and think of the cut bank. "I turned it over to the Lord." She didn't try to stop her tears. "I let Him carry the load, because I couldn't. Is that the lesson you want to teach me, Uncle?"

He surprised her again. "Julia, I've been vacillating and agonizing since our last visit. I must be honest: that's the lesson you're teaching *me*."

"*Me?* How could I teach you anything?" Her hand went to her scarred neck.

*Julia, say the right thing,* she told herself. *Heavenly Father, help me to say the right thing.* She closed her eyes and felt Paul's hands on her head by the stream where she lay after the fire, then at the depot only days ago. She chose her words carefully.

"Paul told me of all the remorse he felt about his first wife and remorse at some of his other regrettable deeds." She touched her neck again. "I suppose some scars are on the outside and some are on the inside, aren't they?" She looked at Albert. "I think you need to tell me what happened to Mary Anne."

She knew it was a gamble. Maybe she was totally off the mark. With his hands on her head, Paul had blessed her to think of others. *I'm trying my best, my love,* she thought.

She sighed when Uncle Albert gave her a hard look. *I was wrong,* she thought. *Why did I ask that?*

As she watched, unhappy with herself, he struck an obvious pose, sitting there in his easy chair. "What do you see, Julia? Let me tell you what the good people of Koosharem and now Salt Lake City see: a successful merchant who survived the handcart ordeal. My, isn't he special? What a good man he is!"

She had to remind herself to breathe. In the painful silence that followed, what he was trying to tell her struck home like a lightning bolt. *What scars are you carrying?* she thought and willed him to continue.

The clock seemed to tick louder. Uncle Albert glanced at it, and suddenly deflated; the pose disappeared. "You see a willful boy who teased his sister and was the reason she was left behind and abandoned by the handcart company."

"No!"

"Yes! Mary Anne was fourteen and I was ten." The words came out of him in a rush. "Before she died near Chimney Rock, Mama told Mary Anne to watch over me. It . . . happened before we reached Devil's Gate, where we stopped for good. Mary Anne had scolded me about keeping up, and I was angry with her. I ran away and made her follow me, then ducked behind a snow bank. She kept walking and calling my name, and I went back to the handcart company. The joke was on her. No one missed her until the next day, and no one knew I was to blame."

"Uncle Albert, I am so sorry," Julia whispered. "It's over now." She reached for his hand, but he pulled back.

"No, you need to hear it all. The very last person on earth I ever wanted to see was Paul Otto. His existence has forced me remember what I tried to bury. I even thought I had, until that letter came from your father." He managed a crooked smile. "Paul was so delighted to meet me. He was the last person I ever wanted to see."

Julia gasped as though some cosmic hand had pounded all the air out of her. She sat back in astonishment. She closed her eyes again, saying her little prayer for Albert Hickman this time.

"Surely it wasn't as bad as all that," she said finally, opening her eyes. "You were but a boy and those were desperate times. Surely no one thought harshly of you."

He raised his eyes to hers, and she saw all the misery and the truth. There was no sense in flogging him, because he was doing a good enough job of that, himself. "You never told anyone, did you?" she asked gently. "Am I the first?"

"The second. I told my wife on her deathbed last

year." He shook his head. "She said she loved me anyway. You can tell Paul my story, if you wish. You should, actually."

"He has his own scars on the inside. I know about them, and I don't love him any less."

He let her hold his hand then. They sat together as the afternoon passed. The enormity of what she had heard and what she suddenly knew made her stand in awe of the Lord. How to tell this good man? He was a valued pillar of his community, a priesthood holder, an honored member of the Willie and Martin handcart companies, no matter how cynical he had sounded. She had needed reminding of what she learned in the cut bank, and she needed to tell him and then never forget it.

She picked her words carefully. "Uncle Albert, I'm no Biblical scholar." She laughed softly. "I'm about as far from being a Biblical scholar as you can imagine. Just ask your nephew! But I do know this, and I learned it in a terrible place. I think you learned it too, in a terrible place, but maybe you just need a little reminder. And I need to never, ever forget."

"And that would be . . ."

"Just leave it in the Lord's hands. Give away your scars. That's what the atonement is about, isn't it? Let's make a pact. I'm convinced the Lord has forgotten all about our scars and moved on to bigger matters. I'll forget my scars if you'll forget yours."

To her own ears, she sounded presumptuous. *I'm only twenty-eight, and what do I know?* she asked herself, hoping she had not offended Uncle Albert. She tried again.

"You need to understand this: Mary Anne was found by wonderful people who took her in and loved her. She married a good man from North Carolina who loved her too. Paul is really happy about the way things have worked out for him." She leaned forward and kissed Uncle

Albert. "I am too. If what happened to Mary Anne hadn't happened, I wouldn't be getting married in March to the man I love. That's where it rests, at least, for me."

He gave her a measuring, thoughtful look, which made her heart turn over, because he looked so much like his nephew just then. "So we just leave these little burdens . . ." He let his breath out in a rush, and she understood the gravity of what she was asking. ". . . these little burdens in the hands of the Lord."

"We do because we can." She traced the words on the tablet with her finger, as gently as though she caressed Paul's face. "We endure."

She walked home again in the dusk, staying longer on the playground, smiling to think that someday maybe she and Paul would visit from the Double Tipi and take their little ones to the playground to swing. She pushed herself with one foot, which meant dragging her foot through the snow, and thought of Mary Anne Hickman, calling and calling for her brother.

A month ago, when she was fretting, Mama had suggested rather timidly that things generally work out for the good. Julia closed her eyes and stopped swinging. "I snapped at you, Mama," she whispered, leaning her cheek against the iron chain. "You were right, though."

After a thoughtful evening in the parlor, when she stood by the window and faced slightly northeast, she laughed out loud when Mama smiled at her. She kissed her mother before she went upstairs.

"Thanks, dearest," Julia had murmured.

"For what?"

"For being right. Things do work out."

There wasn't anything to do but cook between now and Christmas, Julia decided the next morning. At the first meeting of the Relief Society bazaar, the committee had promptly put her in charge of cakes and confections.

Papa was quick to notice the difference. When he came into the kitchen a few mornings after her visit to Uncle Albert, he leaped back in mock surprise to see her spinning sugar around a cylinder. He looked around elaborately.

"All right, where have you hidden Julia Darling, who's been frowning at all cookbooks recently?"

She made a face at him and slid the sugar off the cylinder. "I know I've been a bit of a moper." She handed him the spun sugar to taste. "I thought I'd better practice my confectionary skills. Dear sir, all is somewhat better in Zion."

He smiled at her, but there was no mistaking the relief in his eyes. "Uncle Albert was a bit of a tonic?" he asked.

*If you only knew who helped whom*, she thought as she went happily into his one-sided embrace because he was concentrating on the sugar. "We've agreed to meet tomorrow. Before he leaves for Koosharem, he promised to tell me about Mary Anne's childhood in Devon. I want to write it into a booklet for Paul for Christmas."

"Only 'somewhat better in Zion?' " he asked.

She nodded. "Things won't be entirely better until Brother Otto graces us with his presence at Christmas!"

His presence was felt all the time. She was sleeping better, but even on a bad night, she could reach out with her toes and feel the suit at the foot of her bed. Most nights, she clutched his pillow to her body, even after the elusive scent of bay rum was gone. She wished she wouldn't find herself wrapped into a little ball each morning, as though she tried all night to find safety in the cut bank. *Patience, patience, Julia*, she told herself.

For a week, Julia visited Uncle Albert, who seemed more at peace with himself. It took a little coaxing at first, and banana cake this time, but soon he was telling her about the Hickmans' years in Devonshire, always in sight of the sea, which he still missed. Each night, she sat at the rolltop desk in Papa's study and wrote up her notes.

Uncle Albert had already told her that under no circumstances would he tell her any more about the tragic journey to the Salt Lake Valley, so she was not surprised when he announced after Thanksgiving that he was returning to Koosharem. "I'll return with that daguerreotype of Mary Anne and the rest of us. I'm afraid it has to stay in my family, but I want him to see it," he told Julia.

He looked into her eyes. "An old man couldn't have a better niece," he told her. "Take good care of my nephew."

Paul's letters since his departure were short. She expected that, knowing he and the other ranchers affected by the summer wildfires were spreading out across eastern Wyoming and western Nebraska and Colorado to find each others' cattle, scattered when they cut the fences to let them run. She generally read his letters to her parents, or at least, most of them, but the last one she kept to herself, putting it in her apron pocket and taking it out now and then to read, as she blushed and then wondered. It had kept her awake last night just long enough for Mama to knock on her door and ask if everything was all right.

She took out the letter again after Papa left for work and Mama went to her weekly bridge game. *Dearest Darling, just a quick note here. I'm in Lusk with Matt and James, and we're finding more cattle, mine and McLemore's. I'm so tired. All I want to do is put my head in your lap and sleep for a week. Well, maybe not quite a week, <u>especially</u>* [underlined several times] *after March 17, when we get married. We'll probably think of something else to do. Thanks for the dignified calendar, or at least what used to* *be a dignified calendar. The boys in the bunkhouse are still ribbing me about it. Yrs, Paul, only half dead.*

She felt her face grow rosy, thinking of the staid 1911 calendar she had found and mailed, after circling March 17 in red, with little fireworks explosions radiating from it. *Heavens, what was I thinking?* she asked herself, then smiled because she knew precisely what she was thinking. That was not a letter to read aloud.

Still, that wasn't the hardest part. She turned over his letter, wishing that maybe this time there wouldn't be that postscript, dated a day later and scribbled in pencil, instead of his usual careful print: *P.S. Something happened this afternoon, and I'm worried. More later.*

Trouble was, there wasn't more later, not that week nor the next. She wrote her usual letters, telling of her visits to Uncle Albert, and of the cakes she was making for the bazaar, wracking her brain for topics of interest in her quiet life. In the last one, she included a picture one of her Primary students had drawn, which featured her short hair prominently. " 'He didn't draw a scar , so maybe I am the only one who sees it,' " she wrote.

As November slid into December—literally, because streets were too icy for Papa's Pierce-Arrow—she received a small package, which included a volume of Shakespeare's sonnets to replace the one burned in the fire. She smiled to see Paul had turned down the corner of Sonnet Eighteen, and written "My fav.," in tiny letters on the dog ear.

The letter left her no wiser than before, except he said he was home briefly, and staring at the pile of lumber stacked on the foundation of their new house, halfway between the river and the other ranch buildings still standing. "Wish I had more time," he had written. "See you in two weeks, morning train. Yrs, Paul."

She glanced at the Cheyenne postmark, noting to her dismay that two weeks would be practically Christmas

CARLA KELLY

Eve. Then he would probably be off as soon as possible, because there was the Denver stock show. *I'll make him take me next year*, she thought as she added the letter to the little pile by her bed and put the book of sonnets under her pillow.

As the days crawled by, Julia watched her mother grow more and more silent. Papa was taking the streetcar to and from downtown now, because the roads were so icy. Julia watched him each evening as he approached the house. Standing back from the drapes so he couldn't see her, it tore at Julia's heart to watch his stooped posture, and the way he straightened up and squared his shoulders as he approached the front door, determined not to show his sorrow.

*Iris, we're missing you*, she thought, meeting him at the door each night with a cheerful word, where she felt none as the anniversary of her sister's death came closer.

Nobody said anything until December 18, the day of her death. After an excellent dinner of stuffed filets of halibut, asparagus tips, everyone's favorite duchess potatoes, and prune whip with custard sauce, which all tasted to Julia like tissue paper, Papa looked at them.

"I received a letter yesterday from Paul," he said. "He sent it to the bank and told me not to open it until tonight. With your permission, ladies?"

Her eyes bleak, Mama automatically handed him a hairpin. He slit open the letter, scanned it with his eyes, and looked at Julia.

"You know, Jules, I had high hopes of my daughters marrying well. Iris"—he couldn't help the catch in his voice—"Iris did quite well. I worried about you, though." He managed a smile. "I shouldn't have. Maude, get out your handkerchief. Julia, your apron will do." His smile at his wife was genuine. "I have this entire tablecloth."

"Jed," Mama said softly. "Just read it."

He looked at the postmark. "Sidney, Nebraska. That boy does travel." He cleared his throat. " 'Dearest Darlings, I've been working my way through Revelation. I'd give the world to be with you right now, but I can't. Will this do? 'And God shall wipe away all tears from their eyes; and there shall be no more death, neither sorrow, nor crying, neither shall there be any more pain: for the former things are passed away.' " Papa put down the letter and pressed his fingers to the bridge of his nose, unable to continue.

Julia swallowed and picked up the letter. "You weren't quite done yet, Papa," she said, her own voice strange to her ears. " 'If I were in your dining room right now, and I know it's a far remove from this flophouse in Sidney, I'd be hugging you all. With all my heart, Paul.' "

Then they were all in tears. Papa stood up finally. He gathered Mama and Julia into his arms, walking with them to the parlor, where they sat, all crowded onto the settee, crying until no one had a tear left.

"I've been wanting to do that for about a week now," Papa said. He managed a watery chuckle. "My secretary, bless her heart, has been looking at me with such concern and solicitation that I wanted to pop her in the nose this morning."

Mama's eyes widened. "Miss Halibut?"

Julia laughed. "Mama! We had halibut for dinner. I think you mean Halifax."

"No, Halibut," Mama insisted and blew her nose decisively. "She has buggy eyes." She started to laugh then. "You can thump her once for me too, Jed, if you want." Mama picked up the letter in Julia's lap. "My dear, how on earth did you find such a man, and in Wyoming, of all places?"

"Nothing easier. He was pacing back and forth on a

train platform, waiting for a mature cook to materialize, and he took me anyway," Julia said simply.

They sat in silence then. Julia looked at her parents, both of them thinking of Iris. When she had returned to Salt Lake City, Julia had returned Iris's burned baby quilt to Mama, who washed it carefully and tucked it away. Julia longed to touch it again and remember how it had saved her life in the cut bank. *Iris, you're not so far away*, she reminded herself.

She finally excused herself to return to the dining room, clear off the table, and do the dishes in peaceful solitude. When she finished, she returned to the parlor, where Mama and Papa were still sitting close together, Mama asleep, and Papa's lips on her hair.

He glanced at her, a question in his eyes.

"It's simple, really," she whispered, not wanting to wake Mama. "All we have to do is endure."

Paul's suit at the foot of the bed wasn't close enough that night. After reading the verse again in Revelation, pausing for a moment on "Write: for these words are true and faithful," Julia pulled the suit higher and draped one sleeve over her shoulder. "We endure," she whispered and closed her eyes. "That's all."

# Four

Papa had her recollections of Mary Anne Hickman printed and bound, and the price was only a week of cecils and peanut brittle. Apologizing for the short notice, the stake president hired her to prepare a Christmas dinner on December 21 for the staff of his accounting firm. With her earnings, she went to Auerbach's and bought an extravagant paisley tie for Paul's suit, which was back in the closet, cleaned and ready for its owner; she saved the rest.

The opportunity to really show off her skills for the stake president—starting with consommé, meandering through roast goose and chicken croquettes, and easing to a tasty conclusion with plum pudding and bonbons—should have sent her into culinary ecstasy. All it did was make her sob into her apron while she dressed the lettuce with cheese straws and thought of the men of the Double Tipi, eating out of cans, and whatever else Paul's niece from the Wind River Rez could slap onto a plate. *If they even have plates*, she thought, miserable.

Besides that, Paul was probably still enduring greasy steaks and brittle biscuits in the various hotels and cafes along the route of his wandering livestock. She cried harder to think of the nights he was probably enduring on the open plains, with not a hotel in sight, and nothing to do but hunker down in a dry wash and pray someone would find his bleached bones on the prairie, come spring.

She sobbed all this into Mama's lap the afternoon

after the stake president's dinner and was rewarded with a laugh and a little thump on her head.

"I should have warned you that this is what happens when you fall in love," Mama said. "Paul is far more resourceful than you're giving him credit for."

"But he's lost on the plains and starving!" Julia sobbed, which only made Mama laugh harder.

"You are unfeeling," Julia said, getting up off her knees and trying to leave the room with some dignity.

"Yes, I am," Mama agreed. With a laugh, she turned back to her knitting. She held up one sleeve. "Is this long enough for Paul, do you think? Of course, if he's frozen to death on the Colorado Plains, probably with the lights of Julesburg in the distance and too exhausted to crawl there, it won't matter, will it?"

Julia frowned, then had the good grace to blush. "Mama, I'm a goose," she said. She picked up the sleeve and draped it at her shoulder, letting it curve around her elbow until it hung below her fingers, remembering how nice his arms felt around her. "Yes, it's long enough."

She bullied her father into getting a Christmas tree the next day, even though the best ones were already gone. As he brought it into the house after Mama was in bed that night, Papa confided that for some reason, the tree was still the hardest part of Iris's death at Christmastime.

"I avoided it," he said simply.

"You wouldn't want to disappoint James, would you?" she asked, steadying the tree in the stand while he tightened the bolts.

"Or you," he replied.

The tree was decorated before Mama came down to breakfast the next morning, because Julia had stayed awake most of the night, putting on the ornaments and wishing James were there to help. Before she dragged herself upstairs for a short nap after breakfast, she told Papa of the cranberries and popcorn on Exhibits A and B last Christmas, along with Willy Bill's tin can ornaments, and wondered what James would make of this extravagant effort.

"You'll find out soon, Jules," Papa had said.

When she made her appearance after her nap, rubbing her eyes, her father handed her a telegram. "From Cheyenne. Probably Romeo."

She opened the message with a flourish and held it out so he could see it too. "Are you ready? *Dearest Darling, look for us on the early train from Ogden tomorrow morning. Stop. Yrs, Paul.*" She sighed. "It seems like years and years."

"Or yrs and yrs," Papa joked, which made them both laugh.

Owing to the still-icy streets, Julia told Papa to stay in bed the next morning and keep the Pierce-Arrow from calamity, while she took the streetcar to the train station. She shivered in the early dawn, grateful at least that the snow had stopped. She looked around the depot, her eyes on the magnificent Christmas tree, which reached almost to the rafters in the waiting room.

As eager as she was to see Paul, she felt herself growing anxious as the time passed. For the tiniest moment she doubted and started to finger her scar. She looked over her shoulder at the utility closet where Paul had tugged her two months ago for a blessing and put her hand down. He certainly didn't need to ever know that only two days ago, she was certain he was lying frozen on the Colorado plains.

The train was only thirty minutes late. She hung back a little when the doors opened, shy, until she clasped her mittened hands together and felt the ruby engagement ring, which she had been quite ready to hock, even if he was joking.

Paul was wearing a new Stetson and overcoat, which made her sigh with relief; he wasn't going to freeze to death anytime soon. James was at his side, leaning close, his eyes wide at the sight of all the people waiting on the platform. Paul's hand rested firmly on his head, until James spotted Julia and ran forward.

With a cry of her own, Julia held out her arms to the boy, whirling him around, then holding him close, because Paul had grabbed her too, and James was sandwiched in the middle. James wriggled free when Paul kissed her and kissed her again, after muttering, "Not enough," and holding her so close that, between his embrace and her corset, she had to gasp for breath.

"I have missed you," she managed to murmur in his ear, which led to her hat falling off when he kissed her again.

"Did you have any second thoughts, along about Rock Springs?" she asked, out of breath, even a little dizzy.

He smiled that edgy smile that made her heart pound a little faster. "You're teasing me," he said. "I'll let it go for now, but that's going to get you in a world of trouble after March 17." He looked around for James. "Well, I'll be . . ." He pointed.

Knit cap in hand, James stood in front of the tree, his mouth open. Paul let go of her and walked to the tree, squatting down beside the boy.

"What do you think?" he asked.

"I think this didn't come from your land."

"You'd be right. What do *you* think, Darling?"

She put her hand on Paul's shoulder, grateful to touch him. "I think we'd better get on the streetcar because breakfast is waiting at home."

The streetcar ride was another epiphany to James, who stood, open-mouthed, by the coin and token drop box and only sat down when Paul gave him his familiar, measuring look. The streetlights and Christmas lights were still on, so they captured his attention next.

"I doubt he's ever seen this many people at one time in his life," Paul said, his hand in hers, as they watched James' face. "I know I haven't." He looked at her. "This fall, have you ever just wished that you could be with me on horseback, riding out of Gun Barrel?"

She couldn't help herself, and his expression changed. "Oh, hey now, Julia, I didn't mean to make you cry. I guess that's a yes."

She nodded, barely able to speak. "I think of it all the time."

His arm went around her, and he held her close until their stop. It was just a short walk home, with its welcome Christmas wreath on the front door, a far cry from last year's funeral wreath. Julia tried to see it through James' eyes: the big house, the wide porch, the stone walkway. She stood still a moment, absorbing the dear sight herself and thinking that it would be different next Christmas on the Double Tipi, and for all her Christmases to follow.

Paul looked at her, a question in his eyes. She leaned against his arm. "It's nothing. I was just thinking how much I love this familiar sight, but how much I'm looking forward to Christmas on the ranch next year."

"You won't miss this?"

"Of course I will," she said, after a moment's reflection. "Still, I'd rather be home."

"No home to speak of yet," he said, apology evident in his voice.

"You'll be there, won't you?" she asked quietly. "That's home enough for me."

Breakfast had turned into brunch and was followed by a tour of the house for James, who watched seriously as Julia's father flushed the toilet in the upstairs bathroom, then jumped back at the noise. He was equally impressed with the feather mattress in Iris's room, although the delicate wallpaper didn't meet his expectations.

"I've been learning to read the wallpaper in the bunkhouse," he told Jed Darling. "Haven't I, Mr. Otto?" He thought a moment. " 'Road agent kills three in botched robbery,' " he said. "Or was it two?"

"Two, bub," Paul said and chuckled, to hide his obvious embarrassment. "We read newspaper headlines before bed, since that's all the bedtime story we have right now. I can't count Doc's dictionary."

"Impressive," Papa said.

"'Madam arrested as town council closes bordello,'" James quoted from memory, then frowned. "Mr. Otto wouldn't explain what a bordello is. Do you know?"

Mr. Otto rolled his eyes, and Mama turned away to hide her laughter. "Obviously we are missing your daughter's leavening influence," he said to her shaking shoulders. "March can't come fast enough."

"And that's the truth," Paul said later, sitting in the parlor with his arm around Julia. The house was quiet. Mama had announced after the dishes were done that she and Papa were going to take James downtown on the streetcar to see the mechanized elves and snowmen in the window at ZCMI, and then maybe, if they were lucky, visit Santa Claus.

"Dear Jules, I can hardly keep a straight face when James calls you Mr. Darling," Mama said. "He calls me that too, now."

"He just doesn't seem to understand, or maybe hear, the difference," Julia replied. "I'm so used to it now. I hope he isn't too confused when I become Mrs. Otto!"

"Julia, we trust you to be the perfect hostess while we're downtown," Papa had said with a straight face. "Treat Paul as you would any old fiancé, Mr. Darling."

She did, which made her face rosy with whisker burn and her curly hair even more of a tangle. Paul had decided that the chair across from the settee was suddenly more comfortable, and they both laughed.

"Julia, I miss you so much, but that's all this stockman can stand," he said. He turned serious then. "How are your parents coping? And you?"

"Your letter was a blessing," she told him. "We all cried and discovered we're pretty good at enduring. Sometimes that's what it comes down to."

"More than we know, probably." He leaned back in the chair. "I'm so tired."

"Sleep, then." She went to him and touched his face, then covered him with the throw from the settee. He was breathing deep and peacefully before she left the room.

He found her in the kitchen an hour later, pulling a pan of rolls from the Majestic. He rubbed his eyes and stretched. "Darling, you're probably wondering what kind of an old man you're about to hitch your wagon to."

She pointed to a chair at the table. "Hardly. I can read between the lines in your letters. No wonder you're exhausted. I don't know how you stay in the saddle!"

"Chief is a well-trained horse." He started to lean back in the chair until she put a crock of butter and a jar of raspberry jam in front of him, followed by a knife and half a dozen rolls. "When I'm not dreaming about you, I'm dreaming about food. Blasted unhealthy, eh?"

Julia sat down to watch him eat. He buttered two rolls and handed her one. "Nice of your folks to leave us alone for a little while." He ate and then leaned back. "We really do have to talk."

"What happened in Niobrara County?" she asked, pouring him some milk. "Your letter said 'More later,' but there wasn't."

"I had intended to return to the Double Tipi and

write you a lengthy letter, but I got a telegram from a rancher near Ogallala who had found the bulk of my herd. Off we went for a winter cattle drive. No fun." He sighed. "Sometimes I wonder why I ranch."

"Because you love it," she said promptly. "What happened in Niobrara County?"

He tipped his chair down and turned to face her. "I think one of the ranchers near Lusk recognized James, or should I say Thaddeus Pulaski?"

"No! Surely not," Julia said and reached for Paul's hand.

"I wish I knew for sure." He held her hand, ran his thumb over the ruby, and smiled faintly. "Nice ring." He passed his hand in front of his eyes. "I blame myself. I never should have taken James along, but I just didn't think . . ." He shook his head.

"There's no blame. You probably needed every hand you could get to find cattle. I know how James hates to be left behind."

"So right." He sighed. "The deuce of it is, I really don't know if McAtee recognized him."

"What happened?"

"The usual stuff. Everybody's been really good about sending us telegrams if our cattle are spotted in the vicinity. I got a telegram like that from the sheriff in Lusk, telling me to look around Rawhide Buttes. We were in the saddle the next morning." He eyed the empty plate in front of him. "Darling, there seems to be a hole in this plate."

"More likely a hole in you," she retorted, but got him the rest of the dozen rolls. "Honey?"

"Yes?"

She thumped him, which only earned her a spot on his lap and another close encounter with whisker burn. "You really need to shave," she said but made no move to get off his lap. He put his arms around her and buttered another roll, slathering this one with honey.

She made herself comfortable on his lap. "Keep going."

"But you just thumped me. Ow! All right." He finished a roll and buttered another one. "We found the cattle at Rawhide Buttes, sure enough. We were on McAtee's land, and there he was, watching us. I know him well, and I went to palaver. He said he'd contacted the sheriff, so I thanked him."

"That seems pretty straightforward," Julia said, getting off Paul's lap to take the next batch of rolls from the Majestic.

"It was. We spent a moment more just chewing the fat—my word, I wished I'd just said thanks again and ridden away! James rode up beside me." He pushed away the rest of the rolls, his distress evident to her. "Julia, next thing I know, James is hanging over his saddle, puking and crying. I've never seen him like that. I leaned over to help him, and his eyes were like saucers. He pulled himself up and rode like a scared rabbit back to Matt and the herd."

"Did Mr. McAtee recognize him?"

"Wish I knew. I watched his face, and his eyes kept getting narrower and narrower. I thought it would be best to just gloss over what had happened, so I said something stupid about the kid getting seasick on a loping nag. Sit down again; you're too far away."

She did, her arms around his neck.

"McAtee got really quiet, and his eyes just kind of bored into mine. He said he didn't know I had any children." Paul made a disgusted sound. "I'm not much of a liar. When I assured him that James was mine, he gave me such a look and came this close to calling me a liar." He shrugged. "He's right; I was. I was lying, and he knew it."

Julia put her hands on both sides of his face and her forehead against his. "There are worse things than being called a poor liar."

He kissed her nose. "I know, I know, but it did sting a bit. My reputation may be suffering some."

*Not with me*, Julia thought. She rested her head against his chest, enjoying the sound of his steady heartbeat. "Did you ask James?"

"Yes. He wouldn't say anything, and he kept looking over his shoulder until we were well clear of Rawhide Buttes. I got firm with him that night, when we were all shivering and trying to stay warm in our bedrolls. James still wouldn't say anything. I doubt he ever will, so I doubt McAtee has anything to fear. But McAtee doesn't know that, does he?"

They sat together in silence until Paul kissed the top of her head. "Have you resigned yourself to being curly top now?"

She nodded, happy to change the subject, and told him about the two young women in the ward who had showed up at church with short hair. He smiled and traced her neck scar gently with his finger. "This bothering you so much?"

"Not so much, not after Uncle Albert and I had a good talk about scars on the inside and on the outside. I'll tell you about that later. He's gone back to Koosharem, and said he might be here for Christmas. I . . . I wouldn't exactly hold my breath for that."

"I won't. It's more than enough to see you, and frankly, I don't think my uncle feels comfortable around me."

"He doesn't," she replied equally frank. "You remind him of a hard time, and besides, he doesn't know you the way I know you."

"And you love me anyway."

James and her parents came home when she was finishing dinner and Paul was sleeping in the parlor again. James almost danced as he described the wonder of mechanical elves, all of them moving and gesturing in a store window.

He held still long enough for her to unwind his muffler and take off his coat, which gave him a moment to reflect. "Here's what's strange, Mr. Darling," he told her. "There were people walking by the window and they didn't even stop to look! What's wrong with them?"

"Maybe they've seen it before," Julia suggested.

James rejected that with a frown in her direction, which made Julia smile inside. "Jee-rusalem Crickets," he muttered, sounding very much like Mr. Otto.

"I know it's hard to imagine," she said. "Did you see Santa Claus?"

Obviously James's opinion was mixed, starting with, "He wanted me to sit on his lap," then morphing into, "He just out of the blue asked me what I wanted for Christmas!"

"What did you tell him?" Julia asked, her eyes lively.

James' face fell. "I couldn't think of a thing." He brightened then. "But I did ask for a house for you."

*That's kinder than I deserve*, Julia thought as she hugged him, breathing in the little boy fragrance she had been missing and thinking of all her complaints. *Let me take a page from your book. I know it's not the first time.*

It was a good time to ask. "James, what *has* been done on the house?"

"Next to nothing," came a sleepy voice from the doorway. "I have already abandoned my less-than-spectacular career as a prevaricator."

"What's that?" James asked. "Mr. Otto, your hair is rumpled."

He grinned and grabbed Julia, who shrieked when he

tousled her hair. "Not as bad as Mr. Darling's! Besides, she did it. James, *prevaricator* is a big word for liar. I found it in Doc's dictionary. I am up to the P's now."

"Mr. Otto, you've never told a lie in your life," James said.

"Yes I have, and not too long ago," he murmured. "Julia, point him to the cutlery and plates, and he'll help. You'll have to tell Mr. Darling here how you've been hauling wood for Charlotte."

"I like her," the boy said simply. "So does Matt."

Her eyes merry, Julia glanced at Paul, who suddenly looked inscrutable. "How's *that* wind blowing?"

"Matt doesn't bother me about my love life, and I don't trouble him about his," Paul said, clipping his words and sounding remarkably like Mr. Otto. He clapped his hands together. "Big change of subject: Yes, your house—our house—had a foundation with center supports in place and not much else. No time, Julia, just no time."

She rested her hand on his shoulder, and he covered her fingers with his in a gesture so automatic that she knew she would never nag about something as mundane as a mere house. "Paul, we're still getting married March 17, no matter if we have to spread out a bedroll on the foundation and tack up tumbleweed to cut the breeze."

He kissed her fingers with a loud smack, which made Mama smile as she stood in the doorway. "Mrs. Darling, you certainly raised a daughter with low expectations. She'll do well in Wyoming."

Considering that they were still raw from the pain of remembering Iris a year later, Mama and Papa made a special effort for James. *And me too*, Julia thought, as she popped popcorn in a wire basket vigorously shaken directly over the flames with a stove lid removed. They had been hurting too bad last Christmas to make popcorn balls, but Mama didn't hesitate this year, enlisting James to butter his hands and help her shape the fragrant treats.

"We'll eat some of these tonight and set two out for Santa Claus," Mama explained. Julia's smile trembled a little when Mama said, her voice almost too soft for Julia's ears, "Julia and Iris were my little girls, and they always set out popcorn balls, one apiece. That's for Santa, who comes down the chimney and leaves toys."

James looked at Paul, skeptical. Paul held up his hands to ward off his expression. "That's what they do here in Salt Lake City!"

The boy thought about it, and Julia remembered the deliberate way he reasoned. "What are you thinking, James?" she coaxed, dumping more popcorn in the bowl on the kitchen table.

"Do you think he'll know I'd like a knife?" He hung his head. "I should have told him."

"He'll know," Julia said with a questioning glance at Paul, who nodded.

"It came up a time or two," Paul whispered in her ear when James turned his attention to the popcorn balls.

Julia smiled and watched her mother show James what to do, remembering how Mama had showed Iris. She knew Mama had been looking forward to showing the grandchildren she would never have now from Iris and Spencer Davison. She glanced at Paul, who was watching her.

"Our children, some day," she told him, blushing when he nodded.

"Our child right now," he said. He poured another handful of popcorn in the wire basket. "And that's something else we need to talk about." He wasn't smiling now and kept looking at James thoughtfully. Julia put her hand in his shyly, aware of that envelope of Indian silence that sometimes surrounded him and not wishing to interfere with it.

"He'll be safe, Paul," she said. "You'll keep him safe."

"Can I? It's more than that."

She wondered what he meant, but there wasn't any opportunity to ask until the popcorn balls were finished and eaten, along with the ribbon candy she had made, left over from the stake president's dinner, and the elegant Bûche de Noël that had even impressed Miss Fannie Farmer at the Boston School.

"I got an A in confections for one very much like that," Julia said as she handed around the slices on Mama's best china.

Paul took a healthy bite and rolled his eyes. He gestured at James with his fork, "Son, I've done two really smart things in my life."

"Only two?"

"Believe me, that's a lot for a rancher," he joked. He ate another bite. "One was advertising in the *Deseret News* for a cook, and the other was reading the Book of Mormon. They're pretty much one and two in pretty close order, and the order shifts, depending."

"On what?" Julia asked. "Hold still." She dabbed at his moustache, where some of the whipped cream was lodged.

"Let me take another bite. Right now, it's the cook. But don't you know, when we read tonight about Nephi and that day and a night and a day when Christ was born, the order will likely shift."

"Pretty simple," Papa said. "When she's in your house cooking, you can eat and read at the same time."

"My thought precisely," Paul said. He took a deep breath and set down the plate, unable to say any more.

As long as Julia could remember, they always read the scriptures on Christmas Eve, starting with Luke and then reading the passages in Helaman and Third Nephi. Most years, she and Iris were too excited to pay attention, thinking about the presents coming on the next day, while their brothers suffered their enthusiasm, in that way of the older and wiser.

Last Christmas, still numb with Iris's death, they hadn't read, which left a hollow place in Julia's heart that wasn't filled until a week later, when Paul read Luke 2 to James on the Double Tipi at their belated Christmas.

Here they were again, not so raw, reading, "There were shepherds abiding in the fields," and "On the morrow, come I into the world." The earth's axis may have shifted with a vengeance in 1909, but the sweetness had returned this year. Her eyes moist, Julia looked around at her parents, sitting so close together, and Paul, with James leaning against him on one side and her on the other, his arms around them both. The Christmas she had almost dreaded was gentler and kinder and braver than she could have hoped for. "Thank you" seemed a paltry way to tell Heavenly Father what was truly unspeakable, but it was the best she could do.

# Five

Julia said good night to her parents. She couldn't bring herself to say good night to Paul, not at all. Every instinct rebelled against it, and so she told him, after the house was quiet and dark.

"I feel the same way," he whispered, "but you know we're going to do just that."

She nodded. He took her hand. "There's one more thing I have to tell you, and it's not pretty. In fact, it unnerves me, but I need your advice." He touched her cheek. "Don't look so worried! It has nothing to do with you . . ." He looked away. "Well, yes it does. How about we just sit here on the stairs?"

He took her hand and walked her down the stairs, sitting her on the bottom step, where they could see into the parlor. Mama had left the drapes open, and Christmas lights still winked far below the avenues.

She hesitated, then put her hand on his thigh in a proprietary gesture that made him smile. He tugged it a little higher, and even in the dim light from the upstairs hall, she saw in his face a great need for comfort.

"Paul, what on earth is wrong?" she questioned, almost afraid to ask and wondering what could be worse than McAtee on the range.

"I hate to do this." He leaned toward her, correctly gauging the panic in her eyes. "No. No. It's not you and me! Nothing changes there, but this is still hard. Julia, I told President Gillespie about my encounter with McAtee.

He immediately offered his home for James."

Julia couldn't help her sigh. She just wished it hadn't sounded so ragged and needy. Paul touched her neck. "You've had a tough year, courtesy of me," he said, "and I do regret the pain. Believe me, I do."

"What did you tell him?"

"I told him no, of course, but not for the reason you're thinking."

"What are you so sure I'm thinking? My dear, all I want to know is what's going on!"

He chuckled. "And I'm exasperating you. You don't know this yet, but it looks like Sister Gillespie is . . . uh . . ."

"Good for her," Julia whispered in his ear. "My, but you cowboys are shy." She leaned back. "And you just don't want to burden the Gillespies with another responsibility, with their house already bulging at the seams?"

"So right." He took her hand again. "Julia, when our pesky house ever gets built, it's going to have four large bedrooms. Just so you know."

It was her turn to blush. "My, but you cooks are shy," he teased, and then grew immediately serious. "I assured Heber I couldn't impose that way. He nodded, then asked me if I planned to keep James up there in isolation on the Double Tipi, with no opportunity for school or other advantages that boys his age usually have. I couldn't think of a thing to say to that."

Julia nodded. "I've been wondering about that too."

"Some ranchers move their families into town and visit them on Saturdays and Sundays," he said. "The thought of ever being that far from you again makes my blood run in chunks." He looked at her. "But this isn't about us yet, although it's something we'll have to think about in the future." He smiled. "If we're lucky enough to have the Gillespies' problem."

"What *are* you going to do about James?" she asked in the lengthening silence.

"I asked myself that, after I talked to Heber. I prayed about it too. Oh my word, all the time I was praying about it, sitting there in that cold saddle, when Matt probably thought I was asleep. Amazing how a cold saddle sharpens the mind. You ever pray all the time?"

She knew he was teasing her now, and she pinched his thigh.

"You have wicked fingers, but I deserved that! Well, a funny thing happened the next week. Before I joined the Church, I'd have called it a coincidence. I'm almost smart enough now to know an answer to prayer, no matter how strange it may seem. Julia, when James and I are able to get to church, he likes to sit with Cora Shumway. Remember her?"

Julia thought a moment, remembering a tall, thin woman, all angles and planes. "She teaches the children's Sunday school class."

"The very one."

"And doesn't Sister Groesbeck always hand Sister Shumway her baby, so she can play the pump organ?"

"She does. Cora's husband is Eugene, that meek little guy about half a head shorter than she is, who used to look afraid of me."

*Eugene and most of the people in Wyoming,* she thought, *but you'll never hear that from me.* "I know."

"When Eugene and I are at the Sacrament table, James just gravitates to Cora Shumway. He sits with her, and I've noticed Sister Shumway puts her arm around him. You know how he nestles in when someone does that."

"I do. My feet are getting cold, so you'd better hurry up this narrative," she said, then stifled a shriek when he pulled her slippered feet into his lap.

"Don't holler. I just solved your problem," he said mildly. "The Shumways want to solve mine. I don't know how many months it took, but Eugene worked up his nerve to ask me after Sunday School just last week if I would ever consider letting James live with them in Cheyenne and go to school."

"Oh, my."

"My reaction was a little stronger. I said no right away." He shook his head. "I guess it's almost a reflex with me, but I'll be . . . darned if little Shumway didn't back down an inch. Don't know if you're aware of it, but Shumway is Cheyenne's only automobile mechanic. He stood right up to me and said he'd also be honored to teach James everything he knows about fixing autos when he came to live with them in Cheyenne."

"My goodness." She smiled in the dark. "James may never be a scholar, but he certainly knows how to build things with the Meccano set you gave him."

"James can tinker, that's for sure. I had spent the better part of a week praying about a solution, and there it was, standing right in front of me. Tell me something, Darling: do you think Heavenly Father ever gets discouraged when we pray, He gives us an answer, and we ignore it?"

"Oh, maybe now and then! I've ignored my share of answers too. Why does the Lord bother with us?"

"Beats me." Paul took off her slippers and rubbed her feet. "They're like ice. I suppose you plan to put them on my legs, after March 17."

"I was counting on it. Paul, do the Shumways have any children?"

"No. They never will." His sigh was audible and more than a sigh. "Here's my dilemma: you know very well that if James goes to live with them, one thing will lead to another and they'll want to adopt him."

He couldn't say anything else. Julia leaned forward. "Paul, this *is* hard."

"I love that boy. We've . . . we've been through a lot together. You've been through a lot with him too. It's also a divine solution to the problem of McAtee. Keeping James with a family in Cheyenne is a surefire way to keep him safe, but what should I do? What should *we* do?"

They sat a long time in silence, Paul's hands on her feet. When he moved them up to her knees, she laughed softly and lifted her feet out of his lap.

"You're a rascal, and I love you," she said, putting on her slippers again. "You already know what to do, Paul. It won't be easy, and he'll miss you too, but you know what to do."

"Yeah, I do. My prayer was answered," he said after a long time. He rubbed the back of his head. "It's just leaving me feeling a bit bruised."

"And you're not used to that!"

"Nope."

"Another sore subject: Julia, James and I have to leave the day after Christmas. Don't you dare cry!"

"I won't," she said and couldn't help her tears. "Why so soon?"

He handed her his handkerchief, and she blew her nose. "Before we left Cheyenne, word got to me of more cattle that drifted. A rancher named Bell is keeping them for me, up near Laramie Peak, and I told him I would be there by the end of the week. That's about the last of the missing herd, thank God. Darling, I promise we'll have a boring Christmas next year."

He walked her up the stairs and stopped at the top. "You know what I'm looking the most forward to about March 17?"

"I have some inkling," she told him, glad she had

turned out the upstairs hall light, so he couldn't see her blush.

"That too, but just think of it: I'll be able to say good night to you when you're right *next* to me and maybe sharing the same pillow, and not down the hall off the kitchen, or across the state, and I'm not in some deathtrap of a hotel in Julesburg or Sidney or Ogallala. I'm tired of that!"

She put her fingers to his lips. "Shh! You'll wake my folks, or James, and you know he's already skeptical about Santa Claus."

"There's some logic to that statement, but it escapes me," he whispered back. "Good night, Darling."

She went in her room and closed the door, then just leaned against it, fighting tears of her own at the thought of James in Cheyenne, even though she knew it was for the best. As she stood there, she heard Paul go downstairs again. In a moment he was back upstairs and knocking softly on her door.

"You know I shouldn't let you in," she whispered.

"I promise to behave myself." A pause. "If you will."

She opened the door. He stood there holding the Christmas present for her that he had put under the tree earlier.

"Don't cry yet."

She pulled him in her room, pointing to the chair by the fireplace as she sat on the bed with the present. "I was thinking about James," she said.

He indicated the package in her lap. "This'll give you something else to think about."

"It wouldn't wait for morning?" she asked, tugging the impressive-looking gold cord off the package.

"No," he said. She couldn't see him well in the darkness, but she knew sudden shyness when she heard it. "James might have a whole lot of questions if you open it downstairs." He chuckled. "And your father will probably toss me out the front door."

"Good heavens, what have you done?" Julia murmured. "The wrapping paper is gorgeous." She peered closer at a little gold decal. "Marshall Field's? Isn't that in Chicago?" The ribbon was off, and she carefully removed the paper.

"I was there about this time last year, as you'll recall."

She remembered all too well, thinking again of the telegram from his former wife's parents that had sent him on the next train to Chicago. She looked at the pasteboard box, elegant even without wrapping paper on it.

She started to lift the lid, then set it down. "Wait a minute. You bought me what looks like a fearsomely expensive present in Chicago *last year*?"

"I did, indeed." She heard the amusement in his voice. "Open it."

"In a minute. A year ago, weren't you still wondering if I could breathe and walk at the same time?"

"Open it." He had rarely sounded more patient.

"Very well." She lifted the lid and couldn't help the sigh that escaped her. Even in the moonlight, or maybe especially in the moonlight, she could see exquisite lace and silk, just a shade off-white. Scarcely breathing, she lifted out what had to be the most beautiful negligee in the entire history of the universe. Words couldn't do it justice. It felt no more substantial than cobwebs in her hands.

"Good thing I bought it, because a quick look at ZCMI and Auerbach's two months ago didn't turn up anything remotely like that," he said. "Say something."

"I can't. I'm struck dumb." She got off her bed and held up the nightgown to her robe.

"Don't do that," Paul said quickly. "Just don't."

She put it back in the box. "You amaze me," she said when she could speak.

"Good. That should keep you off balance for a few centuries of our eternity," he told her.

She closed her eyes in utter delight and sat down on her bed again as the realization of the whole thing crashed into her brain, banging cymbals and tooting horns and shouldering all reason aside. "You bought this a year ago."

"We've already been over that."

She leaned toward him and rested her elbows on the brass rail at the foot of her bed. "All right, cowboy, just *when* did you fall in love with me? I'm definitely curious now."

He regarded her in the moonlight. "I knew I was a no-hoping goner when I caught that ridiculous hat of yours on the platform at Gun Barrel."

Julia sucked in her breath. She tried to be severe. "Mr. Otto, *nobody* falls in love that fast!"

"I did," he said simply, and he left her room.

Julia decided that James wasn't up at the crack of dawn on Christmas morning because he had no real idea just what largess meant. Her gift to him last year had been just crayons and paper, and she knew Papa and Mama had been whispering together in the kitchen, wrapping presents for him.

"It's nothing too extravagant," Mama had said last night. Julia wouldn't have cared if Mama had bought out the whole toy section at ZCMI, because James seemed to be bringing out the fun in her mother again.

"Julia, you should have seen him in front of the window at ZCMI," her mother had said, her eyes lively with the memory.

*And you should see your face now*, she had thought. "Tell me about it, Mama," she said, watching her parents, noting how happy her father looked to be seeing his wife take such an interest in one child.

And here they were, gathering in the parlor, watching James open his presents. Julia glanced at Paul, who was yawning. *I don't think you got any more sleep last night than I did*, she told herself.

James accepted each gift of books and clothes and games with cries of delight, but his gift of a more advanced Meccano set from Paul reduced him to jaw-dropping silence. He ran his hand reverently over the box lid.

"Open it," Paul said. "Some of the pieces are pretty detailed, but there are written instructions."

James did as he suggested. He looked at the pieces stashed in their own cardboard compartments and gave the booklet a single glance. Without a word, he began assembling the pieces.

"Guess you don't need instructions," Paul said. He looked at Julia and raised his eyebrows. "Could be you're destined to be a mechanic." His shoulders slumped slightly. He was sitting on the floor, his back to the settee. Julia rested her hand on his shoulder and knew he was thinking of the Shumways. "There are worse things," he said, more to himself than anyone else.

Julia's gift to her mother was always the same: glycerin and rosewater lotion, the better to combat Salt Lake City's perpetual dryness. She had attached a little gold brooch of seed pearls, which made Mama smile her thanks and pin it immediately to her robe. Papa was suitably impressed with a new fob for his watch.

"This is for you and Paul," Mama said, sounding almost shy.

She held out the envelope to Paul, who read the contents and smiled, getting up on his knees to kiss her on the cheek. "I'd rather call you Mother than Maude," he said. "Is that allowed?"

"Please do. That's what Iris's husband did." Her voice barely faltered.

"Thank you for this," Paul said. "Darling, we've been given the 1911 model of the Queen Atlantic, which, according to this note, is waiting for us in a warehouse in Cheyenne."

"Mama, that's so sweet," Julia said.

Paul gave her mother another kiss. "I was practical too, Mother. Since it might be a little while until we can invite you to the Double Tipi, what with the wind whistling through the frame and the snow piling up, I had a Double Tipi beef dressed out and frozen for you two. It'll arrive any day now in a reefer car from Cheyenne. Maybe I should have asked if you have an ice source at a butcher's for it."

"We'll find one," Papa said. "Believe me."

Julia rested her hand again on Paul's shoulder and leaned closer. "Tell me, is this your beef or McLemore's?"

He tried to look shocked. "Julia, I would never give my future in-laws poached beef! I think it's mine. This is for you, Jed."

Papa unwrapped the package and pulled out a copy of *The Autobiography of Parley P. Pratt*.

"That's to repay you for your personal copy that you gave me last Christmas," Paul explained. "Your copy was another casualty of the range fires."

Jed handed over his present for Paul, who unwrapped it and found an identical copy. "Son, I guess we were thinking along the same lines," he said.

Julia handed Paul her package. "I have two things, but this is first."

"Feels like another book," he said and undid the string. "Little too small for another autobiography."

"No, it's a biography this time," she said. "Your mother's."

He was silent as he unwrapped the slim volume, titled *Mary Anne Hickman's Early Years*. "She never talked about her childhood," he said as he turned the pages. "I guess it was too painful." He looked at her. "Thank you, Julia. I don't know what to say."

"Just say you'll treat me as you would any female member of the House of Hapsburg, and agree to my every whim," Julia teased.

"Done, madam." He took the other gift she held out and pulled out the paisley tie.

"It'll look so nice with your new suit," she told him. "In fact, I think you had better take the suit back with you. You can wear it to the Denver stock show in January and impress your poker-playing cronies."

The smile left his face, and he grew thoughtful. "Funny you should mention them. I don't think I'm going to Denver this year."

He had to be joking. Julia laughed. "You told me you haven't missed one in fifteen years! Is the suit too grand for—where was it you told me—the Cattleman's Saloon?"

Paul watched James with the Meccano set, as if to assure himself that he wasn't paying attention to their conversation. She recognized his look of embarrassment. "If you'd rather not say . . ."

"No, no, I've been wanting to get this off my chest, since I got here." He looked at her parents. "I don't know what Julia's told you, but every year I spend two weeks in Denver at the stock show, looking over livestock, sometimes entering my own in competition. It's a general good time."

He must have felt suddenly uncomfortable, because he got off the floor and went to the window, seeing something outside that no one else seemed to see. "There are ten stockmen who get together for what is basically a continuous poker game. We talk, describe our year, and trade information about the range or whatever suits us." He managed a half smile, again with that faraway look. "I've been told that it's a pretty exclusive group. We're the old-timers."

Julia patted the settee beside her, and he sat down, putting his arm around her shoulders, then resting his hand in her curls, which still seemed to fascinate him. "I was near Grover on the Colorado plains last month, following up a lead on my strays. Kaiser ranches there, and he had them. He helped me get them to the train station and onto box cars."

"Kaiser?"

"John and his brothers are big names in land and cattle, there and in Nebraska." Paul twined his fingers in her curls, and she closed her eyes with the pleasure of it. "It's silly, but every year we elect a major domo to call the shots and decide on the saloon. I was major domo a couple of years ago. We take turns. I knew it was Kaiser's turn, so while we were watching my cattle loaded in the box cars, I mentioned that I hadn't received my annual invitation to the poker game."

Julia felt his shoulder tense as she rested against him.

"He looked a little uncomfortable, hemmed and hawed a bit, then told me that Mormons weren't invited."

"It happens," Papa said to fill the enormous silence.

"Sure did to me," Paul said ruefully. "I didn't know where to look either, so there we were, looking everywhere but at each other. Comical, I suppose."

"I'm sorry that happened," Julia said.

"I am too. These are—or were—my friends of longest standing."

"What did you say?" Papa asked.

"I didn't want to grovel or plead. What's the point?" Paul nudged Julia. "I gave him my patented 'look,' at least that's what the Queen of the Hapsburgs here calls it. So then he asked me, 'Well, aren't you a'—I'll modify his response for the ladies present—'aren't you a blamed Mormon?' "

He laughed then, and it was genuine, which made Julia let out a slow sigh of relief.

"I got really angry at first, but I bit the inside of my cheek. Jed, I remembered what you told me about our President Smith, and what happened when he was set upon by ruffians, and all his companions scattered."

"Oh, yes," Papa said.

"I looked Kaiser right in the eye and said, 'Yessiree, dyed in the wool, true blue, through and through.' "

Everyone laughed, including Paul. His concentration disrupted, James looked around, saw everyone laughing, and laughed too.

"What did Mr. Kaiser do?" Julia asked.

"He gave me *his* patented look and walked away. So it goes." Paul picked up his mother's biography and thumbed the pages again. "It stings, though. It does." He looked at Jed. "I gave up drinking and, uh, sporting around. Never did smoke. I still like to play cards and I don't mind the odd gamble or bet. Jed, are betting and gambling not allowed?"

"You're a rancher; you bet and gamble every day."

Paul laughed, and the tension left the room. "That I do. Now I'm asking your dear child to bet and gamble with me."

He looked at her and Julia had to tell herself, *keep breathing*. She felt as though everyone had left the room, and they were the only two people in the universe. "It's been a tough year, Darling. I'm not so naïve to think that roses should have sprouted on every clump of rabbit brush after I joined the Church, and that certainly hasn't been the case."

"It seldom is," Papa said. "Regrets?"

"Not one," Paul said softly. "I'm learning to endure, which I suspect Mormons do almost better than anyone else."

Julia watched the look her parents exchanged, seeing in it all the pain of their own year without Iris and with her own wounds. "I'm learning too," she said. "I'm sorry it's been so hard for you."

Paul looked embarrassed again. "I'm no paragon; another P word. I sulked on the train ride from Ogallala to Cheyenne. It happened to be Sunday, so I went to Sunday School, dressed in all my ranching splendor."

"Oh, horrors," Julia teased, which earned a tug of her curls.

"Funny thing: I stood there in the door and looked around at my fellow Saints, who've become so dear to me in recent months. All I could think of was that scripture in Alma, when Alma runs into his buddies again after all those years trying to shake up the Lamanites. You know that one yet, Darling?"

"I do indeed," she said promptly. "Something about rejoicing to see that they were his brothers still."

"You're on the money. It's true. I felt completely at home, because I was. Darling, we'll go to Denver next year, stay at the Brown Palace Hotel, eat at the Buckhorn Exchange—great elk steaks—and see how much honest trouble we can get into."

"I wouldn't miss it."

"Mama, this is the best Christmas of my life," Julia said later, as they were doing dishes. She peeked into the dining room, where James was intent upon building a drawbridge. She heard Paul and her father laughing about something in the parlor, and smiled.

"Next year will be even better, Jules. You'll be on the Double Tipi and . . ."

The doorbell rang. Julia wiped her hands on her apron. "Can't be the bishop; he's already visited." She looked into the hallway as her father opened the door. "Oh, my."

Spencer Davison, Iris's husband, stood there, hat in hand, as Papa helped him off with his snowy overcoat. He looked at her and nodded a greeting. She smiled back, then went back to the kitchen.

"Mama, it's Spencer."

She noticed Mama's sudden pause and intake of breath, and hopeful eyes, writhing inside to know that just for one small moment, Mama hoped that Iris would be with him and not lying in the Salt Lake Cemetery, patiently waiting for the resurrection. She touched Mama's arm. "It's all right, Mama."

"I know. I just didn't expect him." Her smile was wistful. "For just a second . . ." She shook her head, then took Julia's hand. "I can bear it, if you're with me."

"Always, Mama."

*It's my turn to pick up the pieces*, Julia thought as she entered the parlor with Mama. Papa was just standing there, Spencer's coat in his hand. Julia glanced at Paul, who was mystified.

*Take a deep breath, Jules*, she told herself. *Iris would expect it.* "Spencer, I'm so glad you came. Let me introduce my fiancé, Paul Otto. Paul, this is Iris's husband. He has a dairy farm in Draper."

To her relief, Paul didn't miss a beat. He shook hands with Spencer. "I've been wanting to meet you," he said. "I haven't married into this traveling circus yet, but I suspect we have the best in-laws, don't we, you and I?"

Tears in his eyes, Spencer nodded. Paul gripped his arm and said with all the honesty of his heart that Julia knew so well, "I am so sorry for your loss. If Iris was anything like Julia . . ." He stopped and swallowed.

"She was," Spencer said. It was his turn to take Paul's arm. The two of them stood together, then Spencer managed a small laugh. "Pardon my plain speaking, Mr. uh . . ."

"Make it Paul."

"Paul, then." He glanced at Julia, with that little bit of fun in his eyes that Iris always seemed to bring out and her death had not banished. "I don't think Jules ever realized how often she referred to you in her letters to us. You look about like I thought you would." He stepped closer, his smile growing. "Iris swore that you probably wore a gun."

"Not recently." Paul shook his head. "Spencer, did Iris ever confess to you that she and Julia used to read their brothers' western dime novels?"

The two men laughed together. "Uh, yeah," Spencer said. "She got really indignant about it when I teased her."

Julia let out her breath slowly as Mama smiled.

"Oh, you two," Mama said in her quiet way. "You're starting to remind me of our two sons in St. George."

"Whom I've yet to meet," Paul interjected.

"Oh ho, you will, and with a vengeance," Spencer said. "You can look as fearsome as you like, but they'll take you aside before the wedding—not after—and give you the 'brother talk,' both barrels, one on each side of you."

"Whoa," Paul said. "I was an only child. What is the brother talk?"

"It's the one where they vow to strike you dead if you do anything—a-n-y-t-h-i-n-g—to disrupt their sister in any way."

"I've already done that enough," Paul said. "It's too late."

"Don't tell them!"

Everyone laughed, and it was easy then for Mama and Papa to sit down with Spencer and chat about the dairy farm and how his life was going. Julia pulled Paul into the kitchen with her, closed the door, and kissed him as hard as she could.

"When was the last time I told you that you are magnificent?" she whispered, her lips close to his ear because he had grabbed her up in his arms.

"Can't recall. Maybe when I bought you that ring that we don't have to hock now, because I found my cattle," he teased.

"Well, you are magnificent. Set me down now so I can dish up some pie."

"Kiss me again and then I'll set you down."

She did, he didn't, so she had to kiss him twice more. She knew her face was still red when she and Paul took dessert into the parlor, dropping off some pie for James in the dining room, who looked up, smiled, and went back to his drawbridge. "It's going to have a pulley to raise the bridge," he said.

In the parlor, they ate in companionable silence. When Spencer finished, he leaned back and looked at Julia. "You're still some cook."

"Isn't she just?" Paul said. He winked at Julia. "Sport, how about we gather up the plates and you can tell me in the kitchen how wonderful I am?"

"Just a minute," Spencer said. He looked at Julia's parents. "I was visiting my parents in Sandy most of the day, and it took me most of that time to get up the courage to visit you."

"You know you're always welcome here, Spencer," Mama told him.

"I know. It's just hard," he replied. He took a deep breath to calm himself and pulled a packet out of his suit coat. "Julia, this is for you."

Julia took the packet, feeling cloth inside.

"Open it."

Curious, she put the packet in her lap and untied the twine around the brown paper. She pulled out eight quilt squares and held them up so Mama could see. "You and Iris were the quilters, Mama. What's the pattern?"

Mama took one, running a trembling finger over the colorful design. "My dear, it's the double wedding ring." She caressed the fabric. "I'd know Iris's little stitches anywhere."

"They're hers, all right," Spencer said, taking one of the squares. His eyes were bright with unshed tears when he looked at her. "Julia, she started making this for you last fall."

Julia stared at him, open-mouthed. "Are you certain?" She stopped, amazed. "Last fall, Paul was trying to eat my warm liver salad and probably toying with firing me!"

Spencer looked at Paul and smiled. "We laughed over that letter." He returned his attention to Julia and took her hand, after a glance at Paul, who nodded. "You may not have been aware how many times you mentioned Mr. Otto in your letters, but Iris was. She told me right after Thanksgiving that she knew you were going to marry him." He paused for a long moment, the quilt block tight in his hand. "She even said she'd better hurry up, but she only had eight blocks done when . . . Well, she only had eight blocks done." He handed her the note.

Julia could barely read it because the familiar handwriting swam before her eyes. All it said was "For Jules. Surprise!"

"I found these last week when I decided to box up some of her things. I know there's not enough for a quilt yet, but Mother Darling, maybe you could get it done. My mother said she would help."

He bowed his head over the single quilt block in his

hand. Julia took him in her arms and kissed his head, holding him close. "Spencer, you're the best," she whispered.

He dried his eyes and held out the block. Julia shook her head and pressed it back in his hand. "That's yours, dearest," she said. "We'll make a wonderful quilt for Iris. I promise."

# Six

Spencer left a few minutes later, shaking hands with Paul first. "I don't think Julia's brothers will give you too hard a time, because I think you could take them in a fair fight. Well, maybe separately."

"You're optimistic," Paul said drily. "I doubt brothers fight fair. I'm sure I wouldn't!"

"Be brave," Spencer joked. He kissed Julia. "Make sure I get an invitation to the wedding."

He embraced Mama and Papa, standing close to them in a tight circle by the open door. When the front door closed, Paul put his arm around Julia.

"He'll always be your brother-in-law, won't he?" he whispered.

"Always. Nothing changes that."

"Even if he remarries?"

"We hope he does. But, no, he will always be my brother-in-law." She turned her face into his shoulder. "I could have wished a longer life on earth for my sister, but as you pointed out yesterday, nothing happens by coincidence." She chuckled. "Which reminds me: I'm so sorry I whined about . . . well, you know, a few months ago."

To her surprise and then her profound gratitude, he looked genuinely puzzled. His expression changed, and he touched her neck. "I'd forgotten."

"I'm forgetting, but I'm not perfect yet," she said, kissing his cheek and then detaching herself, because he was getting all too comfortable. "Come on, cowboy, dishes await. We'll wash them in cold water, and you'll keep your hands in the sink."

He did as she said, and Julia glanced into the dining room as Papa sat with James. In a few minutes, the boy was showing her father how to build an elevator. Paul looked too, when he finished washing the dishes. "It appears we have an engineer on our hands. Two of them, maybe." He grabbed the dish towel she had draped over her shoulder and snapped her with it. "James and I will talk on the train ride home. He's already said that the bunkhouse isn't a good place for either Meccano set, what with overcrowding. I think I can convince him that the Shumways have plenty of room."

"It's going to be hard for you."

"Not as hard as Spencer has it. I can endure a little temporary heartache." He rested his arm on her shoulder. "Maybe the Shumways will let James spend some time with us on the Double Tipi during summer, when school is out."

"Maybe they will." She patted his chest. "And he'll be safe in Cheyenne, no matter what McAtee thinks."

"I hope you're right. I think—not certain, mind you—that all McAtee knows for sure is that I'm a liar, and a bad one, at that."

Julia read to James that night from one of the many books Mama had given him for Christmas. At her request, one of the books Mama had purchased was *The Children of the New Forest*. As James settled himself in Iris's bed, she glanced through the pages, nodding.

"James, we've struck gold," she said, aware in the deepest part of her heart how much she loved this boy that Paul was going to have to give away, for his own safety. "I had my suspicions, and now I know it: This is that whole book that Mr. Otto used to read to you and then make up endings, because so many pages were missing." She turned to the last page. "Look. There's the ending. What do you say we start at the beginning?"

The wary look returned, but she knew his natural curiosity would triumph. James nodded and made himself more comfortable, snuggling down in the quilt Mama had made years ago. "Do it, Mr. Darling."

She kissed him. "I'll read a chapter, and then Mr. Otto will read to you tomorrow night on the train." *And after that, it might be Cora Shumway*, she thought. *Comfort me, Jesus.*

She put her finger in the book. "One thing more, James. I think you understand that Mr. Otto is going to marry me."

"High time." He grinned. "That's what Doc says."

"My thoughts exactly."

Surprised, Julia looked around to see Paul standing in the door, holding a tape measure. "Mine too," she told the boy. "If you call him Mr. Otto, maybe you could call me Julia, instead of Mr. Darling. Will you do that for me?"

James nodded. "He'll still be Mr. Otto?"

"Always and forever," she said, opening the book again. "Cross my heart."

"So that's the book," Paul said, after she finished reading, knelt for James's prayer, and turned off the light.

"The very one." Julia closed the door to James's room and took the tape measure from Paul. "What's this for?"

"Your mother says you are to measure me for temple clothes and garments, which she and you will make during the next few months." He handed her a piece of paper. "Here are the measurements she needs." He nudged her shoulder and pointed. "I'm really looking forward to the measurement from my crotch to my ankle."

"Slow down, cowboy," Julia said. "*You're* going to

hold that tape measure at your crotch and I'll handle the ankle part! Mama didn't raise silly women."

"I had to try," he joked. "And I suppose you'll want to do the chest measurements and neck to waist measurements in a well-lighted place like the dining room, where your father is still making that elevator?"

"You are smart, for a cowpuncher."

*Keep it light, keep it light*, Julia thought, after family prayers, with all of them kneeling in the parlor. *I'll miss you dreadfully, Mr. Otto.*

"We'll be going early to catch that short line to Ogden," he said. "I've been on the Overland Express so much in the past year that I think I'll be a conductor, if ranching ever gets boring."

"You'd have to go through Rock Springs several times a week," Julia pointed out, not wanting him to go upstairs to bed.

"That's a scary thought," he said. He hesitated, then looked at Papa. "Jed, would you give me a blessing? I'm just not easy about James, or leaving Julia, or thinking about that house that isn't going anywhere."

"I'd be honored. Kneel down, son." He rested his hands on Paul's shoulders. "When Julia left here a year ago, I blessed her to look at people different from her in new ways."

"And you blessed me to be kept safe from storm and fire too," Julia said softly, kneeling beside Mama.

"So I did," Papa said, his voice thoughtful. "Paul, I know it says Hixon in your family Bible, but we know it's Hickman now. Any preferences?"

"The Bible burned up. I lost everything except my father's medicine bag and Julia, which means I lost exactly nothing. Make it Hickman. We're starting over."

Julia didn't even try to swallow the lump in her throat. Tears coursed down her cheeks as her father blessed Paul with peace of mind and heart and told him not to worry about the house. "The Lord generally provides," he concluded, "even if not in ways we imagine, because His ways are most certainly not ours."

When Paul rose, Julia stayed on her knees. "My turn, Paul," she said simply. "You speak, and Papa, your hands too."

"Walk with me, Darling," he said, when he finished and lifted her to her feet. "We'll be back in a little while."

It was a Christmas world outside, she decided, with snow gently falling, as it had all season; today it was Christmas snow. They strolled arm in arm, taking little glances inside the houses on the block, with Christmas trees and people gathered around them. It was late enough that some guests were leaving, with laughter and arms full of presents or carrying sleepy children.

"You've had Christmases like this all your life," Paul commented. "Going to miss them?"

She shook her head, remembering last year's belated Christmas at the Double Tipi. "Maybe not too much, if you're there."

"I'll be there. No more separations like this one, please. My hands in the bunkhouse are really getting tired of my foul mood. They were all hoping we'd get married at Christmas, but they just don't quite understand that we can't, until March."

"Try not to be crabby," she told him. "Mama is going to keep me very busy sewing!"

"I may be crabby, but I pay their salaries. They'll suffer me."

They came to the elementary school, where the swings were gathering snow, as they had gathered snow a month ago, when she sat there and thought about Uncle

Albert. "It's nice here," she said, dumping out the snow and sitting down.

Paul did the same and sat in the swing next to hers. "I don't know, Julia," he said, shaking his head. "Where is there a school like this one anywhere near the Double Tipi?"

"We'll leave it in the Lord's hands," she said, thinking about the fire and the cut bank, and held out her hand to him.

Holding hands, they moved together in rhythm, enjoying the quiet and the relief from overheated rooms and worries that would press around again on some day other than Christmas.

"I have to ask you something," Paul said finally, and she heard the hesitation in his voice. "It's a personal question, but we need this conversation." He stopped their swinging with his foot. "Julia, I know there are ways to prevent children, at least right away."

She nodded, glad there was only a streetlight to illuminate her rosy face.

"I don't really hold with that, especially since I'm approaching the dread thirty-seven this year, come August." He started them moving again. "I'd like to be able to teach a son to ride and work cattle, before I'm too decrepit."

"And I'll be twenty-nine in January," Julia said. She chuckled, thinking about a similar conversation with Ezra Quayle. "Paul, last year, I scandalized Ezra by assuring him that all my parts would work just as well at twenty-eight as they did at twenty-seven."

"You *are* a rascal," he agreed. "Unlike your former fiancé, I have no doubts that all your parts will work just as well. Are we in agreement on this matter?"

"Most definitely," she assured him. Her embarrassment passed and was replaced by gratitude that her fiancé wasn't one to tiptoe around the delicacies. "One of my recently married friends told me all the reasons why she and her husband were going to postpone a family for a few years. It sounded to me like she was trying to convince herself."

"What did she say?"

"Something like, 'This will give us a chance to get to know each other,'" Julia said. She stopped them both and turned her swing toward Paul. "I think we know each other pretty well."

Paul nodded. "Amazing what a year on the Double Tipi did, eh?"

"Maybe not so amazing." She bumped his swing with hers and he laughed.

He grew serious immediately. "Darling, have I changed much?"

It was a good question, and she thought about it, letting go of his hand and swinging herself back and forth a few times. She stopped the swing. "No, not in those particulars that make you Paul Otto. What you are is wider and deeper." She leaned her head against the chain. "I hope I am too."

"You are, madam," he said. "I'm so much in love I would almost enjoy warm liver salad now."

Julia bent down quickly, gathering a handful of snow into a ball and pelted him, which earned her a snowball too. She shrieked with laughter, which turned into a giggle and then silence when he kissed her.

"Your parts work fine," he said, his lips against hers. He sat down again and started the swing in motion. "One more thing. It's awfully private, but I need to know."

"There isn't anything you can't ask me," she said quietly.

"Same here. It's this: I've already told you about my experience with Katherine. She knew absolutely nothing about what goes on between husbands and wives." He shook his head, as though to banish a bad memory. "Our married life was purgatory. I can't go through that again; I simply can't. If you have any intimate questions, ask me, ask your mother, ask your doctor. I don't care. Just—"

Julia took off her glove and put her fingers to his lips. "Mama gave me the mother talk when I was twelve and becoming a woman." She looked down, shy. "And lately, she's been augmenting the basic discussion." She heard him chuckle and looked up, quite serious, which took the smile off his face. "All I ask is that you be gentle with me."

"Done, sport," he said simply. "I just wish I had a bedroom for that brass bed in storage in Cheyenne."

"The Lord will provide." She made a face at him. "O ye of crabby temperament and little faith, obviously!"

"He might provide the tack room."

"So? Are you going to be in it?"

"Wherever you are, there I'll be." He took her hand and pulled her up. "But right now, my a . . . backside is freezing to this swing. You know you don't want anything to happen to—"

"Paul, it's Christmas!"

"I love your logic," he said. "It gets better every time I kiss you."

Saying good-bye was hard, but not as hard as before, not with Mama and Papa both at the depot with her. Julia hugged James, thinking of their year together on the Double Tipi and her fierce desire to see him safe. For a long moment, all she could do was cup her hands around Paul's face and look into his eyes.

"Don't worry about the house. I mean it," Julia told him. "I know you want the house to be done, but you have so much to do."

"I do, indeed," he said.

"Let me at least be one thing you don't have to worry about!" *Worry about James*, she thought, with a sidelong look at the boy.

Paul's eyes followed the direction of her gaze. "I'll keep him safe, Darling, I promise."

"I never doubted it," she said quietly. "The conductor is giving you the fish eye. Better get aboard."

He nodded and took something out of his overcoat pocket. "I forgot all about this." He handed her a little glass jar, decorated with beads and feathers. "I was supposed to tell you from Doc that if you haven't already tried it, to buy some, um, what was it? Something to do with softening agent . . ."

"Dr. Blair's Softening Agent," Julia said promptly. "You can tell Doc that my doctor recommended it and I have been using it faithfully. But what's this?"

She took it from him and unscrewed the lid, gasping at the odor that rolled up from the jar like swamp gas. "It's vile!"

"My cousin Dan Who Counts—he's Charlotte's brother—sent that to me and said for you to dab it on your scars."

"Only if I had no sense of smell!" Her eyes watered before she had time to screw the lid back on. "What on earth is in it?"

"Julia, I never ask."

The conductor cleared his throat loudly, and Paul glared at him but took the hint. He kissed Julia and whispered, "Just dab a little of that behind each ear to repel any possible Romeos who don't know the fearsome Mr. Otto."

"Absolutely," she said and tucked the jar in her pocket. She stepped back then. "I'll see you in March, darling."

"That's *your* name," he said, but the worried look was gone.

"Yours, too." She surprised herself and him too by grabbing the lapels of his overcoat. "Don't worry! Do I have to get rough with you?"

He kissed her once more, elaborately pried her fingers from his overcoat, and took James's hand, to the obvious relief of the conductor. Julia noticed with a laugh that it was the same conductor who had given them five extra minutes a few months ago when Paul left.

"Won't you be happy when I marry that man and get on the train with him?" she asked him, when Paul and James went aboard and the conductor pulled up the step.

"Lady, I live in hopes of that," the conductor said, which meant she was smiling and waving as the train pulled out of the depot.

She kept a smile on her face all the way home, trying to ignore Mama's anxious glances in her direction. She went into the house with considerable dignity, head high, then announced, "I am going upstairs, but don't worry. I'm not going to cry."

In the quiet of her room, she got Paul's suit out of the closet again and put it back where it belonged at the foot of her bed. She cried until there wasn't a tear left, then dried her face. She felt scooped out and hollow inside and equally determined not to show that face downstairs. In the parlor, where Papa was already removing ornaments from the tree, Julia announced that she wanted to go to ZCMI and buy wedding dress material.

"Hold on, anxious one," Mama said. "Nothing's open today and tomorrow is Sunday. Monday will have to do."

"How on earth does ZCMI make any money, being closed on the Saturday after Christmas?" Julia groused.

Mama accepted the ornaments from Papa and wrapped them in tissue paper. "Jed, this is a far cry from the Jules I took to ZCMI more than a year ago to buy wedding material. You know, when she wasn't interested."

"I want something simple—I like tight skirts—but it should be silk, with a soft pleat in the back."

"Jed, I do believe she's been thinking about this for some time."

"Mama!" Julia said. "We'll buy plenty of muslin for garments too. And there is Iris's quilt to make." She sat down, tired already. "I don't think there's time between now and March for all this sewing."

"No problem there," Mama said with a straight face. "We'll just move the wedding back to June. June is such a lovely month for weddings, don't you think?"

Julia sighed. "Am I already a trial?"

"No more than Iris was," Mama said, and Julia heard nothing in her voice except amusement this time. "I'll turn my dressmaker loose on your wedding dress. The Relief Society and Spencer's mother have already agreed to make your double wedding ring quilt, and we'll sew the garments."

"I do believe you've been thinking about this for some time," Julia teased in turn. "And the temple clothes?"

"Ours to do, as well. Monday, it begins."

It began with such a vengeance that Papa commented over dinner Monday night that President Taft missed a bet by not making Mama Secretary of War, instead of Jacob Dickinson.

"Jed, how you carry on," Mama said serenely. "Secretary of War would be no challenge."

Julia had insisted on being at ZCMI that morning, the moment the store opened. By 8:05 a.m., she had already towed her mother up the stairs to Dry Goods to stand before as lovely a bolt of silk as existed in all the world.

"I noticed it a few months ago, when I was here with Paul," she explained. Her cheeks bloomed with color as she remembered a previous visit, when her whole aim was to ignore the idea that she was marrying Ezra Quayle. *I've learned a lot since then*, she thought, admiring the fabric. "I believe I have the bosom for it. Yes, a slim skirt, with a lot of drape," she said.

Mama signaled to the Dry Goods clerk, who started toward them with a tape measure around her neck and a pair of sheers. "You just needed to find the right man. And, yes, a slim skirt with a little kick to the back." She smiled at Julia. "Sort of like you."

*The things I'm learning*, Julia reminded herself as January rolled through. After twenty-nine years sharing the same house with her mother, she thought she knew her, but Julia began to see another side of the woman she adored, a funny side, a roguish side that must have been kept under wraps all those years.

Of course, in the privacy of her bedroom late at night, when she was restless and couldn't sleep, Julia had to admit there wouldn't have been any reason before now for Mama to tell her such intimate details of her own marriage. Mama wasn't one to dart in with unwanted advice. During one stormy afternoon when snow fell with a fury outside, and they sat so contented in the parlor, doing hand work, Julia finally gathered up enough nerve to tell Mama about that conversation with Paul on the swings at the elementary school.

"After his disastrous first marriage, he wanted to make certain that I knew exactly what goes on between husbands and wives," Julia said, her face on fire as she calmly embroidered her apron. "He wasn't shy about asking."

"You're a lucky woman," Mama said, her cheeks a little pink too. "You can probably bring up any little amorous request and have a willing participant." She touched Julia's knee. "Not all men are so wise." She turned back to the larger apron she was embroidering, then just put her hands in her lap. "My dear, I watched Paul pretty carefully during Christmas. Maybe I just wanted to assure myself that he's the husband for you."

"You did?" Julia asked, charmed. "What did you decide?"

"You know! He likes to sit in the kitchen while you cook and just watch you."

"I wasn't aware."

Mama picked up her needle again. "If you don't mind me saying, Jules, when you're in the kitchen with a spoon in your hand and a pot in front of you, you're rather like a fox watching a hen house!"

"Oh, Mama!"

"You are. Paul just tips back in his chair . . ."

"I wish I could break him of that habit," Julia grumbled.

"Don't bother trying. Save your reforming zeal for things that matter," Mama told her. "He always has his eyes on you, and his eyes look so happy." She stopped sewing again. "I am certain that has not always been the case with a man like Paul Otto."

"No. Far from it. I'm buying into a hard life."

"I doubt you'd have it any other way," Mama said softly. "I could wish you married to a banker like your father, or a doctor or a lawyer, but you want a rancher." She smiled a shy smile. "I think you want him quite a lot."

Julia swallowed and watched the green fabric get a little blurry. Funny how needlework made her eyes water. "I do, Mama. Sometimes I want him so much I wonder if I'm a family embarrassment. Is there something *wrong* with me?" There, she said it. *What will Mama think of me?* she asked herself.

Mama laughed. It was a hearty laugh Julia hadn't heard in a long time. She felt herself relax.

"Mama! I mean, some of my married friends . . ." She looked around and lowered her voice, as if the house was full of disapproving aunties. "They say it isn't much fun for them." Her words came out in a whispered rush. Julia was starting to wonder if it was easier talking to Paul than her own mother. *Who probably thinks she raised me right*, she thought, apprehensive.

"Pardon me, my dear, but some of your friends are idiots." Mama kept stitching.

Julia burst out laughing, then lowered her voice again. "So you think I'm normal to . . . to want that man so much? Not just any old man—*that* one."

"You're so normal that I'm relieved," Mama told her. "He's quite a catch. He has the broadest shoulders, and that straight back, and if you don't mind bowed legs, well . . ."

They laughed together. "I never felt this way about Ezra," Julia confessed. "I could barely get him to kiss me, and it's hard to get Paul to keep his hands from straying around."

"Good for him." Mama touched her knee again. "But thank goodness he's inaccessible on the Double Tipi right now."

"I suppose so."

"You *know* so. Just remember this: nowhere is it written that only the men find enjoyment. And if the mood is on you, just wake *him* up in the middle of the night and see what happens." She stopped. "I'm starting to drop stitches and it's your fault. Let me just say that I have no doubts you and Paul will deal well together." She stopped to pick out the misplaced stitches. "Where *is* my mind?"

Julia leaned closer and spoke in her best stage whisper. "Mama, do you want me to find an excuse to visit one of my brainless friends tonight? You know, give you and

Papa the whole house to yourselves for, oh, I don't know, maybe calisthenics. I hear it's healthy."

They laughed together, and then Julia laughed harder when Mama said, "Actually, yes. Call your friend," in total deadpan.

Julia wrote to Paul that night, not delving very deep in the afternoon's conversation, but telling him how delighted she was to see such a playful side of her mother. " 'I thought I had lost a large part of her after Iris died,' " she wrote. " 'How happy I am to be wrong.' "

She lived for Paul's letters, not that they were anything more than prosaic accounts of the ranch, complete with hiring his two cousins from Wind River, and working when they could on the house, which wasn't often enough to suit him. James was living with the Shumways now, and not a moment too soon. " 'McAtee came on the property yesterday,' " Paul wrote. " 'He said he had a steer of mine, but it was one of McLemore's, and he knew it. He looked around and asked about the boy. I didn't say a thing, and he just glared at me.' "

"Mama, I'm worried for him," Julia said, looking up from the letter she was reading aloud—at least, parts of it.

"He's capable of taking care of himself, Jules, and you too."

She didn't read Mama the next part, where Paul wrote that McAtee asked about her. " 'He had a few too many personal questions to suit me,' " he had written. " 'Julia, if you have no objections—and maybe even if you do—I think I'm going to get a dog. I think I'd be uneasy leaving you alone on the place with only Two Bits as a watch cat. Once we're married and the spring work starts, it'll just be you and Charlotte on the place for a week or so at a time. You remember how it was last spring. I don't want to leave you alone there.' "

No need for Mama to know that. Also no need for

Mama to listen to what made Julia breathe a little deeper: "'I've turned into the worst grouch. I've got an itch I can't scratch. The boys are ready to hog-tie me and set me on the train to Salt Lake City. That would make the itch even worse. Did you ever meet such a horny toad as yrs truly? Oh, for the late lamented line shack. Julia, I miss you.'"

"And I miss you," she said as she sat in her window seat and watched the snow fall.

She fingered the scar on her neck, grateful that the wider ones on her breast and ribs from the burning branch weren't painful anymore. She had been applying the foul-smelling salve from Dan Who Counts, even though Papa reeled around and collapsed in a chair when she wafted into the kitchen in her nightgown and robe one night.

She would have stopped using it, except to her critical eyes, the scars seemed less vivid. Maybe that was only wishful thinking, she decided, as February passed more slowly than it ever had since the Almighty created the earth in six days. What wasn't wishful thinking was the way the noxious stuff did loosen the tension on her scars.

And so she told Paul in one of her many letters, which she knew must be piling up like Melba toast in the Double Tipi post office box. " 'It doesn't hurt to raise my arm now,' " she wrote him. " 'The scars are more elastic. I could probably even beat you at arm wrestling.' "

"'Not a chance,'" he replied two weeks later. " 'I will never play fair, especially with you. By the way, are you ticklish? Yrs, Paul. Really, really yrs.'"

"Really, really mine," she repeated and turned her attention to the snow again.

# Seven

February was a dreadful tease, cold one day and blustery, and then warm, with water dripping from eaves all over the avenues. Cross-legged in her window seat with a writing board in her lap, Julia spent two days addressing invitations to the wedding.

Next to the kitchen, it was her favorite spot in the house, partly because she could watch for the postman. Paul's letters had gone from "'Jerusalem Crickets, the snow!'" to "'What? Snow again?'" to "'If I commit to paper what I really feel about the snow, someone at Church headquarters will yank my membership.'"

That one made Papa smile. "Something tells me it's feast or famine in Wyoming, when it comes to moisture," he told Julia one afternoon after he came home from work and found her in the kitchen, practicing wedding cakes.

Cake had become a family joke. For several weeks, she tried a small version of each cake in Miss Farmer's cookbook, until Papa complained that he was having trouble with the top button on his trousers.

"You only need to sample one bite," Julia told him.

"Agreed, but I'm never sure which bite," he said, then nudged her shoulder. "You know, if you keep rolling your eyes like that, they'll get stuck, Jules."

Her twenty-ninth birthday had come and gone. Paul must have found a way to get through that snow-covered canyon, because her present was a whopping large transfer of money from the First National in Gun Barrel to

Zions Bank with instructions to buy furniture.

"That house he's building must be the size of the Taj Mahal," she told her father, when he came home with a copy of the bank transfer in an envelope.

"As a banker, I'd probably advise you to invest it, honey," he told her. "As the father of the bride, I'd suggest you spend the man's money."

"Papa, he had a bad year!" she protested.

Papa only smiled. "My dear, as a banker *and* father, I'll relinquish privileged information—after all, you're almost married—and assure you that he's good for it. In fact, when my boss sees a transaction from Mr. Paul Otto, he gets all misty-eyed. Spend it, honey."

He touched the envelope. "I think you'll find a note in there from Mr. Money Bags."

The printing was familiar. *Dear Darling, I can just see the disapproving look on your face. Gotcha! I see it this way: Sure I could have bought all this in Cheyenne, but I seem to recall a little miss who only wanted a choice. Get what <u>you</u> want, sport. Yrs of course, Paul.*

"I'll spend it, Papa."

She did, taking the streetcar with Mama to the furniture warehouses on South State Street, picking out a sofa, comfortable leather chair, and a rocking chair for herself.

"I plan to rock my babies in this," she told her mother. Julia sat serenely and rocked, thinking of last year's parlor that went up in smoke.

At Mama's suggestion, she purchased two bureaus and a wardrobe, plus an excellent table long enough for a ranch crew, with a corresponding number of chairs, which made the salesman look at her in wonder.

"I run an orphanage," Julia said with a straight face. "Older orphans."

And so they are, she told herself, thinking of Matt, Kringle, Doc, and now Charlotte and two new hands

Paul mentioned in one of his letters. Her face clouded for a moment, thinking of Willy Bill dead in the fires of summer.

"Are you all right, my dear?" Mama asked.

"Just remembering one of my orphans," she said quietly. "What else do we need here?"

Mama talked her into end tables and kerosene lamps for the brass bed Mr. Otto had already purchased— "Trust a man to think of the essentials and no farther," Mama said drily—and similar tables and lamps for the parlor, as well as several bookcases with glass fronts, the better to keep Wyoming dust at bay. Julia stood for a long moment in front of cribs and bassinets, changing tables and highchairs, and decided not to go that far yet, especially since they were making her blush.

She did buy two beds, dressers, and chairs for two more of the still-imaginary bedrooms. "So you'll have a place to stay when you and Papa visit, and maybe James . . ." She stopped. "I wish, well, you know what I wish about James."

The salesman, looking dazed from Julia's shopping spree, agreed to ship everything to the warehouse in Cheyenne that Paul had specified.

"He wrote me that President Gillespie has a key to the warehouse," Julia said as they rode the streetcar home. "Now let's visit our favorite emporium for dishes and every utensil known to womankind."

To her secret delight, a floorwalker materialized immediately when they walked into ZCMI. *I shall have to write Paul about this*, Julia thought as she smiled like the Queen of the House of Hapsburg and let him escort her and Mama to Housewares. *Maybe Mr. Otto's silent, commanding ways are rubbing off on me.*

After selecting china, everyday ranch ware, silver plate, glasses, bowls, cooking utensils, a clever toaster with four wired sides for the oven, pitchers, and bowls for the wash table and chamber pots for under the beds, even the Queen of the House of Hapsburg needed to rest her feet.

"Shopping is onerous," she told Mama that night as they both sat in the kitchen, their bare feet in a solution of Epsom salts and water. "There's still money left."

"Books for the bookcases," Mama said decisively. "And rugs."

"We'll send Papa on that errand," Julia said. "My feet are going to hurt for a long time."

By the end of the week, they had agreed on two cakes: Miss Farmer's Imperial Cake for the groom and Queen Cake for the bride. "I'll make three layers and put Orna-mental Frosting on it, with spun sugar rosettes," Julia announced.

Papa made her try it more than once. "Just to make sure."

"I received an A-plus for this cake," Julia protested.

"Just to be sure," he said again.

"If you can't button your trousers at all after my wedding, Mama will make you walk around the block a number of times with her each night," Julia warned. "And you know she'll walk you fast."

Everything seemed to happen at once then: a bridal shower at her best friend's house, where everyone got the giggles about sweet, citified Julia marrying a rancher "with a past"; wedding presents of all shapes and sizes, which turned the postman more stoic every day; Iris's double wedding ring quilt, which took Julia's breath away; a doctor visit that could have been embarrassing but wasn't, because she had no qualms; a visit with her bishop and stake president that calmed her heart and left them smiling.

"Our little Julia, going back to cook for hard cases, even though she knows better this time," President Wilkie teased. He held out his hand and ended up patting her hand. "You haven't chosen an easy life, Sister Darling, but you don't seem inclined to change your mind. Someday there might even be a branch in Cheyenne, but I wouldn't hold out much hope for Gun Barrel, Torrington, or Wheatland."

Papa began to complain about the presents piling up in the dining room. "This is even more than Iris got," he said, wading through the boxes and checking the name tags.

He frowned over an engraved silver tray from Zions Bank. "Nincompoops. When will you ever use a silver tray on the Double Tipi?"

"Maybe I'll let Paul coil his calving ropes on that instead of slinging them over the rafter," Julia joked.

He wasn't through. "Grapefruit spoons? Cut glass knife rests? Bouillon cups? Jules, this idiotic stuff shows amazing largess from our family. Why on earth?"

"Simple. My old aunties are so astounded that I'm getting married that their reason has left them."

Julia picked up a present wrapped in brown paper. "Papa, it's from the Double Tipi!" She peered close at the wrapping. "Look. It says to open this *before* the wedding and not tell Paul. Oh, dear, should I worry?"

She opened the package and pulled out a bright blue garter with white lace and little gold tassels. "Something blue," she said, her eyes merry, and held it up for Papa, who put his hands in front of his eyes and peeked through his fingers. She looked at the attached note and laughed out loud. "'Dear Julia, Keep him away from us for two weeks and sweeten him up. We can't stand him. Love from all of us, Doc.' My goodness."

The present was followed a day later by a letter from Paul, brief and to the point. "'Dearest Darling, Look for me on next Saturday's morning train. One problem:

I haven't a single idea for a good spot for our wedding night. I don't know your town. Will you find an appropriate venue (I'm up to the V's in Doc's dictionary), and make a reservation? Yrs, Paul. P.S. Whatever my sweethearts sent you, I probably won't approve.' "

"Yes, you will," she murmured, "especially when I let you remove it."

It was really too late to blush about the matter, but she did just that over one of her many farewell dinners of his favorite foods that Papa had requested. "Any ideas? The new Hotel Utah would be nice, but it's not open yet." She pressed her hands to her flaming face. "I don't want to go to a hotel. Paul's tired of hotels, and I . . . I just want a quiet time with my husband. No bellhop with his hand out for a tip or maid wanting to clean the room. No food that I didn't cook. No sign saying we have to check out by 11 a.m. I want—we want—peace and quiet."

"The Callahans," Mama said. "What do you think, Jed?"

"Precisely," Papa agreed. "How about you two spend the night next door?"

Thoughtful, Julia got up from the table and went to the window, looking at the dark house next door. Horatio and Desiree Callahan, the neighborhood's only Gentiles, wintered near San Diego at the Hotel del Coronado. For years, Papa had kept their furnace going from November to April to keep the pipes from freezing. In exchange, the Callahans always brought him a crate of grapefruit. *For all those grapefruit spoons Paul and I are getting*, Julia thought, amused.

"Yes. We'd like that."

"Jed, go send a telegram."

After another look at his roast duck and mashed sweet potatoes, Papa did just that, grabbing his overcoat and hat. Eyes wide, Julia looked at her mother. "The Callahans? Do you really think they would allow it?"

"Jules, the Callahans have loved you since you picked all their tulips that year you were three and then replanted them upside down when you felt guilty," Mama said. "It's peaceful, it's quiet, and just the place for a rancher about this close to strangling his cowpunchers and a cook on her last nerve."

"I am not on my last nerve!" she declared, indignant.

"Trust me, Jules, you are," Mama replied, all complacency.

The Callahan's reply came the next day, and it was typical of Horatio Callahan, who owned one of Salt Lake's fifteen breweries. Mama handed it to her, along with a hairpin.

Julia opened the yellow envelope and laughed out loud. " 'Yes. Stop. The mattress in the blue bedroom doesn't squeak. Stop. Horatio,' " she read. "Perfect."

When Papa got home that evening, he took them next door and unlocked the front door.

"It's a little dusty," Mama said, looking around. "Nothing we can't remedy."

They went upstairs, looking in the bedrooms until they found the one with the blue wallpaper. Mama prodded the mattress discreetly. "No squeak."

Julia threw up her hands and went down the hall, looking for the lavatory. "Oh my," she said, her voice low. "What a palatial affair! I guess beer pays."

Papa peered into the tub, elegant with claw feet and gilt fixtures. "Big enough for a tall rancher and a short cook at the same time. Desiree *is* from France, after all. Paul will never know what hit him."

"Listen to you two!" Mama scolded.

Papa shrugged. "Maude, you're the one who tested the mattress."

"I can't take you two anywhere, can I?" Julia asked. She looked at them both, her heart overflowing with love for her parents. "And how can I part from you?"

"No parting, Jules," her father said, his arm around her and Mama. "We're all in this for the long haul, if eternity is everything it's cracked up to be." He smiled at her then. "Paul too. The blue bedroom in a brewer's house seems a good place to bed down with your sweetie. I'll probably still get a crate of grapefruit too."

Two days before she was to meet Paul at the depot, Julia sat for a long time on her bed, looking into the mirror over her bureau. She fingered her curly hair, longer now. There was enough to put up into a small bun, so Mama's hairdresser had assured her.

No one had tousled her hair since Christmas, twining the little curls around his fingers. She longed for that feeling of Paul's hands in her hair. She could let it keep growing, or she could cut it shorter again. She knew she was no Gibson girl, with long legs, a swan neck, and luxuriant hair piled high into a pompadour. Slender yes, maybe too much since the fire, and she did have a deep bosom, but she was short and always would be. She thought of Matthew, where her scripture reading had taken her lately: "Which of you by taking thought can add one cubit unto his stature?"

"Not I," she informed her reflection. She touched her hair again, thinking how Paul's eyes seemed to light up when he looked at her. She couldn't help but think of another Paul who called a woman's hair her crowning glory. She doubted that particular Paul would have been pleased with her mop of curls, but she wasn't about to marry that one.

"To the hairdresser tomorrow, and two inches less, maybe three," Julia told herself. She then fingered her scars, familiar with them, hers to keep. Without any hesitation this time, she unbuttoned her camisole, let it fall from her shoulders, and took a hard look. "This is what you will see from now on, Paul," she whispered. "Heavenly Father, I hope he really means it when he says he doesn't mind. I want to be the most beautiful woman in the world for Paul Otto."

She smiled to herself as she pulled up her camisole again, thinking of the times she had asked Mama if she was pretty. Mama always said yes, of course. Young men from her own set had shyly told her the same thing at Salt Lake Stake Academy, and she had almost believed them. She thought about the prophet Samuel, taking a spiritual inventory of the sons of Jesse, rejecting this one and that one until he came to David.

"The Lord looketh on the heart," Julia told the mirror. Maybe a future husband did too. Or wife; she knew Paul Otto's heart already. Even before she would kneel across the altar from him in the temple, she knew his heart. Good to know and not worry about, she decided, now that they were into last-minute details: wondering where to put one more out-of-town relative, or keeping an anxious eye out for the ice man, who promised a double delivery for the aspics and creams.

"Maybe we should have eloped to the temple," she told her father that night as he sat at the dining table, making paper rosettes for the table where a little niece from St. George would sit with the guest book.

"What? And ruin all this fun?" Papa asked.

Julia sighed. She took the rosette from him and twined it around a thin wire. "Festivities take on a life of their own." She put down the rosette. "Papa, what was your wedding like?"

He picked up another strip of paper. "Your mother and I were poor as church mice and I was in my last year at university. We rode in my father's wagon to the Endowment House, got married, and came home to meat loaf and hearty congratulations from your mother's parents. They figured anyone majoring in accounting would be a steady fellow."

Julia laughed. "If I read Paul's last letter correctly, we'll be going home to the tack room."

Papa covered her hands with his. "You know you couldn't be more delighted."

Julia nodded. "I just wish Paul didn't feel so bad about it." She hesitated. She ducked her head a little as she felt the tears behind her eyelids.

"Spill it, Jules," Papa said, his voice kind.

"I don't think he understands how little I care about the house." She swallowed and felt his hands tighten around hers. She took a deep breath. "He wasn't in that cut bank, trying to breathe and not burn. I look on every day since then as a gift. What on earth difference does a tack room make?"

He tipped her chin up with his finger and looked into her eyes. "It's useful knowledge, honey." It was his turn to hesitate. "Since Iris died, I don't think about trivial things in the same way, either. Paul just wants things perfect for you because he loves you."

"They already are perfect," she said simply.

Thinking about her parents' wagon ride to the temple in 1871, Julia took the streetcar to the train depot Saturday morning. Her face fell when the station manager told her the westbound train was stalled because of high water in the canyon.

"But I'm getting married on Friday!" she wailed.

The station master must have had daughters of his own. His expression was kind as he patted her hand. "My dear, the Union Pacific may not always run on time, but we always have a plan. The Ogden-Weber Stage Line is going up the canyon now, to bring'um down. We'll run a later train on the short line, and I promise you he'll be here in time for a wedding . . . ," he paused, staring long and hard at the calendar, " . . . six whole days from now." He leaned across the counter toward her. "The Lord created the earth in six days, miss, so I think the Union Pacific can deliver one groom in six days. He'll be here, unless he gets cold feet."

"Mr. Otto would never," she said, trying to gather up her few remaining scraps of dignity.

"Go home, dearie," he said. "We'll truss him into a tidy bundle and send him to your home, if he looks like he's planning to bolt."

She stood a minute more on the platform, squinting her eyes and commanding the train to materialize. When it didn't, she took the streetcar home, feeling massively sorry for herself. Mama was out hunting for a few more baskets for flowers and Papa had gone to the bank to clear out some work so he could take a few days off. They were planning to come home together, so there was no one at home to listen to her woes. After another squinty-eyed glare at the clock in the kitchen, she did what she always did in moments of crisis: she reached for the cook book.

What to make? The mints were done, the nuts all sealed in canisters. She had successfully hidden the hand-dipped chocolates from both her father and her older brother, David, who was due tomorrow from St. George with his family. Mitchell had to remain behind because her other sister-in-law was expecting confinement any minute.

She ran her finger down the table of contents and stopped at salad rolls, the perfect complement to her dinner of broiled steak, tried-and-true duchess potatoes, and that aspic, cooling so patiently in the ice box—Paul's favorite things.

She prepared a double batch and experimented with rolls shaped like crescents, twists, braids, and bow-knots. Grim and silent, she thundered down maledictions upon the president of that faulty Union Pacific Railroad and made a row of tiny hangman's nooses, which made her laugh. She gradually relaxed and finally caught herself humming as she arranged the last bits of dough into little rabbits—cooking had worked its usual magic on a disordered mind.

The front door opened a few minutes after the rabbits, nooses, and bow knots went into the Majestic. "High time, my dears," Julia called out. "You were a long time getting home and I have *such* a complaint against the UP. Papa, I trust you don't have shares in that miserable company."

"Um, *I* do. What's up, sport?"

Julia gasped and turned around as Paul, his overcoat muddy, scooped her up into his arms and kissed her. She grabbed him tight around the neck until he started to make strangling noises.

Julia held herself off from him. "You're such a tease," she said, then put her forehead against his. "What's so funny about that is no one in Wyoming would believe me if I told them. I love you."

She put her cheek close to his again and whispered softly in his ear. " 'What's up?' I'm looking at the object of my delight. Mr. Otto, I'm getting married!"

"Ditto on both of those statements," he said and kissed her again.

He sat down with her at the table, his arms around her but also in easy reach of the rolls. "Do you mind? I'm famished. The UP nearly drowned me in a mudslide and the dining car was uncoupled at Evanston because the cooking range exploded. You'd better be worth all this trouble!"

She gave him such a look then, one Mama would never approve of and that would have made her great-aunties fan themselves. "I am, Mr. Otto," she said. "I am."

The look she got in return prompted her to get off his lap and retreat to the cabinet where she kept the butter. *Steady, Julia*, she thought as she sparred for time, finding the butter, raspberry jam, and a knife, then threw caution to the winds and sat on his lap again.

"Darling, you're a welcome armful," he told her as he reached around her to butter two rolls. "The past month, I've been wrestling with calves that were in no hurry to come into this cold, cruel world; lassoing beeves out of mud banks; and eating so-so grub since Charlotte went home for a few weeks." He nuzzled her neck with his day-old whiskers, and she shrieked. "And my little sweethearts have told me not to return to the bunkhouse, ever."

She leaned against his chest, buttering another roll for him as he ate, content to stay where she was, even if his ranch hands didn't want him and his overcoat was muddy.

"You're going to be staying next door at the Callahan's place, because my brother David will be in his old room with his whole family, and my great-aunties from Pleasant Grove are taking Iris's room," she told him. "Mama said it would be safer to have you next door. She had Papa dig a moat and put in alligators."

Paul laughed. "Have you gotten all kinds of marriage advice from friends and relatives and unknown passersby?"

"I have! I've discovered that everyone loves a bride."

"I know I do, Darling."

When he finished eating, he set her off his lap, removed his overcoat, and tossed it onto the back porch. "When it dries, I'll scrape off the mud," he told her. "When are your parents coming home?"

"Any time now, and my brother is expected soon too.

And my aunties." Julia sighed. "This is about the only time we're going to have alone together until the wedding."

"Let's make the most of it," he told her as he sat down again and patted his lap. He held her close, his eyes closed. "This has been the longest six months of my life. There aren't enough cold baths in the universe."

There wasn't anything to say to that, so she didn't try. It was enough, for now, just to feel his arms around her and listen to the beating of his heart.

"I do have a matter of business to discuss, Darling," he said. "You smell so good. I like that combination of yeast and . . ." He sniffed. "Vanilla?"

She nodded. "I dab a little behind each ear. Cook's secret. *This* is business?"

"Not this! The business has to do with McLemore."

Julia sat up and looked at him. "Charlie *McLemore*?"

"I want your opinion on something, even if it does dredge up bad memories. Remember when I told you last summer that we cut the fences so the cattle could run and maybe outrace the fire?"

She nodded, feeling that familiar chill and remembering that day. She rubbed her arms.

"I had already cut the fences on my own land and had finally convinced most of the others to do the same to theirs. My cattle were long gone, and so were the ones on the open range."

She thought about what he was saying. "You *are* a gambler. What made you do that before the others?"

"Pa and I had done exactly that years ago, but we were slow then and lost most of our herd. Tough times. I give all the credit this time to the Holy Spirit, because I wasn't sure." He chuckled. "I prayed about it. Just sat there on Chief, with all the others staring at me, bowed my head, and prayed about it. The answer was just two words: 'Cut'um.' So I did, even though the others told me not to, because the wind probably wouldn't shift."

"I hope Mr. McLemore didn't make fun of you for praying," Julia said.

"They all did. And you know McLemore." He nudged her. "Goodness knows he teased you enough about your cooking." His voice was serious again. "McLemore argued with me, stalled, and lost most of his beeves. He was over-extended anyway, and with that loss, he's about to go under. Allen Cuddy—remember him?—shares a fence line with McLemore. So do I, of course, and I wouldn't mind dividing up McLemore's land with Cuddy."

"So you and Mr. Cuddy would buy out Mr. McLemore?" she asked.

Paul nodded, then twined his fingers in her curls. "I've been wanting to do this for a long while. Did you cut it?"

"Just for you, because you like it," she said, her eyes closed, enjoying the feel of his hand in her hair. "How does Mr. McLemore concern me?"

"Before I left the Double Tipi, he asked me to bank-roll him for one year—be a silent partner and help him get on his feet again. If I don't, he'll have just enough to cover his losses when we buy him out, but he'll be broke. If I do, he'll pay me back gradually. What should I do, Darling?"

She turned around to look at him, flattered. "I'm pleased, but why does my opinion matter? This is a ranch decision."

There was no overlooking his surprised expression. "Exactly. It's your ranch too, Darling, or will be in a few days. We're in this pickle together from now on. Any thoughts?"

"I'm an equal partner?"

"None better. I'll be asking your advice on most ranch decisions from now on. That's what my parents did."

She sat a moment in silence, savoring the idea, then patted his chest.

"What's that for?" he asked, amused.

"Nothing in particular, except that you are my best fellow," she told him. She looked into his eyes. "You know what to do, Paul. I see it in your eyes, and I approve."

He hugged her. "I thought you'd agree. You realize that if I become too philanthropic, I'll never maintain my status as Wyoming's stockman to tread lightly around."

"Yes, you will. I doubt Mr. McLemore will want to shout this deal to the rooftops."

"I'm certain you're correct," Paul agreed. "Personally, I can take McLemore or leave him, but his father helped me a lot after my pa died, and I owe his memory." He picked up her hand and kissed it. "What do you say we give Charlie McLemore a year, but that's all?"

She nodded. "It's fair, and I agree."

She heard Papa's automobile in the back alley. "They're home," she said into his chest. "I'd better get off your lap and look like the soul of decorum."

"You could try," he agreed, tightening his arms around her waist. "Or you could stay where you are. I think they'd be more surprised if you were off my lap."

"I'll stay here then. Goodness knows they don't need any more surprises. I've been enough of a trial."

She heard their footsteps on the walk, took Paul's face in her hands, and kissed him. "That's in case you forgot for just the smallest second that I'm mightily impressed with you."

"Not a chance, sport."

# Eight

*C*hurch the next day was an unalloyed pleasure, with the women casting little glances at her fiancé, marvelous in his black suit and vest, paisley tie, and new Stetson (the bowler hat had never seemed right; even Mama agreed).

"Everyone's looking at you because they can't believe my good fortune," she whispered.

"No, they're looking at *me* because they can't believe someone as sweet as you would show such pity on a broken-down rancher," he whispered back.

"You're hopeless, Brother Otto."

"I know, Sister Darling."

Sharing her bed that night with one of her St. George nieces, Julia found herself smiling into the dark, laughing to herself about the way her brother David took Paul aside after sacrament meeting and insisted on a walk, even though it was raining. All Paul had time to tell her when they returned was, "I've been threatened and warned," which made her glare at David. Her brother only raised his eyebrows like Papa and looked more innocent than a roomful of Young Ladies Mutual Improvement girls.

Monday morning saw the Darling men and Paul off to the church office, Paul with his endorsements from President John Herrick of the Western States Mission, his priesthood certificates, and another endorsement from Heber Gillespie, Cheyenne Sunday School Superintendent.

"It's like this, Jules," Papa said as she prepared French toast for everyone. "There's no officially constituted branch or ward in Cheyenne, so permission for admittance to the temple has to come from a General Authority."

"I'm a lot of trouble," Paul said cheerfully, holding out his plate for more French toast.

"I already knew that," Julia said.

By the end of the day, she was standing in the parlor, almost with her nose pressed against the window like a child, willing the men to come home and spare her from one more particle of good advice from well-meaning aunts, a dear sister-in-law, and visiting teachers who seemed to find it necessary to stop by. Mama had wisely retired to the hairdresser's.

*I just want to be married,* Julia thought and sighed, which made the window steam. She breathed on it again when she finally saw Papa stop his Pierce Arrow in front of the house and let out Paul and her brother. She breathed again and wrote "HELP!" in reverse on the glass. She sighed with relief when Paul's head went back and he laughed.

"I mean it," she murmured when he opened the front door. "Get me out of here!"

"Get your coat," he said.

Before anyone could stop her, she snatched up her coat and took his hand as he pulled her outside and into the wet snow.

"There now," he said as he stood with her on the sidewalk and buttoned her coat. "Where do you want to go?"

"Anyplace where I do not have to hear well-meaning advice," she told him frankly. "The swings at the elementary school."

He crooked her arm in his, a look of real understanding on his face. "It would be really precocious children who would give you marriage advice on the playground."

"Precocious? My goodness, did you start reading Doc's dictionary again?" she teased, already feeling better.

"You know I have a good memory."

When they reached the playground, Paul dusted the snow off and made her sit while he swung her. She tipped her head back, breathed deep of the cold air, and imagined herself on the Double Tipi. Paul was right; it *had* been a long six months.

After a few minutes, he slowed the swing and then stopped it. "Better?"

She nodded. "How did you fare today?"

"Better than you did." He patted his coat pocket. "I am now the proud possessor of one temple recommend, complete with permission for endowment and marriage. I almost feel as though I should ask you again to marry me."

"The answer's still the same."

He sat in the swing next to her. "Any questions for me?"

She shook her head, too shy to look at him. "You already answered my only question the last time you were here. You'll be good to me, and that's all I need."

"I couldn't be anything else," he said quietly. "Want to just walk?"

She nodded. "I just want to walk and walk until I wear myself out and drop into a deep sleep of the Rip Van Winkle variety. Maybe when I wake up, it will be Friday morning and we'll be in the temple."

"No such luck, sport," he told her, "although your father and David are taking *me* to the temple tomorrow for my own endowment."

"I thought they might. You'll come home knowing more than I do."

"It's still not a competition, Darling." He raised her

hand and kissed it. "You have to endure another two days of relatives."

She stopped walking. "I just can't," she said, and it sounded to her ears very much like whining. "I want to be married and on horseback and on my way with you to the Double Tipi." She was suddenly tired of overheated rooms and cooking odors and waiting and being polite when she wanted to just sit in her room with the door closed. "I'm whining and I'm sounding so ungrateful for everything. Forgive me, Paul, but thanks for letting me complain."

He held her close.

"I know we've done the right thing by waiting, but enduring isn't exactly a picnic, is it?"

"Nope." He looked up at the sky. "It's stopped snowing, thank the Almighty. A few blocks south of here, we passed a sweet shop. Could I buy my best girl an ice cream cone? Better say yes, because it's a real novelty to me. And don't tell me I'll ruin my appetite."

They stayed in the store until the owner, her ward's newest member, gave her the high sign and started lowering the window shades. Julia smiled her thanks at him. "See you at my wedding reception, Brother Grant?" she asked.

"I wouldn't miss it." He nodded to Paul. "Do you have any idea what a wonderful cook she is?"

"I have an inkling."

They walked home slowly, stopping in front of the big veranda finally, where she and Iris had played almost non-stop jacks one summer until they wore down the nails on their little fingers. She clutched Paul's hand and thought of the games of pickup sticks, the dolls the two of them had dressed and undressed, the whispered secrets. As she looked at the welcoming light, she remembered the trick or treating; the time she had the mumps and Santa knocked on the front door to cheer her up; the boys from Stake Academy who had escorted her home from dances; the neighbor children who had left May baskets on the front step, rung the doorbell and run away, giggling. A lifetime of living seemed to unroll in front of her, and she knew how blessed she was. The whole house seemed to glow with electric lights. Julia watched her relatives inside the parlor: her folks, the aunts, the uncles, the cousins, nieces and nephews—all there to wish her well. She smiled to see some of Paul's Hickman relatives too. "I love them all," she whispered into Paul's sleeve.

"Of course you do." He kissed her cheek. "Take a deep breath and go inside. I'm right beside you."

*And you always will be*, she thought suddenly, *even when I'm crabby.* "Paul, do you ever ask yourself how you ever got so lucky? I do."

"So do I," he told her, his lips on her hair now. "Just nearly every minute of every day."

They were married in the Salt Lake Temple at ten o'clock, Friday morning, March 17, 1911, a year and a day after Paul was baptized in Denver, Colorado. Kneeling across the altar from him and holding his hand, Julia had to remind herself again to breathe. Her whispered "yes" was as soft as his, as though a louder voice would somehow ruffle the serenity of heaven. *I am marrying the best man who ever lived*, she thought, looking into his brown eyes and seeing a mirror image of her own serious face.

Julia didn't try to stop her tears when she saw tears welling in her husband's eyes too, after he helped her to her feet. They stood in front of the officiator, and Paul slid a ring on her finger. With a little cry she couldn't help, she let him gather her into his arms and just hold her, his heart pounding as hard as hers.

"We did it, Mrs. Otto," he said softly, then released her as Mama and Papa gathered close and enveloped them both in an embrace that went on and on, reflected in the mirrors on either side of the altar.

Paul and her new Hickman relatives had arranged for a wedding breakfast at Salt Lake's finest restaurant. She had been properly impressed when Paul had written about it in one of his letters and had been looking forward to the meal for a month now. It might as well have been gritty canned pears eaten at the Double Tipi, because her mind was in such a jumble.

Then it was off to Shipler's Galley for a portrait, wearing her wedding dress for the first time, since she had worn a simpler dress in the Temple. It was Paul's turn to look stunned. "What a beautiful daughter you raised," he commented to Papa.

"I blame her mother," Papa replied.

As Harry Shipler set up his camera, Paul walked around Julia. "I like the pleats in the back," he said after a complete circuit. "Is that on purpose? They really remind me of that skirt you wore on the train platform."

"Useless skirt, wasn't it?" she said, holding still while Mama set her shoulder-length veil on her curls.

"Hardly. It gave me a great excuse to pick you up and set you in that wagon. That was the best skirt I ever saw."

Julia laughed out loud and looked at her mother, who was arranging the soft, shirred folds on the front of her dress. "I told you he'd remember, Mama."

Sitting in the chair with Paul standing behind her, his hand on her shoulder, Julia found it too hard to keep a serious face for the photographer, so she didn't try.

"This is a permanent record," the photographer reminded her.

"Let her enjoy the moment," Paul said in that tone of voice that never got an argument from anyone in Wyoming. "She hasn't seen her new house on the Double Tipi yet."

After she changed into her suit again, Mama and Papa gave her no argument either, when she told them to go on ahead. "Just put my dress in my room, please," she told Mama. "I want to walk around the temple with . . ." She took a deep breath. " . . . with my husband." She glanced at him and wondered for the tiniest moment how it was possible for him to look even more handsome than he had in suspenders and shirt sleeves that morning over bacon and eggs. "Then I think we'll take the streetcar home." She smiled at her father. "You know, Papa, sort of like you and Mama going home in a wagon to a meatloaf dinner."

It was a slow walk. The sun was shining and the air crisp. They stood for a long time, just looking up at the spires. Another slow amble took them to the entrance, where two couples, surrounded by family, were leaving.

"There seems to be a lot of that going on in the temple," Paul said. "Why does it feel like we're the only ones who ever got married?"

It wasn't a question that required an answer, so she just tucked her arm closer and leaned against her husband's shoulder.

She had to nerve herself again outside her house. "Look at all those people," she said, staring through the front window. "The walls are bulging."

"Courage, Darling. I know you're braver than that." He took her hand firmly in his and tugged her up the front steps.

Mama opened the door and stepped onto the porch, closing the door behind her. "It's a madhouse in there," she said. "Julia, your room was full of cousins changing their clothes, so your father and I just took your dress and everything else you'll need next door." She fanned herself and pushed a few stray hairpins back into her pompadour. "Then David said the dining room was too full of all those presents, so he and Papa put most of them next door too. And there is general rejoicing, because we just received a telegram from St. George, saying that we have a new granddaughter. Everyone is fine. Just a typical day at the Darlings'!" She took Paul's arm. "My dear son, your Hickman relatives dropped off such a wonderful gift!"

"Say that again, please," he asked.

Julia almost held her breath at the look he gave her mother.

"My dear son," Mama said softly. "It's true, now and forever." She dabbed at her eyes and released him, looking at Julia this time. "My aunts are in the kitchen, so all is right in their world. Best you avoid it. Paul, take her next door. Be sure to look in the parlor at the painting before you go upstairs. The reception starts at six. Don't miss it." She blew a kiss to them both, then left them standing on the porch.

Paul turned Julia around without a word and started down the steps. "Your parents are simply . . ." He shook his head. "I have no words."

"Yes, aren't they?"

He unlocked the door to the Callahan's house, ushered her inside, locked it behind them, and took her in his arms.

"I think we're supposed to look in the parlor before we go upstairs," Julia said when she eventually emerged from his embrace.

"Parlor?"

"A room with overstuffed sofas, usually a fireplace, lamps, and tables. This way."

The drapes were still closed, but it was only three in the afternoon, so they were able to thread their way through the presents to the painting. Paul picked it up and went to the window, pulling back the drapes to see it better. Curious, she peered over his arm and then leaned against him as the impact of the little painting struck her.

A family of six stared back at them, dressed in clothes stylish before the War Between the States: mother, father, two daughters, two sons. Paul traced his finger lightly over the older daughter, tall for her age, standing with her hand firmly on her younger brother's shoulder, already his protector.

"Mama and Uncle Albert," Paul said. "And my grandparents. Grandmother Hickman is buried on the trail somewhere." He made a soft sound in his throat and said something in Shoshone. "Maybe even near our ranch. Who knows?"

"Uncle Albert told me he wouldn't let the daguerreotype out of his possession, but he was thinking of having a painting made for you," she said, her voice soft, because the moment seemed almost as sacred as the temple.

"If we ever get a parlor—you know, a room with sofas, a fireplace, and a few tables—we'll hang it there. Julia, I'll race you upstairs."

He put his arm around her shoulder as he opened the door to the blue bedroom and just stopped. "My word," he said finally. "Iris's quilt. Your mother must have done this when they brought over your clothes." He chuckled. "I didn't even take time to make the bed this morning."

Julia took off her suit jacket and hung it over a doorknob. She turned around, her back to her husband. "I have lots of hooks and eyes in this shirtwaist. Get started, cowboy."

He did as she said, stopping between each hook and eye to kiss her spine. The flutters in her stomach moved lower, and she wanted him to hurry up. He took his time, though.

He must have read her thoughts. "I'm relishing the moment, sport. You know, with so many hooks and eyes and petticoats, it's amazing that the human species propagates. Another P word, in case you're wondering."

She wasn't. "I never thought I'd say this, but you talk too much, Paul."

"Ah, the complaints begin," he said with a laugh. "Be gentle with me, Julia. I'm a brand spanking new husband."

"Paul? Wake up. It's almost four-thirty."

Julia leaned over and looked under the bed, trying to find her nightgown, then realized she had never gotten that far. There wasn't even a robe in sight, just two piles of clothing, right by the bedroom door. After the tumult of the last hour, she was amazed she could still blush.

She looked at Paul again, ready to shake him awake, but suddenly content to lie down again and just watch him breathe, with even more interest than she used to just watch him eat. He had a half smile on his face, which didn't surprise her in the least. His fine-veined hands lay open on the sheet, as stretched out as he was, completely at ease. *I certainly know what relaxes you*, she thought, amused.

She kissed his bare shoulder and leaned closer to whisper in his ear. "Paul, the wedding reception starts in an hour and a half."

She gasped when he opened his eyes suddenly, growled, and grabbed her. The growl turned into a murmur, and then she forgot about the wedding reception.

"My hair is a total ruin," she said a half hour later as she lay beside him, tucked into the hollow of his shoulder, her head on his chest. His heartbeat had nearly returned to its normal rhythm.

"That's the beauty of short hair," he told her, his hand twined in her hair. "Just give it a fluff."

"Mama's going to arrange a little seed pearl hair net on it, because I don't want to wear that veil."

"How long will that take?"

She laughed and kissed his chest this time.

"Best stop doing that, Darling, if you want me to get out of bed," he warned her.

"It will take five minutes for the hair net, and it's five o'clock now, cowboy."

"Jee-rusalem Crickets, you are a spoilsport," he told her as he sat up and contemplated his clothing by the door. "I should have hung up that suit. Don't know why I didn't think of it." He padded over to the door and picked up his suit, shaking it out, and regarding it with a frown. After draping it carefully over a chair, he put his paisley tie around his neck and winked at her. "A gentleman always feels more dressed with a tie."

"Not in your case," she joked. She sat up in bed, the sheet high under her armpits, feeling shy again.

Paul took the tie off his neck. "Scoot over," he said and sat down beside her. Eyes on hers, he took the sheet and pulled it down.

"I wish I didn't have these scars," she said.

"And I wish you wouldn't give it another thought," he told her, tracing the scars with gentle fingers. "I didn't hurt you, did I? There or anywhere else?"

She shook her head.

"Well, then, Mrs. Otto, better look lively." Paul stood up and glanced at the clock. "We have forty-five minutes now to spruce up and look innocent."

"Paul, honestly, when was the last time you looked innocent?"

He just laughed.

While Paul headed down the hall, Julia went to the wardrobe and put on his robe. The room was cool now. She glanced at the bed and rolled her eyes. At least the mattress was still in place. *It does squeak*, she thought, *but no one will hear that from me.*

She made the bed quickly, smoothing down Iris's quilt with no feeling of sadness. "You may have been younger than I, my dear, but you always were smarter about affairs of the heart," she murmured.

Dressed except for his suit coat, Paul proved useful enough helping her into her wedding dress. "I am becoming an expert with hooks and eyes, but these little pearl buttons are a trial," he complained. "They take so long."

"They wouldn't if you didn't stop and kiss me with every button," she pointed out. When she was dressed, she took the blue garter from the Double Tipi out of her bag and handed it to him.

"That's from your sweethearts on the Double Tipi," she said, sitting down and lifting her skirt. "Do you think they borrowed it from one of the working girls at the Ecstasy?"

"Wow." Paul slid the garter high up her thigh and laughed when she slid it down to her knee. "I don't want to know where they got it! That's the blue. What about old, new, and borrowed?"

Julia handed him a modest gold chain. "Mama wore this at her reception," she said, turning around.

He worked the clasp. She closed her eyes at the feel of his fingers and his breath on her neck. "My dress is new, but I forgot about borrowed."

"No problem." He tugged his father's medicine bag out of his shirt front. "Just stick this down the front of your dress. Or I can loan you my tie."

She gave him a critical look after she helped him into his suit coat and fiddled with the platinum watch fob she had given him for a wedding present. "Excellent. Thank goodness wrinkles don't show much with black wool." She glanced at the clock. "We have five minutes now." She went to the window and pulled back the drapes a crack. "My goodness, people are already there!

Let's sneak out the back door and let ourselves into the kitchen."

"Where your great-aunties are," he said with a smile.

"And probably scandalized."

He shrugged. "This sort of thing doesn't show on your face, sport. We'll just tell them we've been playing strip poker."

Julia groaned and slapped his arm.

"Is there some Church admonition about saving yourself until *after* the reception?" he asked as they let themselves out the Callahan's back door. "Did we break some rule?"

"No," she replied with a laugh. "If I ever get up the nerve, I'll ask my mother about her wedding day."

"I think I already know her answer," he said, opening the back door to the Darling house. "She certainly knew where she wanted *us* this afternoon."

To her relief, the great-aunties didn't say a thing, only gave her sidelong glances in the kitchen, which she passed through with as much dignity as she could muster. After cutting her three-tiered Queen Cake with the spun sugar ornamentation and blushing at Papa's extravagant toast and his welcome of Paul into the family, they spent the next two hours circulating among the guests.

Hickmans were out in force early in the reception, even if Ed and his brother pleaded business further east and a train to catch. "Papa's expecting you both in Koosharem next week," Ed told Paul. Julia was properly awed when President Smith, his counselor Anthon Lund, and their wives stopped in briefly, but touched when Spencer Davison introduced her to a tall blond lady with shy eyes.

"Good for you, Spencer," Julia whispered in his ear as she hugged him. "I know Iris is happy too."

*Everything comes full circle*, she thought as she watched

131

Spencer with her parents. *This only means more people to love in the eternities.*

Mama told Julia on Sunday at church that the aunties left Saturday afternoon, after several surreptitious glances at the Callahan's house and giggles between the two of them. "I think your afternoon antics will become family legend, but who cares?" she whispered. "By the way, glad to see you. Have you done any cooking, or have you been surviving on the wedding cake I left at the back door?"

"Wedding cake." Julia leaned closer to her mother. "I was going to do bacon and eggs yesterday morning, but Paul said it would take too long."

Mama absorbed that with a smile. "Have you opened any of the presents yet?"

"Not one," Julia whispered back. "That will have to wait until we return from St. George."

"I'm happy you took time out for Sunday School," Mama teased.

"And I'm happy we're on the late schedule," Julia whispered, then smiled sweetly at Papa, who was about to shush his flock; she knew all the signs.

They left Monday morning on the Short Line for Koosharem, which meant getting off at Scipio and continuing the journey by stage, over bone-cracking roads where the snow was melting.

"No wonder Uncle Albert didn't come for the wedding," Paul commented, hanging onto a strap with one hand and keeping Julia in her seat with the other. "I have satisfied my curiosity about Utah roads."

Their stay in Koosharem was brief, just long enough to visit Uncle Albert—who seemed more at peace, to Julia's eyes—and to meet more Hickman cousins. Koosharem's only hotel had burned to the ground a year ago, so they spent the night with Uncle Albert, who kept Paul awake until long past midnight, telling stories of the family's experiences in Utah. Julia gave up and went to bed, but she woke up when Paul joined her. She put her cold feet on his legs. He yelped, then gathered her close, his arms around her waist.

"He wouldn't say a word about that handcart journey," he whispered to her, long after she thought he slept. "Said you had some things to tell me about that, and then he clammed up. Better tell me, Julia, because he won't."

She did, whispering of Uncle Albert's lifetime of guilt that he had fooled his sister and left her stranded for the Shoshone to find.

"That would explain him," Paul said, after a long pause. "I don't know if you noticed, but for all that he wants to talk to me, I must remind him of a terrible time. He can hardly bear to look at me."

"I noticed," she said quietly. "I don't know if he'll ever give up the pain of what he sees as ruining your mother's life. He's kept that guilty secret so many years." She rose up on one elbow to look at him better in the moonlight and touched his face. "I told him to let it go." She kissed him. "But that's a whole lifetime of guilt to let go of."

He was silent a long time, and then he ran his hand along her hip. "It's taken me a while to forgive that Mr. Otto who used to drink and sport and cheat his neighbors now and then."

"Oh, him?" she asked, putting her hand over his. "I thought he drowned when you were baptized."

He started to laugh, then kissed her hand when she put it over his mouth to quiet him. "Julia Otto, you are an amazing theologian, but you're precisely right. I like the new guy better too."

"Good thing, cowboy," she whispered, untying her clothing. "How quiet is the new guy?"

"Let's find out."

St. George was warm and welcoming, with a new niece to admire and a sister-in-law grateful to stay in bed, nurse her baby, and let Julia cook. Assuming control of the range, she cooked all her brothers' favorite dishes, pleased to work while her brothers and Paul got acquainted over the kitchen table and in the corral.

It made her heart happy to look out the kitchen window and watch the three men on horseback. She knew she had a critical eye, but there was no denying that Paul was the best horseman. She looked around at Mitch's wife and laughed at herself.

"Sorry, Julia, but Mitch is the better rider," her sister-in-law said and turned her attention back to her baby. "Paul's a close second."

Trust her brothers to do the right thing about housing them. Rather than crowd them into either of their houses on the ranch, David had elaborately handed her the key to their grandfather's little shack closer to the Virgin River, the house he had built when he came south years ago with other pioneers.

She took the key. "Iris and I used to play down there." She tapped David with the key. "And you and Mitch used to peek in the window to scare us!"

David grinned. "Now you and Paul can play down there, and no one will peek. I promise."

There wasn't any reason for the dream that night. After nearly two weeks of married life and no dream, she had begun to think it was over: the terror of the fire as she made herself small and tried to dig with broken finger-nails into the cut bank, and the horror when she couldn't breathe.

"Julia. Julia. Wake up." Paul's voice was soft, but firmly insistent as she gasped for breath and drew up into a small space, her arms tight around her knees. "Hey now. You can straighten out."

"No! I'll die!" she sobbed. She started to shake.

Paul let out his breath in a long sigh. "Oh, honey," he said. "Oh, honey. Just limber up a little. You'll be . . ."

"I'm afraid!" She sobbed out loud, resisting his attempt to straighten her legs.

He quit trying then and just put his arms around her as she shook and cried. " 'Dear Evalina, sweet Evalina, my love for thee will never, never die.' " He sang it over and over until she could breathe again. When he put his hands on her legs to straighten them, she let him, trying to control her ragged sobs as he hummed softly now. "Go back to sleep. I'm here and I'll keep you safe."

She must have slept then, stretched out and held firmly by her husband, as though they were one body. When she woke in the morning, she was alone in the bed. She came awake gradually and smiled to see Paul's long legs propped up on the bed, as he sat in a chair by her. She watched him a moment, loving him with all her heart, as he read the Book of Mormon, something he did every morning, if they weren't otherwise engaged.

His slow smile told her he knew she was watching him. He put his railroad ticket bookmark back in place and closed the book.

"I'm sorry that happened," she said. "I was hoping it wouldn't happen again."

"No need to apologize to me," he replied. He climbed back into bed with her. "I'll never know how terrible that was, will I?"

"No," she said, her voice small. "Do you think I'll get over it?"

"I know you will."

"But *when*?" She didn't want to whine, she truly didn't.

"We have eternity to find out, Darling. I've got the time if you've got the time."

She slept, safe and comfortable. When she woke, the sun was high. She was alone again, but Paul had left his pillow next to her body this time.

He was standing on the front porch, looking at the river. She came up behind him and put her arms around his waist, leaning her head against his back.

"Let's go home, Julia. I'm hungry for my own land, and I want you on it. Let's go home."

# Part Two

## The Double Tipi [TTP]

*C*asting all your cares on him;
for he careth for you.

—*I Peter 5:7*

# Nine

The most happy person to see them get on the east-bound Overland Express—together—was the conductor. With a roll of his eyes, he slapped his hand to his chest and breathed a fervent, "At last!"

"Who knew the Union Pacific hired comedians from a burlesque house?" Paul asked Julia as they sat down. He looked at her. "Darling, you're not paying attention."

"No, I'm not," she replied, all complaisance. "I'm thinking about the Double Tipi. I'm quite reconciled to the tack room, but I believe I will insist on a new privy."

"I'm way ahead of you. That's the *only* thing completed!"

She yawned. Joined by their parents in the Callahan's house, they had opened presents until nearly midnight. Most of them were impractical for life on the Double Tipi, including more sharp-pointed grapefruit spoons, an umbrella stand, a punch bowl, and a miniature potted palm tree.

Mama asked Paul why he shook his head over the umbrella stand. "The potted palm I can understand," she said, "but an umbrella stand could be useful."

"Only in states where the wind doesn't blow the rain sideways," he told her. "And as for the punch bowl . . . Julia, you can use that to wash dishes until we get a kitchen sink. I believe we'll leave the potted palm for the Callahans."

By 2:00 a.m., everything was crated and ready for the

train. "We'll get it as far as Gun Barrel and leave it for Matt or Doc to bring down a wagon," Paul said as he nailed down the last crate. "I guess we can store these in the horse barn."

*Or we could just lose them*, Julia thought as she prepared for bed. Nothing mattered to her now except getting on the high plains of Wyoming again. She glanced into the wardrobe in the blue bedroom, hoping she had packed everything.

There hung the beautiful negligee, neglected and forgotten. "Paul, I never wore it," she said after he returned from the bathroom.

He fingered the fabric. "You could put it on now," he suggested. "Better yet, save it for our fiftieth wedding anniversary, when I might need a little encouragement! Give me a hug; that's potent enough, or so I've observed."

She did, finding herself completely at home in his arms, with the result that when the alarm went off at 5:00 a.m. to catch the early train to Ogden, neither of them had slept. "A honeymoon is not for the faint of heart," Paul joked. "I'm amazed at our stamina." His mood changed then, as he pulled her close to his chest, his fingers gentle in her hair. "We'll never have this much idle time on the Double Tipi. The early work starts as soon as we get back, and then the spring cow gather in May. You'll be cooking for armies again, and I'll have to be Mr. Otto."

"And Mr. Otto will come home in the evenings and fall asleep at the kitchen table," she told him. "If we had a kitchen table."

"I'm a cad, promising you a house I didn't deliver."

She sat up and stretched, savoring the fact that she no longer felt shy in front of him, and pleased with the light in his eyes. "It still doesn't matter. Get up!"

Paul was asleep before they left the depot in Ogden,

his legs stretched out in front of him, his head on her shoulder. Julia kissed his hair and made herself comfortable with her knitting. She put her knitting down soon enough, closing her eyes to think about the past two weeks and her wonderful transformation from Julia Darling to Julia Otto. Paul had whispered to her one night that half of his pleasure was her pleasure. As she grew in love, she came to understand what he meant. It touched her, because she felt the same way.

She knew how hard he worked and knew how difficult his winter had been, rounding up cattle in snowstorms and living in an overcrowded bunkhouse. It made her sad that some of his friends—those men of power— had chosen to ostracize him, and that he had been forced to relinquish James to the care of others. He wasn't used to circumstances beyond his control, and she knew it touched a nerve in a proud man. He couldn't even talk about James without digging deep to control his emotions. That prickly encounter with Kaiser had upset the balance of his hard ranching world. He hadn't mentioned the matter again, but she remembered the hurt in his eyes when he knew he was no longer welcome in a place with his equals.

*I don't know what I can do about that, my love, except feed you and love you, and help where I can*, she thought. *I hope it's enough*. She opened her eyes, happy to see her husband so close to her, where he had been so far away for too many months, both of them yearning for each other. She wished with all her heart that she had the power to ease his way a little in his own harsh world. Maybe it did just boil down to cooking for him and loving him, if that would keep the heart in his body. *And I can pray*, she thought, *which is only what I have been doing for months and months. I'll just keep doing it*. She picked up her knitting again. *And try not to be a bother with my nightmares*.

Paul slept off and on all day, surfacing to look around at Wyoming's bleak Red Desert and Rock Springs, give the landscape his squinty-eyed stare, say something he didn't usually say, and go back to sleep. "We should have taken the night train," he told her, as he made himself comfortable against her shoulder again. "We could have slept through all this." He gave her a slow wink. "Or not."

"Seems like you're sleeping anyway, cowboy," she reminded him. "And you'd be a day later getting back to the Double Tipi, if we took the night train. This way, we can visit James this evening and catch the morning train to Gun Barrel."

They checked into the Plainsman Hotel in time for dinner. "Do you just tell them 'the usual' here in Cheyenne too?" she asked, as she opened her menu.

He nodded and handed back his unopened menu. "The usual, Clarence," he said to the waiter. "Stick with me, sport, and you'll never have to order, either," he said, after she asked for vegetable soup and baked chicken.

"You know I like to try new things," she said. "My rule for the Otto kitchen remains: your sweethearts *and you* will try something new each week."

"Darling, I like everything you do," he told her with a straight face. "Your cooking too. Julia, what are *you* thinking?" he teased.

"That you are a trial that will probably amount to an affliction, now and then. And this is my stern, behave-yourself-in-public look, in case you're wondering."

"Not likely." He started to lean back in his chair, then thought better of it. His eyes lively and alert, after sleeping across Wyoming, he looked around the dining room.

"Well, lookee there," he said softly. "It's Kaiser. I should mosey over and ask him how the continuous poker game went in Denver without a . . . hmm . . . *blamed* Mormon sitting at the table."

She saw the hurt in his eyes. "I think you should say hello. Introduce me."

"No. It's one thing for him to be rude to me. I'd take it poorly if he was rude to you too."

"I'll take a chance on that," she said, putting her hand over his. "You have to live here in Wyoming, and I do too. You're not a man to duck and run."

"I would, to spare you embarrassment," he said quickly.

"Don't worry about me! I'm tougher than I look."

He regarded her seriously. "I won't argue that," he said finally. "Straighten your hat, sport. I'll introduce you to the first in a long line of bigots you'll encounter here."

"Not the first," she reminded him as she tipped her hat slightly to a more rakish angle. "I certainly won't pour gravy on his head, like I did that preacher."

Paul laughed, which caused Kaiser to look up from the menu he was contemplating. *Or maybe hiding behind*, Julia thought. She touched her hat again, the pretty one Paul had bought her at ZCMI.

"Lead on," she said. "He looks harmless enough, especially with that slightly receding chin." She nudged Paul. "Even his handlebar moustache can't hide that!"

"You're wicked," he whispered as he stood up. "Your arm, madam?"

She took a deep breath and twined her arm in his. It wasn't her imagination that the dining room got quiet. Someone—she knew it wasn't Paul—must have spread the word about that testy encounter on the Colorado plains.

To his credit, Mr. Kaiser stood up as they approached. Julia noted the slow flush that rose from his neck.

Kaiser nodded to Paul, his eyes wary. "This your wife?" he asked.

"She is," Paul said, his tone affable. "For your

CARLA KELLY

information, she's also true blue, dyed in the wool, through and through. Julia, I'd like you meet John Kaiser, from near Grover, Colorado. He and I go back a long way. John, this is Julia Otto, certainly my better half."

Kaiser smiled slightly at that.

Julia held out her hand. "Mr. Kaiser, I am pleased to meet any friend of my husband's." *Even if you did insult him and shame him a few months ago*, she thought, smiling her company smile.

She held her breath, willing her hand not to tremble. *Heavenly Father, please, please*, she prayed silently. *We have to live here.*

To her relief, Kaiser shook her hand. It was a light handshake, the kind she expected from stockmen, who seemed to think ladies were delicate creatures.

"My pleasure, ma'am."

"Mr. Kaiser, if you're ever near the Double Tipi, do stop in. You'll eat better at my table than anywhere else."

"So I've heard," he replied, his eyes not so wary. "You're not shy about your gifts."

"No, I'm not," she said calmly, even as her heart pounded in her chest. She glanced at their table, where the waiter was setting down her vegetable soup and Paul's slab of a steak. "Kindly excuse me. I dread cold soup, unless it's supposed to be cold. Mr. Kaiser, so nice to make your acquaintance."

She returned to the table, spreading her napkin in her lap and not even daring to glance at her husband and Mr. Kaiser. She sipped her soup, covered with relief to hear the men talking to each other. *Please, Father, let it be polite conversation*, she prayed again.

"Your steak's getting cold," she said, when Paul returned to their table. She looked into his eyes and saw that inscrutable Indian look. "I hope he wasn't rude to you after I left," she whispered.

144

"Not at all. Uncomfortable, yes, especially after you were so nice to him." He took a bite of his steak. He set down the fork and gave her such a look that she held her breath with the wonder of it. "Julia, thank you. I was just going to ignore him. "

"You can't do that," she whispered, surprised at her own fervor. "We're *not* going to isolate ourselves on the Double Tipi anymore. All I know how to do is kill people with kindness and feed them. Kaiser's a beggar too, and just think how much Heavenly Father loves him. Tell yourself that until you remember it!"

His eyes filled with tears. She swallowed the boulder in her throat and reached for another roll. He took her hand.

"You amaze me," he said. "Just when I think I know you inside and out, I find out I don't. You're planning to keep me humble, aren't you?"

"Humble, but not terribly meek, I hope," she replied. She leaned closer. "Somewhere during the past two weeks, I discovered I *like* making love to a tough stockman. You signed the marriage license, so that's you. And don't forget it."

"I asked Kaiser how Denver went," Paul said, after they left the dining room and started walking to Second Avenue, where the Shumways lived. "He likes to show off his cutting horse, so he usually enters an event."

"And?"

"He just shrugged and said he came in second this year, and that maybe Denver wasn't so much fun."

"Because he came in second?"

Paul navigated her around an icy spot on the sidewalk. "He admitted that the card game kind of petered out after a few days. That's as close as he'll ever come to an apology. I asked him how his early work was going, and he said he's in town to hire more hands."

"I hope you told him that if he needed any help, you'd be there if he sent a telegram."

"I certainly did, sport." He chuckled. "It's almost maliciously fun to kill with kindness, isn't it? Guess I'm not so humble yet." His face grew solemn as he looked down the street. "That was easy. This is hard. Two more houses."

"Maybe not so hard," Julia murmured as Paul rang the doorbell and James came hurtling out and into his arms, and then hers, as if trying to gather them into a tight bundle.

He didn't seem surprised to see her. She looked James over: healthy, well-groomed, hair cut. When he tugged them both inside and then shouted, "Sister Shumway, look who's here in our house!" Julia felt her own heart crack a little and knew that Paul's must be breaking. She didn't even dare look at him, but groped for his hand, when James let go and went in search of Sister Shumway.

"You know this is best," she whispered to him, her lips next to his ear.

He nodded, his face set. "Still hard."

Then Sister Shumway was there from the kitchen, face flushed, apron untidy, which told Julia all she needed to know about supper in progress. There was something more in her eyes; they were softer. Julia hadn't observed the woman in months now, but she wasn't the same lady who had always seemed a bit like a dry twig. Sister Shumway was blooming. Julia saw it in her face, and in the way her arm just naturally went around James' shoulders. *He's her boy*, Julia thought, torn between dismay and delight.

"Can you stay for dinner?" Sister Shumway asked. "It's almost ready." She smiled at James. "I make certain he has finished his homework before we eat. Incentive, there."

Julia laughed. "How are you doing in school, James?"

"School is fun," James replied, smiling up at Sister Shumway. "Sister Shumway helps me with reading." He grinned at Paul. "We don't read the walls here, and I still don't know what *bordello* means."

To Julia's relief, Paul laughed. "It'll keep, James. Believe me, it'll keep. Sister Shumway, we already ate. We just wanted to say howdy to you two and Brother Shumway. Is he about?"

"I'm afraid not. He had a delivery to make. He should be back tomorrow or the day after." She touched James' head. "Go wash up, and make sure you stand a little closer to that bar of soap than you did this morning." She sighed and looked at Julia. "Little boys."

*Little boys*, Julia thought, transfixed by the change in the woman. She was a mother now, as sure as if James were flesh of her flesh. "I know," she said softly. "Little boys."

Sister Shumway ushered them into the parlor. "He's doing well, Brother Otto, but he misses you."

"Not too much, I hope," Paul said. "He's safe here, and from the looks of things, finding a good pasture. It's all I wanted and it's what . . . what James needed."

"I hope you're pleased," Sister Shumway said. She brightened. "You should see him in the shop with Eugene! He can already change a tire." She said it proudly.

"That's more than I can do," Paul said. "I think I'll wait on the porch. Just tell James we'll see him in church soon." He excused himself and left the room abruptly.

Sister Shumway's eyes followed him. "It's hard for him, but we need James," she said simply.

"I know you do," Julia said. "Bless you for taking him."

"Who wouldn't want James?" the woman asked. She sniffed the air. "Oh, my, the meatloaf." She touched Julia's shoulder. "I'll see you in a week or so. You'll sit next to us in church?"

Paul was standing on the sidewalk when she closed the front door behind her. He took her hand without a word, and they walked back to the city center in silence.

She put on the negligee that night, happy to offer herself to a husband in pain and hoping she could relieve some of it. Not that the negligee probably made any difference. He reached for her before the lights were out.

When they finished, she looked under the bed for the negligee. "I have the hardest time keeping track of my bedclothes," she grumbled, her head hanging over the edge. She was rewarded with a drowsy laugh from her husband and a pat on the rump.

"Forget the nightgown, sport," he said. He turned out the light by the bed and held out his arms to her. "Just stay close."

"I'm good at that."

He was silent a long time, but she knew he was awake. He ran his hand down her arm in a gesture so soothing that her eyes closed.

"I'm a lucky man," he said finally. "I'm with my best girl, and we're heading home."

"You'll be happy again."

"I'm happy now, Julia. Just a bit tender. Treat me kindly. You know, as you would the King of the House of Hapsburg."

Maybe it was the tumult in Julia's heart over James; maybe the baked chicken was more elderly than should have been served in the dining room. Whatever the reason, she had the dream again that night.

She could smell the smoke as she had smelled it for weeks last summer, hanging over the valley. In ponderous slow motion, she ran down the hill toward the shallow stream that looked no wider than a rivulet from Papa's garden hose. Her legs started to draw up toward her chest as she watched the flames roar over the ridge and explode in the house. She turned her face toward the cut bank, searching for air.

It was different this time, even though it took her a long, panicky moment to realize. She tried to draw herself into a compact ball, but Paul was pressing on her legs, his hands firm. She fought him for a moment, then woke up, her terror leaving her as he ran his hand down her leg. After a long, long moment, she began to relax. She slept, safe from the fires in her mind.

Julia woke before sunrise, her head on Paul's chest. She moved just enough to admire his profile. She touched his face, tracing the little wrinkles around his eyes. His was the face of a man used to weather, someone who faced the storm. "Let me learn from you," she whispered.

He opened his eyes at her tentative exploration. "I'm all yours," he said. "Any little thing. Julia, are you all right?"

She nodded. He kissed her forehead and settled his arm around her.

"I'm sorry . . ." she began.

"Don't apologize for something you have no control over when you sleep." He rose up on his elbow to see her better in the low light. "We could make a deal, you and I."

She watched his face, then nodded, wary.

"It's simple: you don't worry so much about bad dreams, and I won't gnaw my fingernails off to the elbows, worrying about the house I didn't build for you. A deal?"

"It's easy to say," she temporized.

"Yeah, talk's cheap. I'll worry about your dream, because it doesn't bother me, and you can worry about the house, which doesn't bother you. It's right out of Mosiah 18. I'll bear your burdens if you'll bear mine."

She nodded, touched to be reminded. He sat up and stretched. "If you have nothing better to do right now, Mrs. Otto, I vote we take advantage of that big tub in the next room. I'll scrub your shoulder blades if you'll scrub mine, and then it's back to a tin basin in the tack room. The honeymoon will be officially over."

"Only if you want it to be," she teased. "I like celebrating events early and often."

"Early's always good for a stockman."

After a quick stop at the Gillespies', which meant an awkward hug from Sister Gillespie, who looked ready for her confinement any day, they made the morning Cheyenne and Northern to Gun Barrel with minutes to spare.

"I have to wonder that Heber would go out of town when she looks ready to deliver," Paul said as they sat down. "That's about when I start pulling in my cows, keeping them close to the home place."

"I will *never* tell Emma of that comparison," Julia said, getting out her knitting again. "And you are *not* to sling the calving ropes in the tack room, also known as our house until further notice!"

Paul winced. "I'll be browbeaten and henpecked before we reach my property line."

"*Our* property line," she reminded him, digging him in the ribs with her elbow and not dropping a stitch.

He put his arm around her, his lips on her ear. "Whatever happened to that sweet little cook on the platform in Gun Barrel?"

"She's been replaced by a wife, cowboy," Julia said, trying not to smile. "I distinctly heard you say yes in the Salt Lake Temple."

"I did, indeed. Smartest thing I ever did. Just remember that when I carry you across the threshold into the tack room."

Hours later, Julia expressed her pleasure at being in the saddle again with a yell, making her normally placid horse step sideways in alarm.

"Whoa, boys," Paul said as he quieted Chief and tightened the lead on the pack horse Matt had left in the livery stable too. "We'll make it home before dark if we don't stop at the Marlowes'. Julia, I wish you could see your face. You look about as excited as James on Christmas morning."

"I've missed the Double Tipi," she said simply.

They rode steadily through the afternoon. The snow still lay in drifts and the horses picked their way carefully. Still, Julia could sense spring in the air. She pulled back on the reins suddenly and Millie stopped.

"Blue Corn," she said. "Does he think it's still winter, or has he already left? I hate to think I've missed him."

Paul reined in beside her and just looked at her for a long moment.

She knew; he didn't have to say anything. "He's dead, isn't he?" she asked, her voice soft. She leaned out to touch her husband's knee.

Paul nodded, and sat quietly for a long time, looking into the distance. Julia waited for him to gather his thoughts and compose himself.

He moved Chief even closer to Julia's horse. "He arrived on time last winter, and sure enough, the first snowfall came the next day. Charlotte took good care of him all winter, there in the old tack shed. She speaks a little Lakota, and he enjoyed that."

He sat there, taking deep breaths, for another long moment. "We had some fair weather in early March. When I visited him with Charlotte one evening, I signed that I thought he would be gone by now. Blue Corn just shook his head. And wouldn't you know, the next morning, the last blizzard of the season rolled in."

"He always knew," Julia said.

Paul nodded. "Spring came after that. One night, I told Charlotte he would probably be gone the next day, and . . . and I suppose he was." He couldn't say anything else.

"Did you bury him in the ground?" Julia had a hard time speaking around the boulder in her throat.

"Oh no. Charlotte and I built him a scaffold out where my parents are buried," he told her. "Wind, rain, snow, and Wyoming will do their work."

She saw the tears in his eyes and felt the tears in hers. "Blue Corn saw himself as your protector." It wasn't a question; she knew it was so.

Paul nodded again. "All winter, he wanted to make certain you were coming. A week before he died, I assured him that in ten sleeps, I was going on the iron horse to get you."

He brushed his hand across his eyes in that familiar gesture that she knew meant he did not want to talk. She waited.

"That satisfied him," Paul continued, when he could speak. "He signed to me, 'Your heart will be good again when she comes.'" He just looked at Julia for another long minute. "He was right, as right as he was about the weather. My heart is good again. He knew it was okay to join his ancestors."

He touched her knee this time, then started Chief in motion, riding ahead in silence until the sorrow passed, then joining her again to ride by her side.

The air was brisk, but as Julia rode, she saw the signs of spring in the activity of small birds building nests in the lodge pole pines. She breathed the fragrance of earth waking up, thankful to be away from concrete and buildings. "You had quite a winter," she said, riding close on the places where the trail was narrow because of snow. "There are some real ruts here."

"Strange. Looks like someone pulled a heavy wagon or two. Funny I didn't notice them on the way down."

"Maybe your sweethearts bought a player piano."

"You nut." He looked again at the ruts, and Julia smiled to see his good humor back. "I'm a dunce! I asked the hands to wrestle the new Queen Atlantic up here. They're supposed to have set it up in the horse barn, your new kitchen."

"I'll be cooking for horses?" she joked.

Her husband laughed, and that was his last laugh as they neared the almost-hidden turnoff to the Double Tipi. Julia knew he still agonized over his inability to deliver the promised house. He was a man of his word, and she knew it pained him to fall short. House or not, she could barely resist the urge to race ahead to see the Double Tipi valley.

"Go ahead, Darling," Paul said. "You're itching to see the place again, aren't you? The burned land still looks pretty bad, and I know the river's high now."

Funny she hadn't thought about the river. She slowed her horse and then stopped.

Paul passed her, then obviously stopped to think about it. He returned to her side, leaned toward her with a creak of leather, and kissed her cheek. "Hey now, sport. You'll get used to seeing the cut bank again. You have to let it go."

Julia nodded and kneed her horse into motion again, staying closer to Paul's side.

There it was, full of water from the spring runoff, swift and deep. To her relief, the burned branches had either been hauled away or swept downstream. She looked at the cut bank and felt her breath coming quicker.

"It doesn't look like the same river," she said finally.

"It isn't. I see now why my father didn't build right on the bank," Paul said. "The current's swift, so grip Millie tight with your knees. You know, kind of like you . . . uh . . . hang onto me."

"You are a rascal," she said, blushing furiously, and coaxed her mare forward.

They crossed the river carefully and headed up the valley, Paul looking ahead. Julia watched his face for disappointment, determined not to be unhappy herself. *He has to understand that it doesn't matter*, she thought.

"Whoa." Paul jerked back on his reins. "Julia. Julia!"

His words sounded strangled, unnatural. Alarmed, she looked where he was pointing and sucked in her breath.

A two-story white-painted house with a deep veranda stood halfway between the unburned buildings and the river, the shutters painted sky blue. Was that a porch swing? Maybe it was a trick of twilight. She closed and then opened her eyes. The house was still there, with people coming out of the front door, waving to them.

"Paul, you were teasing me the whole time," she said when she could speak. "Paul?"

She looked at her husband, who bowed his head forward until he was touching Chief's head. He sobbed out loud; she reached for him, clutching his arm as he cried.

"Paul. What . . . ?" She edged Millie closer.

"They built it in two weeks." He sobbed again, and her heart turned over. "As God is my witness, I had no idea."

"I believe you," she whispered and felt her own face grow tight. She leaned forward in her saddle, still clutching her husband's arm, and looked at the people on the porch now. "I see Karl Rudiger, and . . . oh my heavens, the whole Cheyenne Sunday School." She shook his arm more vigorously. "Is that your cousin Ed Hickman?"

Paul managed a watery chuckle. "He did tell me at the reception two weeks ago that he had to catch the east-bound train." He looked at her. "I don't know what to say."

As she leaned closer to kiss his wet cheek, he reached out to steady her. "You're not so good at that in the saddle yet, sport," he told her.

"But I'm great at it everywhere else," she said. She reached into her pocket for a handkerchief and handed it to him. "Dry up, cowboy. You have a reputation to maintain."

"It's gone," he said as he blew his nose. "They can probably hear me bawling in Gun Barrel."

"I don't care," she whispered. "You're the best man in the world, and it appears that you have a lot of very good friends who agree with me. Come on! Do I have to take your reins and lead you?"

"Like to see you try," he said, with his old humor. He took a long, shuddering breath that went right to her heart and kneed Chief forward.

The builders lined the porch. There were Doc and Matt, and even Kringle, as well as Dan Who Counts and Curtis McLeish, Paul's new hands, and a tall Indian girl she didn't recognize. Maybe it was Charlotte Who Counts. With a little sigh, she saw Karl Rudiger, his grin both wide and proud. He stood with two men she didn't know, but they all wore carpenter's aprons. "Oh, my," she said, to see Charlie McLemore and Allen Cuddy, their nearest neighbors. The Marlowes were there too.

"No wonder President Gillespie wasn't in town," Paul whispered, taking his own census of the porch's occupants. He gestured toward the little man next to Heber. "Cora Shumway did say Eugene had some hauling to do. Julia, I can't believe I'm too shy to get off my horse. I'm not sure my feet will hold me."

"Well, I'm getting off," she said. "I want to see this house!"

That was all it took. Paul dismounted and helped her from the saddle. He went straight up the front steps and wrapped his arms around Brother Gillespie, who gestured for her. In a moment they were in the center of the talking, laughing crowd, everyone speaking at once.

Finally, Paul held up his hand. It didn't surprise her even a little that everyone stopped talking. *Oh, and you think you've lost your reputation*, Julia thought, amused.

"Thank you," he said simply. "From the bottom of my heart, thank you. Who . . . How . . ."

"Howdy to you, Chief," Max Marlowe said. "We'll 'fess up after you pick up your bride—Julia, was there a shortage of men in Salt Lake?—and carry her across your threshold."

"No shortage of men," she said, her voice tight. "I got the pick of the litter in at least two states. Maybe Montana, too."

She shrieked when Paul pulled her into his arms, gave her a great kiss, picked her up, and carried her through the open door of her new home on the Double Tipi.

# Ten

Paul set her down gently. They all stood crowded into a hallway that ran the length of the house, with a stairway. Everything smelled of paint and new wood. Julia took a deep breath.

Paul looked around, a dazed smile on his face. "Will someone tell us how this astonishing bit of skullduggery came about?"

"No," Julia said emphatically. "I want a tour of every room and *then* they can tell us."

"I'll go with the brains of the outfit," Paul said. "Who gives the tour?"

President Gillespie pointed to Doc and ushered him forward. "It should be the man whose idea it was—Dr. McKeel here."

"Doc, you really *were* sick of Paul in the bunkhouse," Julia said with a laugh. "Was he so awful that you didn't even want him as close as the tack room?"

Everyone laughed, cutting the tension of tears and unshed tears.

"Julia, you'll never know," Doc said. He glanced at Paul. "Boss, with your permission or not, I'm going to give your wife a kiss and a hug."

"Just this once," Paul said, a slight smile on his face, but only a slight one.

Doc kissed her cheek. "You're as pretty as I remember, my dear. We knew Paul wanted the best for you." He looked around the front room. "First, some explanation,

Julia. After all, you're going to be living here for years and years, and the tour can hold off a moment."

Years and years. Maybe that was when it hit home. She glanced at Paul, who seemed to have the same thought, if the look on his face was any indication. "Years and years," she said softly. "Oh, Paul."

A chorus of groans rose up. "Darling, this is not a sentimental group," Paul reminded her. He looked around. "Years and years, men. I'm the lucky one."

"And it's high time," Cuddy said.

Doc cleared his throat loudly. "We're going to be awash in sentiment any moment. It wasn't just my idea, Boss. About a month before you left for Salt Lake, when I think you were out, I rifled through your ranch papers . . ."

". . . not a hard task now, with most of 'um burned," Paul interjected.

"Made my job easy. I found the name of your lawyer here and wrote to him. Told him I wanted to organize some people to at least get your house started before you returned. I mean, even *one* room would have been better than the tack room." Doc gestured to Heber. "Mr. Gillespie took it from there."

"Everyone in the Sunday School class pitched in," Heber said. "It's what we do."

"Maybe you Mormons do, but I've never seen anything like it," Doc said. "Mr. Gillespie and I decided we needed a few real builders, though, and I thought of Karl Rudiger."

"Ja. I brought along *my* helpers," Karl Rudiger said with quiet pride. "Mr. Otto, I have my own business now in Fort Collins."

"So I've heard," Paul said. He put his arm around Julia. "Actually, Darling, last fall, I had arranged with Rudiger to build cabinets for the kitchen. That is the only thing I knew would be here." He laughed. "Stashed in the horse barn with the Queen Atlantic."

"I am eager to see Mr. Rudiger's kitchen cabinets, but let's start with the parlor."

With a grand gesture, Doc opened the first door and ushered Julia through. *I just can't cry*, she thought as she looked around her in delight at the two large windows, a stove just for warmth in the corner, and all the furniture she and Mama bought in Salt Lake City. The rug was just the right size.

"I have some lace curtains in a trunk in Gun Barrel," she said.

"Lace curtains!" Charlie McLemore snorted in disgust. "Paul, she's going to ruin you!"

Paul laughed. "Too late. I surrendered two weeks ago without a whimper. Will it do, sport?"

Julia nodded. She thought of quiet evenings, rocking in her chair and knitting, with Paul sitting there. She chuckled. And probably asleep, worn out from the bovine business, as he called it.

"Let's go across the hall," Doc said, and they followed him through another door into the dining room, with its long table and many chairs. "I'm already anticipating the food here," he said. "Is it big enough, Julia?"

"Only until they start filling it with highchairs!" someone shouted from the hallway, and everyone laughed. Julia turned her face into Paul's shoulder.

She admired the new china cabinet and the bare sideboard opposite. "Paul, we can put all our wedding gifts there." She couldn't help laughing. "And never think of them again!"

"Oh, no. I *insist* on the cut glass knife rest on full display," he joked and looked around at incredulous faces. "That's right, gents. I have married up and into the gentry in Salt Lake City. I know you don't believe that, but it's the truth."

The door was open to the kitchen. Julia walked through and stood in stupefied amazement. "My stars," she said softly. "Mr. Rudiger, I think I love you."

The German laughed. "Ah, Frau, don't say that. Herr Otto will shoot me. You like them?"

Julia stood in the center of the kitchen, taking in the handcrafted cabinets that lined two of the walls from floor to ceiling. She ran her hand across the light wood, then opened one cabinet and then another, to see the dishes, pans, and cutlery she had bought in Salt Lake. She traced the grain of the light wood.

"Maple, Frau Otto," Mr. Rudiger said. "He wanted for you the best." He bowed in that courtly way she remembered.

Julia turned around to look at the new Queen Atlantic, impressive in its sheer bulk. A large pot simmered on the back burner. She lifted the lid, breathing deep of the stew inside. "Who gets the credit for this?" she asked, looking at the Indian girl standing next to Matt Malloy.

"Charlotte," Matt said and gave her a little push forward. "She's been keeping us fed, since you ruined us forever for bully beef and Vienna sausages."

"I hope you're planning to stay," Julia said.

Charlotte glanced at Paul. "My cousin wants you to have some help."

"I need it," she said. "My doctor told me no heavy lifting because of my shoulder."

Charlotte looked at Paul again. "My cousin also said you would teach me how to make biscuits and rolls."

"Your cousin's right. Where do you stay?"

Charlotte opened one of the three doors, and Julia looked into a neat little room with bed, dresser, closet, and one window, with a washstand. She stood a moment in the doorway, hands clasped in front of her, remembering with painful clarity her little room off the kitchen.

Reduced to ashes, it had been the room where she finished reading the Book of Mormon, and where she stayed so long on her knees last summer, praying for Paul and the men of the Double Tipi. She thought of the time Paul knelt here with her and cried, during that terrible summer. Staring at Charlotte's neat room brought back a gush of memories, as the loss of the ramshackle house punched her with a blow she wasn't prepared for. She felt her breath coming quickly again as she remembered her terror watching the log building burst into flames. She sagged against the doorframe.

Paul's arm went around her waist. "Hey now, sport, what's the . . ."

She turned her face into his shoulder, horrified to have such an audience for her pain. "I was remembering when the house exploded, and the flames started down the hill," she whispered.

She heard a few words softly spoken as she burrowed into his shoulder, her nightmare haunting her, toying with her, in her new home, the last thing she wanted. In a moment, the room was empty, except for Paul, Doc, and Brother Gillespie. She raised her head from Paul's shoulder, mortified. "Forgive me. I didn't think that would happen. Paul, I'm sorry. Everyone is so kind and here I am . . ."

"No fears, Darling." He held her close. "It's been quite a day for both of us. How about I take you upstairs, where I am assuming there is a brass bed with sheets on it."

"There is," Doc said, his voice kind. "Julia, I can give you some sleeping powders . . ."

She shook her head decisively. "I don't need that." She looked at her husband shyly. "What I really want—Paul understands—is just to stay in this wonderful kitchen and make some biscuits. They'll go so well with Charlotte's stew. Is there any butter?"

"Alice Marlowe brought some," Doc said, assessing her as the physician he was and not a ranch hand. "Take a look in that pantry. I think you'll be amazed."

Not letting go of Paul, Julia did as Doc said, admiring the shelves and all the foodstuffs neatly in place. And cookbooks. She sighed to see a row of them.

"We tried to think of everything in here, Julia," Brother Gillespie said. "Emma had fun."

Julia nodded, unable to speak. Brother Gillespie hugged her briefly. "Did we do all right?" he asked.

She nodded again.

"We'll just leave you here with Paul," Brother Gillespie said. "I know there are a few more things to finish up, and we'll do that before supper."

"Thank you," she said simply. "I need to cook and . . ." She took a deep breath. "I need Paul."

When the two men left the kitchen, Julia sat down at the kitchen table. "I didn't mean for that to happen," she said. "I thought I would be fine with the Double Tipi, but this is painful."

He nodded. "We shouldn't have left you alone that afternoon. Don't think I haven't rolled that around in my mind for months."

"You had to do what you did." She sobbed out loud. "I don't want to ruin this for everyone!" She was in his lap then, her arms tight around him, her refuge far more reliable than a cut bank. "It's so hard," she whispered. "Please tell them I'm fine, but this was a jolt."

"You'll be all right if I go outside?"

"I will. Here's how I know: I want to make biscuits."

"Do it, sport. I'll grain and curry our horses, and then I'll come back in here and sit with you, whether or not you want me to."

"Oh, I do." It was easier to smile then. "When was the last time I told you I loved you?"

He thought a moment, and she watched the fun in him that probably no one else in Wyoming would ever have suspected. By the time he spoke, she was smiling. "I believe it was around midnight in the Plainsman Hotel. As I recall, you said it several times. Quite emphatic." He helped her onto her feet. "Of course I may be confusing that with the night before, or was that the morning before? Any day now, I'll probably go blind or lose my hair, with all this love. Remember our deal? I bear your burdens, and you bear mine. See you in a bit."

She knew that only another cook would understand the peace of standing in a beautiful kitchen and doing her best work, even if it was just baking powder biscuits. When she opened the cookbook, a note from Emma fell out. "'My dear Julia Otto,'" she read out loud. "'Our Relief Society really gave this kitchen some thought. Our prayers are with you. Love, your sister Emma.'"

She was giving the biscuits their quick knead, when she thought about her conversation last fall with Uncle Albert. *Julia Otto, didn't you learn anything?* she chided herself as she rolled out the dough and reached for a floured glass to cut the biscuits.

Julia stood there with the glass in her hand, remembering Uncle Albert's anguish at bearing the fifty-year burden of his prank that went so disastrously awry on the bleak plains. *Julia, you told him to give that anguish away to the Lord,* she reminded herself. *The same remedy is yours too. That's what you assured him. Do you believe it or not?*

Deftly and carefully, she cut the biscuits and placed them on the cookie sheets like little soldiers in rank and file, finding peace in the simple task. *You might as well take this burden, dear Savior,* she thought, as the last biscuit went on the sheet. *I don't want it, and you don't mind it. Another perfect division of labor.*

She found a pastry brush and spread each little biscuit top with butter. She smiled to see the butter soak into the moist goodness of the flour. By the time the last round was soaking up butter, her heart was calm.

Julia hummed to herself as she slid the pan into the Queen Atlantic, then laughed out loud when she realized it was "Dear Evalina." When she looked up, Paul was standing in the side door, watching her. He knew her too well to be wary. It struck her that he watched her the way she watched the biscuit dough soak up butter.

"Better?"

"You know what cooking does to me. Cowboy, how about you call in Charlotte and have her set the table in the dining room?"

"I will. Doc said there's a tin of Nabisco Vanilla Wafers that my sweethearts have been saving for a special occasion. Now, don't get all snobby! I know you'll make something better, when you have time."

She tried to look penitent. "Am I a kitchen tyrant?"

"Worst one I know."

The sun had long since left the sky when they all sat down for supper. Julia looked around the table, pleased to see every chair filled. Some of the men watched her shyly, and others, more wary, kept their eyes on their plates.

"I'm sorry I frightened you," she said quietly. "I had a tough time on the Double Tipi last September, and it's been hard to let go of it." Her hand went automatically to the scar on her neck. "I'll be forever in your debt for this house. You're welcome here always. Paul?"

"I agree with everything my lady said." To her heart's delight, he almost caressed the two words. "You're always welcome here. One thing is different: we're going to ask a blessing on the food. We'll do it at every meal, so just get used to it."

"You're watching them eat," Paul whispered to her

when Charlotte passed around the second tray of biscuits.

"Almost my favorite thing."

"It used to be your favorite thing."

"Hush! My priorities have shifted. Don't you laugh, Mr. Otto, or it'll be my favorite thing again."

"Ouch." He pulled back his chair and held out his hand. "Walk with me, Darling. We haven't seen the second floor of this mansion yet." He looked around the table. "There's more stew, and Julia's promised cinnamon rolls and bacon and eggs in the morning."

They went slowly up the stairs as Julia admired the banister. "Mr. Rudiger's work?"

"Yeah. When I was outside, he said he told everyone what to do and kept the finish work for his team. He said they did it all room by room. The only room you didn't see downstairs was my office. They're painting it this evening." He put his forehead against hers. "And then they'll put in some wonderful book cases someone bought in Salt Lake. I believe there's a desk, too."

"Nothing's too good for the man who keeps me in flour, lard, and baking powder," Julia pointed out. "And maraschino cherries."

The first room was their bedroom. Julia touched the brass bedstead and nodded to see how well the bureaus and wardrobe fit. Mentally, she installed the floor-length mirror—provided it wasn't broken and dead in the livery stable—her smaller rocking chair, and a hope chest.

"Matt will take most of the builders down to Gun Barrel tomorrow and bring back your things. They'll look good spread around here."

"Especially Iris's double wedding ring quilt."

"Yep. It's time we got under that again," Paul said, taking her hand. "I am so ready to not do any more traveling for a long time."

"Until the spring cow gather next month?" she teased.

He groaned. "One week away from you! Want to come along?"

"We'll see."

They looked in the other three bedrooms, all of them filled now with bedrolls and clothing from the building crew, along with the beds and dressers she had bought. She looked at Paul, and then glanced away, shy again.

"What?"

"I almost—almost but not quite—bought a crib," she said.

"Why didn't you?" he asked, his arm around her waist now. "It might prove useful. Just saying."

"Iris had baby furniture, and Spencer had to get rid of it all." She rubbed her arms. "I'm not superstitious, but I'm not one to tempt fate. We can buy them later, if we need them."

"We will."

"You're so sure of yourself, cowboy?"

"You got that right."

Her hand in his, she let Paul lead her back to their room. "Boss's orders, sport. Charlotte and Matt—he insisted—will clean up downstairs. I have a few more things to do. Your job right now is to go to bed. It's been some day."

She didn't argue. She made him stay long enough for prayer, then kissed him and pointed him to the door.

He opened the door and looked back at her. "My side's the one closest to the door," he said.

"And why is that?"

"Something my father said. 'Maybe you'll find a wife someday,' he told me. 'When you do, always keep yourself between her and the door.' You're safe with me, sport."

"I already knew that," she said softly.

Julia slept soundly all night, only waking up to mutter something incoherent when Paul came to bed. When she woke, he was doing what he usually did, sitting in the chair pulled to the bed with his feet propped on it, reading the Book of Mormon.

"You were tired, sport," he said, after he closed the book. "You didn't even flinch when I put *my* cold feet on your legs."

She sat up. "I promised everyone cinnamon rolls this morning. I'd better get cracking."

She looked around the room, still delighted with what she saw. "I'm glad I didn't wake up in the tack room and find all this just a dream. We're pretty lucky, Paul."

Her husband just smiled and opened his book again.

She was soon at work, dough rising in the warming oven. Walking quietly to avoid waking Charlotte, she looked in the one room off the kitchen she hadn't seen last night, pleased to see a bathing room with a tin tub. A washstand with pitcher, bowl, mirror, and leather strop completed the room.

*If I'd wanted indoor plumbing, I'd have married a banker*, she thought, satisfied.

As she prepared the filling for the cinnamon rolls, gradually the house came awake. The Marlowes had left for their own property after supper, with a promise from Alice to bring some eggs in a few days. Julia heard footsteps overhead from the other bedrooms, and doors opening and closing downstairs from the parlor and Paul's office.

Rubbing her eyes, Charlotte Who Counts came into the kitchen. With a shy smile at Julia, she filled the well-seasoned coffee pot with water from the pump at the sink and set it on the Queen Atlantic. Julia put her to work slicing bacon.

After the cinnamon rolls were in the oven, and the bacon chuckling in the frying pan, Julia went through the kitchen, opening all of Mr. Rudiger's lovely cabinets, just to see what was inside. Mentally she thanked the Relief Society for the goods, in addition to what she had bought and shipped ahead, and Alice for putting everything right where she would have put it.

Julia was admiring the row of gleaming canisters when Paul came up behind her, grabbed her around the waist, and nuzzled her neck with his day-old beard. She shrieked, which made Charlotte laugh and look away, covering her mouth.

"Like it?" he whispered into her ear, which made her take a deep breath, and another.

"It's better after you shave," she whispered back, moving his hand back to her waist, since Charlotte was in the kitchen.

"I mean the kitchen, sport. Jee-rusalem Crickets, but you get wild thoughts when a guy sneaks up." After a pat on her rump, Paul took his shaving gear into the bathing room.

Embarrassed, Julia glanced at Charlotte, who made no attempt to hide her smile. "Boys will be boys," she said.

Charlotte turned over more bacon. "Mrs. Otto, my cousin Paul never smiled all winter. I like this cousin better."

Julia brought Paul some hot water from the Queen, amused to see him standing there, his clothes pulled down to his waist, looking at his face with a frown.

"*I* think you're handsome enough for general purposes, Romeo," she said, tipping the water into the china bowl.

He pointed to a red welt on his neck. "*You* did that in the Plainsman Hotel."

"And you enjoyed every moment!" Julia laughed and closed the door on him. In another minute, he was singing "Redeemer of Israel." *I need to enlarge his musical repertoire*, she thought. *The Lord will think he's being disrespectful, shaving* to "Redeemer of Israel." For a long moment she just leaned against the door, feeling contentment cover her like a down quilt. "Keep singing," she murmured. "I love it."

Breakfast was eaten in the usual silence she expected from stockmen, Charlotte circling the table a time or two with the coffee pot, and the four pans of cinnamon rolls gone in record time. The only comment came from Doc. "Julia, do you ever break the yolk on a fried egg?"

"I wouldn't dare," she said, passing him the bacon. "You've never known fear until you've fried eggs with Miss Farmer glaring at you, with that clipboard!"

The men laughed, and she looked around the table, satisfied. Everyone was eating, and no one looked wary this morning.

"I want you to know, I missed you all," she said simply, touching her cheek to Paul's hand on her shoulder.

While Charlotte cleared the table, she went down the hall with Paul and President Gillespie to admire the new office. At Julia's urging, Paul sat in the chair behind his new desk. He leaned back cautiously, and his smile widened as the swivel chair obliged.

"Nice chair, Darling."

"It spins around too, if you get bored."

"How would you know?"

"I tried it out. Got a little dizzy."

"You ever plan to grow up?"

"Not now. You married me anyway."

Julia heard the wagon outside. "Matt's ready to haul away the Sunday School," she said. She held out her hand to President Gillespie. "I don't know when we've been so blessed," she told him. "I appreciate everyone's sacrifice of time and effort."

He took her hand and looked at both of them. "I've

never made an easier call for help in a meeting! I was hoping one or two of the men could get away for such a length of time, but everyone came forward. Some came the first week, and the rest the second week." He laughed. "Brother Shumway said that Cheyenne's automobile owners could fix their own flat tires for two weeks. Brother Larsen prayed for a cold spell in case the other mortician in town was too busy!"

"And you were probably here for the whole thing," Paul suggested.

"It was easy, Brother Otto. I work for myself, same as you do. We were all well aware of your long winter, helping your fellow ranchers round up strays. We're here to help each other."

Julia stood taller and kissed President Gillespie's cheek. "That's for Emma. You'd better hurry home, but if I know Emma, she would have been upset if you hadn't done this."

"You know Emma," President Gillespie agreed. He glanced at Paul. "Brother Otto, if she's agreeable, how about you and I bless this little lady?"

*How did I manage so long last year without this?* Julia asked herself as she bowed her head under the gentle pressure of hands on her head from a man she admired and a man she adored. She breathed deep as Paul blessed her with peace of mind and assurance as she began married life on the Double Tipi. "Let her know, Father, how much she is loved by her husband and admired by the people she meets every day," he concluded. "Grant her courage to endure the hard moments, and the knowledge that her welfare is uppermost in my mind, and in Thy plan."

When he finished, he kissed the top of her head. "The view looks a bit different behind the desk, doesn't it? Stay there a moment. President Gillespie has some paperwork for you to sign."

"Business?"

President Gillespie pulled out a document and placed it in front of her. "This is the agreement your husband and Charles McLemore already signed, which entitles Mr. McLemore to a year's assistance to rebuild his herd."

Julia picked up the document and read it. She looked up, a question in her eyes. "You know I agree with all this. It's generous and kind."

"Will you sign it too?" Paul asked. "You're my partner now. I want your signature."

Julia thought about their visit to the banker last year, when he insisted on a countersign from Mr. Otto because she was a single female, and Mr. Otto was her employer and responsible for her. "You're thinking about that banker, aren't you?"

"A little. You are my partner now, Julia. We're in this Double Tipi gamble together. Sign away, sport. If I lose my shirt, you lose yours."

She did as he said, realizing this was the first time she had signed her name as Julia Otto. She gave an extra flourish to the final *o*. "I'll have to practice my double T's," she said, blowing on her signature.

President Gillespie took the document. "I'll register it and give you a copy next time I see you two in Cheyenne. I'll send you a telegram after Emma has the baby. Paul, Emma and I want you to stand in the circle when we bless the baby." He winked at Julia. "Let's give the man a little practice, eh?"

Her arm around her husband's waist, Julia waved good-bye to the wagonload of home builders and cabinet makers, watching until they were out of sight.

"Rudiger and his crew are coming back this fall to build a new bunkhouse," Paul said, as he stood with her on the front porch. "Have a seat, sport."

She sat with him in the porch swing. "What will you do with the old one?"

"I was going to just tear it down or burn it, but Doc had a better idea. Tell me what you think. After a thorough cleaning and a paint job, and then some interior walls, we could turn that into a nice house for a ranch foreman and his wife."

"Charlotte and Matt? I wondered."

"That's the way the wind's been blowing all winter." He tightened his grip on her shoulder. "Can't say I didn't envy them here, all careful and so aware of each other. Of course, he has to work up the nerve to propose. Malloy's so shy he makes me look like Casanova."

"What about Doc?" Julia asked, her eyes still on the horse corral, as Paul pushed the swing idly.

"You planning to pair up the whole ranch?"

"Why not? I told him last Christmas to take over Dr. Beck's practice in Gun Barrel, so you know I'm a busybody," she reminded him.

"Different story there, I think," he said after more swinging. "Doc's never offered much, and I don't ask."

"I wonder if she's remarried."

"Don't know, and it's none of my business."

She nodded, aware of the implication. "Not mine, either, I know. Maybe I just want everyone to be happy." She kissed Paul and rested her head against his chest as he continued pushing the swing slowly with one foot.

He finally stopped the swing. "I could sit here with you all morning, but duty calls. We're heading north to look over the boys and girls. And then we'll check some of my late-blooming mares that haven't foaled yet. Back to business."

"Home for lunch?"

"Nope. Could my best girl make some sandwiches?"

"I'll see if she's around and willing," Julia joked and

was unprepared for the kiss Paul gave her, his hand firm in her hair.

"She's willing," he murmured, his lips against hers. "Tell her to hold that thought until this evening, okay?"

"Okay," Julia whispered. "Paul, how did we ever keep our hands off each other last year?"

"It was a miracle, Julia Otto."

Julia and Charlotte spent the morning reorganizing the furniture in the bedrooms, now that everyone had cleared out, and getting to know each other. Julia knew Indians well enough not to ask a lot of questions, but just let the conversation move where it wanted. They made beds and fluffed pillows, and gradually Charlotte told her about her childhood on the reservation, going away to Indian school, and being so lonely.

"I learned to cook and sew," Charlotte said proudly.

"Your stew was excellent last night," Julia said. She looked around the room at the two beds and dressers. "I suppose we could move this bed into the empty room . . . No. I'll save it."

While Charlotte swept the house, dusty from the work of carpenters, Julia baked bread and fried a mound of bear sign, fragrant lumps of dough seasoned with cinnamon and maple extract and rolled into logs. "I'd prefer to dust them with powdered sugar," she told Charlotte as she mixed sugar and more cinnamon. "I suppose they're better hot, but we don't cook for a picky crowd, do we?"

Charlotte nodded. Julia could see in her eyes that she was pleased to be included. "They'll eat anything that's fried, Mrs. Otto."

"I know. It's my cross to bear. Let's try these nasty things and make sure they're edible."

The kitchen was hot, so they sat on the side porch, which Julia had already decided was an excellent idea.

Some thoughtful soul had nailed together a rough bench just the right height. Julia ate one last bear sign. "Just to make sure," she told Charlotte.

Charlotte was sweeping the front porch when Julia noticed a horseman on the ridge, watching them. She looked closer, wondering who it was, and why he didn't ride in. She almost raised her hand to beckon him down, but something stopped her. She knew the rules of the ranch. A rider would come into the camp or in the yard and just wait on his horse until invited to dismount. Even last summer, when the range was on fire and men were coming and going, no one rode onto the Double Tipi and dismounted without permission. And here was this rider on the ridge, watching, but coming no closer.

Julia stood up slowly. She walked around the corner of the porch to the main part of the veranda, where Charlotte was sweeping.

"Any idea who that is?" she asked, keeping her voice low, even if there was no chance the rider could hear her so far away.

Charlotte looked up and frowned. "He comes around every now and then, always when the men are away."

Julia felt a chill down her back. "Does . . . does he ever come any closer?"

"No. I tried to wave him down once, but he left." Charlotte leaned the broom against the railing. "It's like he's looking for someone in particular."

"He's giving me the willies," Julia said. "Maybe Doc knows."

Without knowing why, she went upstairs to her bedroom. She knew that Paul always carried a gun, even though he didn't wear it. Even in as civilized a place as the Plainsman Hotel, he had taken it out of his valise and put it in a drawer.

She went to his bureau and pulled open the top drawer. His pistol lay there among his socks and garments. She touched the gun, then closed the drawer quickly. "You're too jumpy, Mrs. Otto," she told herself as she sat down on the bed, carefully looking through the uncurtained window. The rider was still there, watching. She went to Paul's bureau again and just stared at the drawer pulls. When she looked back through the window, the horseman was gone.

Dinner was broiled steak, green beans, applesauce, and bread, hot from the Queen. "Timing is everything," Julia told Charlotte. She took the last loaf out of the oven as Paul and Doc rode in, accompanied by the others, who must have ridden out too. *We were all alone here*, she thought as the chill traveled her spine again.

Comfortable in familiar routine again, after so many months away from it, she knew precisely when to begin broiling the steaks, after the men went into the horse barn.

"Miss me, sport?" Paul asked as he came through the side door later. He sniffed the air. "Me oh my, the head cook has been busy." He kissed her. "I didn't know what the menu was, but I've been thinking about it anyway, all afternoon."

"You were thinking about food?" Doc asked, all innocence.

"Now and then," Paul said, unperturbed. "Treat me with respect, Doctor McKeel, as you would any newly married man with a hickey on his neck."

Julie rolled her eyes. The men laughed and went into the dining room. With shy smiles, the rest of his crew trooped through the side door a few minutes later, followed by Kringle, who scowled at her as usual. Julia felt her calm returning as she watched them eat, silent and appreciative, with a glance in her direction now and then.

"Soo-perb," Paul said when he finished and pushed back his chair. "I will get fat again."

"You've never been fat in your life, cowboy," Julia said. "We're not done yet. Charlotte?"

A chorus of "ahs" went up as Charlotte returned to the dining room with a platter of bear sign. Paul leaned over and kissed Julia's cheek. "You read my mind," he whispered.

"I'll bet I did," she said drily, which earned a chuckle from Doc as he applied himself to a bear sign, dipping it in his coffee.

"You know, you're missing out, having abandoned coffee for life among the Mormons," Doc said.

"They're just as good in milk," Paul replied. "Darling, should we get a cow?"

"That's such a funny question, coming from a stockman," she said.

"None of us are brave enough to milk a range cow," he told her as he ate another bear sign. "I could locate a Jersey, if you or Charlotte might be interested in milking it. Something small and harmless, to replace last year's cow."

Julia looked at Charlotte, and they both nodded. "Consider it done," Paul said. "There might be someone at the roundup willing to turn loose of such a bovine."

He started to rise, but Julia put her hand on his arm. "We need to tell you something."

The look he gave her was alert and attentive. "What happened?"

"There was a rider on the ridge, just watching us," she said, her hand still on his arm. She felt the sudden tension. "He stayed at least an hour."

"I've seen him there before," Charlotte added. "I

never said anything, because he just stayed on the ridge and never came down."

Paul glanced at Doc, then back at Julia. "Doc told me about the rider this afternoon. He just waits, like he's looking for someone."

Julia's throat felt suddenly dry. "It's Mr. McAtee, isn't it? He's looking for James."

# Eleven

*I* fear so."

Julia reached for another bear sign, her eyes on her husband. "Just sitting there, he frightened me. Can we do anything?"

"I wouldn't know what it could be," Paul said. "If I confront McAtee, he'll just say he's passing through, or that he's still looking for strays." He pushed back from the table and stood up. "Walk with me, Darling."

She stood up without a word and put her hand in his. He took another bear sign as they left the table. Outside, his arm went around her waist.

"Where are we going?" she asked.

"Nowhere in particular." He gave her a sideways glance. "I can't tell you how many times a year ago, I wished for an excuse to say 'walk with me.'" He stopped and stared at the ridge, his lips in a thin line. "Blast the man, anyway. He has a ranch of his own to run! Let's go up there."

They walked to the rise. Paul stared down at evidence of the horse. "He was here a while. Smoked a few cigarillos too." He looked to the north. "And then he lit off for the Niobrara country."

"Charlotte and I didn't realize that all the men were gone until you all rode in together tonight. The only man on the property was Kringle, I guess."

Paul gave her a faint smile. "Kringle's tough enough. I'll have a word with him and he'll keep an eye out. No fears, there."

"He's not going to the cow gather?"

"Not this year. He's having a harder and harder time walking, and I have plenty of harness work here for him to do while we're gone."

"We?"

He took her hand again. "Yeah. Come along with me." He kissed her hand and kept walking. "Doc told me that Angus Clyde rode in here a week ago to make sure that you were coming to the cow gather too. He and his brothers Malcolm and Laird are the roundup bosses this time."

"I'm the greenhorn."

"Yep. You'll come in for some ribbing, I am certain."

"I don't know anything about roundup cooking."

"No fears there, either." He patted her hand. "Your chief duties will probably be peeling spuds and watching that the beans don't burn. You're going to meet the ferocious and legendary Cookie Brown. He's worked for Clyde Cattle Company for years, and he's the boss of the chuck wagon. You keep Cookie happy, and all is well."

"You don't call him by his last name?" she teased.

He shuddered elaborately. "I wouldn't dare! We're all afraid of Cookie."

Sitting up in bed a few hours later, running a brush through her short hair, she watched Paul as he sat on the end of the bed, staring out the window.

"Matt will be back tomorrow. Charlotte and I will put up all those lace curtains and find good homes for useless doodads," she said. "I'll put the cut glass knife rest on top of the sideboard. What a joke."

She doubted he heard her, so intent was he on the window and the darkness beyond. "Hey, cowboy, are you in there?" she asked.

"Strange, isn't it? Logic and everything else tells me

that McAtee is miles away and back on his own property, but once someone's spied on you, you're never quite sure." He laughed softly. "I *was* listening! With lace curtains on these windows, at least we won't scare the horses."

She threw her pillow at him. "They'd have to be awfully tall horses."

He threw it back. "Starting something? You'll lose."

"I was hoping to, Romeo."

Later, drowsy and satisfied, Julia listened to Paul's heartbeat. "Good thing no one's upstairs except us," she whispered.

"Then why are you whispering *now*? You're a bit of a rascal, wife."

"No. I'm just the standard issue," she assured him.

"Still . . . have you noticed anything different?"

She closed her eyes, content. "No. You're the same cowboy I gave the hickey to in the Plainsman Hotel."

He ruffled her tousled hair. "No, I meant around the place. Things have changed. Used to be I paid your wages every month, and you basically did what I asked." He laughed softly. "When you weren't doing what you wanted to, instead. Funny how that didn't bother me much."

She thought about what he was saying and understood what he meant. Now she was giving orders to Charlotte, and the house was hers. "It *is* a different outlook now, and it may take some getting used to. For you too?"

He nodded, his fingers gentle in her hair. "Before the fires last summer, I was all work. Well, you know that. A spread this size will never run itself." His hand pressed more firmly on her head, and she had a fleeting memory of his hands on her head at the edge of the shallow river. "After the fire, I learned something about high stakes. Oh my word, I did. You were the center of it all, and not the ranch anymore."

"Oh, Paul," she murmured.

"There you were, wet, wounded, burned, and determined to live." He traced the scar on her breast. "Julia, you have the same fire inside you that I have. That tough time cut you close to the bone, but it didn't stop you."

"I'm afraid of McAtee. I'm afraid of my nightmares."

He put both arms around her now. "Let me tell you something, Darling. I've never told you much about my father's death, partly because it's still hard, and partly because it shows a side of me that only you will ever know."

"You've never told me anything about his death, my love," she said.

"I love it when you say that."

"My love. My love."

He kissed her cheek. "It was about this time of year in '89, and we were doing the early work, getting ready for the cow gather." He released his grip on her. "I'm squeezing you too tight."

"I don't object."

"We were roping, and he was leaning out over his saddle when his horse stepped in a prairie dog hole and broke its leg. Pa was thrown and the horse landed on him."

He stopped, and Julia pulled herself closer again. She rubbed his chest until he sighed.

"Pa got up and kind of shook himself, and said he was all right. I shot Blackie for him. I hated that. Blackie just stared at me with those big brown eyes. Not a sound, but he knew."

She felt the shudder that went through him almost as though it went through her too.

"Pa wasn't all right. I got him back to the ranch, and he just sat there at the kitchen table, like he was listening to his insides. Then he started bleeding from his mouth. I didn't know what to do. Julia, I was fifteen."

She nodded, thinking of her life at Salt Lake Stake

CARLA KELLY

Academy at fifteen, with friends, visits to the malt shop, and buying shoes.

"When he started to convulse, I tried to put him in the wagon and take him to Gun Barrel. He just shook his head and said it was too late." His hand was back in her hair again, idly pulling her curls through his fingers. "I had no one to turn to except Dawes McLemore, Charlie's father, and he was almost two hours away."

"What did you do?"

"What could I do? I just held his hand."

He was silent, and Julia caressed his face.

"Darling, when I saw you at the river's edge, I thought of my father." He took a deep breath. "Here's the difference: I held the priesthood. I knew there was something I could do."

*God comfort this good man*, Julia thought. *I am the lucky one. He will never take the priesthood for granted.* "Thank you for what you did. I'm not sure I ever told you."

"You did. I'm not surprised you don't remember. What a horrible afternoon." She knew better than to fill his silence with chatter. "Before my father died, he motioned me to put my ear close to his lips. He kissed me—blood on his lips, blood on my ear—and he told me the place was mine. Then he grabbed my hand and told me to be the brave man he knew I was. When I say no fears, Julia, I mean it. You're part of me now. You're Mr. Otto's woman. He's tough and you have to be too, or this country will devour you. It will chew you up and spit you out."

"And when I'm afraid?" she asked, her voice small.

"You lean on me and the Lord. I had no one to lean on, once Pa died. Now I do—you and the Lord. I'm rich in support, and so are you. Don't ever forget that. You're Julia Otto now, and Ottos don't blink."

Her sigh was audible, and he chuckled. "Heavy doings tonight, Julia. We make love and I show you the deepest part of my heart. You all right with that, sport?"

"I'm more than all right."

"I'll go another level deeper then. I know this is a sacred subject, but funny thing is, our home seems like a sacred place now. It never was before. When you and I were kneeling across that altar, and the officiator was sealing blessing after blessing on us, I guess the businessman in me surfaced for a moment."

"Businessman?" she asked in surprise. "Paul, are you always going to keep me a little bit off balance?"

"I hope so. You know what I heard? Potential. Together, we have endless potential, where before I had land and cattle, which amounts to absolutely nothing. When I look at you, I see eternal worlds now."

Julia closed her eyes and didn't try to stop her tears, not with her best man so close and well aware of the deepest part of her heart too. "I simply don't know what to say, Paul."

"You already did, sport, when you said yes across the altar. Go to sleep now." She woke him up later in the middle of the night, wanting him, and he was ever so obliging.

The men rode out every day the rest of the week, checking fences and watching for cattle that all winter had been drifting around through fences weakened by the fire. Kringle stayed behind, but Julia noticed that he sat outside while he mended harness, his eyes going now and then to the ridge. She made sure he had his favorite ginger snaps.

Julia thought of what Paul had said as she went about her tasks. *Our home is a sacred place,* she thought as she and Charlotte put up curtains and pictures. Mama had sent along a photograph of the Salt Lake Temple. Julia had thought of putting it in a private place upstairs, where only they could see it, but after Paul's words, she hung it right in the parlor. When Charlotte had questions, she answered them.

Charlotte exclaimed over the wedding presents, then gave Julia a knowing smile when most of them went into the storage space in the office or in the sideboard.

"Your people have never been to Wyoming, have they?" Charlotte asked, after counting all the grapefruit spoons.

"Their parents crossed Wyoming, but nobody came back and settled here," Julia said. She held up a spoon. "Maybe I could use these to plant flowers."

Charlotte exclaimed over the lovely dresses Julia hung in the wardrobe. Julia just shook her head, wondering where she would ever find a use for most of them. Thank goodness she had insisted on more plain shirt-waists, skirts, and divided skirts for riding.

She started keeping Paul company in the bathing room in the morning while he shaved. It became their substitute for "Walk with me, Darling," where he told her of his plans for the day, and she shared the menu for the evening meal.

When he finished shaving this morning, he gave her an appraising look. "I have an idea, sport. I've been mulling it around. Tell me what you think."

"I think you're awfully handsome."

"That too. The Clyde brothers are expecting you on the cow gather. I don't like them and I don't trust them, and I know they don't like me. You'll be helping Cookie, but you'll be the amateur and fair game for jokers."

"Ooh, I thought being Mrs. Paul Otto would keep me safe."

"It'll help," he agreed as he patted on some bay rum. "So will the fact that you're pretty, and you have a reputation for courage and good cooking."

"Thank you, Mr. Otto. What kind of jokes?"

He pulled up his garments and shirt and started tying and buttoning. "Does Fannie Farmer have a recipe for Rocky Mountain oysters?"

"Oysters? *Here*?"

He rolled his eyes. "That's what I was afraid of! Sport, you have a lot to learn. Tomorrow after breakfast, put on your riding clothes and I'll saddle your horse. We're going to hunt the elusive Rocky Mountain oyster, and you're going to learn how to cook 'um. Believe me, it'll save you from disaster at the roundup."

"I'm taking you to work with me today," Paul said the next morning as he twined his gloved hands together. She put her booted foot into them. "Up you get. This is a better horse than Millie. I named her Suzie Q, and she is a well-bred lady. Sort of like you."

Julia looked down dubiously. "I'm up pretty high. I can't ride Millie?"

"Nope." Paul swung himself on Chief. "Mr. Otto's woman rides blooded stock. Besides, I want you to keep up with me better. Suzie Q knows what to do."

They rode north out of the valley. The air was brisk for late April.

"I've never been this way," she said. "Come to think of it, I've never actually seen you at work, have I?"

"No. It's high time you discovered what a competent stockman you married. Race you, sport."

With no discernible command, Chief sprang forward. Suzie Q didn't hang back, which pleased Julia. Her father had never allowed her to race whatever horse her brothers set her on, when she went to the ranch. Julia laughed out loud as her hat fell off and dangled from its strings down her back.

"How do you keep your hat on?" she asked when Paul reined in by a small herd milling around in a corral.

"Practice. What else?"

She set her hat back on. Doc set two irons in the fire and waved her closer.

"Stay in the saddle, Julia," Paul said. "I'll tell you when it's safe to dismount."

She watched as Paul spoke to Chief in Shoshone and left her side, cutting smoothly through the cattle, dodging and weaving until the calves were in the pen with their mothers bellowing outside.

"Pretty impressive man, your husband," Doc said.

"Poetry," she said, her eyes on Paul. "Doc, what on earth is a Rocky Mountain oyster? I know Paul must be joking."

"No. Don't let this embarrass you, Julia, but the boss is going to save you from a whole lot of ribbing. In a stab at gentility, let's call them bull's private parts. Paul wants to brand a few of these calves and castrate them. Then he'll show you how to pop out the oyster, because they're a range delicacy. Since you're going to be *the* greenhorn, the gents will bring you a pan full of oysters in their handy dandy carrying pouch and watch you throw up."

"My word, but I have led a sheltered life," Julia said finally, when she could speak. She pointed at Paul. "That scoundrel over there on his smart horse asked me last night if there was a recipe for Rocky Mountain oysters in my cookery book." She started to laugh. "Do they . . . do they taste good?"

"I like'um. Watch your old man now."

She did, and what she saw took her breath away. He had cut out one good-sized calf and followed it with his rope swinging. With a backhanded twist of his wrist, the lariat snaked out and snagged the young bull around the hind legs as neatly as if the animal had calmly stepped into the loop. It all happened so fast, she wasn't sure what she had seen.

"Wow," she said under her breath as the calf went down.

"He'll take a dally to allow some play," Doc explained, "and drag him toward the branding fire. Watch Matt now," Doc told her. "Since it's a smallish calf, he'll just sit on his neck. Otherwise, Matt would rope the front feet, and they'd stretch out that yearling. There! Come inside the corral."

She followed Doc, watching Chief clamp down as though he was a statue, stretching out the bawling calf, trapped now by Matt's leg on his neck.

"Paul will dismount and Chief will not budge an inch. I've wondered how long it took Boss to train him. Come on. My turn now. You won't like this."

Julia followed Doc to the fire, where he selected an iron. She recognized the Double Tipi TTP brand. Doc branded the protesting calf, as its mother bawled, maybe in sympathy.

Julia recoiled from the odor of burning hair and flesh. She backed toward the fence, then leaned over and retched. She hoped the calf was making enough noise to cover the sound as she retched until she threw up, but Paul watched her. He blew her a kiss.

"Better now than at the cow gather," she murmured, wiping her mouth. He motioned to the canteen hanging from the fence post. She took a long pull.

Paul motioned her closer, and she obliged. "Sorry. You'll be smelling that all day at the gather, so get used to it. Watch now. Or not."

He flashed down with his knife across the tip of the bag. Julia gasped as he reached his fingers inside and pulled out one testicle attached to a cord, which he stretched taut, then severed. Working fast, he repeated the operation and the knife flashed again. The calf set up a louder racket, joined in volume by his anxious mother. Julia put her hands over her ears, but she couldn't help a look, surprised at how relatively bloodless the swift work was. The calf noise made her flinch.

"Who can blame him?" she murmured, repelled and fascinated at the same time. She felt the gorge rise in her throat again, but she subdued it this time, especially since she had nothing left to offer the range gods. "Why do that?"

"Makes'um easier to handle on the range and gives us better meat." He grinned at her. "You know, so I can keep you in flour, lard and sugar. Hand me that tin cup, sport."

She handed it to him, and he plopped in the pink-tinged handful and gave back the cup. "Stand back now, and we'll let up this former bull."

She retreated to the fence as Paul loosed his rope and Matt stood up and away. He nudged the calf and he rose, still bawling, looking for his mother. Doc opened the fence, and the much-put-upon calf scurried through to sanctuary from knives and irons. Both mother and son took one last look as they hightailed it away.

Julia stared at the cup in her hand. "Rocky Mountain oysters," she said. "Miss Farmer, I'll never be able to write you about this."

Julia watched Paul cut out another calf as neatly as before. He repeated the process again, and then again, until three calves were bawling and battle scarred. Each time, Julia held out the tin cup for its offering.

When they finished, Matt and Doc swatted away the remaining cattle with their lariats. Paul draped his arm around Julia.

"You did pretty well, sport," he said, and his eyes were kind. "Sorry you lost your breakfast, but better now than at the cow gather, eh?"

She nodded and surprised him by kissing his cheek. He chuckled and took the cup from her. "Come on over here now, and the lesson continues."

She followed him to the shady side of the wagon, trying to squat down like he did, but ended up poking herself with her spur. "That looks easier than it is," she grumbled.

"Just sit cross legged," he advised. "Can't have you hurting your tender parts, sport."

She laughed. "Paul, do you realize how many things have happened on the Double Tipi that I can never, ever tell my folks? What now?"

He took a bull part from the tin cup. "We could take these back home to fix them, but you'll be out on the range next week, and this is what you'll face. Watch closely."

Julia stared at his bloody hands as he took one testicle, held it tight with two fingers and cut a slit across the top. "They're slippery as all get out, so you have to be careful not to cut your fingers," he said. "Make that slit a little larger, then work your thumbs inside and pop out the oyster."

He did it easily, and the gleaming white testicle popped out. "Take off that gristle and cut the cord. What do think? Want to try?"

She nodded, swallowing a few times before picking up the testicle. After several tries, she draped it between two fingers. "Wish my hands were bigger," she muttered. She took another deep breath and cut a slit. She couldn't help smiling as she put her thumbs in the right place and popped out the oyster.

"That's my girl," Paul said, and she felt that same glow

of pride she always did at a compliment from the boss. "Do the rest of them now."

She wasn't fast, and her incisions weren't as practiced as Paul's, but she skinned the oysters and added them to the others in a piece of waxed paper. Paul twisted it shut and tucked it in her front pocket, patting her.

"Ordinarily, we'd just cook them on a flat stone next to the branding iron fire."

"That's it?" she asked dubiously.

"You could add salt, if you're particular," he said.

"You eat these?" she asked, skepticism high in her voice.

"Whenever we can. Come here and hold out your hands."

He poured water on her hands from his canteen, and she did the same for him. "What'll probably happen, unless Cookie has gotten really mellow since the last cow gather, is that the boys will be grinning from ear to ear as they bring you a few of these." He smiled. "I remember a few years ago when Allen Cuddy's sister was new to the range. She fainted dead away."

"Mr. Otto's woman won't do that," Julia said proudly.

"I didn't think so. Let's go home, sport, and I'll cook them for you."

She washed her hands for a long time at the pump in the kitchen while Paul took care of the horses. By the time he finished, she had changed clothes and found her most enveloping apron. She took the glistening, slippery oysters from the waxed paper twist and washed them.

The Queen was warm, and only needed a few more sticks of wood to produce a moderate heat. She put a cast iron skillet on the range and added a small amount of lard, under Paul's directions.

"Just put them in and fry them," he told her. "You can

poke them around until they're a uniform brown."

She only put in two. "Do'um all, sport," Paul said.

"I have another idea. Let's just try two now."

She moved them around the skillet until they were done, then put them on a cloth to drain.

"Just add a little salt, and maybe pepper, if you're feeling fancy," he said.

When she finished, he popped one in his mouth, chewed, and swallowed. "Excellent, Darling. Your turn."

She picked up the Rocky Mountain oyster and just stared at it. Paul watched her and grinned.

"Don't let me embarrass you, sport, but I haven't seen such a doubtful expression on your face since our first time together at the Callahan's, and remember how nicely that turned out."

She laughed out loud and popped in the oyster. *Heavens, this is dreadful,* she thought. *Maybe if I just don't think about what it is, I'll brush through this. Still . . .* "It's not habit-forming, but I suppose if I were starving . . ."

"Four more to go."

He reached for the oysters and she stopped him. "Nope."

It was his turn to look dubious. "I'm the expert here."

"Maybe you are," she said in her sweetest voice, "but who's the cook?" As he watched, she got down a small bowl and found the flour. "What do cowboys enjoy most of all?" she asked, as she added flour and cracked an egg.

"My blushes, Julia," he said. "What does that have to do with cooking?"

She let out an exasperated snort. "Fried food, you ninny! Would you add two cups of lard to that skillet?"

He did, and she added enough wood to produce a hot fire. She stirred the flour and egg mixture and added some canned milk and a little cornmeal for crunch. When a cube of bread browned and floated to the surface of the lard, she put the oysters in the flour mixture and coated them liberally. One by one, she dropped them into the lard, where they sizzled and popped.

"You could be on to something, sport," Paul said, his gaze intent on the skillet.

"I can't help thinking how your sweethearts devoured those bear sign I made a few days ago."

"When are they done?"

"When they float to the surface. I'll get some ketchup."

She let them cool on the cloth, then salted each little golden nugget. She held the plate out to Paul. "Try that, cowboy."

He did as she said, dipping one oyster in ketchup. He chewed and swallowed and such a light came into his eyes that Julia wanted to dance around the kitchen. "Do we have a secret weapon here?" she asked.

He nodded, unable to speak, and reached for two more. "My word, Julia."

"Save one for me," she said and dipped it in the ketchup. "Perfect." She smiled at her husband. "Stick with me, cowboy."

"That's a guarantee," he said. "I am such an easy mark."

"You are, indeed. Good thing I married you."

"You will be the hit of the roundup."

"I'll pass the greenhorn test?"

"Maybe." He picked up her cook book. "Anything in here about uh . . . sonofagun stew?"

She shook her head, mystified. "Sonofagun stew?"

"I'm being polite, because there are ladies present. That'll be another trial. Basically, it's the insides of one poor little unfortunate calf. You can add one onion, if you're a fancy chef."

"Good heavens," she said and sat down with a thump. She rested her chin on her hand. "I'll probably throw up in that."

Paul kissed the top of her head. "If you do, no one will ever know the difference."

# Twelve

They left for the open range a week later, as the sun was rising. Julia rode beside Paul, with Matt in the wagon, his horse tied on behind. The wagon was piled with equipment and bedrolls, as well as canned peaches and tomatoes and a veritable mound of bread wrapped in waxed paper, Julia's personal contribution to the cow gather. The others rode beside the wagon, careful not to pass Paul.

"Range etiquette," he told her. "I ride first."

She was still dubious about leaving Charlotte, her cousin, and Kringle behind. "You needn't worry," Paul assured her. "I have enough hands with me to gather my cattle, and I'd rather leave the lights burning on the Double Tipi."

She had soaked for a long time in the tin tub that morning, knowing it was her last bath for a week. By the time Paul came in to shave, she was wrinkled and the water barely warm. "Darling, haven't you ever gone without a bath for any length of time?"

"I have not," she had said, standing up and motioning for a towel, which he tossed her way. "I seem to recall that when you returned from the gather a year or so ago, you were pretty rank."

Lathering his face, he had eyed her in the mirror as she toweled dry. "Be sure of this: no matter how gamey you get, you'll still smell better than all of us cowmen types put together."

"That is devoutly to be desired," she said and snapped her towel at him. They were a while getting back to business after that, but at least the hands were too polite to comment on the lateness of breakfast that morning. She hoped she had wiped all the shaving soap off her face before passing the biscuits.

"How far are we going?" she asked as they trotted along, then laughed. "I sound like Iris. She used to whine and ask 'how long,' as soon as Papa turned the corner from the house."

He pointed north and west, through a gap in the hills surrounding the Double Tipi. "We'll be half a day getting there."

"How much of that time are we on your land?"

"*Our* land. Probably three hours. I sent Doc ahead to stake us a good spot. This will be a bigger gather than usual, because I know many are still missing their livestock." He smiled to himself. "This is where all my winter riding paid off, Darling, as much as I hated doing it. Most of my cattle are accounted for. We lost so little. We'll see a lot of reps from other outfits, checking brands and watching the babies." He leaned over and set her Stetson on more level. "Keep the sun off your face and neck, sport."

She touched the scar on her neck, remembering the salve in her blanket roll. "Why so many reps? I'm such a greenhorn."

"The cows that scattered will likely have calved on open range or on other ranches where the fences were cut because of the fires. A branded cow will be followed by her cleanskin calf—that's a calf with no brand. Because mothers and kiddos pair up, the ranchers will know whose is whose, and brand accordingly. If they can't come in person, they send representatives."

"Does anyone get into fights over that?" she asked.

"All the time. I've seen men shoot each other over a cow and calf dispute. Not a pleasant sight."

"You don't ever wear a gun, Paul?"

"That just invites trouble. I keep it in my bedroll, though." He looked down. "And my rifle's always there in the scabbard. Behave yourself, sport, so I don't have to get ugly with some range Romeo."

She gave him such an arch look that he burst out laughing and startled Chief. "Do I have to swat you with my towel again?" she asked.

"Better not. Look where that led."

Julia blushed and suddenly found a tumbleweed fascinating as it blew by in front of them. "You're fun, Paul, even in the bathing room," she said finally, which made him look away this time, his shoulders shaking.

They stopped to noon in the shade of a cottonwood grove along the Laramie River, running high with the snowmelt. Julia brought out roast beef sandwiches with horseradish spread that she had made the day before, and pickles. Everyone was pleased with the Lemon Queens she produced from a tin labeled "lima beans," an old trick she learned from her mother.

"Gents, do you realize that we eat better than any other outfit in at least southeast Wyoming?" Paul said, holding up his fourth Lemon Queen.

"Aye, Boss," Matt said. "And are *you* aware just how many gents want to ride for your brand? When I'm in Gun Barrel or Wheatland, I get asked all the time if you're hiring."

"I've heard it's a considerable number," Paul replied. Julia smiled to hear the pride in his voice. "Maybe they like my bunkhouse."

"I'm certain that's it," Matt replied. "Pass the Lemon Queens. Mrs. Otto, did you bring along any of those chocolate covered cherries?"

"They're hiding in the tin marked 'lard,' so now you know my deepest secrets," she said. "Better eat them now before they melt."

There was a general rush to the wagon. "You spoil us," Paul said, watching his men. "Should I still be paying your salary?"

"You do, Paul," she said simply. "It's called marriage, and I'm in favor of it."

The sun beat down, even if there was a cooling breeze. Paul made Julia put more salve on her neck. "You really don't want that to burn," he said, his fingers gentle on her neck, saying more with his gesture than words.

"Tell me something about this tyrant cook at the gather," she asked as they rode into the afternoon.

"Cookie Brown? He was a former slave in Georgia, I think. After the war, he and a lot of his kind were cut loose from plantations and started to drift. He somehow ended up with the Clyde Brothers Cattle Company, the first foreign consortium here."

"Are they Scots?" Julia asked.

Paul nodded, and Julia couldn't overlook his grim expression. "You never met a tighter-fisted, meaner-spirited bunch." He set his lips in a firm line. "After my father died, they tried to cheat me out of my land."

"Good heavens! You would think they would want to help a fifteen-year-old boy," she said, indignant.

"Not in my world, Darling. You're so tender. I was fair game, as far as they were concerned. Land is everything here."

"It was *your* land, wasn't it?"

"Of course, but the Clyde boys wanted it. They intimidated in little ways: cut fences, spooked cattle, no hands willing to hire out for a boy." He sighed, as if the memory was still too strong. "Dawes McLemore helped me until

I could keep everything together myself. I was seventeen before I knew I wasn't going to be driven off. Dawes was my only friend, and he protected me. Rumor says he put a bullet in one of the Clydes, but Dawes never said and the Clydes weren't talking. I didn't ask, of course."

"I probably would have cried myself to sleep every night," Julia said frankly.

Paul gave her a wry look. "I did. Those were two long years." He chuckled. "Almost as long as the six months we just endured." He leaned toward her, and she breathed in a pleasant whiff of bay rum. "What were you doing at seventeen?"

She thought a moment. "Agonizing over algebra and pining away because the captain of the football team decided to take my best friend to homecoming and not me."

"He was a drooling idiot," Paul said mildly. "My pa scratched a hold in this land, and I've kept it and added on." He looked into that distance she had no part of, then gave himself a little shake. "Cookie is tough too. Do what he wants, and you'll be fine. He'll have a tent set up for you, Alice Marlowe, and Elinore Cuddy, if she comes."

"Can't I sleep with you?" she asked, lowering her voice.

"Certainly you may. I put enough blankets in my bed roll for both of us. It's out on the open prairie, Julia, with not a tent in sight."

"I don't mind," she said shyly. "You're my best guy."

He leaned closer. "No privacy, Darling. I'll give you a handshake and a kiss."

"That'll do. We *really* don't want to scare the horses here."

She heard and smelled the gathering almost before

she saw it—cattle milling about and bawling, and above all that din, the sharp whistles of the cowboys.

"My goodness. How many cows are there?"

"Couple thousand. A lot of ours are fenced on our land already—I'm trying to keep my polled Herefords separate—but I have other cattle here. What happens is we'll separate our herds, settle the disputes, brand the calves, castrate most, and generally leave them on the open range to grow fat on this grass. I'm not shipping any to Chicago this summer, but I will in the fall, of course." He gestured with his lips, Indian fashion. "And there is the famous Clyde Brothers Cattle Company chuck wagon. I'll introduce you to your worst nightmare for the next few days. Or your best friend. It'll depend on you."

*I'm on display*, Julia thought as she rode with her husband past cattle, horses, and cowmen, the dust rising in lazy puffs. She was too shy to look around. She forced herself not to put her hand to her neck and rode as tall as she could, chin up.

"Darling, you're the prettiest lady that has ever graced a roundup," Paul told her as they rode knee to knee. "My stars, you look good on horseback."

"Oh, Paul!"

"I am the envy of nations, and let me tell you, Darling, it feels pretty good."

*He's just saying that to bolster my courage*, she told herself, but couldn't help the real pride she felt, riding beside one of the best—no, the best—stockman in southeast Wyoming, the man who held her heart and soul in capable hands. She smiled at him. "You look pretty good on horseback too, cowboy. *I'm* the envy of nations."

"My, but we are a self-satisfied couple," he said in a low voice meant just for her ears. "These gents will probably start to gag any minute. Rein up here, Julia. We take the rest of the distance on foot. Chuck wagon rule: no horses near to kick more dust in the food."

She dismounted, and they walked toward the chuck wagon. Julia smiled to see Alice Marlowe peeling onions and a thin woman who had to be Elinore Cuddy slicing them. Paul's hand rested naturally on her shoulder, reassuring her. *I am Mrs. Otto*, she thought with quiet delight.

Her courage nearly deserted her when she saw Cookie Brown. He was a massive man, looming over Alice and Elinore, who were both tall women. He held a slab of bacon in one hand as though it was no heavier than a slice of toast.

"Does he eat small children for breakfast?" she whispered to Paul.

"There is that rumor," he teased. They came closer. "Cookie, got a minute? Let me introduce another flunkie. This one's mine, and she's on short loan."

Cookie set down the bacon and wiped his hands on his apron. With a frown on his face, he looked her up and down. Julia gazed back, fascinated, at his leathery, dark skin that looked as though it had been hung in a smokehouse and cured for a year or two.

He nodded, and his voice was surprisingly gentle. "Mr. Otto, pleased to see you. How'd you winter?"

"It was tough, Cookie." Paul put his hand in the small of Julia's back and pushed her forward a step. "This is Mrs. Otto. She's new to cow gathering, but she can cook. Malloy will bring up a sack of bread that she baked for you."

"I'll take it with pleasure, sir." He continued his perusal. "Not much to her. Looks a bit fragile."

"Looks are deceiving. I'll leave her in your hands, Cookie. Just two things to remember about this lady."

Julia looked around at the crowd of interested cowboys that had gathered. *I'm the nine day wonder*, she thought in dismay. Her heart started to pound.

"Just two things?" someone called, and there was general laughter. Julia felt her cheeks burn.

Paul looked around, taking his sweet time to eye everyone in the small gathering. Some of the men started to move restlessly, and all were silent.

"Two things to remember: First, she's *my* wife. Second, she doesn't do any heavy lifting." He looked around again, knowing who his real audience was. "Most of you know what happened to her in that range fire. No heavy lifting. Julia, I'll see you later." He tipped his hat to her and left her there. The crowd parted like the Red Sea.

Silence, then Cookie clapped his meaty hands. Julia nearly jumped. "I have a pile of potatoes with your name all over them, Miz Otto," he said. He made a shooing motion with both hands, and the cowboys all simultaneously decided they had business elsewhere.

"I brought my own knives," Julia said, surprised that she still had a voice, since her throat was so dry. She had carried them with her in a canvas satchel, slung over her good shoulder. She spread out her prized knives at the work table, where Alice was peeling onions, her eyes managing to be red and merry at the same time.

Cookie nodded. He picked up the French knife and flicked his thumb on it. "Miz Otto, you have my permission to stick this in anyone who gets uppity."

"I'll focus on the potatoes first," she said, sitting beside Alice. "But thank you."

Cookie carried over a fifty-pound burlap sack of potatoes with all the effort of a maid carrying a dust bunny and set it in front of her. He put down a pan big enough to bathe a small child in and returned to slicing the slab of bacon.

"My goodness," Julia whispered as she picked up the first potato.

After Alice introduced Elinore Cuddy, they worked

quietly and efficiently. By the time Julia had finished peeling and slicing the potatoes, the sun was much lower in the sky, and Matt had brought up the bread in waxed paper. Cookie looked it over and nodded, his expression inscrutable.

*It's the best bread around*, Julia wanted to tell him. Instead, she started on the next burlap sack of potatoes, even though her back ached. No one else was complaining, and she wasn't going to be the first.

But there was a matter that had been on her mind for at least an hour. She whispered to Alice, "Where do we go, you know, to relieve ourselves?"

"I didn't mention that?" Alice asked, all innocence. She gestured with her knife toward a small tent on the edge of what she was already recognizing as Cookie's domain. "We have some of the comforts of home."

"Probably not what you're used to in Salt Lake City," Elinore added, her first comment of the afternoon.

Julia excused herself and walked toward the tent. *It appears to me, ladies, that you are testing me too*, she thought. *I suppose I am fair game, even to a friend.*

Julia had hoped Cookie would put her to work frying the potatoes, and he did, plopping down a massive frying pan on the grill over the trench fire. She added lard and reached for the pan of potatoes, but Cookie was there first.

"No heavy lifting, Miz Otto," he reminded her. "Tell me how many you want in there at once, and let me know when they're done."

Her heart warmed to the big man. "Thank you, Cookie," she said simply. "I'd do it myself if I could."

"I expect you would," he replied. "Mr. Otto never hires any slackers, and I doubt he would choose a wife so inclined."

She stirred the potatoes, content, even as she wiped

sweat out of her eyes and brushed away flies. *This proves it*, she thought, humming softly. *I'm happy as long as I have food to deal with*.

When the fried potatoes were crispy just the way she liked them, she added salt, and then forked out a piece. "Almost," she murmured and turned back to the table where she left her knives. She pulled out a packet of dried rosemary and brought it back to the trench fire. Leaning over carefully, she stripped several leaves and sprinkled them in.

"Stop right there!" Cookie thundered behind her.

Julia gasped and put her hands behind her back. "It's . . . it's just rosemary," she quavered, as she looked up and up to the tall man's frowning face. "Try it, Mr. Cookie?"

Cookie glowered at her a long time, and she gazed back, determined not to look away. *Oh, Heavenly Father, I've done it again. Here comes a foolish prayer. Please let him like rosemary with my potatoes*, she thought.

After what seemed like years, he came closer and set her aside as though she weighed nothing. "You're too close to the fire, Miz Otto," he told her, but in a more normal tone of voice. "Hand me a fork."

She did, interested more than frightened now. He stirred the fork around in the aromatic potatoes and plucked out a crispy one, blowing on it. He ate it and she held her breath. It was such a small thing, and she truly hadn't meant to cause trouble. She watched his eyes, and then let out her breath slowly. She had cooked for enough prima donnas to know satisfaction when it was writ so large.

"That'll do, as long as no one complains," he said finally. "Do you have enough for all these potatoes?"

"Probably enough for all week."

He shook his finger at her. "If I get objections, that's

the end!" He stirred it around with the fork again. "I'd better try another and make sure. Yep. I'll move these and bring over some more."

Julia fried the rest of the potatoes with rosemary. The urge was strong to ask Alice if she could have some of those raw onions and caramelize them for the steaks that Cookie was frying at another trench fire, but she decided against it. Rome wasn't built in a day, after all.

Elinore had sliced a mound of her bread and placed it on a platter next to the raw onions. When her skillet was empty of potatoes, Julia took off two slices of bread and set them in the skillet to toast crispy, fortified with the lard and potato bits. When Paul came through the line, she handed them to him.

"What makes your old man so special?" Cookie growled, but there was no denying the humor in his voice.

"He just is, Mr. Cookie," Julia replied. "He likes toasted bread. It's even tastier than plain white bread and onions. Would you like to try it?"

"Shore would. Toast me some later." Cookie turned his attention back to the diminishing pile of raw meat. He forked a half dozen onto his massive meat fork and plopped them on her grill. "How about you wrangle these, Miz Otto, since you're not busy."

The cowboys looked at each other in surprise. Even Paul stared.

"Of course, Mr. Cookie." She whispered to Paul when the cook returned his attention to his own steaks. "What just happened?"

"The earth moved," he whispered back, his eyes on Cookie like a kid hoping not to be caught talking out of turn at school. "Only Cookie ever does the meat. Looks like you're on, sport."

*I can do this*, she thought, relishing the challenge more now than fearing it.

"You can put some onions on mine, like you do at home," Paul said, forking his steak to someone else. "I'll wait."

There was still room on the grill for the frying pan, so she added a little more lard and a generous handful of onions, after separating them into graceful rings. "Timing is everything," she murmured as Paul's steak was ready at the same time as the caramelized onions. "Hold out your plate, cowboy."

"I'd like that too."

She looked up and smiled at Mr. Kaiser, holding out his plate. "Nice to see you, sir," she said and put the rest of the caramelized onions on the steak he had taken from her grill.

He nodded to her and then Paul, and turned away. "Well, what do you know?" Paul said, a little amazed.

When Cookie finally turned her loose, after washing a mound of dishes, the stars were out. He had already dismissed Alice and Elinore, so she knew all those dishes must be some part of her probation. "Be here before daybreak," he said, chewing on the toast piled with onions that Julia had caramelized just for him. "Bacon and eggs and hash browns." He pointed a fork at her. "You any good with flapjacks?"

"No one throws them back," she said.

"We'll add that too, then. I have some maple syrup." His laughter boomed out. "No rosemary on them, though!"

"Would you object to some vanilla extract?" she asked.

He gave her the same measuring look as when he ate the rosemary potatoes. "As long as no one complains," he repeated. He looked beyond her. "Mr. Otto, you can have her now, but I get her at daybreak."

"Just for you, Cookie," Paul said and took her arm.

"I am so tired," she said.

"Good tired or bad tired?" he asked, his hand in hers. "He put you through it, sport."

"Good tired."

They walked slowly away from the chuck wagon. The stars were out and the moon just rising. She saw the prairie littered with men in bedrolls, some of them snoring already.

"Thought I'd try a spot a little closer to the outer circle, near the wagon," he said. "Guess I never noticed how noisy they are."

While she watched, he circled his lariat around their bedroll. "What's that for?" she asked.

"Snakes. They never cross rawhide." He grinned at her expression. "You don't believe me."

"You're making fun of the new girl too," she said, "but I still love you."

"Suit yourself," he said with a shrug, as he unhooked his suspenders and pulled out his shirt. "I've been doing this for years and haven't been snake bit yet."

After a long and cautious look around, Julia unhooked her skirt and pulled it down. He held up the blankets for her and she slid inside, taking off her shirtwaist with a sigh. "He wants me there before sunrise," she whispered as she wriggled out of her petticoat. She sniffed herself. "I already smell."

He rose up on one elbow and took a whiff at her neck, which sent prickles down her spine. "Still better than the men. And is that vanilla extract behind your ears? Julia, you amaze me."

At Paul's whispered suggestion, he prayed for them both. "Don't think I'm afraid to do that in front of the others, but let's not terrify them totally," he said when she said "amen." He stretched out his arm, like at home, and she pillowed her head on it. "Learn anything so far, sport?" he asked.

She closed her eyes, peaceful, even though the ground was hard. That pebble under her hip was probably going to feel like a boulder before morning. "I'm starting to think it's the same lesson the Lord has been trying to teach me for years," she said. "I'm learning to endure."

He kissed her. "What if that's the whole lesson? It could be, you know."

"It could be," she echoed. She turned over and backed closer to him, because the night air was cooling the dusty land. "Now be quiet. You'll disturb these other gents, and I'm sleepy."

"Yes, ma'am." He put his hand over her stomach and pulled her closer, to whisper in her ear. "Branding starts tomorrow, sport. I predict you'll get a wash basin full of those handy little baby bull pouches."

Julia sighed. "Loan me your little knife?"

# Thirteen

Even with flies, dust, and cattle bawling, breakfast was flawless, right down to the vanilla-flavored pancakes. When one of the cowboys swore and complained about the fancy food, Cookie gave the man such a look that he was rooted to the spot, somewhat like Lot's unfortunate wife.

Julia busied herself with peeling potatoes again, looking up now and then at the men and cattle milling around far enough away from the chuck wagon not to raise the dust. Soon came the dreadful smell of burning hair and flesh as the branding began.

She must have passed some test yesterday, because both Alice and Elinore were talkative this morning. "I fainted the first time I smelled that atrocious odor," Elinore said. "You must be made of stronger stuff."

*I owe it to my husband,* she thought, her attention on the potatoes again. "Just lucky, I suppose."

She looked for Paul and saw him and the men of the Double Tipi riding and roping. She wished she didn't have to peel potatoes. The fun was obviously going on by the iron fires, where there was loud laughter and cussing, all of it punctuated by the bellows of cattle and the snorting of horses. Dust was everywhere. She finally gave up trying to brush it from her hair.

Lunch was much like supper the night before: endless beef, beans, and potatoes. She chewed her food thoughtfully, always aware of texture and taste.

"You're a good cook," she told Cookie, when he sat down beside her with his own tin plate. She held up a forkful of steak. "I believe that's the best steak I ever ate. What's your secret, or do you share?"

"A cow chip fire," he said. "You don't even need pepper."

She laughed out loud. *Keep smiling*, she told herself later, when a whole delegation of cowboys came toward the chuck wagon. Cookie had laid out coffee and lemonade on his sawhorse table, to accompany a washtub filled with bear sign that Julia and Elinore—not a talkative woman—had made.

"Here it comes, Julia," Alice said. "Ready for this?"

"As I'll ever be."

With barely suppressed smiles, the men carefully brought over a wash basin brimming with testicles. The basin was so full that two men had to steady it. Paul had been right; the range fires had meant more stray cattle, which meant even more branding and castrating at the cow gather this May.

"Set it on the work table, please," she said, taking Paul's little knife out of its sheath.

"We like'um all nice and crisp," someone ventured, before Cookie shooed them toward the coffee.

"Drink up, gents," Cookie boomed out in his usual ear-busting voice. "As I live, these ladies made you dirty, vile wretches a washtub of bear sign. Now aren't you ashamed of yourselves?"

All that little speech earned was raucous laughter. "Sure you know what to do with them little balls, Mrs. Otto?" someone called.

"You'd be surprised, gentlemen," Julia said. She took a deep breath and plunged her hand into the mess, commanding her dinner to stay where it was, digesting merrily somewhere inside.

Several cowboys squatted down to watch as she began her task, slitting, popping, and cutting until she established a rhythm to it. The smell of the blood bothered her less after an hour of work, but Paul had not prepared her for the swarm of flies that appeared from out of nowhere, or maybe from their last engagement in Exodus as one of the ten plagues of Egypt. Attracted by the blood, they swarmed around her nose and eyes until she wanted to scream, but that would only have invited them into her mouth.

She could barely breathe as she slit and popped. She felt panic rise in her, a weird sort of claustrophobia out in the widest of open spaces. Only the greatest stubbornness she had ever known kept her seated there, skinning the oysters. Absurdly, "If thou endure it well, God shall exalt thee on high," jumped into her mind, even though she was pretty sure the Lord never had Rocky Mountain oysters in mind when he told that to Joseph Smith in Liberty Jail.

"That's enough. It really is! Julia, stop."

She looked up in relief at Paul's familiar voice. She absorbed the pain in his eyes right into her own body and shook her head. She doggedly continued at the task set for her by a cow gathering full of rough men, who took their fun where they found it, living out their own dangerous lives on the range. She decided right then that she would die before she would stop. She had cast her lot with a cowman and that was that.

*Heavenly Father, just let there be a breeze,* she prayed as she worked, ignoring Paul, who was talking to Cookie now. Paul seldom raised his voice, but she could hear him now. *That's all I want; just a breeze. Don't worry about me, Paul.*

The breeze never came. The crowd of men squatting on the ground grew quieter as she continued her way through the bloody basin, her breath as shallow as she could make it.

"Move over, sport."

She looked up and shook her head fiercely as Paul sat down beside her, knife in hand.

"You're a boss. You don't need to do this," she whispered, even as she felt the tears start in her eyes.

"Yes, I do," he said, picking up a bloody sac and draping it over his fingers. "I guess I never realized quite how cruel this is to the newest tenderfoot until I saw my eternal companion sitting there. Shame on me. 'Evelina' or 'Redeemer'? I'll just hum, or I'd swallow way too many flies."

"Redeemer," she said. She was crying now, but it didn't matter, because her face was covered with flies, and no one could see her tears. The tears slid down her dirty face. She moved closer until they were touching shoulders.

"Got another knife?"

Julia glanced over to see Mr. Kaiser squatting down by the basin. "Thanks, Cookie," he said, when the cook silently handed him a knife. "Three of us ought to see this finished. Nice tune, Paul. I didn't know you were so talented." Mr. Kaiser reached into the basin too.

His voice was so calm in the middle of all this chaos. When she looked up again, the baiting cowboys had drifted away.

"We'll be done in no time," Mr. Kaiser said. He swatted at the flies, then gave up too, and just applied himself to the task. "What plans do you have for these jewels?" he asked, when the last oyster was shucked.

"Big plans," she told him, appalled at the flies that clung to her clothing and face, and finally yielded to panic. "Paul, help me."

Quickly, he picked her up, blood, flies, and all, and carried her toward the river. He called over his shoulder to Mr. Kaiser. "There's a valise in my wagon and some towels. Just leave them on the bank."

"Will do," the stockman said. "How about when I get back, I just sit on the bank, facing away, with my rifle?"

"Good plan. We'd rather not be disturbed."

"You got it, Paul."

She couldn't stop her tears as Paul stripped off her clothes and put her in the cold water. She gasped, then held her nose and went under, finally free of the torment of the flies. Paul was bare and beside her in a minute, just holding her as she sobbed.

"I knew it would be bad, but I didn't realize how bad. Julia Otto, why'd you marry such a big fool?"

"Because I love you!" she wailed.

He started to chuckle then, and it grew into a belly laugh that come from somewhere deep inside. She couldn't help herself and started to laugh too. She had tapered off to a giggle that grew again, when a bar of soap came flying over the bank and into the water.

"Are you two all right?" Mr. Kaiser hollered, and there was a noticeable quaver in his voice.

"Couldn't be better," Paul hollered back. "I'm still the envy of nations."

"I don't doubt that. I'll just sit here with my rifle until you lunatics are done."

Still humming "Redeemer," Paul scrubbed her from hair to heels. When he finished, she took the soap and worked him over.

"Stay in the water," he said when she finished. He climbed the bank and brought down some towels and the valise. "Wrap up in this," he said as he handed her a towel, and took the other one for himself.

He helped her dress when she was dry. "What a relief to be clean," she said finally. She sat down on the bank and took the comb he handed her, grateful for short hair. She watched him dress, her eyes going to the awful scar under his armpit and down his ribs, put there by his former wife in her insanity. *This is a hard place*, she thought. *Not for every woman.*

"Paul, do you know what I was thinking while I worked?"

"How much you'd like to bean me with a barrel stave?" he asked as he sat down beside her.

"Not at all. A scripture from the Doctrine and Covenants just popped into my mind. "You know: 'If thou endure it well, God shall exalt thee on high.'"

Paul glanced up the bank, where she could just see the back of Mr. Kaiser's head. "Remember the rest of it, sport? 'Thy friends do stand by thee . . .' I'm not sure I would have thought him a friend, not after what happened this winter. What now?"

"Back to work," she said. "I'm clean and the flies won't be interested."

"You still going to make those fancy oysters you cooked for me?"

"Better believe it, cowboy."

Cookie had a few weak objections, but they amounted to nothing, considering the remorse on his face. "You can make some of the oysters the way you do, on that griddle," she told him, calm and confident, "but I think I've earned the right to do the rest my way."

He didn't argue. Paul nodded and walked away, leaving her alone. As she watched the set of his shoulders as he walked away, Julia had a sure idea how hard that was for him, but how necessary for her.

"Do you need some help, Julia?" It was Alice, and there was something close to remorse on her face too. She looked down at the ground. "I . . . I never had to do that. Max wouldn't let them. Why did Paul . . . ?"

Julia knew why. She had figured it out in the river, but it wasn't anything she could put into words for Alice. Max Marlowe was a good man, but he had a small ranch. He didn't control a large chunk of southeast Wyoming. Max had no real reputation to maintain in their hard society, where a man's word and deed could mean the difference between life and death. Maybe that man's wife too. Julia understood clearly what had happened, and why.

"I had all the help I needed, but thank you, Alice." And it wasn't just Paul and Mr. Kaiser, she knew.

It was a nourishing thought that kept her content through the rest of the afternoon, as she breaded the Rocky Mountain oysters and fried them in the kettle full of lard. Cookie agreed that salt was all the seasoning they needed. A smile on her face, she watched him dip the crisp little package in ketchup and then pop it in his mouth. His expression changed from skeptical to beatific.

"Don't change a thing," he said. "I'll fix a few of those puny ones we used to cook on hot rocks, but I doubt we'll get many takers, once they try yours. Miz Otto, if you ever get tired of old Paul, there'd be a place for you to cook with the Clyde brothers."

*Cook for the men who tried to drive out my darling?* she asked herself. *And maybe me too? I'd die first.* "Cookie, that's a compliment," she said instead and called it good.

Supper was a signal triumph. Julia chewed her steak—cooked medium rare the way she liked it, and not blasted to a crisp—and watched the men eat.

"You're doing it again," Paul told her in an undertone.

"I know. They look pleased," she whispered back. "I hope I never see another Rocky Mountain oyster . . ." She stopped and smiled at her husband. ". . . until the next cow gather, or even tomorrow, where Cookie will assign a man or two from each outfit to skin and shuck their own. I'll be happy to fry them, though." She leaned closer. "Cookie doesn't know this yet, but I'll tell him."

"You'll *tell* Cookie Brown? Julia, I doubt even the Clyde brothers tell Cookie Brown what to do in the kitchen."

She gave him her best look. "Paul, I am prettier than the Clyde brothers. I smell better, and I might even be beautiful."

The satisfied smile he returned told Julia exactly what had happened to her. Her heart grew lighter as she realized she wasn't the young woman hiding in her bedroom last fall, afraid to even look at her own scars. *When did this happen?* she asked herself, wondering, as she watched her husband.

"I know you are," was all Paul said, but it was enough to put that demon behind her forever. "Let me tell you one more thing, and I hope it doesn't swell your head: no greenhorn has ever done what you did. None of them ever lasted more than an oyster or two."

"You're joking," she said, even though the hard look in his eyes belied her words.

"Nope. Usually the cowboys just bring over one or two to be shucked and everyone laughs. The boys cut the rest themselves, and the initiation is over. I thought there might be maybe a dozen, since you're my wife, and everyone likes to kid a boss, but not hundreds." He looked in the direction of the Clyde's camp. "Apparently Malcolm instigated this. I'm so sorry. I had no idea he would go to such lengths to humiliate you." He sighed. "And me. You still my friend, sport?"

"You know I am," she said quietly. "We got through it."

Julia couldn't help but notice the change in mood at the roundup. When the next day's branding finished, each outfit brought their own prepared oysters to the chuck wagon, where Julia breaded and fried them, adding just a pinch of sage this time. No one objected. Maybe they were afraid to; maybe they liked it. She didn't care. Her only food critic was Paul Otto, and she saw the delight in his eyes. And there was no denying the respect in Cookie's eyes, especially since it was reflected in the other men's faces too.

Besides the Rocky Mountain oysters that night, and everlasting steak, Julia had convinced Cookie to flavor the rest of his pinto beans with molasses and maple syrup left over from flapjacks the day before. It did her heart good to see some of the cowboys lingering around the trenches of Dutch ovens, looking for more.

"Walk with me, Darling."

*I'll never tire of that*, she thought as she glanced at Cookie, who nodded, and then took Paul's hand. "I have to get back to wash dishes," she said. "Where are we going?"

"I was minding my own business, when some of my former poker-playing colleagues said they want to meet you."

"I'm skeptical," she said, tucking her arm in his. "These are the same gentlemen who didn't want a blamed Mormon at their precious poker table in Denver?"

"The same. We can leave, if it goes south."

Julia had watched this group earlier in the day, some of them riding and roping, like her husband, others sitting in chairs under the cottonwoods, the only men at the cow gather with chairs. She remembered some of them from last summer's range fires, sitting at her old kitchen table, some of them bleak, and others indignant, as though blaming God for making their empires vulnerable.

"Gentlemen, you wanted to meet Mrs. Otto," Paul was saying as she looked around the little circle. All they needed was a round table in front of them, a deck of cards, and poker chips. "Here she is. Some of you remember her."

The men nodded. A few of them stood up. *Your mothers raised you right*, she thought, linking her arm through Paul's again.

They were looking at her, expecting something. Maybe she should remember her manners too. "Gentlemen, it's a pleasure to meet you," she told them. "You are always welcome to our home on the Double Tipi, if you're in the neighborhood." She wanted to cross her fingers behind her back, thinking how rude they had been to her husband.

Some smiled, some did not.

"You're a good cook," Malcolm Clyde said. He poured amber liquid into his shot glass and held it up to her, as if in salute. She felt Paul's arm stiffen.

"Thank you, sir," she said. "Now if you'll excuse me, I have to do a mound of dishes for Cookie."

"Maybe *you* should stay awhile. The black man can do his own dishes," Clyde said. "We'll fill you in on your husband's Denver exploits. Paul ever tell you about his checkered career at Mattie Daw's?"

Julia felt the blood drain from her face. This was worse than flies. She hadn't the courage to look at Paul, but from the startled expressions on some of the smug faces in the circle, she knew he was giving them his squinty-eyed stare.

"Let's go, Julia," he said, through clenched teeth.

"In a moment, my dear." *Help me, Heavenly Father*, she prayed. "Of course he told me about Mattie Daw. He also told me about Jennie Rogers and her House of Mirrors." If Paul could glare to good effect, she could see what serenity did to this group of men she hoped never to lay eyes on again. She forced herself to look around that smug circle, stopping for a moment on Mr. Kaiser's stricken face. She smiled at him, grateful all over again for his help at the river. "Mattie Daw is old news, gentlemen, and it's over. So is this conversation. Good day."

"One more thing. You're making SOB stew tomorrow?"

She flinched at the baldness of the word. "I wouldn't miss it," she said. One of the ranchers laughed. She dug her toes into the soles of her shoes. "You're still welcome at our home, every one of you."

"Not if it's warm liver salad."

Julia suddenly remembered large indignities and small ones in Boston during cooking school, and thought about Paul's comment last year about Mormons being fair game. "That warm liver salad is destined to follow me to the ends of the earth, I suppose," she told them. She could feel Paul relaxing slightly. "Nothing much has changed at the Double Tipi, except that neither of us holds with cussing . . ." She glanced at Paul. ". . . In the house, anyway," she added, relieved to hear some chuckles now. "And one or the other of us always asks a blessing on the food." She sighed. "Even on the warm liver salad. Good night. So pleased to make your acquaintance."

She forced herself to walk slowly with Paul. *Never show fear, never show fear*, she thought until she heard her husband take a deep breath.

"I hate those men now," he said, his voice ragged.

"They don't know any better. I hope I killed them with kindness." She leaned against his shoulder as they walked steadily away from his former friends. "Paul, do you have the feeling that this roundup isn't just my initiation as a greenhorn, but yours too as a Mormon?"

"Are we passing?" he asked her, and his bleak tone

pained her heart. He was a proud man, not used to such treatment.

"Probably the only person who could answer that would be Mr. Kaiser. He looked pretty shocked."

"Odd. He's the one who told me I wasn't welcome anymore. I don't know, Julia."

She washed dishes in silence, while Paul talked with Doc and Matt. When she finished, he walked her to the river. They stood there a long time, watching the water.

"Sonofagun stew looks dreadful, and I can't prepare you for that," he told her finally. "You'll be on your own."

"I'm never on my own, Paul," she said quietly, then stood on tiptoe to kiss his cheek. She laughed. "Have I told you before that I like the way your moustache tickles my nose?"

"Boy howdy, can you change a subject, sport." He patted her. "That hickey of mine is starting to fade."

"Guess I'd better give you a new one, when we get home."


If there was a worse mess than sonofagun stew, Julia wasn't sure what it could be. Her stomach lurched when some of the cowboys brought her a heaping bucket of what Cookie called innards, after the noon meal. She was struck by the serious looks on the men's faces. There was none of the joshing and ribald commentary that accompanied the Rocky Mountain oysters yesterday. Word of her treatment by their bosses must have leaked out. The very air at the cow gather seemed charged now.

"I'll do my best," she told them.

"We thought you would, ma'am," the bravest among them said, tipping his Stetson to her.

"Cookie, this might defeat me," she said, after they walked away. "What on earth do I do?"

"How about 'we'?" he growled, which touched her heart. "I'll stay by you."

Her knees felt weak as Cookie poured off most of the blood, then started pointing at the various parts in the pan. "Sweetbreads, lung, liver, brain, marrow gut—that's important—tongue, heart, kidney. You'll want to boil that tongue first, and pull off the skin. They left you the skirt steak too. Let's—"

"Cookie!"

They both looked up, startled. Angus and Malcolm Clyde came striding toward the chuck wagon. Malcolm pointed to the ground in front of him.

"We need you here, Cookie."

"Yessuh. Just let me show—"

"Now!"

"They're going to make you leave me alone," she whispered. "Just tell me what to do."

She watched the strain on his face, sorry he had been put in such a position.

Cookie opened his mouth, and Angus Clyde shouted, "Now! She can ask God to help her!"

"I hate them," Cookie whispered. "I never knew how much until now, but I have to work, Miz Otto. You understand."

"I do," she said clearly, her head up. "I cut it up small? What about the brains?" She gulped as her gorge rose.

He was walking away from her now, leaving her alone. "Put the brains in last, about fifteen minutes before you serve it," he called. "Squish'um."

The Clyde brothers laughed. She looked at them, calling on every ounce of calm she had ever possessed, and nodded. The cowboys standing around looked at each other. No one spoke.

She found the biggest pot and tried to lift it, until she felt a sharp pain in her shoulder that made her wince.

"She can't do that!" Cookie shouted. "Let me lift it for her!"

"No, Cookie. I'll be fine. Just get Paul."

"He's not getting anyone. Your Mormon doesn't need to do woman's work."

*There it is*, she thought. *Now I know.*

One of the cowboys swore and started forward.

"Take another step, Wagner, and you're off my crew," Malcolm Clyde shouted. "No one will ever hire you again on this range."

"You're on the Double Tipi payroll as of right now," Paul snapped, and he walked toward Julia, coming from the direction of the branding area, an iron smoking in his hand.

With a grin, the cowboy beat him there, lifting the pot for Julia. "Name's Colby Wagner, ma'am," he said. "I'm a good wrangler, Mr. Otto."

"You're a gentleman too. Find Matt Malloy and give him a hand with my beeves. We're finishing up. I'll help the cook. You're riding for my brand now." He handed Wagner the iron. "In fact, here it is."

"You okay, sport?" Paul asked.

She nodded, rubbing her shoulder. "I did need some help, but you're not going to do my work. I have to do this myself. Just tell me how small to cut these parts."

"Really small. Put in just enough water to cover them and let'um boil. Save the brains for last."

"Seasonings?"

"Salt. Pepper, if you're adventurous." He kissed her cheek, then rubbed the frown between her eyes. He whispered so their audience couldn't hear him. "Don't worry about the Clydes! They've never been my friends, so there's no love lost." He looked around. "No Alice? No Elinore?"

"Alice and Max already left. I'm not sure where Elinore—"

221

"Right here!"

Julia looked around and clapped her hands. "Bravo! But didn't you faint over Rocky Mountain oysters once?"

"What a ninny I was. Shoo, Paul. We'll be fine."

The flies came back in abundance, but Julia kept her head down, cutting quickly. She had trimmed many a tongue of its skin back in Boston in the cooking school, so she spared the very green and wobbly Elinore Cuddy that experience. *You've done this all before in Boston, just not in these amounts*, she told herself over and over, as she diced and minced her way through the endless afternoon, until everything except the brains was bubbling in the pot.

Paul came back when she was stirring the mess. He looked in. "Ah, you added an onion," he said. "One's enough. No sense in muddling up a good stew. Want to visit the river again?"

"I've run out of clean clothes. I'll just wash my hands and keep going."

"Why aren't you puking over this?" he asked.

"I owe it all to Fannie Farmer," she told him as she pushed up her sleeves and washed her hands and face, driving away a few flies. "We spent a whole week on sweetbreads. My classmates dropped like flies." She couldn't help a glance at the brains, covered in a bloody cloth, with flies circling overhead like vultures. "Not so sure about brains, except the Clyde brothers must share one between the three of them."

Paul laughed. He looked around. "Where's Elinore?"

"Lying down. She was looking puny."

"I almost hate to ask: have you tasted it yet?"

She shook her head. "I'm not that brave, Paul, no matter what you think."

He took a spoon. She flinched as he sampled the grayish-green mess in the pot.

"It's missing something." He lifted the cloth over the brains, which upset the flies. "Ah! Sport, you left out the marrow gut."

"It didn't look like anything I've ever seen before," she said, highly dubious.

He brushed away the flies and set the tube of marrow gut on the slimy cutting board. He handed her the knife. "It's a part found in unweaned calves. Cut it in small rings and add it. Marrow gut makes all the difference."

She did as he said, trying not the think about the little calves she enjoyed watching as they cavorted almost like lambs in the pastures on the Double Tipi. She held her breath as she added it to the stew, trying not to retch. It was one thing to cut up all the innards, but quite another to stir them around.

Before he had been ordered away, Cookie had produced an enormous pot of chili. Through the hot afternoon, she stirred the chili and kept an eye on the sonofagun stew. None of the cowboys said anything as they trailed by the chuck wagon for coffee and the last of the lemonade, but she felt the sympathy in their eyes. One of them got brave enough to whisper, "He . . . heck, Mrs. Otto, we all started out green on the trail." He blushed fiery red, but none of his bunkies teased him.

"How does this work?" she asked Elinore, as suppertime approached. "Is it like all the other meals?"

"Pretty much. The bosses always go first. Since the Clydes are the gather bosses this year, they go first." Elinore took a deep breath and puffed out her cheeks. "You can't avoid it, Julia. You have to put in the brains."

Julia managed a tiny smile, if only because Elinore was looking green again. "I'll toss you for it," she joked. "Heads, I put it in; tails, I put it in, and we both go lie down and die."

Elinore put her hand to her mouth and started toward

her tent. As Julia watched, she stopped, her hand still to her mouth, and turned around. With what looked like a massive attempt to control her insides, Elinore started walking back to Julia. Her eyes narrowed as she stared at the pan. "I can't abandon you to this mess," she declared.

"Elinore, believe me, I understand if you don't want to—"

"Here goes, Julia," Elinore said, a study in grim determination. She pulled back the cloth, stared at the convoluted gray mass, and squished it between her fingers.

"Bravo," Julia said and joined Elinore, shuddering as she worked her fingers through the brains.

"Tomorrow I am back to the Double Tipi and my own bed," Julia said, more to herself than to Elinore, whose resolve had stiffened her. As she tightened her lips, Julia felt that peculiar drooling that always preceded a good puke and forced it down.

When the brains were reduced to small particles, Julia picked up the pan and dumped it into the larger pot. The smell that rose like an evil cloud made her dizzy. She turned away to wash her hands and sank to her knees. Elinore reached her quickly and helped her to her feet.

"I think I stumbled into a hole," she said, embarrassed. "Thank you."

She washed her hands, wretched with humiliation, wondering why none of the cowboys waiting for supper laughed. She turned slowly around to face the Clyde brothers, watching her and gloating. "Give it another minute or two," she told them, digging down deep and finding dignity somewhere.

Julia stood behind the trench fire, hands clasped tight together. She sighed in relief as Paul approached. He started toward her, but one of the Clydes reached out to stop him.

"We're the gathering bosses," Malcolm Clyde said. "Where are your manners?"

Paul just gave the three men a withering look. He walked behind the trench fire. "Sorry I couldn't be here sooner. Angus and Malcolm sent me on a tomfool errand. Is it done, Julia?"

She nodded, not trusting herself to speak.

"Better try it, Mrs. Otto," Malcolm said. He took the lid off the pot and peered inside. He glared at her. "What the Sam Hill is *that*?"

She looked in too, swallowing over and over as her stomach heaved. She had to smile as the humor of the whole thing took over. *My stars*, she thought, *that vile man is afraid of a little bay leaf.*

While everyone watched and no one breathed, Julia ladled a small amount into a bowl.

Deftly, she plucked out the single bay leaf, dropped it in the fire, and picked up a spoon. She took a small sip, and then another, nodding to herself.

"All it needed was bay leaf," she said, giving all three Clyde brothers a level stare. "Gentlemen, supper is served."

The applause that rose around her was better than music. *We passed, Paul*, she thought. She let them spoon up their own sonofagun stew and handed out bread and dried fruit at the other table. When everyone was served and sitting cross-legged or squatting, she excused herself, walked down to the river, and threw up everything she had ever eaten since at least her sixth grade birthday party.

When she finished, she dipped her hand in the river and drank, relishing the cold water down her sorely tried throat. She turned around to see Paul sitting there, watching her.

"I don't think I'll come to the roundup this fall," she said.

"You should. You're the roundup queen now." He gave her a hand up. "Sit a spell. This gather's going down in Wyoming history." He gave her a solemn look. "Did *I* pass, sport?"

She leaned her head against his shoulder. "You did. You're an official blamed Mormon, and you didn't shoot anyone."

"I wouldn't waste one bullet, let alone three, on the Clyde brothers."

Silent, they sat close together on the riverbank until the sun went down.

# Fourteen

"I never saw anything so beautiful," Julia said, when—after a half day's ride—they topped the ridge from the north and looked down on the Double Tipi. She sniffed the air, enjoying the fragrance of lilacs by the bunkhouse, put there by Paul's mother, in some attempt to make the place more homelike. She traced the path of the burn to the water's edge, and then to the other side where it jumped the river. She sighed and looked away.

Maybe the same scar was on Paul's mind too, because he pointed to the area where the house used to be. "We're going to leave bare earth there. I don't want any growth around our home."

"Maybe a lawn and some zinnias?" she asked, hopeful. "Hollyhocks too?"

"For you, Julia, a lawn and zinnias." He chuckled. "Maybe even hollyhocks, but nothing tall that I can't burn if we ever need a backfire. I won't take another chance with your life. No arguments."

"Not from me, Mr. Otto," she agreed.

At the side porch, Charlotte greeted her with a welcome smile, but her eyes were on Matt, who was sitting with Colby Wagner by the horse corral.

"I followed one of your recipes and made a poppy seed loaf," she said. "Would you like a slice?"

Julia watched the trajectory of Charlotte's gaze. "I would, but I think Matt, Colby, and Doc have been eating more dust that I have. Take some out there first. Do you have any lemonade too?"

Charlotte's smile was heartfelt. "You know I do. Thanks, Mrs. Otto."

Julia hoped her face wasn't too rosy when she added, "You needn't hurry back. I don't have any particular duties for you right now."

Julia rubbed her neck and then the small of her back as she watched her husband lead their horses into the horse corral. She had lost that argument earlier, when he insisted that it was never any trouble to tend two horses, rather than one.

"I know you, Darling," had been his clincher. "If I get distracted, you'll probably try to lift off that saddle, and I won't have it."

*It never does to argue with Mr. Otto. Paul, maybe, but not Mr. Otto*, she thought as she dipped hot water from the Queen Atlantic into a small bucket and carried it into the bathing room. A number of trips back and forth were no strain at all. By the time her husband finished unloading equipment from the wagon and caring for the horses, she was wearing clean clothes and was fragrant with rose talc.

Paul sniffed her as he walked into the kitchen. "My word, Julia." His lips were on her neck then. "I miss the wood smoke, but maybe not the flies."

"You know, there's plenty of hot water left in the Queen, and Charlotte made a stew that relieves me from afternoon kitchen patrol."

"That's a blatant offer, if ever I heard one," he said. "See you upstairs. Want me dry or wet, wife?"

"Just clean, husband."

*Heavy doings*, Julia thought later. "Maybe there's nothing like a cow gather to sharpen the senses," she murmured to her husband.

No answer. "You've been chloroformed," she whispered, pleased with her power. She reached for her clothes.

"Not so fast," Paul said, groggy but awake, his hand on her hip. "I was just resting my eyes."

She had no objection to pillowing her head on his chest. His fingers just seemed to go automatically to her curls, twining them around his fingers.

He didn't say anything for a long time, just fingered her hair, then kissed the top of her head before drawing her closer. "I've never been so mortified," he said finally. "I believe I would have suffered any indignity, rather than hear those men—I can't call them friends—drag Mattie Daw and Jennie Rogers into a conversation with you."

"I just considered the source," she whispered into his chest. "I meant what I said to them: it's old news. You've repented, you've been baptized, and I'd stake my life on it that you haven't returned to Denver's Tenderloin District."

"True."

"End of story." She raised up to look him in the eye. "I've noticed something more important to me than Denver ladies. Do you realize I haven't had that . . . that dream in weeks?" She made a face. "Not even after that awful day when I seem to have cornered the Wyoming market on Rocky Mountain oysters." She put her arm around his waist. "I can't decide if that was worse or if the sonofagun stew was worse."

Paul started to laugh. "I would almost—not quite— go through some of that again, just to see the look on Malcolm Clyde's face when you pulled out that itty bitty bay leaf!"

"It *did* make the stew better," Julia insisted, laughing too. "Almost edible."

He kissed her and ran his hand down her arm. "Since the president of the Double Tipi and his executive officer are not busy right now, I suggest we have a shareholders meeting."

She looked at him, interested.

"It's this: I want to give Malloy a raise and name him my foreman. I mentioned this before."

"Can we afford that, Mr. Otto?" she asked. "It's my job to ask questions like that."

"We can, especially since I'm not paying for the employment of that expensive but beautiful cook any more. I can give Malloy a raise and pay Colby Wagner what he's worth, and still come out ahead. Does the executive officer agree?"

"She does."

"How about this? Suppose I tell Malloy I plan to refurbish the old bunkhouse into a home for the foreman? Think that'll speed his wooing a bit?"

"You are a matchmaker!"

"Guilty as charged."

"The executive officer also agrees with that proposal."

"Done and carried," he said with a yawn. "Now, I am somnolent."

"One of those S words from Doc's dictionary?" she teased. Silence.

As her husband slept, Julia dressed. She stood a long moment just looking at him, satisfied. She looked out the window and up toward the horse barn and the bunkhouse, where Doc, Colby, and Paul's two cousins sat. She heard the murmur of two voices from the side porch below and smiled to herself. *Matt, you're about to get a real nudge from the president of the Double Tipi corporation*, she thought.

Leaning against the window frame, Julia twisted her wedding band on her finger. She had removed her ruby engagement ring before the cow gather, not willing to chance its loss. Humming, she went to her bureau and opened the top drawer to retrieve her ring.

Her ring rested on top of a note in pencil: *I know he's here somewhere.* She sucked in her breath, then hurried to Paul and shook him awake. He sat up quickly, rubbed his eyes, then grabbed the note she held in her shaking hand.

"Where . . . where was this?" he demanded.

She couldn't speak; she pointed to her bureau and the open drawer. He got out of bed and went to the drawer.

"Anything missing?"

Julia shook her head. "How did he do this?"

Paul stared at the note in his hand. "We don't even know it's from McAtee," he told her, his expression bleak.

"You . . . you told me you saw him at the gather."

"He rode in that second day with some stockmen from Niobrara County. They looked around, checked a few brands, but didn't stay." He reached for his clothes. "Julia, go ring the triangle, and let's get everyone in the dining room."

She did as he said, stepping past a surprised Matt and Charlotte on the side porch to ring the triangle. She looked down the valley toward the river and then up to the ridge. The peace was gone from her quiet afternoon.

When Paul explained his reason for asking his crew into the dining room, Kringle, Charlotte, and her cousins looked at each other. Doc stared thoughtfully around the room. Colby Wagner sat back with a frown, his arms folded. His expression hadn't changed since Paul took the time to explain what had led up to the note.

"James is safe somewhere else, and that's all I'll say. The less you all know, the better. Wagner, I have to trust you, because you weren't aware of James or the way his family was burned out in Niobrara County four years ago," Paul said. "The way you defended my wife at the cow gather assures me of your character. I trust you."

Wagner nodded. "You can, Mr. Otto. Let me

understand this: McAtee of the Bar Lazy S knows—James, is it?—is the only living witness to what happened?"

"Yes." Paul looked at the note in his hand. "This confirms my fear that McAtee did recognize James. I was doubtful before, but not now." He looked around the dining room table, his eyes troubled. "The only way he could have put that note in my wife's bureau drawer was for everyone to have been off the Double Tipi," he said. "Please tell me what you know. Charlotte? McLeish? Kringle? If I can't trust you . . ." He didn't finish his sentence.

Charlotte cleared her throat, looking at her cousin, Curtis McLeish. "We weren't sure what happened," she began. "We didn't think anything had, until now."

"Better explain," Paul said, his voice more gentle now. "Curtis?"

"It was three days ago, about noon." McLeish looked at Charlotte. "Wasn't it?"

She nodded, and he continued. "I noticed quite a cloud of smoke to the north and east, so I saddled up for a look. After last year's fires, I'm not inclined to ignore smoke."

"How far did you ride?" Paul asked.

"About two miles. By the cut in the bluff."

"Yeah, that's two miles. You can't see the ranch buildings from there, if I recall."

"Nope."

"What was it?"

Curtis shook his head. "Just a pile of brush to start a hot fire, and then green wood to make it smoke. I looked around and didn't see anyone, so I kicked out the fire. I stayed there until it was out. I guess I was gone about an hour and a half." He shrugged. "That was it."

"You didn't see anyone?"

"Not a soul."

Paul turned to Charlotte and spoke to her in Shoshone. She nodded and took a deep breath.

"I was in the kitchen making biscuits when I heard someone banging on the wall by the horse barn."

"'Twas me," Kringle said. "I had to bang really loud. It was a windy day, and I thought the wind had blown the door to the harness room shut. You know how it can latch."

"I do. I got stuck in there once," Paul said. "Charlotte?"

"I heard the banging and went to the harness room. It was like he said. The door was latched. The wind can whistle through there, if the barn doors are open." She swallowed. "I feel so stupid! I opened the door and went inside, and it slammed shut behind me. I should have known better."

"How'd you get out?"

"When I came back, I heard both of them hollering," Curtis said. "I let them out—laughed at them—and then we fixed the door so it wouldn't happen again." He looked at his cousin, as if for reassurance. "We looked around and couldn't see anything out of place, so we chalked it up to the wind. Couldn't explain the fire, though." His expression changed. "Maybe now I can."

"You didn't see anyone?"

"No one," Charlotte said, her voice emphatic. "You know how dark the horse barn is by the harness room. Someone must have been there." She shivered.

They just looked at each other. Paul stared at the note again. "McAtee's smarter than I thought," he said. "I'm not sure what to do. The note's unsigned. If I take any of my unfounded concerns to the marshal in Cheyenne, he'll laugh me right out of his office." He sighed and leaned back in his chair. "Burning out those homesteaders four years ago means nothing in a state that doesn't much care about farmers. We're on our own."

Julia put her hand over his. "What do you want me to do?" she asked, her voice soft.

"My first thought is to send you back to Salt Lake City," he said quickly, looking into her eyes.

"You know my answer," Julia said. "This is my home. I belong here with you."

He nodded, his eyes never leaving her face. "Well, sport, it looks like I'll have to teach you how to shoot." He touched her face. "I know you shot my gun last year, but can you aim at a target and hit it?"

Doc cleared his throat. "Boss, uh, I've only used a rifle to scare off varmints. Shooting's not a pastime much in Indianapolis."

"Aye to that in Cork," Matt said.

Kringle held up his arthritic hands. "I'm doubtful."

Paul threw up his hands. "Wagner, please tell me that your checkered career with the Clyde brothers included some shooting."

"It did. I can help you teach them," the cowboy said, amused.

Julia watched her husband's face, searching for something beside concern. "We'll learn, Paul," she assured him. The others nodded.

"You'll have to," he replied simply.

The lesson began the next morning, after breakfast and chores. Julia hadn't expected to sleep at all that night, but Paul held her close and sang "Dear Evalina," until she drifted off. When she woke, he was in his usual place, reading from the Book of Mormon, with his feet propped on the bed. She tickled his bare foot, and he looked up.

He smiled at her, and she felt relief cover her. "Nothing's too bad in my world, if you smile," she told him.

"Julia, you're about as easy a mark as I am," he said. "Hopeless. I'll have to tell your father that the more I read the Book of Mormon, the better I get at remembering where things are."

"Me too. What'd you find?" She sat up cross-legged on the bed.

"Oh, there's a real scoundrel, Amalickiah, up to serious no good. He gets on Moroni's very last nerve, going around and destroying the church. This verse, Julia: 'And we also see the great wickedness one very wicked man can cause . . .' There's more, but that's McAtee." He put his finger in the place and closed the book. "So Moroni has to drum up help from his neighbors." He sighed. "I can't invite my neighbors into this mess, especially since no one knows much about James except us here and some folks in Cheyenne." He opened the book again, his expression sour. "And McAtee."

"You can depend on us."

"I do." He set the book aside. "I'll have to tell your father someday that he neglected a major part of your education by not teaching you to point, squeeze, and fire, up there on the Avenues in Salt Lake City."

"You forget. I was supposed to marry a banker."

"For someone so bright, you show a remarkable lack of judgment now and then," he joked. "Feed me, wife, and then we'll see if you're much of a shootist!"

She wasn't. The theory interested her, and heaven knows she wanted to set her husband's mind at ease, but there was another matter that made the whole exercise in gunfire complicated. She didn't notice for a few days, because he and Colby Wagner had lined the bunch of them up, and guns in hand, had them practice pointing, squeezing, and firing without bullets.

Paul was distracting enough when he stood next to her and put his arm around her to demonstrate the proper technique. He even blushed one morning when she suddenly turned and kissed his cheek, then he burst into laughter and grabbed her around the waist while the others watched, not sure what to do.

"Paul, behave yourself," she said severely.

"You started it."

Charlotte got the giggles and turned away. Doc just shook his head.

"All right. Line up again, people. If we all behave," Paul said, giving Julia the patented Mr. Otto look, "we'll try some target shooting with real bullets. I feel confident that there are enough liniment bottles from the bunkhouse—some of them mine—to line on the fencepost. Julia, what about vanilla extract bottles?"

She had been feeling out of sorts for several days, blaming the cow gather, and then the upset caused by McAtee's note. It just seemed worse that morning. The pleasant odor of lilacs had faded now as Matt lined up a row of mismatched bottles on the fence. She wrinkled her nose against the pungent aroma of horse and cow, which up to a week ago had troubled her not at all. Well, never mind. She was looking forward to actually firing Paul's pistol and not doing it in the desperation of last summer, when she tried to warn them of the approaching fire.

Paul loaded his weapon and handed it to her, after making sure everyone else was ready. Two of the Colts were his and two belonged to Wagner, so they would take turns.

She, Charlotte, Matt, and Doc stepped to the line Wagner had drawn in the road. "Just remember: squeeze deliberately. Don't rush. Keep your eyes open, Julia," Paul cautioned. "Fire when you feel ready."

Matt fired first, and Paul nodded as a liniment bottle shattered. Charlotte was next, with a miss. Doc took his time and broke another liniment bottle.

Julia raised her gun to fire as the smoke from the guns drifted back across her face. The smell made her drop her gun, turn away, and stagger toward the bunkhouse, retching as she went.

"Julia!" Paul called, alarm in his voice.

She waved him away and leaned against the rain barrel, bent double, hoping to ward off the nausea before she really embarrassed herself.

While the others hurried toward her, she felt her face burn with shame. She heard someone rush inside the bunkhouse, and then Doc came out with a tin cup of water. He handed it to her, after Paul wiped her mouth and sat her down on the bench outside the bunkhouse.

"Drink it, Julia," Doc said.

"That smell!" she exclaimed, when her stomach quit lurching.

Paul looked at the others. "Let's give her some room. Wagner, how about you keep the others practicing. I'll help Julia into the house."

"I'll invite myself along," Doc said. "In fact, Boss, how about you get them started again, and I'll give Julia a hand."

A slight smile on his face, Doc helped her down the road the short distance to the house, as the gunfire continued behind them.

"Want to sit on the front step a moment?" he asked, when they reached the house. "Are we far enough from that smell?"

She nodded. "Oh, Doc. I think . . ."

His smile grew. "Julia, want to tell me a few more of your symptoms, or may I guess?"

She had been too shy to say anything to Paul, which had surprised her, considering that there wasn't anything she thought she could keep from him. And here she was, telling Doc—a man she knew well, but who wasn't her husband—about the calendar that she had forgotten to mark and the dizziness and the nausea.

She finished and was too shy to look at anything except Paul, who was coming toward them now. "I think what I have isn't contagious," she said cautiously.

"It's not. You'll feel better in a few months."

"Months!"

"Well, let's call it eight weeks, maybe twelve, if that helps," Doc said, eyeing Paul as he approached. "Any idea when this big event took place, so Dr. McKeel can make a long range forecast?"

She put her hands to her red face. "We had a real dry spell during the cow gather. Had to have been before that."

Doc turned away, his shoulders shaking. "In other words, you haven't a clue," he said when he could speak, his eyes merry.

"Clue about what?" Paul said, concern on his face. He sat down beside Julia.

Doc stood up. "I think I'll go shoot a few more liniment bottles. Julia, talk to the boss. He's generally reasonable and a whole lot sweeter since you married him."

"All right, sport. What have you done?" Paul asked, when Doc was out of hearing.

"What have *we* done, you mean," she said, speaking softly, as though the whole crew sat on the porch. "Paul, I'm anticipating."

*Poor man*, she thought. *Here he is, anxious about McAtee, and protecting me—all of us—and now I tell him this*. "At least, I think I am," she said, when his silence continued. "Pretty sure, in fact." She finally worked up her courage to look at him. "Nearly positive."

His eyes were closed. As she watched, a tear rolled down his cheek.

"Please don't cry," she whispered, dabbing at his eyes

with her apron, her nausea forgotten. "I know the timing is awful, but . . ."

He opened his eyes and put his arms around her, still silent, but breathing deep of her hair until he seemed to collect himself.

He still hadn't said anything, but maybe he didn't have to. "I guess you're okay with this," she ventured.

He shuddered, and she hoped he was laughing. "'Dear Evalina, sweet Evalina, my love for thee will never never die,'" she sang softly. "Maybe you'll want to expand your repertory and learn a lullaby."

"Count on it," he said finally, his voice not quite his own. "I never thought I would ever be a father."

"Silly cowboy," she whispered. "You're the man who bought the negligee in Chicago."

"Julia, I will prize your logic until I am bald and toothless," he told her, more himself. "That's *not* what causes babies."

"Yes, it is." She kissed him. "Of course, I only wore it once, so maybe it was that hickey in the Plainsman Hotel."

"I'll explain it to you someday, sport."

# Fifteen

The shooting lessons had continued for everyone else as well as new rules on the Double Tipi. "No one rides alone, and no one leaves Julia alone here," Paul had said a few nights later over dinner. "Julia and I are going to church in Cheyenne, so be watchful."

It had taken only a small argument to allow Paul to let her take the usual ride on Suzie Q down to Gun Barrel to catch the train, and Doc had swayed the matter.

"She's not fragile, Boss," he had assured her husband. "Another month or two in the saddle won't hurt. Still, this might be a good time to order that buckboard you've been thinking about."

The horseback ride down to Gun Barrel was a test of her insides. Julia had stopped once to liberally douse some sagebrush, and Paul kindly handed her his canteen when she finished.

"Sport, I love you, even when you redecorate Wyoming," he assured her, helping her back into the saddle.

For the most part, they rode silently. Julia glanced at Paul now and then, noting the furrow between his brows. *I wish you didn't have to worry about me*, she thought, determined to give him no cause for more alarm. She enjoyed the silence—the peaceful quiet between two people who know each other well.

Gun Barrel toasted in the June sun. The train was going to be an hour late, according to a salesman in the livery stable, so there wasn't the need for a mad dash to the depot. Their first stop was the post office, where Paul handed her a thick letter from her parents. He glanced at the statement from his cattle buyer in Chicago but held a telegram in his hand for a long moment, just looking at it.

Julia looked around his arm. "It's addressed to both of us. Grover, Colorado?"

"Here goes." He opened the telegram. "Huh." He handed it to her. "I'm surprised."

She read out loud. "'Sorry. JK.' Mr. Kaiser?"

"Yeah." He nudged her shoulder. "He's a man of even fewer words than I am."

"I wonder what prompted that?"

"It's not impossible to imagine he has a conscience, Paul."

"No, it isn't." He put his arm around her shoulder. "Care to chance a bowl of clear soup and soda crackers? I've noticed that's your current diet. I'm hoping that will change. You're still a bit slim."

"I'll chance it," she told him. "Usually by noon I feel a bit more like Julia Otto."

"Music to my ears."

"What? So I won't give you cause to blush in the restaurant?" she teased.

"No. You can puke where you want. I like to hear Julia Otto."

According to Paul, she fell asleep first on the train, which didn't surprise her. That was another symptom she had forgotten to mention to Doc: she was tired all the time. When she woke up, Paul was reading the Doctrine and Covenants. The frown was gone between his eyes, which relieved her.

"Find something to cheer you up?" she asked, leaning against his arm.

"Nothing in particular. I just like it where Jesus

Christ tells the early church, 'Doubt not, fear not, little flock.' Sounds like good advice." He put his arm around her. "If he helped those Saints, he'll help us."

Paul had sent a telegram in Gun Barrel, advising the Gillespies that they would be staying at the Plainsman Hotel, but Heber was there at the depot anyway, with his boys and a dinner invitation.

At the house, it was an easy matter to coo over the newest Gillespie son, who regarded Julia as solemnly as Buddha as she held him. "Our house is too crowded for any guest's comfort," Emma apologized. "I've put Mabel in with Amanda. Besides, you probably enjoy a little privacy with your husband."

Julia nodded, admiring the baby in her arms. There was so much she wanted to ask Sister Gillespie about little ones, and childbirth, but it could wait. She thought of Mama and her matter-of-fact remark that Relief Society was the best place for "all knowledge," as she put it.

"Maybe you'd share that little guy," Paul said suddenly.

Julia couldn't help her wide-eyed amazement. The last time Paul held now bigger-sister Mabel, it had been a toss-up to decide who looked more wary. Julia glanced at Emma, who nodded, her eyes lively. She handed Paul the infant. "Now keep your hand under his head," she cautioned. "Up on your shoulder."

Paul's look of extreme caution faded as the little one nestled close in that compact way of babies and turned his head into her husband's neck. His hand gentle on the baby's back, he walked toward the parlor, where Heber was standing.

"Julia, I think you have something to tell me," Emma whispered, her eyes on Paul. "Don't be shy. That looks suspiciously like early practice. I must say, he's doing well, for Mr. Otto."

Julia nodded. "I didn't know he'd do that," she whispered back.

"What? Get you in the family way?"

"No! Hold your baby like a professional."

"Come in the kitchen and tell all. And while you're at it, show me where I went wrong with this angel food cake."

"Looks like some stray yolk got away. Just turn it into trifle," Julia said as she surveyed a lethargic angel food cake in the kitchen. "Break it up in little pieces, and add fruit. I can make a pudding, and maybe you have heavy cream?" She folded her hands in her lap. "Oh, Emma, I've never been so sick and happy at the same time. I never thought cooking would be so trying. Please tell me it passes."

"By the time you get to four months, you'll feel like conquering the universe," Emma assured her, then chuckled. "Of course, it starts getting hard to bend in the middle, so maybe the universe can wait." Her face grew serious. "What are you going to do about a doctor?"

"We've been having a mild argument about that," Julia said, mixing the ingredients for vanilla pudding. She set the pan on the stove and started to whisk. "Paul says I should go back to Salt Lake City, or Cheyenne, or even Gun Barrel, but I can tell his heart is not in that. Mine, either."

Emma took the spoon from her and pointed to the chair again. "Sit! You're looking a bit green. There's something about cooking smells . . . No, you need to stay on the Double Tipi. Brother Otto was miserable all winter, and I still remember how you wouldn't turn loose of him when they brought you to my house. No, you need to stay there."

"We've both been thinking about Doctor McKeel, who works for him, but it's hard to say whether Doc will agree." Julia sighed and started breaking the angel food into smaller bits. "Having a baby shouldn't be so . . . so daunting!"

Julia heard the men laugh in the parlor. "I shouldn't worry. On the train, Paul pointed out that passage in the Doctrine and Covenant where the Lord says, 'Doubt not, fear not, little flock.' That would be us too."

"Counsel from the Lord was never just for Joseph and our grandparents, Julia," Emma reminded her. She set the pudding aside to cool and started slicing bananas, handing her half of one. "Eat it, my dear. Any questions, or should I mind my own business?"

Julia had some, which Emma answered as they put the trifle together.

"And I'm wondering—hmm, how to ask this: is it written any place that we can't . . . Oh, my . . ."

Emma shook her head and leaned closer, whispering. "My doctor tells me that by the time you get to the seventh month, you make Romeo settle for a peck on the cheek after the lights are out."

"The lights have to be out?" Julia asked innocently and then laughed at the expression on Emma's face.

"Sister Otto, you're an advanced beginner," she teased.

"You two are having way too much fun in there," Heber said from the parlor, which made Emma put her hand over her mouth.

The women looked at each other. And there was Paul in the doorway now, watching her, the Gillespies' baby sleeping so peacefully against his shoulder.

"I am a lucky woman," she said to him. Paul's only response was that edgy smile of his that she knew by now meant a pleasant evening at the Plainsman Hotel, lights on or off.

The sweetness continued the next day at Sunday School, with James hurtling himself into her arms, a reminder how much she had missed him too. He was taller, even since her last glimpse of him, and he seemed more confident somehow. As much as she wanted James close by her side, she couldn't help her relief that he went, as a matter of course, to sit with Sister Shumway. Julia noticed the disappointment on Paul's face and took his hand.

"You know it's better if he sits with them," she whispered.

"I know. Still . . ."

She looked at Sister Shumway, who was whispering to James now, her arm around him protectively. To Julia's pleasure, James glanced over at them on their bench and patted the spot next to him. Paul took Julia's hand and they moved.

"Never think we won't share," Sister Shumway said. "We owe you a debt we can never repay."

*That sounds so decided*, Julia thought, startled. She leaned closer to Paul and looked at him, a question in her eyes.

"Tell you later, sport," he whispered as the chorister stood up to lead the opening song.

He didn't need to tell her anything, she realized, as they held the hymnbook and sang. He had already given James away to them.

There wasn't time to talk about it, not with Paul joining the other men, hands on each other's right shoulder, as they all held the Gillespies' infant and added their priesthood support to President Gillespie's blessing. Then there was the sacrament, and Sunday School, and a rush for the train, after hugs and kisses.

"Have they adopted James?" she asked finally as the Cheyenne and Northern began their return trip. "You've given them permission, haven't you?"

Paul nodded. "I had to. I watched them all winter, forming a tight bond. I did it just before I came to marry you."

"Even before we knew we could have children."

"It felt right, Julia. I hope you don't mind that I didn't ask you first."

"I don't mind. Not at all. It wasn't my decision to make. How did you arrange it?"

"Heber and I sat down with the governor and told him as much as we felt was safe to tell." He chuckled. "Sometimes it's nice to lean on my status as one of the first ranchers in Wyoming. There wasn't any argument. Governor Carey listened and placed a call to his attorney general. Done. Thaddeus Pulaski James Otto is now James Eugene Shumway. The Eugene was James's idea and tickled Brother Shumway no end."

Paul leaned his head back against the cushion and stared at the ceiling for a long moment. Julia tucked her hand in his vest.

"Getting proprietary?" he asked finally. His voice sounded ragged, but she overlooked it.

"Yes, I am, cowboy. You're my hero."

He sighed. "Remind me now and then."

They spent the night in Gun Barrel, debating whether to visit old Doctor Beck in the morning, and finally decided against it.

"He's delivered many a baby, but there is simply no guarantee we could ever get him to the Double Tipi in time in mid-winter," Paul said as he finished breakfast. "Oh, these eggs, Darling. You've ruined me."

Julia looked at her dry toast and swallowed a few times.

"Need to make a quick exit?" Paul asked, his eyes kind.

"No. It's mind over matter," she said. She took a sip of water. "We need to ask Doc, don't we?"

"We do," Paul pushed away his plate. "He assured me years ago that he'd always doctor my crew. And you probably saw him at the cow gather, tending to everything from broken bones to hangover." He shook his head. "A baby is a different matter. I don't know what he'll say. It's far more private and you're the patient, not me or my men."

"If he won't?"

He took her hand and looked into her eyes. "My father delivered me. That work for you, sport, if need be?"

She nodded. "There's no one I trust more."

Doc didn't seem surprised when Paul asked him to sit with them in the parlor after supper. Without blushing this time, Malloy volunteered to help Charlotte with the dishes. Julia nodded, keeping a straight face.

Paul sat a moment, looking at Doc. "I'm certain you know what we want to ask," he said finally.

"I wondered when you would," Doc replied. "I'm out of practice, Julia. You know that."

"I know. If . . . if you're afraid I'll be embarrassed, I won't be."

"Hard to say about that. You see me every day, the Boss's hand. Taking care of you during a pregnancy is something entirely different. It's far more intimate, and I'm still a ranch hand." He looked down. "I know you both think I should be more, but I'm safe from myself here."

"If you'd rather not, I have no hard feelings," Julia said, after a glance at Paul. "I will insist you teach Paul everything he needs to know to birth our baby. There won't be any calving ropes!" she joked, and the men chuckled as she hoped they would.

*This is hard,* she thought, thinking of Iris and how her mother would worry, if her only living daughter had no physician except a willing husband. Julia couldn't help her sudden tears at a time when she wanted them both to know how determined she was. "I *refuse* to go back to Salt Lake City, or Cheyenne, or Gun Barrel. I can't be that far away from my husband. It would kill my soul."

"Steady, Julia. Tears come easier when you're expecting. I would never suggest you and Paul be separated during this time. I don't think either of you could survive it."

Doc's voice was calm. As she listened to him, holding tight to Paul's hand, she heard a difference. Doc was never one to intrude. She blew her nose, remembering how he had calmed her in the dreadful days after the telegram came from home, telling of Iris's death. Maybe he was just a ranch hand now, but he would always be more. She could hear it in his voice, even if he couldn't.

"We'll be all right, Doc," she said simply.

Doc stood up and went to the window, looking out at the waning sunlight. "I love this place," he said, speaking to the window. "Physician, heal thyself. Well, this physician healed himself here, with considerable help from Mr. Otto. You too, Julia. I never did properly thank you for your Christmas gift of Gray's *Anatomy*. It put the heart back in my chest."

He rocked back and forth on his heels for a few moments, then turned around and clapped his hands together. "I owe both of you. I'll do it." He was all business. "I'll go get my bag. Boss, escort this little mother upstairs and help her into her nightgown. You lovebirds can give me some estimates on when this blessed event could, uh, conceivably have taken place. I'll provide my best guess after an exam, and dimes to doughnuts, your child will probably arrive when it feels like it. Welcome to the exact science of childbirth. It's no wonder they call it a medical practice. All we do is practice! Go on, now, before I change my mind."

With some pondering, the three of them decided on February 15, 1912. "We'll be ready for anything after January, for certain," Doc said as he put away his calipers. "Boss, mid February is generally when we start calving. Don't you two know that farmers and ranchers have their babies in August and September? I even remember that from Indiana."

"What on earth do you mean?" Julia asked.

Paul and Doc looked at each other and grinned. "I can answer that one, sport. November and December are slow months for ranchers. Nothing much to do on the place except make a little more whoopee than usual. I can't speak for farmers, but *I* was born in August."

"You two!" Julia exclaimed. "Maybe I *should* go back to Salt Lake City."

"Don't even think it," Paul said quickly, as serious as she had ever seen him.

"I was teasing," she said softly. "I won't say that again."

After much crossing out and crumpling of paper, Julia sat at Paul's desk that night and tried to write a letter to her parents. "Why is this hard?" she grumbled to Paul, who sat in a straight chair with his feet on the desk, going over a ledger.

"It's hard because of Iris."

She nodded and folded her hands together across her latest bungled attempt at correspondence. "I could wait until I'm farther along, and then write."

"You could," he agreed. "I'm probably going to Gun Barrel later in the week to inquire about a buckboard. I'll mail any letters you feel like sending." He smiled at her. "I think you should tell them."

She yawned and frowned at the letter again. Paul stood up and looked over her shoulder.

"How about this? You lie down, and I'll write the letter. You've been yawning for an hour, and I know I'm not *that* boring. They're my parents too, now."

"You're on. I'll just rest my eyes for a little bit. That's all I need."

She stood up, and he sat down. "Better put on your nightgown before you 'just rest your eyes.' Last time you said that, I had to wake you up in the morning to fix breakfast."

"Am I already a trial?"

"Yep. Go to bed."

Julia rested her eyes until morning, coming awake easily. Lying beside her husband, she edged a little closer, not wanting to wake him but liking his warmth. She watched the lace curtains flutter in the early-morning breeze, as cheerful as her mother's curtains in Salt Lake City, a brave symbol of civilization. Trust ladies to know how to make a house a home.

Still, she couldn't overlook that Mr. Otto's original ranch house, with all its eccentricities, had become home to her quickly enough last year. She carefully turned sideways to admire her sleeping husband. "You're what makes this my home," she whispered, barely moving her lips. "And maybe this." She put her hands on her abdomen, pushing in gently where Doc had pushed. There was only the barest indication of a baby, a small gift no one would notice yet. It was their child to grow in peace and quiet on the Double Tipi, surrounded by people who cared deeply about them both. *This is my job*, she thought, her hands gentle on her belly. *I doubt I'll have a better one.*

She got up quietly, pleased not to disturb Paul. He had come to bed late last night, so she suspected the letter to her folks hadn't been any easier for him. She carried her clothes downstairs and dressed in the bathing room, happy not to disturb Charlotte, either.

Julia didn't need her cooking book for cinnamon rolls. She sat at the kitchen table eating soda crackers until her stomach settled. When it did, she worked quickly, and soon had rolls rising in the warming oven. Quietly, she padded on bare feet down the hall to the office, where Paul's letter lay on the desk.

She sat in the straight chair, not trusting the motion of Paul's swivel chair so early in the morning. Since he had left the letter on the desk, Julia knew he meant for her to read it too. She picked it up, read it, then set it down, nearly overcome with the love Paul had for her.

*Dear Folks, for so you are,* he had written. *I doubt anything I write here will surprise you. Julia feels a little tender about sharing this news, for reasons we all know too well. Somewhere in the middle of February, you'll find yourselves with another grandchild. Babies are plentiful in this world, but this one will be ours, on loan from the Lord, so there is no more special child in all the universe. Julia is doing fine, except for nausea. Even with her hand over her mouth, she keeps me in line. I've never thanked you for rearing such a woman, and for your own courage in not objecting when she declared she was going to cook for a Wyoming rancher. I'm certain you had many objections. I doubt I would be brave enough to let my child go into the wilderness. I thank God every day that you did. My life B.J. (before Julia) was a barren desert, sort of like that stretch of parched misery between Rock Springs and Rawlins. Those days are over, and I thank God for that too. Life will never be easy on the Double Tipi. I wish I could tell you it will be, but I would be lying. What it is, is heaven on earth for all the Ottos lucky enough to call it home, as we do. Thank you for your daughter. Her life brings life to me. Love, Your son Paul.*

"Will that work, sport?"

Julia looked up into smiling eyes, even if his hair was a regular tumbleweed and his moustache rumpled. "It'll work," she replied, shy at so much love on paper. "Thank you."

"Any time. You're my special girl."

He slapped the lintel of the door, and she listened to his measured tread heading toward the kitchen. She inclined her head and waited, first for a ferocious yawn, then there it was: "Redeemer of Israel" this morning.

Even with nausea and exhaustion, Julia felt herself drawn into the predictable and ordinary rhythm of ranch life. She knew it well from her previous year on the Double Tipi, but there was an added layer to it now, as she relished being mistress of her home.

She swallowed her discomfort and did what was expected of her without complaint, because Paul never complained, even the afternoon he came home with a large flap of skin dangling from his forearm, the result of a slip with the fence stretcher. His face impassive, he let Doc stitch him, then grimaced, reached over, and tugged her down in a chair with the comment, "You're starting to wobble, sport."

She knew how much he liked her cooking, even though morning sickness that lasted all day sometimes left her trembling with nausea. *Ottos don't wobble*, she reminded herself as she held her nose, cooked his favorite food, and broiled the everlasting steaks. *I can always die when the meal is over.*

Charlotte helped everywhere she could, but Julia understood her distraction when Matt Malloy came around the kitchen on any little excuse. His attentiveness provided enough diversion to keep Julia's mind off her own discomfort. *If I drank that much coffee, I'd spend every waking moment in the backhouse,* Julia thought. *Lovers must have kidneys of steel.*

The matter resolved itself nicely in mid-June, when Paul took Matt walking by the horse corral one evening to announce a new position for him as ranch foreman, a raise in pay, and the additional bonus of the old bunkhouse refurbished as a home. Sitting on the front porch with her knitting, Julia watched the whole job interview, from the handshake right down to Matt's purposeful return to the kitchen through the side door, a few quiet moments in the kitchen with Charlotte, then a whoop, followed by more silence.

"It appears that the Irishman's wooing has been successful," Doc said from his perch on the front steps.

"High time," Julia said, casting off. *What about you?* she wanted to ask, even though she knew better.

"Doc looks so sad," she told her husband that night after prayer. She made herself comfortable against him as she settled herself for sleep.

"That may be, but I wouldn't meddle in Doc's life," Paul said. "Just because you're happy doesn't mean everyone is." He sighed. "Or maybe can be."

"You used to think that," she pointed out.

"So did you, I believe," he said, toying with the tie to her nightgown. "Were we two nincompoops?"

"Ancient history, cowboy," she said. "Do you have designs on me right now?"

"Any objections?"

"Just watch the motion, Romeo."

"My specialty."

Her nausea lessened as July wore on, to the point where the horseback ride to Gun Barrel endangered no bushes by the side of the trail. They stayed in Gun Barrel long enough to place an order for a buckboard, complete with springs. Paul asked the liveryman to keep his eyes open for a smooth-walking horse to pull it.

Marriage had not hurt Paul's negotiating ability. One long, Mr. Otto look changed the "I can't have it to you any sooner than late September," into "August 15? Certainly."

Word must have got around in the Cheyenne Sunday School, Julia decided. It couldn't be her imagination that most of the sisters eyed her waist. She did her best to suck in her stomach, but the effort wasn't successful.

"If you keep trying to do that, you'll start breathing out of your ears," Paul warned in a low voice.

She laughed out loud, then gave him a sunny smile, which led to a massive throat clearing from their Sunday School teacher.

"Do I have to separate you two?" Brother Mitchell asked.

"Too late," Paul said cheerfully, which made the class dissolve and answered any questions that the slower among them might have wondered about.

"It's a good thing you were never able to inflict yourself upon an actual school," Julia scolded as they hurried to the depot after church. "You'd have gotten rid of many a schoolmarm."

She looked at him, expecting at least a chuckle, but his face was serious. He took her arm and moved her toward a café, with its large front window.

"What's the matter?" she asked, critiquing the menu board outside the café because she would always be a cook. Maybe he was hungry.

"Just keep looking at it," he told her. He leaned forward a little and stared into the window's reflection. "Well, well." He took her arm again and continued toward the depot. "I do believe we've been followed."

"What?" she exclaimed.

"Don't look around, but McAtee is a block behind us."

Julia gulped. "No! Do you think he knows we came out of the Odd Fellows Hall?"

He shrugged. He stood there a moment, indecisive, a trait she was not familiar with in her husband.

"Let's go say hello to him," Julia suggested. "I've never met the man, and you'll have to admit my introduction to Mr. Kaiser was successful, as far as it went."

"True. All right, Julia. About face. Let's call his bluff."

They turned around and stood there. McAtee was nowhere in sight.

"We didn't both imagine him," Paul said, frustrated.

"*I've* never seen him," Julia said. "Well, that's a sour look from my best guy."

"I didn't imagine him," he said pointedly. He shook his head and gave a self-deprecating laugh. "Or maybe I did. He's getting on my last nerve, rather like Amalickiah."

The journey home was quiet. When they were nearly at Gun Barrel, Paul took her hand. "I know we've been stopping in Gun Barrel overnight, because I don't want to tire you, but would you mind if we push on? It's summer, so it'll still be light."

"You know I don't mind." She patted her middle. "Neither will Junior."

When they left the train, Julia headed for the depot office. Paul lingered on the platform, watching the cars. He walked toward the front of the train and stood there, half-hidden by a post, as passengers got off and on. In a few minutes, the conductor called "All Aboard!" and the train started to move. Paul remained where he was, watching the cars as they moved slowly past.

She saw him nod as the last two cars flashed by on the way north to Wheatland, then Glendo, Orin, and Douglas.

Paul pushed himself away from the pillar where he had been leaning and strolled toward her, hands in his pockets. He didn't try to hide his unhappiness. "He was in the second to the last car, just staring back at me and grinning."

She put her hand on his arm.

"He'll probably get off in Orin, and then ride cross country to his ranch near Rawhide Buttes." He slapped his hat against his leg. "How did he know we were in Cheyenne?"

"It might have been a coincidence," she said as they left the depot. "People go to Cheyenne all the time."

He nodded. "Maybe. Let's write a letter to the Shumways tonight and tell them our fears. It'll pay to be extra vigilant until we find out if the whole thing today was a fluke."

Paul was steering her toward the livery stable. "Julia, I'm officially worried. I want to get home. Ready to ride?"

They rode steadily into the afternoon and early evening, stopping only when Julia requested a break.

All was in order on the Double Tipi, even to Julia's less-practiced eyes. She glanced at her husband as they rode past the house and toward the horse barn, relieved to see the calm return to his eyes. *You would never be happy anywhere else, Paul*, she thought, letting him help her from the saddle and hoping no one was close enough to observe the way he held her against his body as he lowered her to the ground. *And if you weren't happy, neither would I be.*

He was quiet that night, looking at his ranch hands at the dining table. She knew what he was doing: measuring each of them, as if wondering who informed Mr. McAtee they were going to Cheyenne. She sipped peppermint tea, which never failed to settle her stomach.

"Not much of a meal, Julia," Paul said after the others

left. Charlotte had cleared the table, and the two of them were still sitting there. "I thought you were supposed to be eating for two."

"Until my stomach settles, I'm just eating for your little Cherokee, and he likes consommé princesse," she said. "Doc says—no, I'm going to call him Dr. McKeel, when he's my doctor—Dr. McKeel says we'll be fine." She took his hand. "It's you I'm worried about."

"Not James?"

"No. We'll write that letter to the Shumways, and they'll keep him safe. I want to know what you're going to do to Mr. McAtee."

He leaned back in his chair. "I'm not sure. He may have been in Cheyenne on perfectly innocent business. It may be I am starting to suspect people who would never, never be anything but loyal. He may have had nothing to do with that note in your bureau. James may have been wrong. I wish I knew."

They went up the stairs together. While she prepared for bed, he stood a long time looking out the window. "I always feel better on my own land," he said. "Ready for prayer?"

He was quiet that night, his arms around her. She thought he was asleep, until he whispered in her ear, "Julia, let's set aside McAtee for a while and call a brief meeting of the Double Tipi corporation. Is the executive officer willing?"

"Certainly," she said, smiling in the dark.

"Good." He patted her belly. "Newest board member is obviously present, as well."

"Obviously."

"I'm wondering what my executive officer would think if we pulled off the open range and kept our stock exclusively on Double Tipi land."

"Why would you pull off the open range entirely?"

"It's something your brother David said when we were in St. George."

"David?"

"Yeah. He asked me how long I thought the open range would last, even in Wyoming. I told him I see it shrinking every year—more and more homesteaders trying to stake out the last open land in the West. He asked me, 'What are you going to do about that?' I didn't have an answer then."

She turned around to look at him. "I'm so new at this. Behind fences, you can't support so many cattle."

"True." He touched her face. "You're pretty in the moonlight. Any light for that matter."

"That has nothing to do with corporate business."

"Actually, it does." He kissed her forehead. "I don't want this land to grind you down. That roundup was too much. Oh, I know you'd never be treated that way again, now that you've more than proved yourself, but life could be simpler on our own land."

"You can't shut out the world, Paul," she said, her hands gentle on his face.

"I can, a little. Besides that, my two beautiful Denver bulls are giving us some wonderful boys and girls. I'm developing the best herd around here; I could see that at the gather. I want it on my land, and not at the mercy of the open range. If I keep breeding superior stock, our reduced herd will pay out better than our current herd."

She thought about what he was saying. "Executive officer agrees. Sounds like you can still keep me in flour and sugar. Maybe one new dress a year."

"And then some. Times are changing, sport. The day when the Peter and Mary Anne Otto family could hide from the rest of Wyoming Territory are gone. The Paul and Julia Otto family is here to stay, with superior beef that refrigerated cars can take to the farthest markets."

"If you're going to stay behind fences, will you need more winter forage?"

"Julia, you're proving to be an excellent executive officer. I will, indeed. The Sybille Ditch is making the bottomlands bloom, just like the Pathfinder did in Nebraska. I could contract for more hay from the farmers around Gun Barrel and Wheatland. Maybe even grow my own hay." He chuckled. "Be a da . . . blamed farmer."

"I'm in favor. But the executive officer reminds you not to cuss. How will you go about this?"

"Mind my mouth. Oh, you mean . . . Things are running well here. I'll take Doc and visit some of the farmers." He pulled her closer. "You'll be safe here."

She could feel his hesitancy, and gave his moustache a tug. "All right, Paul. What *else* are you going to do?"

"My word, you know me well," he exclaimed. "We'll go north to Lusk. I'm going to make a discreet inquiry—feel out McAtee's circumstances. There's something not right about this whole odd situation. What those ranchers did to James's family is not the first time something of that nature has happened in Wyoming. For years, everyone has turned a blind eye to such evil."

"You don't know why he's so worried about James."

"I really don't."

# Sixteen

The letter to the Shumways and one to the Gillespies went to Gun Barrel two days later with Paul and Doc. She noted, as they sat around the table with the hands after breakfast, that Paul had only told everyone they were going to Wheatland and Gun Barrel. She also noticed that when he left their bedroom, he had strapped on his gun.

His eyes followed her gaze, and he rubbed gently at the frown between her eyes. "Just insurance, sport." They went down the stairs together, his hand on her shoulder. "Walk with me?"

"Always."

He chuckled. "Just as far as the horse barn today: last-minute instructions for the next-in-command."

"Which would be Matt, since he's your new foreman," Julia reminded her husband.

"Nope. You're the executive officer of this cowpunching corporation. Matt has his instructions, which he will tell you every morning. Yours are to see that he follows them. He'll make a full report each evening over supper. Ask him all the questions you want."

She nodded. "I can do that."

They stopped by the horses and watched Doc swing into the saddle. "Doc said he has a few orders of his own," Paul said. He kissed her and mounted.

"I do, indeed," Doc said, "and I'm speaking as Doctor McKeel. Absolutely no heavy lifting over ten or fifteen pounds. That's an order, and you'll obey."

"Yes, sir," she replied, saluting.

"No joking, Mrs. Otto." He leaned down, and his gaze reminded her of Paul's. "If you have any troubles at all, even minor things, send Colby for Elinore Cuddy."

"Not Alice? She's closer."

Doc shook his head. "I watched Elinore at the cow gather. Sure, she got a little green over the oysters, but she stuck with you at the sonofagun stew." He straightened up. "I rode over to the Cuddy's place yesterday and asked her."

*Oh, you did?* she thought. "I hope you told her to come visiting."

"I actually did."

*And you blush better than my husband*, she thought as Doc tipped his hat to her and started from the horse corral. *Oh, I do love to see a grown man blush.*

Paul leaned down from the saddle for another kiss. "I know that look," he whispered, on his way back up. "Behave yourself, sport."

"Paul, you . . ." She stopped and gave him her sunniest smile. ". . . know me rather well."

His grin said it all.

"Where you headed, Boss?" Colby asked, as he saddled his own mount.

"Big doings in Wheatland and maybe Torrington. I'm on the prowl for farmers who'd like to grow me hay."

Paul tipped his hat to Julia too. She stood by the corral and watched until he was just a speck through the cut in the ridge.

"He's not settled in his mind about that note or the bonfire, is he?" Colby commented as she stood there, watching the two men leave the valley.

"No, he's not. Better to be safe, wouldn't you say?"

"A thousand times better." He nodded to her and

walked his horse toward Matt Malloy, who stood with Paul's cousins. After a moments' discussion, the men mounted their horses and headed in the opposite direction. Julia noted with some relief that Colby looked back at her, then gave her a small salute.

*Thank you, Paul, for leaving me with protectors*, Julia thought as she looked for one last glimpse of her husband.

Julia kept Charlotte busy all week, letting her assistant do the strong-smelling cooking that sent her into the parlor to lie down. By afternoon, when her insides were tamer, she instructed her willing helper in the fine art of yeast dough. Charlotte worked diligently, not saying much, because that wasn't the Indian way, but paying close attention to Julia's directions. By the end of the week, Julia turned over the bread making to Charlotte.

"You've obviously been taking good care of your cousin's little sweethearts for six months," Julia said. Shy, she touched Charlotte's arm. "I think you've done a wonderful job."

Charlotte's normally solemn face glowed with the pleasure of the compliment, reminding Julia forcefully of her own delight in a compliment from Paul, back when he was Mr. Otto, and she was his cook.

As the week passed, she began to sense something different about herself, and it had nothing to do with the child she carried. She realized how gracefully she had settled into her new role on the Double Tipi, that of the stockman's wife, trusted by her husband. She regretted that Matt called her Mrs. Otto now, instead of Julia, but she understood. When he gave his report each evening over supper, describing what he and the hands had done, she paid close attention, asking questions. She didn't worry about appearing foolish and ignorant, because she was coming to understand ranch work. When she didn't understand, she said so frankly.

"Why's my husband doing this, Matt?" she asked one night, when the others had returned to the bunkhouse and he still sat in the dining room with Charlotte. "You know far more than I do, and we all know that."

"He told me once, 'Malloy, every time you put yourself in the saddle, you court danger and death. Anything can happen.'" He took a sip of his coffee, his eyes serious, reminding Julia that he had changed too, with new responsibilities. "He wants you to be able to run this ranch."

She nodded, disturbed by his candid reply.

Matt must have seen the discomfort on her face, because he spoke with a certain shyness Julia found touching. "I think he's already taking care of his children by making you strong."

"I believe you're right, Matt," she said as she rose from the table. "Thank you for putting the matter so plainly." She smiled at the two of them, sitting close together, their shoulders touching. "I'd be happy now if you'd help Charlotte with the dishes." She laughed. "Charlotte would be even happier."

Charlotte beamed at her and rose to clear the table.

Julia sat for a long time at the desk in Paul's office, going through the journals he had left there with a note: *Take a look at these, Julia.* When she had helped him occasionally last year with the ranch accounts, he had often sat with her at the old kitchen table, writing in his journal. She looked through them now, reading his careful notations about early work, branding, ear marking, diseases, and weather. Every event was dated. She closed the book, impressed with what she held in her hands. With capable hands and a willingness to work hard, anyone could run this ranch by following Mr. Otto's journals.

He must have known what she would be thinking,

as she looked at the most recent journal and found a note there addressed to her. *My darling, my ranch is your ranch*, she read. *I'll never fear for our children, because you are here, looking after all of our interests, even as I do.* The responsibility he had placed on her took her breath away. No one had ever depended so much on her as her husband did now. Remembering what he had told her about eternal potential, what he asked of her humbled her.

She spent a long time on her knees beside their bed that night, grateful for a careful husband who was leaving nothing to chance. She missed him with every fiber of her being, still a little amazed at herself, the independent Julia Darling, who had become so twined with Paul Otto. She had come to the Double Tipi with nothing in common with her employer. Here she was a year and a half later, in love, married, carrying his child, sharing his beliefs because they were her beliefs. They had everything in common now, but she knew such a blessing would always be a bit of a mystery to her. She had read somewhere—she knew she would never be a scripture scholar—about the Lord's tender mercies. The phrase had baffled her, but she understood it perfectly now; she saw tender mercies everywhere.

After praying, she climbed in bed and pulled his pillow close to her body, breathing deep of bay rum and a little wood smoke, comforted because he had left men he trusted in charge of his growing family.

Funny how seeing that rider on the ridge the next morning could thrust comfort far from her mind. There he sat on his horse, surveying the sleeping ranch below. She dressed quickly and hurried downstairs, still running her fingers through her short hair. Paul had been right—it was easy to fluff it. As she went to the side porch, to stand there in the angle of the house and see the rider without being seen, Julia decided it was better to see him on the ridge, rather than to wonder if he had already circled behind the buildings and made a stealthy approach.

To her relief, Colby Wagner, spurs and jingle bobs setting up a racket, came from the horse barn toward the house. Julia motioned to him. He glanced at her and then looked in the direction of the ridge where she pointed. He nodded and headed into the corral.

Not taking the time to throw on a saddle, he bridled his horse and swung up, keeping himself between the barn and the ranch road.

Julia sighed with disappointment. The rider on the ridge swung his horse about and set off at a gallop, away from the ranch buildings.

"Be careful, Colby," she murmured, hoping now that their mysterious visitor had ridden away and was not preparing to ambush her protector. She closed her eyes, hoping not to hear gunfire.

Except for the wind rustling the cottonwoods along the river, all was silence. She stood for a long while on the porch, hands on her belly, unaware she was doing that until Colby rode into the ranch yard again. She looked down at her hands, shaking her head over her puny protection of her child. *I suppose I will do that now*, she thought. *It must be a reflex.*

She went inside the kitchen and started the coffee brewing, then hurried to the horse corral, where Colby was now saddling his horse. She leaned her elbows on the fence rail, and he walked toward her, slapping one glove in the other hand in obvious frustration.

"Was he even there or a figment of my imagination?" she asked.

"Oh, he was there," Colby said, the disgust high in his voice. "Big as life, for a scrawny . . ." He paused. "Can you clue me into a polite word for someone who preys on women and children?"

"There isn't one." She thought a moment and drew a ragged breath. "Call him a sonofagun, the gentleman from Rawhide Buttes."

He pushed his hat back and gazed at her. "Mrs. Otto, you're way too polite to last long on the Double Tipi."

Something in his words made her want to dig down a little deeper and not let him see her fear. "Colby, I am on my second year on the Double Tipi, I'll have you know," she told him, her voice crisp. "I have no plans to ever leave this ranch."

"Sorta thought you'd say that," Colby admitted. "I'm saddling up to take a harder look for our, uh, gentleman from Rawhide Buttes."

She started to agree, then shook her head. "No, not until you ask Matt Malloy."

"You're the boss when the big boss is away," he countered.

"Then the little boss is telling you to ask Matt Malloy," she stated. "No arguments, Colby, even though I know you mean well."

He shrugged. "Have it your way, Mrs. Otto," he told her, then touched his fingers to his hat brim and returned to saddling his horse. "I'll go ask him when I'm finished with this."

*I do intend to have it my way*, she thought, *even though I greatly appreciate your concern for me.*

She returned to the kitchen as Charlotte came from her room, braiding her hair, a question in her eyes. Julia told her what had happened, and she frowned.

"Do you think that rider knows my cousin is off the place?" Charlotte asked.

"I have no idea," Julia replied. "Of course, he may have seen him in . . ." She stopped, remembering that Paul had asked her not to mention Lusk. ". . . in Torrington or Wheatland," she finished, sitting down at the kitchen table.

Two Bits jumped into her lap, and she petted him, drawing comfort, as always, from his oversized purr. "Let's have flapjacks and sausage this morning, along with fried eggs, Charlotte. Let me see if I'm brave enough to attempt the sausage."

She was, even though she had to go to the side porch a few times to take deep breaths of air that wasn't redolent of grease and sage. She knew Charlotte wouldn't have minded taking over, but Julia continued to mull over Colby's words, hoping others didn't see her as too light weight for ranch life. It was one thing to cook for hire, and a far different thing to invest her heart and soul into the Double Tipi.

"But it's done and I have," she murmured as she poked the sausage around.

Over breakfast, Matt vetoed Colby's wish to track the ridge rider. From the thin-lipped look Colby gave the new foreman, Julia could tell he didn't agree.

"No argument, Colby," she said, passing the biscuits. "Anyone out there is long gone, and there's work to be done here."

"I'm just thinking of your safety," Colby replied.

"I know, but Matt's right," she told him, even though his concern touched her heart.

"Thanks for backing me up," Matt told her later after the hands were preparing to mount up for a day's work checking fences.

"You're the foreman," she said. "It's as simple as that."

He nodded, pleased, and started to leave the kitchen. Julia stopped him with a light touch on his arm. "Matt, what did we do to get so lucky?" she asked.

"I've asked myself that ever since he found me rooting

through that garbage can behind the Trail Café," he said, his eyes on Charlotte at the sink. "And now there's Charlotte."

Alice came by at the beginning of the second week with eggs, and two promised chickens and a rooster, trussed up and indignant. Kringle had grumbled the day before when Julia asked him to make a chicken coop, but the new residence was done, painted with white left over from the house, along with sky blue slats that matched the shutters and underside of her new porch. In a fit of fancy unlike the familiar Kringle, who generally glowered at her, the German had added a medallion with *Wilkommen* written in careful script. Julia knew better than to show much appreciation over the coop, but she gave Kringle an extra piece of rhubarb pie that night.

The next day, when Elinore Cuddy rode over to visit, Matt remarked, "This place is a regular watering hole—two visitors in two days. Faith, Mrs. Otto, I'm not sure we can stand all this society!"

To Julia's delight, Elinore came with a present: a pair of soakers she had knitted. "Elinore, this is our very first baby gift," Julia said, pleased, as they sat down in the parlor with chamomile tea and prune almond cake.

"Soakers? It's nothing fancy," Elinore protested, but Julia could tell she was pleased. "Doesn't take much yarn to whip out a soaker, when I have my feet up after dinner." She peered closer at Julia. "And don't let me have to remind you to put your feet up after dinner."

"Doc told you to keep an eye on me, didn't he?" Julia asked, tickled with this side of what she already knew was a no-nonsense woman.

Elinore nodded and took another sip of tea. She smiled one of her rare smiles. "Doc told me I could even get belligerent, if you gave me any difficulties."

They laughed together. In a few more minutes, both of them were knitting, their silence companionable in the peaceful room, where a soft breeze ruffled the lace curtains and the sound of cottonwoods was better than balm.

She wasn't sure what made her do it, but Julia started to talk about Doc and how kind he had been to her last winter, when she received the telegram about Iris's death. "He just knew what to do," she said, then leaned forward, confiding. "For Christmas I gave him a copy of Gray's *Anatomy* and told him he ought to be practicing medicine again." She put down her knitting. "I admit to being a rank busybody, but I hope he does, someday."

Elinore nodded. She knitted another row, then looked up, a question in her eyes. Julia waited for her to speak, but she chose not to, returning her attention to her knitting. Julia observed her—thin, capable, not young any more, but not old, either. Paul told her Elinore Cuddy had come west from Iowa to help her brother seven years ago, possibly in the hope that she could find a husband in Wyoming's bachelor-heavy society. Perhaps some things weren't meant to happen. Julia frowned at her knitting, sensitive to the woman sitting beside her, a woman that no one in their ranching region had decided to look twice at. Maybe the humiliation of that, in a state where even the plainest woman generally merited a second and third look, had served to turn Elinore Cuddy quiet.

Impulsively, Julia put out her hand to Elinore. "I never did thank you for enduring with me over that wretched sonofagun stew."

Elinore flashed one of her rare smiles, which made her ordinary brown eyes brighten. "I wasn't about to give any of those Clydes the satisfaction of making you cry uncle!"

She coaxed Elinore to stay for supper, which hadn't been difficult. "Let's say I'd like to see you at work in your natural habitat," Elinore said, "and not fly-covered and bending over a trench fire."

"Colby will escort you home," Julia said.

"I don't need an escort," Elinore said quickly.

"Of course you do," Julia insisted. "Colby will be delighted."

Colby wasn't delighted. Julia could tell that easily enough as she stopped him on the side porch before supper and told him, after he had finished washing his face and hands, one of her rules.

"Miss Cuddy doesn't need any man's help to get home," he said.

"She's a woman, and I won't have her riding alone," Julia told him.

"She got here alone, didn't she?" he asked. "No one's ever going to bother Elinore Cuddy."

Julia took a deep breath and stared into his eyes. "Just do it," she said finally, clipping her words.

Colby nodded and didn't meet her eyes once during supper, which was a silent meal, anyway, since talking while eating wasn't approved manners on the range.

Julia thought about Elinore that night as she said her prayers. "And please bless Elinore too, Heavenly Father," she whispered. "I need a friend like her. And maybe she needs me."

Paul and Doc returned late in the afternoon at the end of the second week, trailing a Jersey cow and her calf behind them.

"Slow going, with this menagerie," Paul said as he dismounted and put both arms around her, rubbing her cheek with his substantial growth of whiskers. "I've been thinking about cream and butter and milk and you."

"In that order?" she teased.

"Nope. I hope there's lots of hot water in the Queen

Atlantic. Is supper ready or do you have any old free time just lying around, waiting to be occupied?"

"Supper's waiting for you, once you wash off that trail dust," she told him. "I'll keep until after dessert."

"Sport, you *are* dessert," he whispered into her ear, biting her ear lobe delicately.

What was it about a smelly rancher that made the bottom drop out of her stomach? "Supper first, Romeo. You'll find me upstairs after at least one fairy bite of Charlotte's raspberry jam tarts, chewed and swallowed without bolting your food," she said, holding him close. "You wouldn't want to be rude to your cousin and not try one."

"Well, I would, except that my uncle never did discard his scalping knife, and I like the way you tug on my hair, when life gets lively upstairs," he said, and he walked with her toward the house.

"I can't take you anywhere," she said, blushing.

"Guess not." He stopped in the road. "I nearly forgot." He pointed up the road toward the cut in the bluffs. "That's the last member of this traveling circus. Darling, let me present Magnus. He's way overnamed, but as you can see, he's persistent."

Julia looked where he pointed, at first seeing nothing more than a dust puff. As she squinted into the afternoon sun, the puff resolved itself into a low-slung dog, loping along, his tongue hanging out of his oversized head and his short legs churning up the distance. As she watched, wide-eyed, he tripped on one of his long ears and tumbled in the dust. He righted himself and continued on.

"What on earth?" she asked, mystified.

"Don't you know a dog when you see one?" Paul squatted down as the dog came closer. "Here, boy, come meet your new boss. She's pretty, she smells great, and you'll like her."

Julia stared. "He looks like a cross between an

ottoman and a badger," she said. "That's the ugliest dog I ever saw. *Magnus*?"

"That's what the bar tender at the Silver Dollar in Lusk called him. Here, boy." The dog stopped in front of Paul, eyes hopeful, tail going. "Grandiose name for pretty much nothing. The bartender claimed Magnus was the booby prize in a raffle. Pet him, Julia."

Cautious, she knelt beside her husband and put out her hand, the way Papa taught her to approach strange dogs. She touched one of Magnus's long ears, surprised at the velvety feel, so incongruous in a dog obviously designed by a committee. To her further surprise, Magnus flopped in the dust and rolled over to expose his belly.

"Reminds me of you," Julia murmured. "You do that too when you want something."

Paul laughed. "Julia, I can't take *you* anywhere."

"I'll rub your belly later," she assured him as she rubbed Magnus, who groaned with pleasure. "Hmm. Same reaction. Does he snore too when he's satisfied?"

"Oh, you are saucy," Paul said. He looked toward the porch. "Uh-oh. Trouble."

Two Bits had hunched himself sideways in the doorway, hissing. "Jerusalem Crickets, if Two Bits still had a tail, it would be as big as a broom, about now," Paul said. "Magnus, don't make any sudden moves."

Magnus's grasp of English was obviously not any stronger than his ability to understand the nuance of social situations. Interested, tongue still hanging out, he trotted toward Two Bits as Julia held her breath.

With a yowl, Two Bits launched himself onto Magnus' back, digging in with his claws. The dog bellowed in surprise and pain and turned in circles, trying to shake the enraged cat off his back. With a despairing yelp that made Julia wring her hands together, Magnus took off running, tumbling in the dust when his ears got in the way, but righting himself as Two Bits hung on grimly.

"Do something, Paul!" she said.

"Not me," he told her. "That's more than my life is worth. We'll have to let Magnus and Two Bits sort this one out." He put his hands on his hips, watching the dog with the cat run toward the barn. "Could be Magnus isn't much of a bodyguard. Guess we'll have to depend on his all-purpose ugliness to ward off any bad guys."

Julia gave him his own look. "Mr. Otto . . ."

"Oh, Jerusalem Crickets . . ."

"Do something!"

"For you," he said, picking up a bucket by the horse trough. He filled it and went into the barn, walking so cautiously that Julia turned away, laughing.

In another moment, she heard water splashing and outraged protests from both cat and dog. Solitary now, Two Bits streaked back across the yard. Charlotte opened the screen door as the cat raced through. Julia laughed to hear his claws scrabbling against the floor as he failed to make the turn by the icebox.

"I believe Two Bits would have gone through, whether that door was open or not," Paul said. He looked over his shoulder at the barn. "Magnus, all you have to fall back on is ugly. Happy?" he asked her.

Julia just laughed, yanked off his hat, and swatted him with it. "Wash up, cowboy," she said as she went toward the house. "You reek."

"Honeymoon's over," Doc said, still sitting on his horse.

"Nope. She didn't tell me I stink," Paul said. "She likes me."

# Seventeen

Paul was right; she did. Julia watched him finish two of Charlotte's raspberry jam tarts without even sitting down, after he came out of the bathing room. She noticed how thin his face was, which brought out the prominence of his cheekbones and accentuated the weather lines around his eyes. *You work so hard, while I am comfortable here*, she thought, understanding his love on a deeper level that touched her heart. *You probably wouldn't even call it a sacrifice.*

When he finished supper, Paul accepted another tart from a beaming Charlotte and leaned back, looking around the table at his hands.

"Gentlemen, Doc and I have been braving the wheat and hay fields of both of our newly named Goshen and Platte counties, courtesy of the state legislature. We have drummed up hay business. We were successful, thanks to the new Sybille Ditch. I signed contracts with three farmers. We're going to keep Double Tipi cattle behind fences now. No more open range."

"No more roundups?" Colby asked, disappointment evident in his voice.

"We'll still help our neighbors, of course," he said, "but we'll be nursemaiding our own cattle right here on the Double Tipi. Times are changing."

"Does that mean you'll need fewer hands?" Dan Who Counts asked, his expression serious.

"Not sure yet, Dan. We'll see how it goes. I'm not laying anyone off.

"That's all I have," Paul said. "Charlotte, you make a superior raspberry tart. Think how good they'll be with whipped cream from that Jersey. May I assign you milking duties? Julia can fill in, now and then, if she's willing."

"You know I am."

Charlotte nodded. "We'll have eggs soon too."

"Jee-rusalem Crickets, the Double Tipi is turning into a farm," Paul joked. He nudged Julia. "I suppose you'll want a garden next."

"It's small but it's already planted," she told him. "We'll have lettuce in a few weeks and other green stuff to counteract all that fried food you sweethearts like. Times are changing."

"I think we can stand the strain." His expression grew wistful. "My mother tried to grow green beans and squash, like she did on the rez. A garden would have pleased her."

"Come to think of it, she'd have been completely delighted with you," he told Julia an hour later, as he eased his arm around her bare shoulder, and she nestled closer.

"I wish I could have known your parents." She closed her eyes, then opened them again, not ready to sleep yet, not with daylight still streaming in the windows. "What happened in Lusk?"

"I got a really ugly dog," he teased, "who is probably halfway back there, by now."

"You know what I mean." She sighed. "The ridge rider was here once."

"That's what you're calling him?"

Julia nodded. "Colby looked for him, but came up dry."

"Anything else happen?"

"Kringle built a magnificent chicken coop, and don't

275

you dare twit him about it. Elinore paid me a visit, and we knitted soakers. I can't button my skirts anymore."

He chuckled and rested his hand on her belly. "Losing your little waist? I can't say that bothers me."

"Me, either. I've been keeping my food down."

"Good news. No bad dreams?" He kissed her shoulder.

"Not one. All I did at night was wish that empty space beside me had your amorous carcass in it."

"Believe me, I'd rather have been here." His hand went to her hair. "We rode around McAtee's land at Rawhide Buttes. It doesn't look prosperous at all, Julia. There's some serious neglect. I went to the courthouse in Lusk and looked at land deeds. Sure enough, McAtee and three other ranchers divided up those sections belonging to the Polish families."

"How did they do that?"

Paul's expression turned sour. "They got a Denver lawyer, someone who knows just enough and not too much, and who wasn't too bothered by the process of the law." Idly, he traced her scar from her neck to her waist. "I found out a lot more in the Silver Dollar, where Doc had two or three beers to cut the dust—can't deny I miss that now and then—and I drank a virtuous sarsaparilla followed by a water chaser, to everyone's amusement."

"You're still my hero," she whispered in his ear. "I'm sorry they laugh at you."

"Never to my face. I'm Mr. Otto. Give me a kiss, sport."

She did, happy to assuage whatever pain, real or imagined, he had suffered in the Silver Dollar.

"Anyway, there's always at least one broken-down cowpuncher in a bar in early afternoon, willing to chat for a beer and a bump. We found our man. He looked around the room and kept his voice low, because he had quite a story to tell."

"About Mr. McAtee?" she asked.

"More than that. According to our cowpuncher, that whole thing went wrong. The deal was to just frighten away the Polacks. It's been done before: burn a haystack or two, trample a field of wheat, maybe harass the women when they come to town."

"Then why . . ."

"I asked my new best friend that," he told her. "I think he must have been there, because he had such a look in his eyes." He shuddered.

She kissed his head. "Go to sleep now."

With a sigh, he did, cradled in her arms until she slept too. When they woke up, he felt like talking again.

"According to the cowboy, the whole scheme just went wrong." Paul sounded grim then. "He says he can still hear them screaming."

Julia shivered and Paul tightened his grip on her arm.

"Sorry, sport. Apparently those four ranchers divided up the land the way they wanted, everyone getting an equal share. Here's the kicker: after that land—that blood land—was divided, the other three ranchers didn't want to have anything to do with McAtee." He gave a snort of disgust. "I guess even greedy murderers have some sense of morality, strange as it seems. McAtee was ostracized, Julia, and my rummy old friend thinks it unhinged him."

"That makes him really unpredictable," she said.

"Quite so. McAtee was always a bit skittish; I remember that from earlier dealings with him. Now he's scarier. We'll have to be on our guard."

When she woke up, morning had barely started. Eyes still closed, she put out her hand, but Paul wasn't there. She opened her eyes and sat up to see him seated in his chair. His scriptures were open in his lap, but he stared out the window.

"Is the ridge rider there?" she asked, trying to keep

her voice neutral, even though prickles of fear ran down her back.

"No, no. It's something else."

He hesitated. Julia reached for her nightgown and pulled it on, padding quietly to his chair, picking up his scriptures and sitting herself in his lap. He smiled and put his arms around her, resting his hands on her belly, over her hands. She looked down at the book, and it was the Doctrine and Covenants, open to Section 121.

"What's the matter?" She looked at the scriptures, noticing he had underlined part of verse 7: *thine adversity and thine afflictions shall be but a small moment.* "What else happened in Lusk, my love?" she asked, resting herself against his chest.

"I've been expecting it. There was a letter from the Wyoming Stock Growers Association waiting for me in Gun Barrel." He chuckled, but there was no humor in his voice.

She couldn't help her sudden intake of breath. "Oh, please don't tell me you've been dropped from the association because you're a Mormon."

"I won't then. I think you remember that the annual meeting was in Laramie in June. I didn't go because it was Sunday and we were in church. Oh, Julia . . ." He made no attempt to disguise the hurt in his voice. "They took a vote to kick me off the association. Didn't give a reason, but we know, I think."

"I'm so sorry, Paul," she said, unable to help her tears, which she dabbed with his nightshirt. "You're paying a high price, aren't you?"

"One vote saved me. I'm still in, but just barely. Me, Paul Otto! It chaps my pride more than anything, I suppose, if I'm honest." He looked down at her. "Maybe almost as much as having those blamed fools at the roundup mention Mattie Daw and Jennie Rogers to your face. Julia, you're the dearest part of my life, and I can't bear such humiliation for you. I think we're in for a long haul of trouble. The association schedules cattle shipments to Chicago. This could mean real trouble, if they ship me late."

She shook her head and burrowed closer. "I wonder whose vote kept you in."

"Who knows? I do know this: I won't be laying anyone off here, because I don't think I can count on even my neighbors to help out with my roundup next spring, once we're behind barbed wire exclusively."

"You'll help them, though," she said, pulling back to look him in the eye.

"I could never do any less."

She cupped her hands around his face. "Mr. Otto, it's a rare privilege to be married to a man of character. I don't know what I ever did to deserve you, but I'm not complaining."

"Somehow, I knew you wouldn't complain. What you see is what you get, Julia."

She kissed him. "I like what I see."

They sat together until the sun rose, Paul's chin on her head, her arms around him.

While she and Charlotte served cake and cold milk from their Jersey cow that afternoon, Paul gathered his hands together and told them about the Stock Growers vote.

"I want you to know, because we could find ourselves isolated here," he said. The words came hard, and Julia's heart went out to him, a proud man considerably humbled now. "If you want to draw your pay and have nothing more to do with the Double Tipi, believe me, there are no hard feelings. With you or without you, we're still the best ranch in southeast Wyoming. I picked you all carefully, and I want you to stay, but it's your choice. I'll never interfere with your agency to choose."

Julia sat beside him, her hand in his, so proud of her husband she could hardly breathe. She glanced at her ruby engagement ring. *You wanted me to have a choice,* she thought. *Just a choice.*

No one left, and they all went to work. With no monstrous range fire to fight this summer, there was time for the ranch. Her morning sickness became a thing of the past as she cooked, cleaned, and did her best to make life easy for her stockman, considering the burdens he bore.

"I'm fasting today," he told her one morning while he dressed. "I'm not easy in my mind about any of this, and I know it always helps."

"I'll fast too, then," she said promptly. "I'll remind you I'm executive officer of this cowpunching corporation."

"And I'll remind you that you're finally eating right again, and junior won't like it much if you skip some meals. Neither would Doc or I or the powers that be in Salt Lake City," he said just as promptly.

"I forgot. You're right."

She worried about him all day, knowing how hard he worked and how hot the sun was. *If I can't fast, I can pray*, she told herself after the noon meal, while Paul worked in his office and the others wondered what was going on.

"It's this," she said, as the rest of them ate. "Mr. Otto is fasting. He's in a tough position, courtesy of the Stock Growers Association, and he wants to pray about it. We believe the Lord needs to see our commitment, if we ask Him for blessings." Her face was red. She had never been one to share the details of her church, but they needed to know.

"Does it work?" Doc asked.

"Oh my stars, it does," she said, her voice soft,

thinking of her own fasting last summer, when she had so many questions and no answers in sight. "I think mainly fasting channels your mind, because you're not thinking about food. It brings you closer to the personage with the answers."

"I'd be thinking more about food than ever," Malloy joked. They laughed, Julia too.

"Matt, I'm sure many would agree with you," she told him, passing the biscuits his way. "Have a biscuit! The Lord needs to know we're serious." She put her hand to her warm face. "I'd fast with him, too, except ladies in delicate conditions are not allowed to."

"Your doctor is glad to hear that," Doc told her later as the men left for the range again. "Tell you what, though: your doctor can fast in your place."

"You're so kind." She took a deep breath. "Say a prayer for him."

He nodded, even though there was an unsettled look in his eyes. "I haven't prayed in years. Not since my son died."

She touched his sleeve. "Then this is a good time to start again. And say a prayer for yourself too. Thank you, Dr. McKeel."

"You *will* remind me I'm a physician," he said, his voice rueful now.

"I will remind you," she answered. "We pray for you too, each night, and all the people of the Double Tipi."

"I thought you did," he said as he left the dining room.

Paul had little to say that night before they went to bed. After prayer, they lay there quietly together, his arms around her as usual. She drifted to sleep, fully aware that he was still awake, but unable to keep her eyes open. This was his time to think, and she added her silent prayers to his.

In the morning, they knelt together, and he prayed, asking not so much for the Lord to remove their obstacles, but for the strength to endure them. "We live here, Father," he told the Lord, "and we're doing the best we can. We call down the powers of heaven on us here on the Double Tipi. You know our situation, and we know You love us. Above all, keep Julia and our baby safe, and help me to lead my family and my hands. If it's possible to soften the hearts of stubborn, proud men—men I know well because I'm stubborn and proud too—we'd think it a real favor. If not, help us endure what comes."

He said amen, then stayed on his knees, eyes closed, resting his forehead on their bed. She kissed his cheek. "I love you, Paul," she whispered.

Eyes closed, he was still there when she dressed quietly and hurried downstairs to begin breakfast. When he came downstairs and sat at the head of the table in the dining room, he had a thoughtful look on his face.

Breakfast was silent, as usual, the men looking at him with expressions she couldn't quite divine. The atmosphere wasn't uncomfortable. She took a deep breath as the impression struck her powerfully that the Lord was quite mindful of the Double Tipi. With a jolt that brought tears to her eyes—she would have to ask Doc if her over-active waterworks were somehow connected to the baby she carried—she understood quite clearly that the Double Tipi this year was worlds different from last year. It was a holy place now. The reality of that was so huge she could only take another deep breath and another until her mind settled.

"Well, gents, let's cowboy."

He said it quietly, but everyone was listening. She looked at the dear faces around the table, most of them rough men with salty tongues and bad habits aplenty: Matt Malloy, who had been found in an alley, hungry;

Doc, who had crawled into a liquor bottle and stayed there for years; Kringle, unemployable because of arthritis; Paul's Indian cousins, who other ranchers might not have hired, and certainly not at top-hand wages; Colby Wagner, who had defended her and lost his job. *We're so blessed*, she thought.

"Yes, go cowboy. I'll have a pie or two available for consumption at noon," she said, getting up from the table and starting everyone in motion. "I'm trying a new recipe on you for supper, so keep up your courage."

They laughed and trooped outside. Paul hugged her. "Walk with me, Darling."

It was only as far as the porch, where he sat with her in the porch swing. "Funny. When I got up off my knees upstairs, I had the distinct impression that the Lord just wanted me to quit worrying and get to cowboying."

"Good advice. Can you?" she asked.

"We'll see. I've always tackled problems head on, so that might be a new approach. Just turn it over to Him." He nudged her shoulder. "Kind of like what you did in the cut bank."

She gave him a little push. "There's a horse in the corral there with your name on it. Does the executive officer have to get tough with the president?"

"You're a fearsome thing."

She smiled at him as he walked away, hoping, and then sighing with relief when he started to sing "Dear Evalina," about halfway across the road. " 'My love for thee will never, never die,' " she whispered as she watched his jaunty walk and heard his jinglebobs.

Magnus came back mid-morning, looking around the corner of the house, wary and ready to bolt. She and Charlotte were sitting on the side porch, peeling the last of the winter apples for pie. Julia pointed her paring knife at the dog, and Charlotte shook her head.

"Magnus, as a watchdog, you're pretty useless," Julia said. "I guess we'll have to depend on your general ugliness to frighten off road agents and malefactors. Oh, don't give me that hangdog look!"

"You're talking to a dog," Charlotte teased as she finished peeling the last apple.

"I figure a dog that ugly must be smart, as compensation." Julia held out her hand to Magnus, who sniffed it and started to wag his tail. He offered no objections when she petted him, even flopping down on the porch and showing his belly again. "You're hopeless, of course," she said. "Just stay shy of Two Bits, and you'll have a long life on the Double Tipi."

She tipped some meat scraps in a bowl and put it on the porch for Magnus, who got to work immediately. A bowl of water went down next, and then he collapsed again under the porch swing, long ears wet from dragging through the water bowl.

When Two Bits came to the side door and hissed, Magnus opened one eye, sighed with the resignation of a martyr, and closed it, expecting the worst obviously, but not inclined to move after that meal.

"So, so much like Mr. Otto," Julia said. "Two Bits, behave yourself. Magnus means well. You're not so handsome yourself, with a tail missing."

Two Bits arched his back elaborately, made a few feinting punts with his claws out, then retired to the kitchen again, still in charge and full of dignity.

"I guess you're here on sufferance, same as I was, Magnus," Julia said, bending down to give him another pat. "And I suppose you're my protector." She laughed and ran her fingers along one velvety ear. "Let's hope I never need one."

Paul's birthday came a week later, which meant an elaborate Imperial Cake, because she had plenty of raisins and the walnut meats were threatening to go rancid. She iced it with White Mountain Cream, and the hands took turns at the ice cream crank, while Paul watched, amused.

"We are far gone to becoming civilized," he said as she handed him the paddle and a spoon since he was the birthday boy.

"You know you love it, cowboy," she said. Charlotte carried the ice cream churn into the kitchen, followed by the entire crew. "Here's your present." She handed him a package with nothing more exciting in it than a new pair of riding gloves, which Mama had smuggled to her at her request, inside a box with three Mother Hubbards from Mama's dressmaker. On her instructions, Kringle had made him new leather wrist protectors.

He smiled his thanks. "Got anything else, sport?" he asked. "I'm taking the afternoon off."

"Feeling frisky?" she teased. "Keep your crew busy, and I'll put Charlotte to work snapping a gallon of string beans. But first, cake and ice cream. You know, to build up your strength."

"Happy birthday, Romeo," she said later in their bedroom. "Thirty-seven. Yikes." She snuggled close. "At least you have all your teeth, and other things."

"Especially those other things. Funny, last year when I turned thirty-six in the middle of all the range fires, I felt so blamed old! I don't feel old this year. Far from it." He patted her fanny.

"You're my guy."

He rested his hands on her belly again. "Your waist is but a memory, Darling. When did Doc say you might feel a quickening?"

"Another month. I declare it's like waiting for

Christmas!" She closed her eyes, content. "I've been resisting wearing those Mother Hubbards Mama sent, but my clothes are getting so uncomfortable."

"Vanity, thy name is Julia Otto," Paul said. "I'm glad you're writing often to your folks. They need the reassurance that you're blooming." He kissed her shoulder. "Let's convene a meeting of the corporation. There's some news, and I'm not sure how it affects us."

"Only if it's good news, because it's your birthday," she told him.

"I'm not sure what it is. Mundane matters first: Marlowe met me on the trail with a note from the liveryman, saying the buckboard was ready, and he'd found a good horse to pull it. I'll send Colby to Gun Barrel tomorrow to bring them back, and I'll teach you to drive it, if the horse is gentle enough."

"I'm in favor. That way, I can visit Elinore."

"Good. Here's the other news: McAtee's ranch has been sold to those three other stockmen who were his partners in crime."

"Where . . . where did he go?"

"Nobody knows. I hope he's left the state, but I don't trust him."

She nodded, grateful that Cora Shumway had taken James to Springville, Utah, to spend the summer with her parents. "At least we needn't fear for James."

"I don't want to fear for us, either. Wish I felt easy about the matter, but I don't, so we'll table that issue. Here's something else: Marlowe had a letter for Doc, from his former wife. He read it right there on the trail, then asked me if you had written to her, telling her how well he's doing. Did you?"

"No," she said, mystified. "I wanted to, but you didn't think it was a good idea, so I didn't. I'll have to assure him I didn't. Did he tell you what was in the letter?"

"No. Not my business. Not yours, either, sport."

"Was he upset?"

"I don't know what he was," Paul said frankly. "I'd have gotten the cold shivers if I had ever received a letter like that from Katherine, but that is, as you put it, ancient history. He seemed a little pleased."

"Maybe he still loves her."

"Could be."

Paul hesitated. She knew he had more to say. "Need something else for your birthday?"

"One more thing. I've already told Malloy to keep everyone off the trail toward Gun Barrel tonight. Julia, you and I are going bathing in the river by the cut bank."

"I can't," she said quickly.

"You can. Every time we come back from Gun Barrel, you avoid looking at the cut bank. It's time you faced it and moved on."

"Why, for Pete's sake?" she burst out.

"Because this is our home and our ranch and our river. You're in charge, not some stream, and for sure not last year's fire. Let all of it go, Julia."

Julia was silent through supper, feeling her fears gather again from some place where they still hid. She wanted to be angry with Paul for forcing her hand, but something else in her told her he was right. *It's just water*, she thought, taking her towel and a bar of soap from the bathing room and scuffing her feet into the moccasins Charlotte had given her.

They walked hand in hand to the river as the shadows fell in the valley, another hot day done and gone. She knew she was squeezing Paul's hand too tight, but he didn't complain.

The water had gone down considerably since they had ridden onto the Double Tipi in April, but it was still much higher than last year's drought-blighted stream. The cut bank had a more generous overhang now, thanks to the pull and tug of a strong current.

She stood still as Paul undid the buttons on the back of her shirtwaist. He chuckled a little to see the top two buttons of her skirt undone. "Time to tuck those away," he whispered, his lips on her shoulder now. "In you get." He gave her a little push, and she went into the water, gasping out loud because it was cold and then wading deeper before she lost her nerve entirely.

She stood there shivering, more frightened than cold, until Paul joined her. He took her hand and towed her toward the cut bank. She drew back and started to cry, and he stopped, just holding her.

When he spoke, he was matter-of-fact. "I've toyed with the idea of damming this little pool and keeping it deep right here. That way, if we ever need it again, you won't have such a hard time, you and our children. We'll be safe here. The river will protect us. You're the executive officer; what do you think?"

She sobbed until her nose ran, and Paul wiped her face with a washcloth, humming "Redeemer" this time. Then it was over, her tears done. She looked at the cut bank and moved closer to it, remembering where she had barely stayed alive last summer, the roar of the burning trees overhead blotting out everything. She looked up. The trees were gone, and she saw the stars coming out.

"I . . . I think I was more afraid of the trees than the water," she said finally. "It was as if the whole world was on fire. And then when those branches fell . . . Paul, I was so afraid, and I didn't want to die, because I loved you so much."

"I'm still here, sport. I had the closest cottonwoods chopped down and hauled away last winter. I'll keep this area clear of trees, I'll add a dam, and we'll have a nice swimming hole for our children. Is that okay?"

She thought about it and touched her growing belly. "I'm a pretty good swimmer, and children should learn to swim. Yes, that's okay."

She waded back to the bank and found the soap, breathing deep of the carbolic in it. "I like Lifebuoy. It's nice and red and cuts the dust on cowboys. Turn around, Paul. I'll scrub your back for a birthday present."

"I already got my present, sport. Thanks for being as brave as I knew you were."

# Eighteen

Paul had ordered a single-bench buckboard, because he wanted to keep the rig light. "We can get a bigger one with more seats, if your waist expands a few more times." He scratched his head. "Wonder what causes that."

"You're hopeless," Julia said as she stood nose to nose with the most beautiful bay she had ever seen. "And you are gorgeous, Maisie."

"Maisie?"

"I used to name all my dolls Maisie. Don't look for logic, Paul. You know me too well."

Considering how busy he was, Julia was flattered that Paul took the time to show her the whole process of getting Maisie to the buckboard. Colby had volunteered, but Paul had waved him away, which made the cowhand grin at her and tip his hat as he followed Matt.

Paul helped her onto the seat and took the reins, speaking to Maisie in Shoshone, as he always spoke to his horses.

"She's bilingual," Julia joked.

"I only get smart horses, same as me. Oh, she does have a gentle mouth. Julia, I can't see this will be a problem for your shoulder at all. Here. Put your hands in front of mine and I'll gradually back off."

She did as he said, holding her breath and then letting it out as Maisie seemed to straighten up, even from her perfect stride, and feel her lighter touch on the reins.

"I think she knows it's me," Julia whispered. "She likes my touch."

"So do I. Take her out on the road and let's go visit the Cuddys. Keep the reins even and loose in your hands. You can trust Maisie."

"Paul, can you take the time? That fall roundup is getting closer and closer."

"For you, sport, I make the time. I want to make sure you can get to the Cuddys without pain."

She would have liked the trip to the Cuddy's ranch to have lasted longer. Everyone was preparing for the fall roundup, and the only time she saw Paul alone was in their bedroom. She smiled to herself as she watched Maisie's ears. "This is nice. I like some time alone during the day with my best guy."

"Things'll slack off after we ship the cattle." He sighed. "The Association has moved my shipping schedule back two weeks. We won't ship until late October."

"Oh, Paul!"

"Could have been worse," he said with a shrug. "I've been in touch with my Chicago buyer, and he has no real problem with it. I'll have all my cattle behind bob wire for a longer time, which means I have to start feeding them hay sooner. So I'll buy more hay from my Goshen and Platte county connections." He took off his Stetson and kissed her cheek. "Don't you worry, sport! That's an order."

"I will though," she told him. "It's what I do."

She wouldn't have admitted it to Paul, but the hour and a half to the Cuddy ranch taxed her to the limit. Or maybe he did know, by the way he kept glancing at her when he thought she wasn't watching.

"Too much?" he asked, as they came to the ranch house.

"Almost," she admitted, as she gently pulled back

on the reins and Maisie stopped like a lady. "Of course, once I make a good visit of at least an hour, I'll be rested. Honest, Paul."

He nodded and helped her down, as Elinore Cuddy opened the screen door and waved them inside. "You won't be doing this after snow flies, I'm afraid. Or if you do, I'll be along."

Elinore embraced her and took a good look at the buckboard and Maisie. "You're rigged out in style!"

"I don't think I'm destined for the saddle anytime soon," Julia said. She leaned closer. "My shoulder hurts a bit, but if you don't mind a long visit so I can rest it, I can manage by myself."

"We'll plan on that," she said, hugging Julia again. "Sometimes I get so hungry for a visit from a lady." Elinore led her into the parlor, which reminded Julia forcefully of the Double Tipi ranch house last year. "I've been knitting soakers for you." She looked at Paul, who stood in the doorway, hat in hand. "Paul, Allen's in the barn, unless you want to knit."

He laughed and left the room.

Julia's eyes followed him. "He's my best guy," she said, her voice soft.

"I'm still amazed at the difference a year and a half can make in one stoic, rather dour rancher," Elinore said. She took up her knitting again, then put it down. "Where are my manners? Julia, do you feel more like eating now?"

"Anything that isn't nailed down or clearly labeled poison."

They adjourned to the kitchen, where they could see Allen and Paul talking by the barn. Elinore put cookies on two plates and took one to the men, while Julia poured lemonade. Back in the parlor, they both knitted.

Julia was quiet, concentrating. She propped her feet

on the footstool and observed her friend, grateful that Doc had thought to involve Elinore when the men of the Double Tipi were off the ranch.

"I want to thank you for being so willing to help me, if I needed assistance while Doc and Paul were gone," Julia said. "Doc said he came over here and talked to you."

She watched Elinore, surprised to see a slow flush rise from her neck and into her blonde hair. She tried to think of what she had said that would have embarrassed Elinore, whose face grew redder. *It's almost as if you're in love*, she thought, then gulped and looked at her needles as the reality came home to roost. *My goodness, sometimes I am so self-centered and dense*, Julia scolded herself. She put down her knitting.

"Elinore, I'm a dunce," she said quietly. "Doc . . ."

Her friend looked up quickly, her face troubled. "It's nothing. How could it ever be anything?"

"There are lots of reasons," Julia said. *In for a penny, in for a pound*, she told herself. "Last week, Doc got a letter from his former wife. He certainly didn't share it with me, but Paul told me she had written because someone wrote her to say that he was a reformed man and maybe she ought to take another look."

Elinore was silent, her eyes on her knitting, even though her hands were still. Julia leaned forward. "You wrote to her, didn't you?"

Elinore nodded. She chewed on her lip, still not raising her eyes.

"Why? Call me slow sometimes, but why would you do that? Why tell her that her husband has changed? I mean, especially if you . . . if you like him a little."

"I like him a lot," Elinore said finally, still staring at her knitting. "I doubt he has any idea how I feel about him."

"You could let him know," Julia said. "There are ways, even for ladies. Trust me."

She looked at Julia then, and Julia saw the pain in her eyes. "If I were pretty like you, I would," she said finally. "I'm not." She held up her hand. "And you're too honest to try to convince me otherwise."

*Please, Father, help me say the right thing*, Julia thought. *I like this kind woman.*

"Elinore, when I saw you coming toward me at the cow gather, determined to help with that dreadful sonofa-gun stew, I knew you were solid and true," Julia said. "I've been long enough on this hard range to know that those are the qualities that endure." She touched her scarred neck. "I . . . I used to be just pretty and a good cook. Now I hope I'm solid and true too. Why did you write to her?" she asked again, coaxing as if she spoke to a stubborn child.

Elinore went to the window, her knitting balled in her hand, her voice filled with intensity. "I thought she ought to know how wonderful her husband was and that he had changed. I told her to give him another chance."

"What if she agrees and wants him back?"

"Then I've done my duty."

"And if she doesn't?"

Elinore turned around, her eyes bewildered now. "If she doesn't, who says he would look at me?"

Julia dabbed at her eyes and continued knitting. "Silly girl, who did he think of first, when he wanted to make sure I had the care I needed? Alice Marlowe is closer, but you were on his mind."

Elinore sat down and started knitting faster. "I suppose I was," she said, her voice hesitant, as if afraid to let the idea take root anywhere.

"Let's leave it at that for now," Julia told her gently. "There's time."

Time. She thought about that on the way home, Paul handling the reins. She watched the slight smile on his face, wondering if he was happy about Maisie's ladylike gait, but sure it was more. She tucked her arm through his, and he glanced at her, that same smile on his face.

"I've spent my life keeping busy and doing things, some more productive than others," she said.

"You're describing most of the human race, sport," he replied.

"True, but now all I have to do is breathe and eat, and I'm involved in the biggest production in all the universe," she told him. "It simply amazes me to think what's going on inside my body. I think I never really understood tender mercies until right now."

Paul spoke to Maisie and stopped the buckboard. He gathered Julia in his arms, and they sat close together until the wind picked up and Maisie shook her harness politely to remind them that time was passing and grain waited in the horse barn.


They took the wagon to Gun Barrel on Saturday because on Monday they were transporting Karl Rudiger, his crew, and their tools to the Double Tipi to build the new bunkhouse. Along with some windmill parts, there was a box marked Singer and addressed to Julia Otto, waiting for them in the freight office. Julia patted the crate, which made Paul chuckle.

"Mama said it would be arriving soon," Julia said as Paul signed the lading bill. "I'll set up my Singer in the dining room. You might even get a shirt or two out of this, if you play your cards right, cowboy."

"Put it in the office," Paul told her. "I always like your company in there."

"Maybe I will. I could use your desk to cut out patterns."

He winced. "Marriage."

"You know you love it."

As much as she wanted to be with the Cheyenne Deseret Sunday School Union, Julia had to screw up her courage to even think about walking down the stairs in the Plainsman Hotel. She felt supremely conscious that there wasn't any disguising her interesting state, in a dress without a waist.

"You know, Paul, there are some ladies in my folks' ward who won't leave the house when they start to show," she told him as he hooked the clasp on her necklace. She looked around the room, speaking softly in case the bell-hop lingered outside, his ear to the door panel. "I mean, everyone knows what we've been up to!"

He laughed. "Do you mean what we were up to in May, or the other night? Julia, you're a funny one. Men see the matter differently. I think I'll like parading you on my arm, as obvious proof to the world what a stud you married."

She rolled her eyes. "You have a regrettable tendency to speak in ranching terms."

"But you love me anyway. Come on. We'll be late to church."

Funny she had ever thought it strange to attend church in the Odd Fellows Hall, with a picture of Custer dying at the Little Big Horn behind the pulpit. She looked around with pleasure to see her Cheyenne friends—the men talking in one corner and the ladies in another, with children running when they should have been walking. She knew what Elinore meant by enjoying the fellowship of women, a rare commodity in Wyoming.

"I was a little embarrassed to start wearing anticipation dress," she admitted in a whisper to Emma Gillespie.

Sister Gillespie fingered the delicate lawn, the color of

cornflowers. "This is a pretty one. Believe me, you'll get mighty tired of the same few dresses by the ninth month!" Her hand went to Julia's cheek. "Motherhood becomes you, now that you're over the icky stage. You have that glow."

Julia's hand went to her other cheek. "That's what Paul says, but I look in the mirror and see the same old me."

"He's right. Come, my dear, Heber's looking at his timepiece. If you're game, you can hold the newest Gillespie for practice while I struggle with Mabel. Good thing I memorized all the hymns years ago. What mother can hold a hymnal?"

After an evening at the Gillespies' and a visit to Eugene Shumway, who was packing his bags for a trip to Utah to retrieve Cora and James, they spent another night in the Plainsman Hotel. They met the Denver train early in the morning, with Karl Rudiger and his crew aboard. By noon they were in Gun Barrel again.

"Don't forget my sewing machine," Julia said as the liveryman hitched the horses to the wagon.

She walked over to the wooden crate, a smile on her face, thinking about the baby clothes to come and a shirt or two for her best beau. She looked closer at the crate and felt her face go pale. She took a deep breath and looked again, then backed away as though the crate were on fire. Scratched next to her name were the words, *If I can't find James, you will do.*

"Mr. Rudiger, get Paul," she demanded, sitting down suddenly on a bale of hay because her legs wouldn't hold her. "Please hurry!"

Once glance at her white face kept him from asking questions. Paul was there in moments, his hand on her shoulder.

"Darling, what's wrong?"

She pointed at the crate. The puzzled look on his face changed into shock and then fury as he read the message. "Slattery!" he shouted to the liveryman as Julia started to cry. "Come here!"

She had never heard that tone of voice from her husband before, and it frightened her as much as the message on the crate. It must have startled the others too, because no one moved a muscle except the liveryman, who couldn't get to Paul fast enough.

The man looked where Paul pointed, then at Julia. "Mrs. Otto, I don't know what to say."

"Someone already said it," Paul snapped. "Get the sheriff. I want him to see this."

He sat down heavily beside her on the bale. He took her hand, and she was startled to find that he was shaking. "That's it, Julia," he said in a low voice. "You're going back to Salt Lake City on the next train."

"No, I'm not," she said in a louder voice, a voice that sounded strangely fierce to her ears. "If you put me on the train, I'll just get off at Laramie and come back. Don't you dare think I'd ever leave you."

The look he gave her took away her breath. She had never seen such anguish in someone's face. "Please don't send me away," she sobbed. "I couldn't bear it."

"Julia, I won't toy around with your life," he said, his voice softer, but no less intense. "This discussion is over."

"No, it isn't," she said, matching her intensity to his. "Not by a long chalk."

She might have been sitting next to a stranger on the long, painful journey to the Double Tipi. The men in the wagon were silent, and so was Paul as he stared straight ahead into the warm afternoon. For a change there was no wind, and the air was mild, even teasingly cool, as though summer was having second thoughts about hanging around much longer in Wyoming. On any other day, it would have been a beautiful ride through the pass to her beloved home. Now all Julia could do was turn away from the man she loved and stare at the sagebrush and the occasional meadowlark, stirred to motion and song by the passing wagon and horses.

*I won't go back to Salt Lake*, she thought as they made the turn to the Double Tipi. *I couldn't survive another separation.* Just the idea of days stretching into months without him made her shoulders start to shake. She cried great, gulping sobs that she could no more have contained than a narrow stream could hold back the spring runoff.

"Julia," was all Paul said. His arm went around her, and she turned her face into his shirt, weeping.

He stopped the wagon and motioned to Karl Rudiger, sitting grim in the wagon bed. "Rudiger, take the wagon in and unload. Matt will help. Julia and I are going to walk." He turned to look at her. "You *will* walk with me, Darling, won't you?"

He sounded so uncertain that her heart broke. "Only with you," she whispered and held out her arms as he helped her down.

"There's too much at stake now, Julia," he said as they walked slowly along. "I'd sell out here before I would take such a risk with you and our child."

"I never imagined I would hear you say something like that," she said, when she thought she could speak without tears. "I know what the Double Tipi means to you."

"You mean more."

She stopped and just held her hands to his face. She took a deep breath. "Paul, if we can't face this together, then how are we going to deal with everything else in this wonderful, terrible, amazing place?"

She felt angry then as he stood there with that inscrutable look, his hands at his sides, making no move to touch her. "I'm convening a meeting of the cowpunching corporation. Don't think I'm not aware of what you're doing, putting my name on all legal documents, making sure I can harness and drive a buckboard, letting me read your journals so I could run this ranch if I had to. You know how hard it is, and you're preparing me."

He opened his mouth to speak, and she gave him a look so fierce that he closed it. "I nearly died in a fire last summer. The Lord didn't keep me alive to cut and run when a madman decides to toy with us. The range could burn up again. I might lose this baby. Chief could step in a prairie dog hole and throw you like your father was thrown. Borrow my light, my dearest; I borrowed yours last year. I didn't survive to run away, and I won't. You can't make me. Meeting adjourned."

She started walking rapidly toward the ranch, praying so hard that there weren't even any words to express the deepest feelings that tumbled through her tired brain. *Take this burden too, dear Lord*, she prayed, when she was coherent again. *I can't handle it and I don't want it. I'm calling down all the powers of heaven to keep me safe. I have a share in Paul's priesthood now, and it's my right to ask.*

She stopped and took a deep breath as the greatest feeling of relief she had ever known covered her whole body. She turned around. Paul hadn't moved.

"Are we in this, Paul?" she asked, never more serious in her life. Her mind became a jumble again as she prayed without words.

"We're in this, sport," he said, equally serious after a long, excruciating time. "You're not going anywhere except our ranch."

He walked toward her, and she watched the determination grow on his face, turning him again into the man she loved. She sighed with relief, then felt something strange.

It felt almost like a hand was strumming fingers gently against her belly. Fascinated, she put her hand to her abdomen, touching lightly in response to the touch within. "My stars," she whispered as she felt a responding touch. There it was again, not her imagination, but their child. "I guess you wanted a say too," she said, looking down.

"What's that, sport?" Paul asked, taking her by the shoulders and gently pulling her close to him.

"Wasn't talking to you," she said, her voice calm now, where it had been so fierce. "I feel the baby, Paul."

She didn't have to say anything more. She went to her knees again, not from anxiety this time but conviction. Julia knelt on Double Tipi land and her husband's firm hands went automatically to her head as he asked the Lord to bless her and their child and called on heaven to protect them.

# Nineteen

"You don't fight fair, sport," Paul spoke into her hair that night. "You cry, and you're right."

That ended the argument. Julia spent the week cooking, her greatest solace, next to Paul and the Lord. She cooked until her mind was clear, and the hands and building crew cried uncle. The bunkhouse went up rapidly, and she marveled at Karl Rudiger's German efficiency.

Paul didn't mind a bit when she cut out a baby nightgown on his desk, but he did draw the line at letting her use his green desk blotter as a pin cushion.

"Don't give me that soft-eyed look. I'm immune," he declared. "Well, maybe just that corner, but that's all, or I'll banish you to the dining room." His expression turned serious. "But no further."

He wanted to keep her in his sight, and she had no objection. She knew he had asked all his hands to do the same thing. Solitary rides to the Cuddy ranch were vetoed, if she had bothered to object. She didn't. When Paul couldn't ride along, he enlisted Colby, who always entertained her with stories about cowography along the Big Horn range, where he used to work.

"How did you end up with the Clyde Brothers?" she asked as they returned to the Double Tipi one afternoon. She had insisted on handling the reins, and Colby was her passenger.

He shrugged. "You drift and winter comes, and you ride the grub line until someone takes you on and lets you ride for their brand, if you're lucky." His expression turned rueful. "Those stories about the Clydes squeezing a penny until it screams? All true."

She returned her attention to Maisie. *It's nice to have a champion,* she told herself, *but I'd rather have Paul along.* He had ridden to Wheatland yesterday by himself to arrange for hay deliveries while he and his hands went to the roundup. "I'm glad it's not far as the spring gather," he had told her yesterday. "I'm uneasy without you in my sight."

When she and Colby returned, Julia went to the new bunkhouse, enjoying the fragrance of newly sawn wood. Two of Mr. Rudiger's men were glazing windows now as he hung the door. She walked inside, please to see a larger, lighter bunkhouse, with two heating stoves and a bathing room too. The wooden bunks were gone, replaced by iron frame beds with genuine mattresses, and tables and chairs enough for everyone. No more need to turn over Nabisco boxes for additional seating.

"It's mighty fine, Mr. Rudiger," she said. "Will you still have time to refurbish the old bunkhouse? Charlotte and Matt are so hoping."

"Ja, Frau, so they have told me. We finish this tonight with the painting and start on the old place tomorrow. Two days more, and then to Fort Collins we return."

She cleared her throat, wondering if she ought to speak her mind, as executive officer of the corporation. "Mr. Rudiger, you really haven't charged Paul enough for this project."

He opened and closed the door several times, until he was satisfied with the fit before he answered. "Frau Otto, have you any idea how much I owe your good man for finding me work in Fort Collins?" He gestured toward the other builders at the window. "I have my own business now. In Germany I could never have hoped for such a thing. There is a German proverb: do a good deed and be twice blessed. Herr Otto and you, Frau, are proof of that." He gave her that courtly bow she remembered from her gift of tar paper to him almost two years ago. "I have been amply paid."

"Very well. I know better than to argue," she said simply. "Mr. Rudiger, you're a peach."

"That is an expression I do not know," he told her.

"It means you're extra special."

He bowed again, and she could tell he was pleased.

"Frau Otto, I took the liberty . . ." He gestured toward the house. "You will find something up the stairs from me and Ursula. I assembled it and showed it to Herr Otto before he left this morning. Go look in the room across the hall from your chamber."

Curious, Julia did as he said, going upstairs and into the room for the baby, which was still empty.

It was empty no longer. She put her hand to her mouth to see a crib with beautifully turned slats. Her astonished gaze lingered on the hand-carved headboard and footboard, with a smiling wooden cherub at each end that looked remarkably like Danila, Karl and Ursula's older daughter. "Oh, my," was all she could say.

Ursula had knitted an elaborate afghan. Julia ran her finger over the delicate design, knowing it was far beyond her own competent skills with knitting needles. There was a note in German on it. She took it downstairs and out to the bunkhouse, silently handing it to Mr. Rudiger.

He took it from her, and his own struggle began. "It is from the Gospel of St. Matthias. Matthew, you call him." He took a deep breath. "So simple, what you did, when you were Fraulein Darling last year." He cleared his throat and gave her a look so kind that tears started in her eyes even before he began to read. "It's something like this: 'When I was hungry, ye gave me meat . . .' "

Julia sobbed out loud, her hand to her mouth.

"Frau, you make this difficult," he said gently. "'Thirsty and ye gave me drink.' And then this: 'If you have done this to one of no account, you have done it to me.'" His eyes were kind. "You fed us, when no one else would. How could we ever be out of your debt?"

She could barely wait to show the crib to Doctor McKeel when he came upstairs that afternoon after chores to listen to her baby's heartbeat, something he did every two weeks now. Charlotte or Paul always accompanied him, so Julia would not feel uncomfortable. When he finished, and she sat up again, he dismissed Charlotte.

"Any questions for your physician?" he asked.

"Not this time," she said. She went to the window. "I have to tell you something, though. Elinore probably wouldn't want me to, but I'm going to, anyway. She wrote that letter to your wife."

He didn't seem surprised to Julia's relief. "You told me you hadn't, and Elinore is the only other person I could think of who would do that." He hesitated, looking unsure of himself. "Did she tell you why?"

"I asked, of course. She told me that your wife ought to have another opportunity, since you have changed so much."

"She's kind."

"She likes you too," Julia added, shy. "I wouldn't dream of treading on her feelings, but she's certain you would never give her a second glance." Julia couldn't help her exasperated sigh. "I wish I could wave a magic wand and give her confidence!"

Doc was silent a long moment. "I'll tell you something private about Elinore, which might help you understand why she is so reluctant to express herself." He looked around. "Let's go to the parlor," he said.

"Elinore Cuddy came out here four years ago, about

305

the same time Paul poured me out of a bottle and gave me a job," Doc began, when she was seated downstairs with her knitting again. "Her brother had invited her out to be his housekeeper. She had taught school for ten years and had no prospects there. I think Allen took a look around, saw all the bachelors, and figured the odds might be better in Wyoming for a woman." He hesitated again. "Well . . ."

"She'd be the first person to say she's plain," Julia said, when his silence lingered. "I see other qualities that mean more, but she doesn't."

"True." His expression hardened then. "The Clyde Brothers decided to play a prank."

"I wish I could say that surprised me," Julia said.

"Your bay leaf in that sonofagun stew was probably the first time that anyone has dared to tease that trio of bullies."

Julia sighed. "Paul is too kind to admit it, but I think that little bay leaf led to his near ejection from the Stock Growers Association."

"I *know* that bay leaf has been the subject of amusement to lots of stockmen from the Powder to the Platte! You have more champions than you know, Julia."

"The Clyde brothers are not among them."

"No! It was Malcolm's idea to send Elinore a letter, saying that his younger brother Angus was smitten with her, and asked if she would enjoy corresponding with him."

"Oh, no."

"Yes. She started writing to Angus, and it went on for some months. Apparently all the brothers took turns writing flowery letters, the kind of letters that would give any woman the notion that marriage was in the cards." He stood up and took a turn around the room, stopping to straighten up the photograph of the Salt Lake Temple. "In his last letter, Angus arranged to meet her in the restaurant in Gun Barrel. She went there, all expectant, and sat and sat, waiting for him to arrive."

"And he never did," Julia finished.

"He never did. When it was late afternoon, she pulled together what shreds of dignity were left to her and walked out of the restaurant. The Clyde brothers were standing across the street, laughing at her and pointing for everyone in Gun Barrel to see. To make it worse, they had placed bets all over town that she would show. Imagine money changing hands over a bet about a lady. I was appalled."

Julia leaped to her feet and took her own circuit of the parlor. "That is unspeakable!" she declared.

"The Clydes thought it was hilarious. Rumor has it that they collected over one thousand dollars on that awful bet. It was two years before Elinore set foot off Cuddy property. I never saw anyone so whipped looking. I admit I was surprised, to see her at the spring roundup. When I chatted with her, she told me she only came because she wanted to meet you."

"Doc, how can people be so heartless?"

"It's a mystery."

They sat down again, both of them silent for a long while. *If you won't speak, I will*, Julia thought. "If I'm not prying too much, have you heard from your former wife?"

"You're not, and I have," he said. "She's asked me to return to Indiana."

"Oh, no," Julia said before she thought. She put her hand to her mouth again. "I mean, well, isn't that nice? No, I don't mean that! I want you to stay here and deliver my baby, and get to know Elinore better and . . ." She stopped, embarrassed, then doggedly continued. "I would never be as kind as Elinore if I loved you! I'd fight and scrap."

"I imagine you would," Doc said, amused. "I pity any

female who would ever try to get between you and the boss."

"It wouldn't be pretty!" Julia declared. "But Elinore is too nice. Well, tell me. I'll hound you if you don't let me know. Did you write her back?"

"Nora? I did, and don't worry! I'm not leaving you without a doctor. I asked her to move out here, because I think I might want to take over old Dr. Beck's practice."

"Oh," she said, disappointed.

"We were married six years before our son died, and they were good years. I want to give Nora and me another chance, Julia," he said quietly. "If I owe that to Elinore's kindness, well, I do. If Nora decides not to come, then we'll see."

Exasperated, Julia thumped her hands into her lap and glared at her doctor. He laughed out loud, then sobered immediately. "Julia, don't pout! Paul will think I've been troubling you, when he returns. Be Elinore's friend, my little friend. All right?"

She nodded, embarrassed at her tantrum, and gathered her own dignity. "I don't usually act so childish, Dr. McKeel. I am going to blame my baby."

He grinned at her, his own equanimity restored. "You're entitled to do that. Maybe someday scientists will figure out why ladies who are anticipating get a bit, uh, high-strung, at times. I'm sure I don't know. Paul tells me you cry at dominos now." He put up his hands in self-defense at the thunderous look she gave him. "He did!"

She laughed. "He's right. Trust my best guy to put it that way."

After Rudiger and Company left three days later, the new bunkhouse had been painted inside and out, with sturdy shutters over the windows to keep out Wyoming winters. The old bunkhouse had been divided into three rooms and painted. Mr. Rudiger's carpenters had cut out more windows and glazed them. These had curtains, made from extra gingham Julia had brought from home.

Hands folded behind her back, as she had been taught at Indian school, Charlotte just stood in the open door, gazing at her future home.

"I have one too many rugs for my house," Julia said, standing there with her. "It'll look nice in your parlor. I hope you don't mind such a small kitchen, but I'd like you to keep cooking with me, and the two of you taking your meals with us."

"We will," she said.

"When you and Matt return from Wind River as Mr. and Mrs. Malloy, we'll have the furniture in place that Paul ordered."

Charlotte turned in the doorway to look at Julia. "When my cousin invited me here to cook and keep house for him while you were away, I almost didn't accept. I had just finished being lonely for four years at the Indian school in Kansas, and I didn't want anything more to do with white people." She ducked her head, embarrassed. "I shouldn't say that."

"Sounds honest. What changed your mind?" Julia asked, interested.

"Something my father said. He and Paul's mother had been raised together and they were close. He told me to not be afraid to look at people different from me with different eyes."

"My father told me the same thing when I left for the Double Tipi!"

They looked at each other with complete understanding. "I will always want to cook for you," Charlotte said, proud. "This is the best kitchen in Wyoming."

"You may, at least, until you start your own family," Julia said. "And that's 'with me,' not 'for me.'"

"Who will help you cook for all the hands then?" Charlotte asked.

"The Lord provides."

With Charlotte and Matt gone to Fort Washakie, Paul took Julia with him to finish the work before roundup, so he could use Colby's services. Julia rode in the buckboard, grateful for its springs. September had turned hot again, and she sweltered, knitting doggedly, disliking the discomfort, but determined not to show it, not with Paul anxious for her.

For seven straight days, she kept up with them on the range as they repaired the fences and put up new ones, rising before dawn every morning to cook for the whole day, and load it in the back of the buckboard. There was no privacy for calls of nature, beyond asking the men to look the other way. It embarrassed Julia that her pregnancy made those calls more frequent. The constant wind in her face made her edgier as each day passed. How on earth did Paul stand this?

"Paul, I can't do another day of this," she said one morning as he came into the kitchen to help her lift the skillet for frying bacon.

"I can't leave you here, sport, because I need Colby, with Matt gone," he reminded her, pulling her down to sit on his lap. "Getting crowded on my lap."

She nodded, but there was no laughter in her. "I didn't want to complain," she started, but he put a finger to her lips.

"And you haven't. How about I drive you over to the Cuddys? I'm pretty sure Allen is closer to done with his fence work than I am. Doc's worried about you too."

Julia sighed with relief.

"I have about three more days of this, and then Matt and Charlotte will be back. Up you get. Need any help in here?"

"You have plenty to do elsewhere," she reminded him, then kissed his cheek when he came closer. "Yes, take me to the Cuddys."

Elinore met her with open arms and a smile for Paul. "Allen's working right here, and we can keep an eye on one little lady," she said, after Paul's hurried explanation.

"I'm sorry to be a burden," she told Paul as he hugged her at the Cuddy's doorway.

"No burden. You're still the toughest wife I have." He touched his forehead to hers. "It's hard to be tough for two, though. Let Elinore spoil you for a few days. You'll do that, won't you?" he asked her friend.

"I'll start right now. Go away, Paul."

With a smile and a wave of his hand, he left Maisie and the buckboard, and untied Chief, who had been following behind. He hesitated a long moment after swinging into the saddle.

"I'll be fine," she said from the porch, even though her heart sank to watch him turn into a speck in the distance.

She stayed with the Cuddys three days, enjoying Elinore's company and Allen's matter-of-fact way of making her think everything was tidy and safe, when she knew it wasn't. She told them everything about James and Mr. McAtee, who for some reason now had transferred his obsession with finding James to her.

"Paul's afraid to leave me alone," she said that first night as they sat around the kitchen table. "Since Matt and Charlotte are gone right now, and he needs every hand, Colby can't watch me."

"You're safe here," Allen assured her. "Maybe you should just stay here during the roundup."

"Aren't you going?"

He shook his head. "Julia, I'm small potatoes in this particular roundup," he told her. "I've already separated out my beeves heading to Chicago. Your husband is moving out a big herd, and so are the Clydes and some others. Stay with us."

She was tempted, but as kind as the Cuddys were, she wanted to be home on the Double Tipi, free to cook away her misgivings and see her husband. "I'll be fine when Charlotte and Matt return, and Colby is able to stay with us," she told them. "He wasn't too happy to miss out on the roundup, but he does what Paul says. I'll be fine."

At the end of the third day, Colby rode back to get her. "The boss said for me to get you home, so here I am," he told her cheerfully.

He hitched Maisie to the buckboard while Julia put the finishing touches on a cookie sheet of macaroons ready for Elinore's oven. "Just five minutes or until lightly browned," she told Elinore, then hugged her and hurried outside, not wanting to keep Colby waiting, eager to get home.

Colby seemed uneasy, looking around as he drove faster. Puzzled, Julia looked behind and sucked in her breath to see a lone horseman following them. He kept far enough back to be unrecognizable.

"We're being followed," she said.

"I know." He smiled at her. "I'll get you home, Mrs. Otto."

*This is nothing to smile about*, she wanted to snap, but she pressed her lips together, resisting the almost uncontrollable urge to look behind again. "How does he know I was on the Cuddys' ranch?" she asked.

"Beats me. Matt and Charlotte are back now, so you won't be alone."

She nodded, determined not to look around. "And you'll be here to keep us safe," she said, grateful for him.

"You can count on me."

# Twenty

Julia decided not to say anything to Paul about Mr. McAtee's apparent knowledge of her whereabouts. He had enough on his mind, and here were Matt and Charlotte, with eyes only for each other. They had arrived from Gun Barrel with the load of furniture that had been waiting at the depot. Charlotte's delight over the simple furniture touched Julia's heart. And sure enough, her extra rug looked fine in the Malloys' new parlor.

There was enough to do without thinking about Mr. McAtee, so she put him out of her mind, only dragging him out at night, after Paul was asleep and holding her, to wonder why on earth he followed and tormented her. She wanted to wake up Paul so she didn't have to be alone with her thoughts, but she didn't; he looked so tired. *I won't bother him about Mr. McAtee,* she told herself.

Still, she couldn't help the chill she felt when Paul announced over breakfast that they were leaving for the gather in two days.

"I heard through the usual sources—rumor—that Cookie Brown asked specifically for you. I hate to disappoint him, but I will. I've also heard that he's planning to fix any Rocky Mountain oysters a la Julia," he told her.

"Please tell me that's not their name now," she said with a sigh, which made Paul laugh. "I think I'd rather be remembered for warm liver salad than . . . than . . ."

"Little bull pouches?"

She put her head in her hands as everyone laughed.

Julia spent the last day counting supplies in the wagon, trying not to pout and wishing she could come along. Charlotte had baked extra bread for Cookie this time, and Julia made sure there were enough canned peaches and canned tomatoes for her men of the Double Tipi to eat when they were parched.

"Walk with me, Darling."

She looked up from her inventory, pleased. Paul took her arm and walked with her to the river. The water was lower now; he sat her on a sun-warmed boulder and edged himself next to her.

"I want to come with you," she said, not wanting to sound pitiful but not willing to appear stubborn, either. "I just want to be with you."

"Was it tough at the Cuddys?" he asked, his fingers in her hair, just the way she liked it.

"They were so kind to me, and I liked just putting up my feet and knitting, but you weren't there," she said simply. "Please let me come with you."

"Sport, even if you weren't in the family way, I wouldn't want you on this particular roundup. We're pulling in bigger herds and older cattle, and the potential for stampede is greater. It's not safe."

*I'm not safe here*, she thought but didn't say it out loud.

"When I get back with the herd, we'll keep it here a few weeks and then drive the beeves to Cheyenne and the railroad. By then it'll be early November."

"May I come along in November?"

He shook his head. "Nope, and for the same reason." He took her hand and kissed it, resting it on his thigh. "I wish I could take you to Salt Lake City after the Cheyenne drive, but Dr. McKeel would rather you didn't go that far." He kissed her. "Afraid you're stuck with me on the Double Tipi."

"There's no one I'd rather be stuck with," she said and kissed him back.

"Hold that thought," he told her. "In fact, let's not let Charlotte and Matt be the only couple on the Double Tipi with something on their minds tonight."

Julia loved him into a drowsy coma that night as the wind picked up and the curtains fluttered. As her eyes closed finally, she kissed his arm where her head rested and was rewarded with a sleepy pat.

"Keep that rawhide rope around your bedroll," she whispered. "You can't be too careful."

No answer. She smiled into the dark and rested her hand on her belly. If she couldn't sleep, at least their baby would keep her entertained until she could.

The ranch was so quiet after the men rode out. Even Two Bits knew they were gone. He stalked from room to room, meowing and ignoring Julia completely, as though she was responsible for their disappearance. Magnus had followed the men for a while, but late in the endless afternoon, she watched him return, his tail between his legs.

"Looks to me like someone named Mr. Otto told you to head back home in no uncertain language," she said, smoothing his velvet ears. "In English or Shoshone?"

That first quiet after the men left never failed to unnerve her a little, but she had never felt such an urge to hitch Maisie herself, if she had to, and follow them. *You're being foolish*, she scolded herself, even as every part of her mind told her to leave. She went to the side porch, and Colby waved to her from the horse barn. And there was Charlotte in the kitchen, frowning over a cooking book and reminding Julia of herself so much that she smiled.

"Let's make something truly magnificent and gorge ourselves," Julia told Charlotte, who looked as glum as she did. "What do you eat when you're miserable?"

"Those little bits of leftover pie crust with cinnamon and sugar baked on them," Charlotte said promptly. "I snuck a lot of that in Kansas at Haskell when I had to live there."

"We needn't bother with pie filling," Julia said, and Charlotte giggled.

An hour later, they sat at the table, stuffed with pie crust and licking cinnamon and sugar off their fingers. Charlotte looked at the clock. "I should go milk the cow," she said, shaking flecks of sugar off her apron. "It'll be dark soon."

"Take the rest of this pie crust to Kringle and Colby," Julia said. "If I eat any more, I'll be ashamed of myself. But I do feel better. It's a pretty good remedy for misery, Mrs. Malloy."

Charlotte smiled at the sound of her new name. "Nice name, isn't it, Mrs. Otto?"

The house seemed to echo when Charlotte left, carrying the extra pie crust. Chiding herself for being such a ninny, Julia went upstairs, going first, as she always did now, to look at the beautiful crib Mr. Rudiger had made. She went next to her own room, going to Paul's pillow to sniff the bay rum. He told her once that he always put a dab or two on it when he left. She breathed deeply, satisfied.

When she came downstairs again, Julia went into the dining room. The cut glass knife rest on the sideboard never failed to make her smile. She thought about the other perfectly useless wedding presents inside. She put the knife rest in her apron pocket to show Charlotte.

"I'll have to ask Charlotte if she got anything useless," she said out loud. "Where are you, Charlotte? The cow's about dry. There can't be that much milk."

She went to the side porch and stood in the doorway, looking toward the barn. "Charlotte?" she called. Then louder, "Charlotte?"

No answer. That was strange. She looked for Colby, but he was no longer in sight. *That'll make Paul angry, if I tell him*, she thought, willing herself to remain calm. "All right, Colby. You know you're not supposed to tease me like this."

Silence. *Heavenly Father, I'm afraid*, she thought, remembering the strong impressions she had felt earlier to hitch up Maisie and leave. *I ignored them, didn't I? Perfectly good counsel, and I ignored it.*

Unsure of what to do, she went into the kitchen again, edging toward the Queen Atlantic for no reason beyond the fact that it was still hot from baking the pie dough, and she was suddenly chilled.

She could have collapsed with relief when she heard footsteps in Charlotte's old room, forgetting for a moment that Charlotte didn't live there anymore. When she remembered, her hand was already on the doorknob, but it was too late.

She stepped back in terror as the door opened, and Mr. McAtee stood there. He swayed a little, and she smelled liquor.

She took another step back, and he came closer, smiling at her in a way that she found profoundly disturbing. Her heart began to race.

"Why Mrs. Otto, we've never actually met," he said, slurring his words. "Where are you keeping James, you naughty girl? You're so rude to keep him from me."

"I don't know what you're talking about," she said, her voice barely a whisper.

"James. James. James! James!" he demanded, each repetition louder until she covered her ears.

"Really, sir, you should lie down," she quavered, trying to sound reasonable. "There's another woman on this property and a cowboy, not to mention Kringle."

"An Injun and a cripple," he spat out the word. "You take me for a fool?"

She shook her head, wondering wildly how to placate a half-crazy drunk. Her prayer only got as far as *Oh, Father*, so she trusted him to know her needs. She edged toward the side door.

Maybe the stern, schoolmarm approach was best. "Mr. McAtee, I'll have you know Colby Wagner is here, and he can shoot."

He smirked at her. Before he could speak, a shot rang out from the direction of the barn.

"Charlotte!" Julia screamed and tried to reach the door.

McAtee was there first, slamming the door shut with his fist. She stopped, focusing on his face, her eyes on his. His glance wavered, but it was no victory for Julia as he leaned against the door.

"That gunshot will bring Colby," she said. "You really should leave, Mr. McAtee."

That peculiar intensity came into his eyes again, and he smiled, which further unnerved her. "Maybe that gunshot *was* Colby."

"I mean it," she said, forgetting the schoolmarm approach, which was proving monumentally ineffective. Quite possibly someone like McAtee had never prospered in the classroom. "Colby's here to protect me."

He laughed, which made Julia's skin crawl. "You've been duped, you and your oh-so-smart Injun. Colby's my half brother, and I guess that Injun girl was more trouble than she was worth. I told him he could do what he wanted with her, but he's picky about women. Me oh my, Mrs. Paul Injun Otto—the joke's on you!"

Julia felt her face go pale. She sank down into a chair at the table. "What are you saying?" she asked as every miniscule strategy she had cobbled together on short notice fled her mind.

"My half brother!" he crowed, triumphant. "Not

worth much to anyone, but blamed if he ain't loyal."

"Colby helped me at the cow gather. We thought—"

"You thought!" he said bitterly. "Not enough, apparently, you and your half-breed. I told ol' Colby about James and set him to figuring how he could get hired on the Double Tipi to find him. He was tired of working for the skinflint Clyde brothers. And there you were, all helpless. Me oh my, you were a pigeon for the plucking."

Silent, Julia thought back through the spring and summer, and the times McAtee had made his shadowy presence known through the campfire and notes. "Colby knew when we were going to Cheyenne. And when you showed up on the ridge, he rode right up there to investigate. Did you two have a nice chat?" she asked.

"We did, little missy." He chortled. "Kinda made me laugh, all that trouble your Injun's been having with the Association. He's not so proud now."

"No, he isn't," she agreed. *Maybe if I keep him talking,* she thought, then her mind went blank again. What possible good would come from keeping him talking? There was no one around to help. All the stockmen were at the cow gather, with the exception of a few smaller outfits. Allen Cuddy was an hour and a half away, and she knew the Marlowes had gone to the gather. She could keep McAtee talking for days, and it would make no difference in the end.

Funny she should think that last summer's fires were the worst punishment Wyoming could throw at her. She put her hands over her belly, cradling her child. The stakes were so much higher now. If she died, so would her child. She couldn't help the sob that rose in her throat, thinking about Mama and Papa and another horrible telegram. And Paul. *Are you strong enough for that, my love?* she asked herself. *I know I couldn't manage without you. I wouldn't know how to begin. I have to stay alive*, she thought. *No matter what happens to me, I have to stay alive.*

"Ah, Mrs. Otto, I didn't mean to make you cry," McAtee said, his false sympathy obscene to her. "Where's James?"

Julia swallowed, forcing down her terror. "He is far away from here and you'll never find him, Mr. McAtee."

Before she could react, he grabbed her shoulders, which made her cry out with the aggravation to her old injury. He lifted her and shook her like a doll, his face right in hers, then threw her back down in the chair. Her hands went to her belly again, her protection so puny that it made him laugh to watch.

"You don't seem to understand what I can do to you both," he said. "Let's see. A pistol. A knife."

"I do," she gasped, blinking back tears. She kept her voice low, forcing him to listen. "What *you* don't seem to understand is that James is even more terrified of you than you are of him. He will never tell anyone what happened that night, when you burned down his home with his family inside it. I don't think you meant to do anything beyond frightening them away."

*Do I sound reasonable?* she asked herself as he stared at her. "I'm sorry that tragedy is weighing so heavily on your mind, especially when you didn't mean to do it."

She allowed herself an even breath as he sat down at the table, his face a study in confusion. There may have been remorse mingled there too; she couldn't tell. He looked like a man driven beyond compassion by the horror of a fire deep in winter, with people screaming and dying. Julia couldn't imagine where the emotion came from, but she suddenly felt sorry for Mr. McAtee. *He's a beggar too, isn't he, Father?* she thought, as her mind calmed down. *I'm having trouble with it, but you love him.*

She folded her hands in her lap. "James is no threat

to you. Your secret is safe with him. And me too, if you'll just leave this range."

*Please, Father, my husband and I have prayed together for our protection*, she told the Lord. Her mind cleared as she remembered standing with Paul and her parents in the Salt Lake Temple and looking into the mirrors that reflected them through the eternities. Life was tough, dirty, and difficult, but she wanted more hard times on the range; more time with her child, kicking her right now; more time with her husband, whom she loved so much that the knowledge of it stunned her; more time with her parents and brothers, enjoying their gentle companionship.

*If this is all I have, Lord, I thank thee for it*, she prayed, calm now and in control. *More would have been sweet. I'll just have to turn what remains of my life over to thee.* For the second time in as many years, she gave it all away.

They stared at each other.

"I'm not going to kill you," he said finally. "Just ruin you, so the Injun won't want you back."

*You have no idea who you're dealing with*, she thought. "He will always want me, Mr. McAtee," she said quietly. "He's mine forever."

Julia saw uncertainty wavering somewhere in Mr. McAtee's wild eyes. She jumped when a second shot rang out, and he jumped too, then leaped to his feet to look out the window.

*Colby must have found poor Kringle*, Julia thought, rubbing her arms. "Kringle was a good man, even though he didn't say much," she told Mr. McAtee. "Colby didn't need to do that. Kringle is so arthritic he can barely get around."

"Shut up!" McAtee roared at her, and she flinched.

He opened the door to the side porch as a third shot sounded, followed by a high-pitched yelp. Poor Magnus.

McAtee laughed and closed the door again, coming toward her, one hand on his belt, his pistol in the other.

*It's my turn*, she thought. Her throat grew dry and her palms sweaty. There it was again, twice in one life, that moment when all her being centered on giving everything away without complaint. She was silent, her eyes on Mr. McAtee's face, taking some small satisfaction from the fact that he could not meet her gaze. She made no attempt to stop the silent tears that slid down her cheeks.

As she looked so fixedly on Mr. McAtee's face, she noticed the back door open slowly, slowly. *Colby too?* she thought. *Oh, please, no, Father.*

"Get up and move back."

Julia heard it distinctly, but no one had spoken. The words came from somewhere right behind her head, even though she knew no one stood there. *You've ignored a lot of good counsel today, Julia Otto*, she admonished herself. *Pay attention.*

She stood up slowly as the side door continued to open and stepped back toward the dining room door. Her hand brushed against the forgotten knife rest in her pocket. She slowly put her hand in her pocket and wrapped her fingers around it. The door was wide open now, but Mr. McAtee was concentrating on his trouser buttons and trying to hold his gun on her at the same time. She took a deep breath and then another as she recognized John Kaiser in the doorway, his pistol out, motioning to her to move sideways. She moved without question, then spoke clearly.

"Mr. Kaiser, don't kill him. I don't want a dead man in my kitchen."

McAtee quit fumbling at his buttons and stared at her. "You're not a very good actress, Mrs. Injun Otto. Colby's a lot better."

"He certainly is," she agreed. "I'll never be as good as Colby. He fooled us completely." She looked at Mr.

Kaiser again, noting that his pistol was cocked and level. "Just wing him, Mr. Kaiser. He's probably deranged, and I know he's drunk. Let the law deal with him."

Kaiser nodded. He motioned his pistol sideways one more time, and she moved quickly out of range. At the same time, she threw the knife rest—the most useless wedding present anyone moving to Wyoming ever received.

McAtee's shooting arm exploded in blood at the moment the knife rest connected with his forehead. He screamed and collapsed in a heap in her kitchen. The Queen Atlantic broke his fall, but it was still hot from all that pie crust baked in misery. He shrieked again as his one good hand smacked against the hot stove. Julia dropped to her knees. "Oh, Father," was all she said as Mr. Kaiser picked her up. She wrapped her arms around him, safe.

Kaiser held her close. "Are you all right?" He kept her firmly in his embrace until her breathing slowed. "Can you stand?"

She nodded and then struggled to get out of his grasp. "Charlotte! Kringle! Mr. Kaiser, there's another man out there!"

"Steady. Colby had a tall woman—Charlotte?—cornered in the barn. She had her knife out, so he wasn't paying any attention to me," Kaiser said, sitting her down. "I coldcocked him. So satisfying. Took a minute to explain to Charlotte that it'd be better not to kill him. She wasn't convinced, but he might be still alive." He rested his hand on her shoulder and gave her a gentle shake. "Kringle's all right too. He fired that shot at *me*!"

She nodded. "My dog?"

"Winged a bit. Mrs. Otto, you can't kill something that ugly. Charlotte is tending him."

Julia stared at her savior in amazement. "I don't

know why you're here, but I've never been happier to see a friendly face in my entire life."

"I'm not sure why I'm here, either," he said, squatting by McAtee. "He's really bleeding. Should we staunch it, or ignore it?"

"Better try. Here. I have dishcloths." She opened a drawer, taking one deep breath and another until her hand stopped shaking.

He accepted the dishcloths. "Seems a shame to ruin these on such a skunk. Still . . . Help me tug him away from that monster cookstove. He's getting crispy. Smells worse than a branding."

He worked quickly, and none too gently, pressing on McAtee's arm until he moaned. He made a tight bandage of the days-of-the-week dishcloths she had embroidered under protest in Primary and stuck in her hope chest. It took Monday through Thursday to stop the bleeding.

Holding Friday, Julia pressed the cloth against the open wound in McAtee's forehead as he cried out.

"You have quite a throwing arm, Mrs. Otto," Kaiser commented, squatting on his haunches as he watched her.

"I have two older brothers who forced me to play baseball, if I wanted to be part of their world. Hold still, Mr. McAtee." She observed her efforts. "Maybe you could tie him to the Queen Atlantic . . . my stove."

Kaiser went outside to find a rope as Charlotte ran in. The women hugged each other, crying. "Charlotte, what happened?" Julia asked.

"I was milking the cow, and Colby put a gun at my waist." Her face darkened. "I'm glad I gave the rest of that pie crust to Kringle! Mrs. Otto, Colby's the one who's been telling—"

"I know. And to think Paul and I trusted him."

Arm in arm, after another long look at Mr. McAtee, still unconsciousness, Charlotte and Julia went to the barn, where Two Bits sat on a rafter, hissing at Mr. Kaiser.

"I tried to tend to your ugly dog, but your ugly cat had other ideas." Kaiser grinned at Julia. "Don't you have anything pretty on this place besides yourself, Mrs. Otto?"

"Mr. Kaiser, I like my ugly pets! Charlotte, do you think Two Bits is *defending* Magnus?"

"I wouldn't be surprised." Charlotte dipped some milk in a dish to tempt Two Bits from the rafter. The cat jumped down, hissed at Kaiser again for good measure, and walked away, ignoring him. He curled up next to Magnus, who was too groggy to object. Charlotte shook her head in amazement. "I'm going to check on Kringle," she said.

As Julia and Kaiser watched, Colby opened his eyes and looked around. He tried to move, and Kaiser stepped on his wrist. He gave him a push until Colby was face-down in the straw. Yanking Colby's arms behind his back, Kaiser trussed his hands to his feet as neatly as he would incapacitate a calf objecting to a branding iron.

He rolled Colby onto his side. "You're an ugly customer," Kaiser commented, all the while keeping his tone conversational. He put his hand on Colby's bloody hair. "I cracked you good. Still seeing double?"

Colby glared at him, then threw up in the straw. Kaiser watched him in disgust, then yanked him away from the mess. "What do you want me to do with this one?" he asked Julia, who was perched on an overturned bucket.

"Let him go," she said.

Kaiser stared at her. "After what he did? Pardon me, but I won't."

"Yes, you will," she said calmly. "Do you realize what will happen to him when Paul gets here? Mr. Kaiser, he will kill this wretched specimen, and I won't have murder on my husband's hands."

"*I'll* kill him, if that's all that's bothering you," Kaiser said mildly. "No jury's going to care, trust me."

Julia looked at Colby, fully conscious now, his bloodshot eyes filled with terror. "Maybe you have some inkling how I felt in there, Colby, while your . . . your half-brother threatened me and my baby! How dare you leave me defenseless when we trusted you!" She nodded to Kaiser. "Untie him and prop him against that post."

Kaiser did as she asked. "I can keep my gun on him, can't I?" he asked, his voice almost wistful to Julia's amusement. "I mean if he so much as twitches . . ."

"Be my guest," she said, equally affable.

When Colby was propped up none too gently, Julia took a deep breath. "I'm doing this for your own good," she told him. "I can excuse Mr. McAtee. I think he's deranged, and I know he was drunk. But you? *You?* Your ailment is worse—a serious lack of character."

Colby wasn't glaring now. He looked at her and sighed, chewing on the inside of his lip.

Julia didn't raise her voice, but she had never been more emphatic. "My husband trusted you with my life and the life of our unborn baby. He trusted you with *me!*" She didn't try to hide the menace in her voice now, even though it was no louder than before. "I'd hate to be in your boots when he shows up here, because I mean more to him than the Double Tipi."

She glanced at Kaiser, who was looking at her with wide eyes too. "Mr. Kaiser . . ."

"Call . . . call me John," he stammered.

"John? When will Paul get here? Did you send someone ahead?"

He nodded, in control of himself again. "My little brother. We were heading to the cow gather and were close to your place when we heard gunfire. What did you shoot at, Colby?"

"The dog," he replied. "I thought he was going to chew my leg off."

"*Magnus*?" Julia asked, amazed.

"Wagner, you're a lousy shot. I told my brother to ride like the devil for Mr. Otto." Kaiser gave Colby an appraising look. "I'd say you have about another five hours to live, if you don't clear out now." He rubbed his chin. "Of course, there is a full moon, so riding's easier, and Mr. Otto will be angrier and more worried than any man I know. Four hours, maybe less."

Colby began to sob, his tears mingling with the blood and vomit on his shirt. "I told Mac it wasn't a good idea, but he was past listening. Mac's insane, isn't he?"

Julia nodded. "That's why I can forgive him. But not you, Colby!" she continued, her voice passionate now. "Not you! Not where my husband and child are involved. If I were you, I'd get on my horse and ride. I wouldn't stop at the border, either. You might be safe if you get far enough north in Montana, or maybe North Dakota, but there's no guarantee."

She looked away in disgust as Colby wet himself.

Kaiser's eyes bored into the desperate man's face. "My brothers and I live on the Colorado and Nebraska plains. Best you not show your face in those states at all. Just sayin' . . ."

Kaiser looked at Julia then, and she saw the hesitation in his eyes.

"There's more, isn't there?" she asked quietly. "Tell me, John. I have to know."

"I think there is. Not sure, but I have my suspicions." Kaiser glanced at Colby. "Let him tell you, if there is."

"Colby, you'd better spill it all, or I'll tell Mr. Kaiser to keep you here until Paul returns."

Colby stared down at the ruin of his clothes, not able to look at her. "Malcolm Clyde put Mac and me up to it." He sobbed and his nose ran. "What you saw me do—coming to your rescue like some *hero*"—he spit out the word—"some hero at the roundup, was a big show, even more than Mac probably told you. Clyde wants to ruin your husband." He sighed. "With Mac, Clyde knew he was working on a sick mind, and I guess I'm stupid enough."

Julia could hardly breathe. She put out her hand blindly for John, and he held it firmly in his grasp.

Colby looked at her, then glanced quickly away. "I don't know why Clyde has it in for your husband. Mr. Otto seems a fair man to me. Maybe they have some long-standing feud."

"They do," she said, remembering how the Clydes had bullied her husband after his father died. She stared at Colby. "But how . . . you must be wrong. How could Malcolm Clyde know about James or the fire or . . . anything?"

"I think I can answer that one, Julia," John said, his eyes troubled now. "I remember. It was three or four years ago at our poker-playing confabulation in Denver. Paul told everyone, Malcolm included, about the boy that had just wandered onto the Double Tipi. McAtee wasn't there, of course: he's small potatoes." He looked at Colby. "Did Clyde know about the fire McAtee set, and the dead people?"

Colby nodded. "Those other three ranchers couldn't help blabbing over their whisky, and word got to Malcolm Clyde. He put two and two together. He figured out how to work on Mac's delusions, and paid him a visit. I guess Clyde couldn't resist an opportunity to do Mr. Otto some harm." There was disgust in his voice. "Trust Clyde to get someone else to do his dirty work and come off smelling sweet."

"But that was four years ago," Julia said. "And it's

been twenty years since the Clydes tried to drive out my husband!"

"He's a patient man, Mrs. Otto," Colby muttered. He sighed. "And he never forgets a grudge."

Julia was silent a long moment. *I am so naïve*, she told herself. *I can't imagine that much hatred.* She looked at John Kaiser. "This is a hard country," she said. He nodded, and she saw the weariness in his eyes, familiar because it used to be Paul's expression.

She returned her attention to Colby. "What were you and Mr. McAtee supposed to get out of this? Money? Land?"

"Money. The Clydes don't give away land."

Julia felt growing sympathy as she looked at Colby's bowed head, sympathy she knew she couldn't show. "Did it never occur to you that it's wrong to ruin people who have done you no harm?"

Colby had no answer for her; she didn't expect one. Cold, she instinctively moved closer to John Kaiser. She waited another long moment before she spoke, thinking through what must not happen, not ever.

"John, Paul must not know of this. He'll kill Malcolm. Colby too."

"They'll deserve it. No jury would think otherwise, Julia."

"Doesn't matter. Paul will kill Malcolm," Julia repeated, her voice stronger now. "I know it. John, you have no idea of the depths of my husband's love for me." She blushed to say it, but he had to know how serious this was. "It goes far beyond death." She grabbed John's shirt. "Paul can't ever know of this conversation. He can't ever know that Malcolm Clyde engineered this! He can't have murder on his hands."

John looked at her for a long moment. "I have some idea just how much a man can love a woman, Julia," he told her finally, his voice far quieter than hers. "My word of honor, Paul will never know of Malcolm's part. If I have to kill Colby to stop any possible chance, I will! Say the word."

The two of them were silent, measuring each other, as Colby sobbed.

"I think he should leave now," Julia said gently, releasing her grip on Kaiser. "Promise me, Colby, if there is any honor in your worthless hide, not a word to anyone of Malcolm's involvement. Never! Go now."

"You really mean it?" Colby asked, still unbelieving.

"I really do. The longer you sit there and mess yourself, the greater the probability that Paul will arrive." She looked at Kaiser. "John, did I forget anything?"

"Not a thing." He reached out to touch her hands, balled into fists. "Calm down, little missus. You're about as ferocious as your man. Are you completely sure about this? Clyde is still capable of mischief."

"I know that," she said, her voice soft now. "It may be that I have to leave it in the Lord's hands. Get out, Colby. John, please make sure he leaves."

Kaiser helped her to her feet and fanned her face with his Stetson until she pinked up again. He pointed her toward the front door of her house. "Don't go in the kitchen. Sit on that porch swing and cool off, tiger. I'll take out the trash."

Julia did as he said, closing her eyes in relief when she heard a horse begin to gallop.

Charlotte came from the barn and sat with her a few minutes. "Kringle's sleeping," she said. "He's just irritated now, so you know he's all right." Charlotte pushed the swing with her foot, as Kaiser spent a long time in the kitchen.

The two women listened to their rescuer walking through the hall toward the front door. "I think I'll go home," Charlotte whispered. "You have a real champion there."

"And I am grateful," Julia whispered back. "Good night, my dear."

With a sigh of his own, John sat down beside her and kept up the gentle movement Charlotte had started. "You all right?" he asked finally.

"Yes." She leaned back, and John put his arm across the back of the swing to pillow her head.

"I wouldn't dare do this if Paul were anywhere about," he told her.

She rested her head against his arm. "Thank you, John," she told him simply. "For me. For my baby. For my husband."

They sat there for a long time, then she sat up, wondering what he must be thinking. "Oh, I should never . . ."

"No fears. You needed a good arm, and it happened to be mine." He sat up too and appraised her. "Pardon me, Mrs. Otto, but you look like death on hardtack." He hauled out his timepiece as though it weighed a ton. "It's one o'clock in the morning. Go to bed. I'll stay on the porch and explain things when your man rides in here like all the hounds of . . . Hades are after him."

"No, Mr. Kaiser," Julia said with a shake of her head. "If he sees you before he sees me, he might shoot you." Her voice faltered, and she took several gulping breaths. "He can't think for even one second that I'm not all right! I'll just bed down in the parlor, if you'd be so kind as to get me a blanket from upstairs. I'm not sure I'm equal to the climb right now."

Without a word he did as she said, bringing back the throw from the foot of her bed. She took it with a smile of thanks and went into the parlor. *I'll never sleep*, she thought as her eyes closed. The last thing she remembered was the creak of the porch swing as Mr.

Kaiser continued his watch over her on the other side of the wall.

Julia heard the vibration of horses' hooves through the pillow on the sofa. She threw back the blanket and sat up in one motion, hurrying to the front door as Paul and Doc rode into the yard. She was down the steps before her husband dismounted, holding out her arms to him. He leaped from Chief and gathered her close. She whispered a modified version of what had happened.

Kaiser watched them, his watch out. "You made good time, Paul," he said. "All's well."

The expression on his face inscrutable, Paul tucked her next to him and climbed the steps to the porch. With a long look at Kaiser, he gathered the man in his other arm and stood in silence with them both.

"I will never be out of your debt, John," he said finally.

*Neither will I*, Julia thought.

"I have a first name now?" Kaiser joked, but his voice was strained too. "Actually, you might be out of debt, but it can wait. Let's see what Doc has to say about that lump of . . . carbon on your kitchen floor. Paul, make her stay here."

"I can try," he said. "Your choice, sport."

"I'll stay here."

"He's in bad shape," Paul said a few minutes later as he returned to the porch. He sat down beside her and pulled her close. He kissed her hairline above her ear. "Doc and John are moving him into Charlotte's old room. If McAtee survives the night, Doc's going to take him to the sheriff in Gun Barrel." He peered closer at her. "What on earth did you hit him with?"

She pressed her face into her husband's shirt. "The cut glass knife rest!"

"Wow. I'll clean it up, put it back, and remember

never to have an argument with you in the dining room!" He laughed a little, then sobered. "Julia, when I think what could have happened . . ."

"Don't think about it," she told him, her fingers gentle on his face. "It'll make you crazy if you think about it."

"Excuse my baser instincts, but is there anything to eat? I noticed some pie crust, but I didn't see a pie."

Julia stood up and stretched. "Charlotte and I made pie crust with cinnamon and sugar baked on top."

"Just pie crust?"

"Yep. It's Charlotte's antidote for misery. We were missing our guys." She held out her hand. "Come on, cowboy. I'm pretty sure there's currant cake somewhere, and milk."

Kaiser stood in the doorway to Charlotte's old room, watching Doc with McAtee. At Julia's invitation, he sat down with them, demolishing the currant cake and drinking two glasses of milk before leaning back with a sigh. "Sun's coming up soon," he said. "Mrs. Otto, may I bed down somewhere?"

She smiled at him, happy he had called her Julia when her need was so great but understanding she was Mrs. Otto now. "Of course you may. There are two guest bedrooms upstairs." She felt shy then but had to know. "Mr. Kaiser, tell us. Why were you here in the first place?"

The Colorado rancher looked at Paul. "We had our roundup a week ago. I told my little brother I wanted to look at some of the Clyde brothers' bulls, but I really wanted to talk with you, Paul. I had planned to stop and see if you had left for the roundup yet." He shrugged. "That's why I'm here."

"Talk to me about what?" Paul asked, and Julia heard the wary tone in his voice.

Evidently, Mr. Kaiser did too. "You say you're in my debt."

"I'll never be out of debt to you now."

"You can pay that debt easily. This is the real reason I came this way. I was wondering, will you give me one of those books? You know, the one you Mormons read."

"The Book of Mormon?" Paul asked.

"That's the one." Mr. Kaiser looked down at his empty plate. "You know how quiet it gets in the winter. Something new to read is always welcome in Colorado too. I mean, if it's all right to share it."

"I'll be glad to give you a copy," Paul said, and there was no overlooking the amazement in his voice. "Sport, do we have an extra one?"

"You can have mine, Mr. Kaiser," she told him. "I'll get it for you. It's all marked up. I hope that's all right."

Kaiser nodded his thanks.

"Why, John?" Paul asked simply. "I thought you didn't approve of what I did."

Kaiser stared into the distance, obviously embarrassed. "Yeah, I convinced the others to boot you out of the poker-playing club in Denver, didn't I?"

"That's the way I see it."

He got up and went to the window, standing there with his hands shoved in his back pockets. "Paul, I've been watching you since I had you blackballed. You never backed down an inch, when a lesser man would have. It's hard out here, and you did something so radical it stunned me. Made me angry too, I guess. Don't know why."

He looked at them both. "I watched you two at the spring roundup. You bore that inexcusable nastiness with uncommon grace." He spoke to Paul. "You used to be a proud man, almost insufferably so, if I may say."

"Go ahead; it's true."

"You had the best cattle, the finest range." His gaze lingered on Julia. "And then the prettiest wife." He shook his head. "You still have all those things, but you're some-thing else besides proud now. I'm not sure what it is, but maybe it's because of that book. Will I find out?"

"You might." Paul stood up and went to Kaiser. "I'm still too proud. But now I wake up every morning, know-ing in whom I trust."

"You're sure it's in that book?" Kaiser asked, sounding doubtful.

"It's in that book." Paul held out his hand. "Friends again?"

Kaiser shook it. "Friends."

Julia left a note on the table for Charlotte, and they went to bed, Mr. Kaiser in her best guest room across the hall. "Just hold me, Paul," she whispered when he came to bed. "I'm still shaking."

He obliged her, and she slept, secure in his grip.

When she woke, the house was still quiet, even though the sun was high. Paul sat in his usual spot. He looked at her, hesitant; she knew what he had to say but just couldn't.

"I know you and Mr. Kaiser have to ride out of here this morning," she said, sitting up. "Charlotte and I will be fine. There's nothing to fear now." She chuckled, because he still looked so serious. "After all, I have a knife rest, and I know how to use it. Time to cowboy."

While Doc prepared a pallet in the back of the buck-board for the still-unconscious Mr. McAtee, the three of them went into Paul's office and wrote down their own interpretation of events. Still fearing the Niobrara ranch-ers, they agreed not to mention James's involvement and wrote instead that McAtee had somehow developed an unhealthy obsession with Mrs. Paul Otto. Julia watched John hesitate, but he never said a word about Malcolm Clyde, to her relief. Over her objections, the men included Colby Wagner's part.

"I doubt he'll ever come back," Julia argued. "I think I scared him sufficiently."

"Amen to that," Kaiser said under his breath. "Paul, your little missus has the patented Otto treatment down in spades."

"Good. Still, I'm not leaving any wiggle room for that scoundrel."

After Doc was on his way to Gun Barrel with his patient, the documents for the sheriff, and sandwiches, Julia fixed a massive breakfast that left Mr. Kaiser a little stunned.

"You eat like this every morning?"

"Generally," Paul said, passing him the maple syrup for his flapjacks. "If I didn't work it off during the day, I'd need a block and tackle to get on Chief. Maybe you need a real cook on your place, John."

Julia brought her copy of the Book of Mormon downstairs while the men were in the horse barn. She opened it to her favorite passage in Mosiah 4, running her finger over the beloved words of King Benjamin. " 'O then, how ye ought to impart of the substance that ye have one to another.' "

She closed the book, thinking of the Rudigers last year whom she fed, and who had returned blessings to them both. She thought now of John Kaiser, who had saved her life, or at the very least, her virtue, and probably kept her husband from committing murder. *Read it and believe it, John*, she thought. *This is the substance we can impart.*

She was standing at the sink washing dishes, still thinking about Mosiah, when Paul came into the kitchen. He put his arms around her as she stood there. She leaned against him as he put his hands on her belly, content.

"Some action inside you this morning," he spoke into

her hair. "Feels like somersaults. Not a dull moment on the Double Tipi for you, eh?"

She nodded and put her soapy hands over his.

"I just had the strangest conversation with John," he told her. "He gave me the brother talk."

"*What?*" She turned around to stare at him.

"I kid you not, sport. He told me that I had better behave myself, because he'd be more than happy to look after you if I should either come up short and make you unhappy, or slough off this mortal coil. Julia Otto, you have an admirer on the Colorado plains. Incidentally, he has more land than I do."

She leaned against him, laughing. "My stars, Paul! I'm sticking out to here and my apron's riding high, and I have an *admirer*?"

"Face it. You'll always be the prettiest lady in Wyoming. Best one too. Guess I'll keep watching my back."

He kissed her so long that she wished there was time for a trip upstairs. "Hold that thought," he said in her ear. "I'll be back in nine days. Walk with me, Darling."

She picked up the Book of Mormon and walked her best guy to the horse barn. She handed the book to him, but he shook his head.

"You give it to Kaiser."

He kissed her, mounted Chief, and started up the road, kind and confident enough to give her a moment alone with the man who saved her life. Julia took a deep breath and held out the Book of Mormon to John Kaiser. He took it from her, ruffled the pages the way Paul had done nearly two years ago, then stuffed it in his saddlebag.

She watched him, hesitated, then asked what had been on her mind since last night. "Mr. Kaiser, was it your vote that tipped the balance at the Stock Growers Association meeting?"

Her question seemed to embarrass him, as if she had

found him out in a secret good deed. "Yeah. I'd caused Paul enough problems." He wouldn't look at her. "I did it for both of you."

"Then I thank you for both of us."

Julia held out her hand to him, and he held it a long moment. "If you ever need help or something happens to Paul, I'm easy to contact: Kaiser Land and Cattle, Grover, Colorado."

"I'll remember that, Mr. Kaiser," she said, her voice equally serious. "I'll also remember how you kept me from being shamed and kept my child safe." She couldn't help feeling shy then. "And thank you for my husband's life too. You're always welcome on the Double Tipi."

"I know I am." He squeezed her fingers, then let go of her hand. "I'll keep an eye on Paul at the roundup and make sure Malcolm doesn't come near. Word of honor, Julia."

She raised up, and he bent down. She kissed his cheek. "You're a good man." Julia turned and went into the house, not wanting to hear both men ride away.

# Twenty-one

$\mathcal{P}$aul and the men of the Double Tipi were back in nine days, dirty and reeking of sweat, the same old clothes, and wood smoke. "I think I almost like *eau de corral*," Julia whispered in his grimy ear as she hugged her husband. "But what do you know: since that monster herd whipped up miles of dust, we saw you coming. There's already hot water in the tub, cowboy. Use it."

"Keep me company?"

Julia shook her head. "Charlotte and I have dinner to get on the table." She kissed him again. "Maybe if I don't think you're clean enough, there will be an encore later tonight in the river. I'll scrub you myself."

"You're on, sport."

Dinner was a far cry from her pitiful effort more than a year ago, with watercress soup no one ate, the now-infamous warm liver salad, and a roast cowering under an oyster blanket. To the appreciation of Paul's veteran crew, the newcomers he hired for the drive to Cheyenne, and two buyers, they began with oyster soup and crackers, segued to roast turkey moist and crackling in its skin, mashed potatoes so fluffy Kringle had tears in his eyes, and onions in cream, which banished all skepticism. Fruit pudding in sterling sauce sent the home team skidding around third base, with Maraschino cherry ice cream completing the grand slam.

"There has never been a meal like this in the history

of Wyoming," Charlotte whispered to her as she held out an empty bowl for more mashed potatoes.

From the Queen Atlantic, where she whipped the sterling sauce into submission, Julia could see into the dining room. Satisfied, she watched the whole meal unfold before her as Charlotte served. *Mr. Otto's not the only member of this family who is too proud*, she thought. *So is his wife. I suppose every yolk will crack for tomorrow's fried eggs, and I'll deserve it.*

While the crew and guests sat or lay on the front porch, stunned, Paul and Matt helped their ladies with the dishes.

"Was it a good roundup, Paul?" she asked, handing him the last platter.

Paul looked at Matt, and they both shrugged. "I'm hard put to say what it was. Entertaining maybe, Malloy?"

Matt nodded. "At the very least."

Paul draped his damp dishtowel over a kitchen chair. "Cookie fixed your recipe for Rocky Mountain oysters to general acclaim. A fight even broke out over the last three or four oysters. Good thing you weren't there. I haven't heard so much bad language since that cow stepped on my foot last month." He laughed and ducked when she grabbed the towel to swat him. "But here's the good part: Cookie made your sonofagun stew right down to the bay leaf."

"I'm certain that thrilled the Clyde brothers," Julia said drily.

"That's not the half of it," Matt said, jumping into the narrative. "Guess what Cookie did then? He glared at his employers and tossed in a whole handful of bay leaves. He stared at that unwholesome trio and declared, 'I quit, you, uh, sonofaguns. They named this stew after you.' "

"My word!" Julia exclaimed.

"Kaiser hired Cookie on the spot," Paul concluded.

He nudged her. "By the way, he just started Second Nephi, and he told me to tell you howdy."

"Something unfortunate did happen as the roundup ended," Paul told her much later, when she lay with her head pillowed on his chest. "I'll probably have to repent of this, but I didn't feel too sad." His hand just naturally went to her belly. "Hmm, Pete's pretty subdued right now. He's probably wondering, 'What the Sam Hill just happened?'"

"Oh, hush," she said. "I'm amazed that you can still make me blush."

"It's my other special gift," he teased. "Well, we had separated our herds." He stared at the ceiling. "Julia, I doubt we'll see such a roundup again, not with the range changing so fast. Wish my dad . . . he'd have enjoyed it." He took her hand and twined his fingers through hers. "The Clydes had moved out their herd and camped just over a little knoll, away from the rest of us. I don't know what caused it—it never takes more than a sneeze or striking a match sometimes—but their whole herd stampeded."

"I hope I never see that!" she said with a shudder.

"I'll see that you don't, my love. Malcolm got caught in it and was trampled. They could hardly find enough of him to bury."

Julia digested what he had said, thinking of Malcolm's cruelty to Elinore and his own nastiness at the cow gather, when he humiliated them both over Mattie Daw and Jennie Rogers, and his scheming with Mr. McAtee and Colby Wagner. "Poor man," she said.

"You're kinder than he deserved. Here's the really rough part: Angus and Laird decided to bury him right there." He shrugged. "Good a place as any, when there's not much to bury, I suppose—Scottish economy. Outside of a few stockmen, no one bothered to come."

"You were there," she said quietly. "I know you were."

"I was." He raised her hand and kissed her fingers. "Angus even asked me to pray. Not to be too mean, here, but it kinda taxed me." He yawned. "You wore me out, wife. Let a husband get some sleep now?"

"In a minute, Romeo," she said. "Did any of the other herds stampede?"

"Not one. My Double Tipi critters were as well-behaved as debutantes at a finishing school. It gave me pause to wonder how the Lord works, sometimes. Maybe He really does fight our battles."

"I know He protects us," she told him, thinking of John Kaiser and wondering about that stampede. "Maybe in ways we never would have imagined."

"I forgot to tell you—there is one thing more," he told her when he woke up an hour later. "What with the Clydes still hunting strays from that stampede, the Association moved my railroad schedule back into its original slot. We head out in two days for Cheyenne. That's probably a five thousand dollar difference." He held up her ring hand. "Your ruby is safe for another year."

Julia and Charlotte waved good-bye to their men two days later, as they trailed the Double Tipi's largest herd south to the railroad. Without a word, but obviously mutual consent, Charlotte made a batch of pie crust, experimenting with a pinch of mace this time. Butter cream frosting was Julia's brilliant stroke. "You know, we could make this for our best guys," she said , dipping the last of the crust into the last of the frosting. "Miss Farmer would be horrified at how I have slid, but Jee-rusalem Crickets, this is good!"

Eight days later, their best guys returned with a hand-ful of mail, more comfortable dresses from Mama, and a glum Doc.

"He got a letter from his former wife," Paul whispered to her as she watched Doc standing at the horse corral, arms on the top rail, staring at the horses. "After all this time, she's still thinking about it, and he's pretty much fed up."

"She could still say yes, once she stops being coy," Julia whispered back.

"She could." He returned to the kitchen table and pulled out a large envelope. "Speaking of coy, it appears that my poker-playing buddies think all is forgiven." He held it out to her. "Go ahead. It won't bite too bad."

"*I* might," she grumbled. "Your *buddies* are despicable." She pulled out an elegant, embossed invitation. "What on earth . . ."

"That's one of the rules. You're supposed to emboss the earthiest words on the classiest invitation. I wouldn't sully your eyes with it, except that since March 17, you're considerably wiser in the ways of men, and you're game."

"At least I'm not gamey," she retorted. "The bath awaits you." She read the invitation, her cheeks rosy and toasty warm. "Good heavens: 'Post-game entertainment at the House of Mirrors. Bring your own . . .' Goodness." She looked around. "Is that another word for . . . ?" She whispered in his ear.

He nodded. "The boys are scrupulous about not reproducing with ladies of the night."

She laughed and pointed to the RSVP. "Well, cowboy?"

"I already sent a polite reply, via telegram. Told this year's major domo that I had better things to do."

"Do you think Mr. Kaiser will go?"

"I asked him when I saw him in church yesterday. He just laughed."

Julia gasped. "He was in *church*?"

"Yep. He has a better voice than I do. I even think he

can read music." He draped both arms on her shoulders. "I don't know what will happen there, but we must be doing something right."

Julia grabbed him around the waist and hugged him. "We're doing a lot of things right."

He held her as close as he could, considering.

She had been dreading a winter like last year's, but snow didn't fall until early December, covering up ranch ugliness. She spent a lot of time in Paul's office, warm and comfortable, rocking and knitting as he worked on ranch books or sometimes just watched her.

"Surely you've memorized my face by now," she said once, when she caught him at it.

"I know one of your chief delights is watching people eat. Mine happens to be watching you. You're just so pretty."

Julia gave up arguing with him about that. Obviously when she looked in the mirror and saw herself rounder of cheek now and definitely bigger of belly, he saw something else. She didn't even consider her scars anymore: ancient history. She still felt shy when they went to church and there were all those people, but he reminded her they were living in a modern world now, and anticipating ladies weren't supposed to hide.

"Times are changing everywhere, Julia, not just in ranching."

They didn't change for some. The worst day that winter came just before Christmas, when Charlie McLemore, more serious than she had ever seen him, spent an hour closeted in Paul's office. She knew Charlie liked Boston cookies, so she made a batch and brought them in when Paul, his face serious too, asked her to join the meeting.

"Julia, Charlie's come to end our agreement early," he told her.

"Charlie, I'm sorry," she said sincerely.

He nodded, the pain sharp in his eyes. "I'm in a hole too deep to climb out of." He took a handful of cookies. "Your husband wants to extend our agreement another year, but he'd be throwing bad money after good." He sighed. "That's why I've made myself scarce this year. It's embarrassing to face ruin and know everyone knows."

*Poor, poor man*, Julia thought. He and his father had ranched here so long, through seasons so difficult that only the strongest survived. And now it was gone. She glanced at Paul, in his inscrutable mode that didn't fool her for a minute. She knew he was hurting too.

"I'm here to offer my land to you first, if you want it," Charlie said, the words pulled from his mouth by pincers.

"I don't need it, McLemore, but I know Cuddy is interested. He'll give you a fair deal."

"He will." Charlie stood up and held out his hand. "Thanks for being square about this, Mr. Otto."

They clasped hands across the desk. "McLemore, you're welcome to ride for my brand now. I have room for you here."

Charlie shook his head. "It'd be too close to home. I think I'll drift a while." He nodded to Julia. "Ma'am."

Paul saw him to the front door and then returned to the office, sitting in his chair with a sigh. He held out his arms for her, and she sat awkwardly on his lap.

"I hate that," he spoke into her hair. "His father kept me alive after Pa died. I wish it could have ended differently, but this is a hard place."

There wasn't anything more to say.

By everyone's agreement, the Sunday before Christmas was Julia's last venture off the Double Tipi. The road through the pass was clear enough, but she couldn't disguise her discomfort, even in a buckboard with such good springs.

"Dr. McKeel is afraid you'll go into early confinement, if we keep making this ride," Paul said before the trip. His words were tentative, but he got no argument from her. She knew it was time to stop.

She thought she might dread that last Sunday, probably the last one until spring came. She looked at James, happy and sitting close to Cora Shumway; Emma Gillespie managing her own brood so capably while Heber presided; John Kaiser paying such earnest attention to the Sunday School lesson, the same as Paul did. The last Sunday was sweet instead, as she looked around and saw friends of like mind, gathered in the pungent, cigar-smelling Odd Fellows Hall, worshiping Heavenly Father in Wyoming. Paul had given the Sunday School an early Christmas gift of a painting of Christ, which replaced Custer behind the portable pulpit. She almost, but not quite, missed Custer.

When the meeting ended, no one left. As she watched, amused and then teary-eyed, ladies brought out baby gifts and there was cake.

"Not as good as yours," Cora apologized, "but no one could figure out how to get you to make a cake for a baby shower without getting suspicious. Julia, we'll be thinking about you and praying for you."

A week before Christmas, Paul and Matt rode to Gun Barrel for supplies, burdened also with thank-you notes and last-minute invitations to a New Year's party on the Double Tipi. "We have the most room now, and I've discovered I do like a party," Paul had said in his office, over-ruling her reluctance to host such a gathering in all her almost-eighth-month glory. "Charlotte can do the heavy work and you can supervise." He grinned at her. "You're giving me quite a look there, sport. Am I still your best guy? Hey now, don't cry!" He stared at the ceiling. "I wish there was a manual for husbands."

"There is, cowboy," she said, not sure if she cried because she was sad, happy, grouchy, or just pregnant. "It's called a marriage license, and you signed it. I just wish we could have gone to Salt Lake, that's all." She tried not to sound wistful, she really did, but it was hard.

"Next year, darling," he told her gently. "Next year."

While Paul and Matt went to Gun Barrel, Doc took Julia walking to find a Christmas tree. In her mind, she was already calling it Exhibit C, picking up where they had left off during her first Christmas on the Double Tipi, where everything went wrong, except James's pleasure in celebrating the holiday a week late.

She mentioned that Christmas to Doc as he held her arm and made sure she was steady on her feet. "I'm not sure I could have managed without your kindness." She stopped as tears welled in her eyes, thinking of Iris. "Doc, does the pain ever go away entirely, when we lose a loved one?" She put her hand to her mouth, ashamed of her whining as she remembered his loss of an only child. "Doc, I'm an idiot. Forgive me."

He kissed her forehead. "No, it doesn't ever go away completely. You know that now too. We all belong to a club no one wants to join."

She let him dry her tears with his handkerchief. "Thank you, Dr. McKeel," she said. "I just wish my parents weren't alone in Salt Lake right now." She looked around and pointed. "That tree."

Doc was doubtful as he circled Exhibit C. "It's a little pathetic from this side."

"That's the one," she insisted, tears forgotten. "We work with what we have on the Double Tipi."

She and Charlotte had been making cookie ornaments since Thanksgiving, keeping them hidden from the hands in that tin marked Lard and left on the side porch to stay cold. "We'll surprise our best guys when they come home," Julia said, stringing cranberry ropes Mama had sent, while Charlotte hung the ornaments. He had grumbled, but Kringle had made tin ornaments. The crude angels and trees gave her pause, as she thought of the lumps of tin that Paul told her he had found in the ruins of his home last summer, Willy Bill's ornaments.

After a moment to consider the matter, she had Kringle punch a hole in one of the lumps. She put a ribbon through it and hung it, too. "That's all it needed," she told Charlotte. "Now we'll just cook a little more and see what it was they were hauling that took the wagon instead of the buckboard."

She should have known, considering that she had married the best man in the world, what he hauled home from the depot. Even after Paul opened the front door, ushered in her parents, and said, "Gotcha, sport," she still couldn't believe her eyes.

"Mama," she said finally, her lips trembling. "Mama, I've been wanting you."

Christmas was peaceful, which made it bliss for Julia, who did nothing more strenuous than put her feet up and let everyone else manage the holiday. The popcorn balls for Santa Claus from her own childhood became an Otto tradition. "I like popcorn balls," Paul had said, and that was enough for Julia.

"You're going to spoil him," Mama said, when she and Julia sat in the kitchen, shaping the balls on Christmas Eve.

"He's already spoiled, Mama," Julia said complacently. "But so am I, so I don't mind."

The only thing she insisted on doing for the holiday feast was the Bûche de Noël, which turned out so breathtaking that Charlotte burst into tears, throwing her apron over her face and sobbing into Matt's shoulder.

"All right, Charlotte, I know all the signs now," Julia said. "Paul says I cry at dominos, and you're crying over French pastry. When?"

Charlotte dried her eyes while Matt beamed at her. "July."

Julia hugged her awkwardly. "Perfect! Mama had her dressmaker put deep hems in my anticipation dresses, so you can wear those when I'm done. We can hand baby clothes back and forth. What's mine is yours."

Mama was right: Christmas in her own home was better. Leaning against Paul while he read the Christmas story in their own parlor, admiring Exhibit C, suited Julia right down to the ground.

They were still sitting in the parlor at midnight, long after the Malloys had returned to their house, the hands were back in the bunkhouse, and Mama and Papa had cried uncle and retired.

"We could go to bed," Paul said finally, his hand fluffing her short hair. He made no move to rise.

"I suppose," Julia agreed, her hand resting on his thigh higher up, now that Mama and Papa were upstairs and sleeping.

They laughed.

"Next year, we'll have toys under the tree and probably diapers drying in the kitchen on a clothesline, which you will string for me," Julia told her best guy. "We probably won't be getting as much sleep, either."

"We don't now," Paul reminded her as he moved her hand a little higher. "And in February, the calves will start coming, and then it's the early work and spring cow gather, and summers riding fence." He kissed her head. "What would the executive officer say if we bought our own haying machine and baler and took on—steady now—a farmer to show us how to cut and bale our own hay?"

"She would think that was smart. Would our own hay be as nutritious as the hay grown by the Sybille Ditch?"

"She's a shrewd executive officer. No, it wouldn't, but a menu of both kinds of hay would serve our bovine partners pretty well. I'll ask 'um."

"Do that." Julia struggled into a sitting position, helped by a firm hand at the small of her back. She went to the Christmas tree and rummaged around.

"Can't you wait?" he asked. "You're too old to be rattling your presents."

"Not mine," she told him, bending down. "Yours. Open it now, Paul, because it's for you and me."

He took the flat box she handed him, a question in his eyes. He shook it.

"There's the whole world in there," she said, sitting down beside him again. "I'm no great shakes at embroidery, but . . . well, open it."

He did and pulled out a framed square of cloth. He held it close to the kerosene lamp, reading the words. He made an inarticulate sound, which made her wink back tears.

"It's a sampler. You can decide where to put it."

"Julia," he whispered. "My goodness. You have a knack. I think I want it right next to the Salt Lake Temple. That work for you, sport?"

She nodded. He put the sampler in her lap and went into the kitchen, where she heard him opening and closing drawers until he found what he wanted. She smiled to hear him whistling "Redeemer of Israel" low, so he wouldn't bother anyone.

In the parlor, he gave her a hand up. "You hold it while I pound the nail."

Two taps and the nail was in. He took the sampler from her and hung it on the wall, leveling it to his satisfaction. "Yep, that's it."

He sat her down on his lap this time. "Holding my whole family," he said.

They stayed there until the moon rose, admiring the sampler with the embroidered TTP brand, the date March 17, 1911, and the words: "We have endured many things, and hope to be able to endure all things."

"Best Christmas ever, sport," Paul told her finally. "I'm awfully happy not to be a desperate rancher anymore."

"You never got your mature cook."

"Yes, I did," he told her. "I did."

# Twenty-two

"Oh, me of little faith," Julia said to her mother in the early afternoon of the New Year's Eve party as they watched a procession of buckboards, wagons, and horses bringing their neighbors from miles around. "I didn't think anyone would come. Mama, I'm so big!"

Trust Mama. "You're just the right size," she said calmly, taking out another bear sign from the hot grease with tongs. "You're about six weeks from confinement and everyone knows it, and no one looks prettier than an expectant mother. Jules, gone are the days when ladies-in-waiting hide in the back room! Go stand by Paul before I paddle you."

"Mama was going to paddle me if I didn't stop hiding in the kitchen," Julia whispered to Paul as they circulated in the parlor, greeting friends.

"Good for her." He leaned close, his lips near her ear. "I wouldn't *dare* paddle you. There aren't enough cold baths in the universe, since all I get is a handshake at night now."

"Paul!"

"You know me," he whispered. "Now let us mingle like experts. Our neighbors came to eat, say howdy to us and each other, and maybe dance a little." He took a deep breath. "And they don't seem to mind that we're Mormons. I wondered if anyone would come."

"I did too," she said. "Guess we're a pair of sillies."

Julia glanced at their little orchestra: a harmonica

courtesy of Max Marlowe, and Allen Cuddy with his guitar were known quantities at many a cow gather. The surprise was the Wheatland farmer Paul had invited who brought along his autoharp. Matt Malloy had a drum he called a bodhran, and Papa embarrassed her only a little bit with his spoons. To her immense gratification, Doc and Elinore were dancing the two-step to "Turkey in the Straw."

The party started at noon with oyster stew, chicken and dumplings, and roast beef sandwiches, followed by cakes, pies, bear sign, rice pudding, and the surprise hit of the afternoon: pie crust cookies dipped in butter cream frosting. Julia watched her friends eat, a smile on her face. *Miss Fannie Farmer, I wish you could see me now*, she thought. *You probably think people bay at the moon in Wyoming, but they just like to eat too.*

The party spilled over into all the rooms on the bottom floor. Upstairs, the Rudiger's crib was put to use by three little ones in a row. Julia admired two older children napping on her bed, their cheeks still red from the cutting wind they had faced to get to the Double Tipi.

She looked out her bedroom window, wondering if there would be a time when her glance wouldn't first go to the ridge. McAtee was held now in the jail in Cheyenne, mainly because there didn't seem to be any place better for him. It hadn't been hard for her to convince Paul to send a little money to the jail each month for his expenses. *Poor, poor man*, she thought. *Why must people be so land greedy?* She wondered if this would always be a hard place, this land she had come to love because it was Paul Otto's home.

The ridge was quite empty. It delighted her to see more adventuresome children attempting a game of horseshoes in the snow, while others rolled a snowman. Someone had brought a sled and was going in search of a slope.

"Happy, sport?"

"You're so quiet," she whispered. "I didn't hear you coming."

"I already know better than to wake up sleeping children," he whispered back.

"Yes, I'm happy. Think how much fun a party will be this summer, with croquet on the lawn, and maybe badminton," she said. "I can make summer slush and all kinds of cookies." She sighed. "I'll have my waist back."

They walked down the stairs together. Paul stopped halfway down. The dancing had swirled out into the hallway now. "This is so far removed from anything that *ever* happened on the Double Tipi before," he told her, wonder in his voice. "Julia Darling Otto, you came to cook, and you changed every single thing about my life except the cows."

She laughed softly. "I like to think they're not cussed at so much!" She winked back tears then. "To think I was on the verge of settling for someone I sort of liked, and then I saw your advertisement. Do you ever just want to pinch yourself?"

"Nah. I just want to pinch you."

The door opened then, and the Shumways came in. Paul was instantly alert. He reached for her hand, but she shook her head. "I'll take a more sedate pace, cowboy. You go ahead."

She stayed where she was, watching Paul hurry down the stairs, and James grab him around the waist. They stood together, hard man and frightened boy who had been through so much, and then the boy dashed out the door and joined the others his age in the snow. "Good for you, James," she whispered. "You're a boy now, too."

"Thanks for coming, Cora," Julia said as she hugged her. "It means a lot."

"You're sure you have room for us?" Cora asked

doubtfully, looking at all the people laughing and talking.

"We do. We started the party early so those who live close by can make it home before dark. We have room." She couldn't help laughing. "You should know. If it hadn't been for the Cheyenne Sunday School, we'd probably be having this party in the tack room!"

She hadn't expected Mr. Kaiser to walk in the door later that afternoon, but there he was, looking around appreciatively, greeting the ranchers he knew, and catching her eye.

He crossed the room to her, and Julia held out her hand. "Mr. Kaiser, you came a long way."

He took her hand. "I like a party. Mrs. Otto, you look like you're blooming."

"I am, sir. Things could have been so different, but because of you, they aren't," she said frankly. "I hope you have a wonderful New Year. Thanks to you, I will."

He just nodded, squeezed her fingers, then released her hand. In another minute he was talking to Paul. She relaxed, watching the two of them together, friends again. Her pleasure turned to surprise as Paul suddenly stared at Kaiser, then stepped back, his mouth open.

Julia held her breath, apprehensive, and then wondering, as Paul put his arms on Kaiser's shoulders. In another moment, he was gesturing to her.

When she reached Paul's orbit, he took her hand and pulled the two of them into the kitchen, the only empty room downstairs.

"What's the matter?" she asked, concerned.

"I think your husband is at a loss for words," Kaiser said. "I asked him to baptize me, and now he looks like a trout tossed up on the bank." He laughed. "And now you do too, Mrs. Otto! I'm serious." And he was, his expression solemn. "You know a person doesn't joke about a thing like that. Not here and not in Colorado." He shook his head. "My brothers think I'm crazy, but I don't think you do."

"No. We don't," Paul said, when he could speak. "I'd be honored. When?"

"I was thinking maybe when the ice is off that nice little area you dammed up, by your cut bank," Kaiser said, with a hint of a smile. "Did you build a font on purpose?"

"Maybe I did," Paul said, wonder still in his voice. He tightened his grip on Julia. "Maybe it's not a scary place anymore, eh, sport?"

"How could it be?" she asked, banishing the last demon completely.

"I'll be back in April then," Kaiser said. He nodded to them both. "Now I'm off to Gun Barrel and the train. Brother Gillespie said I should visit someone in Denver named President Herrick."

Paul laughed. "Tell him howdy from me, will you?"

When Kaiser left, Julia just looked at Paul. He put his arms around her, wordless, until Mama came into the kitchen with an empty platter.

"You two!" she declared. "Out there! Circulate!"

They did as she said. Julia looked around at the noisy room, people chatting, dancing, laughing, eating. She took a deep breath and smelled the pungent aroma of hot cider, the subtle nutmeg of egg nog, just a hint of a distant ocean in the oyster stew: winter flavors.

Almost without even knowing how, she had surrounded herself with tender mercies.

Her parents left in early January. Papa had to get back to Zions Bank, where he had just been named senior vice president. Paul urged her mother to stay until after the baby came, but Mama had said no.

"This is your time with your wife," she told him gently. "From all indications, Dr. McKeel will be fine.

Julia tells me he has a pretty good helper in that nice Elinore."

"You can change your mind," Paul coaxed.

"I know I can, but I won't. You and Julia have everyone here you need. Mostly each other, I think." She touched his face. "Dear, dear Paul. Just make sure I get a prompt telegram, even if you have to ride through a blizzard!"

He saluted, and she laughed.

"I love your parents," he told Julia after he returned from taking them to the train in Gun Barrel. The wind had picked up, and she had started to worry. She had been knitting in his office, getting up every few minutes to look through the swirl of snow for her husband. Julia sighed with relief when she heard his familiar step on the side porch. She listened and was rewarded with "Dear Evalina," so it must have been a good trip.

Still wrapped in his overcoat with his muffler high around his face, he peeled it back and kissed her, then dropped a frozen letter in what remained of her lap. "Better open this one right now. I'm curious, and I was tempted to open it. Who do you know in Nome, Alaska?"

"No one." Puzzled, Julia opened the letter, which had no return address. "You could have read it, Paul. I wouldn't have minded." It was one lined sheet, with laborious printing. She glanced immediately to the signature. "It's from Colby Wagner!"

"No wonder he didn't add a return address," Paul said, looking grim.

"Don't gripe, cowboy," she said her voice soft. "Listen to this: *Mrs. Otto, is Nome, Alaska, far enough? Don't you worry. I won't return. I'm cleaning and packing salmon now. I'm so ashamed. Sincerely, Colby Wagner.*" She looked at her husband. "Is it far enough?"

"Not for me," he said, but he looked less grim. "He

broke the most important trust I could ever have given another man."

"He's a beggar too."

He smiled and fluffed her hair, newly short again because she had prevailed on Mama to give her a good trim before she left. "It's going to take me a while to agree, but I'll try," he assured her. He took the letter she handed to him, read it to himself again, then crumpled it into a ball and lobbed it in his trash basket. "Kaiser said you put the fear of death into Wagner, Mrs. Otto. *Nome!* I guess you did."

He had another piece of news. "Maybe it's just a rumor, but I heard in town that Angus and Laird Clyde are selling out." He let Julia help him off with his overcoat. "I can't say that wouldn't be an answer to prayer. Probably just gossip, though."

That blizzard, the first of the blizzards of 1912, tore into southeast Wyoming and hung on like a tick on a cow's neck. Julia spent a lot of days standing at the office window, watching for the men of the Double Tipi, who rode out in pairs to herd the expectant cows closer to home. More and more, she rested her hands on what Paul was calling her shelf now, talking to the baby within. "Papa's out there, and we'll watch for him until he returns," she said, determined.

Doc made her cry when he told her not to stand so long in one place. This led to a rare scene, when Doc, Matt, Paul's Indian cousins, Kringle even, and both new hands told their boss to stay closer to home himself. "Doctor's orders, Boss," Doc said finally, which ended the argument. "We can nursemaid in your beeves as well as you can, and Julia's distressed. Fire me. I don't care. Fire us all. Julia will hire us back."

Paul had the good sense throw up his hands in

surrender. "You win, Julia. I'll let my sweethearts do the hard riding this year." When his mutinous crew returned to the bunkhouse, he cupped her face gently in his hands. "I didn't mean to scare you. I'm just so used to doing this, no matter the weather. You still love your best guy?"

She held him sideways. "I wonder if there will ever be a time when I feel completely easy to have you out of my sight."

"I feel the same way," he told her.

"You realize we're fueling an unhealthy addiction to chocolate," Julia remarked the next day to Charlotte, as she stirred yet another pot of hot chocolate to perfection on the Queen Atlantic.

"It's no worse than their addiction to bear sign and nutmeg doughnuts," Charlotte said. She beamed at Julia. "Do you think Miss Fannie Farmer would approve of her graduate from Salt Lake City?"

It was food for thought, Julia decided, long after Charlotte had grasped the clothesline strung from the side porch to her own home and disappeared in the swirling snow. Satisfied, she looked around her beautiful kitchen, remembering the mound of dirty clothes, the mice, the bloody calving ropes, and the original Queen Atlantic with the bad foot that had greeted her that September in 1909, when she had stared, horrified, at her workplace.

"Am I actually missing that?" she said out loud, running her hand over the handsome cabinets Karl Rudiger had made. Everywhere she looked was order, from the calendar with a smiling baby representing January 1912, to the sweet potato growing in a mason jar, to the sparkling windows with red and white checked gingham curtains. She breathed deep of the cinnamon-spiced bear sign. Someone was stamping on the porch now, and she knew who it was. *Heavenly Father, I doubt it's legal to feel this happy*, she thought. She never really called them prayers—her running commentary to Heavenly Father—especially since Paul told her that he was certain the Lord Almighty had a special spot in his heart for mothers-to-be.

Paul came into the kitchen, unwinding his muffler, then shaking off his coat outside the door. She knew he would go to the Queen Atlantic first for a look and a sniff, following that with a lopsided embrace and a kiss that always hit the mark.

He sat down so she could serve him bear sign and hot chocolate, even though he had assured her he still possessed the strength to do that himself. She watched him eat, which only made him smile.

"Be extra kind to your doctor," he said, when he finished. "He told me today that he's written a letter to Indiana, telling Nora McKeel he's tired of waiting for her to decide, and the offer is withdrawn."

"Do you think he'll take a good look at Elinore now?"

"No idea. I barely understand my own good luck with one particular lady, let along anyone else's attempts." He held out his cup. "Any more of that?"

"He just said it was time for him to move on," Paul continued, when his cup was full. "I hope he doesn't mean that really."

The February wind blew away most of the snow, except in the deeper drifts, then swirled around and redeposited it. "I wonder if that happens in other states too," Paul asked her as he came away from the window and pulled on his nightshirt. He got in bed, and she went into his arms, resting her belly against his side. "Pa used to say that it never really stopped snowing in the spring, but the wind blew the snow back and forth until it wore out." He patted her. "I wish . . . oh, I do wish my parents were here."

She kissed his cheek, surprised to find it wet. "Hey now, cowboy, I'm supposed to be the one who cries," she told him. "That was my kiss. Here comes my handshake."

He laughed and shook her hand. "*How* long after the baby comes?"

"Doc said six weeks, but he's praying for at least four, Romeo. Good night."

The calves started coming then, beautiful bawling calves from Paul's Denver bulls, the second generation. He and his crew were out day and night, assisting where needed, as cows grunted and gave up their calves to the cold world of the Double Tipi, snow-covered, bleak, and unforgiving in winter.

"Why not breed them later, so it's not so miserable in February?" she asked, when Paul came into the kitchen after another late-night delivery, his eyes tired and his moustache frozen.

"Oh, I don't know," he said. "I could ask why you and I didn't plan this whole thing a little better, ourselves. Maybe the mood was on them."

"That's no answer, Paul," she said with as much dignity as she could muster, considering that he was giving her the edgy look that even now, at her most awkward, excited her.

Two weeks later, another two-day blizzard bowed out. Julia glared at the calendar as her supposed date of confinement came and went. "We could have figured it wrong," she said to Paul and Doc as she finished the breakfast dishes. "Just as well, I suppose. I am desperate to clean the parlor this morning and reorganize the pantry this afternoon."

Doc smiled at her then, the first genuine smile she had seen on his face since he mailed that letter to Indiana. "Boss, best you send Matt for Elinore today. Julia, that's the surest sign I know of that your baby's coming soon."

"Really? I have lots to do then. Stand back, boys."

Matt was gone within the hour. By late afternoon, Elinore, her eyes merry, had unpacked her valise in the best guest room.

"You're pretty cheerful," Julia said as she finished rearranging the spices in the pantry. "Doc says anticipating mothers get a sudden burst of energy right before the big day. That doesn't sound too scientific to me."

"Move over, Julia. I'll help," Elinore told her. "You're going to argue with your doctor now?"

"Heaven knows I've argued with everyone else lately," she said with a sigh. "You're still my friend, I hope."

Elinore hugged her as Paul opened the kitchen door. "Julia, are you getting stir crazy? Put on your coat. Let's go to the cow barn."

She did as he said, embarrassed that she could only button the top three buttons of her coat.

"Waddle with me, Darling?" he teased after he closed the door on the overheated kitchen and they were out in the swirling snow.

She laughed out loud and punched his arm for good measure. "You know I'll waddle anywhere with you!"

He took her hand and led her into the barn where the men had brought as many gravid cows as they could. A grunting cow with an inward expression lay straining on the straw.

"I'll have you sit on one of these remarkable bales of hay, courtesy of my new best friends, the farmers of Wheatland. Comfortable? Or at least as comfortable as you're going to be?"

Paul sat cross-legged by the cow's straining hindquarters. "I was missing you, sport, so far away there in the kitchen. Heavens, Julia, but I love you."

"I've been cross and contrary, and you love me.".

"I do. Plain and simple, you're my girl. Well, here we go."

She watched as a dark-colored sac began to squeeze slowly from the cow's hindquarters. The cow grunted softly and nosed at the hay in front of her. Julia's interest grew as the membrane inched out.

"Does she know what's happening? She seems a bit casual."

"Give her a few more minutes."

More of the sac spilled out. Julia looked closer, awed to see the dark calf inside, head between its front legs. After another grunt from mama, Paul slit the membrane with his fingers. Fluid gushed out as he grabbed the slimy front legs and gave a tug, all that was needed to finish the birth.

Julia wanted to protest when he took a firmer grip on the legs and unceremoniously dragged the calf, already bawling, around to his mother's head and plopped him there. With a moo that sounded almost maternal, the cow began to lick her baby. Julia clapped her hands in delight.

Paul lifted a hind leg for a good look. "Another bull for the herd. Steaks for Chicago, eventually. Here, sport. Take this burlap sack and rub him down. She could use some help."

Julia took the sack as Paul helped her down beside the cow. "Just a good rub. It gets the circulation going."

She rubbed the calf, wrinkling her nose at the earthy odors. Paul had returned to the nether end, where he tugged out the afterbirth and tossed it aside, spreading the straw around with his feet to cover the blood.

She rubbed the calf gently, smiling to herself when the cow's rough tongue tickled her hands. Paul squatted on his haunches and watched them.

"You love these little critters, don't you, husband?" she asked.

"I like husband even better than cowboy," he told her, his voice cheerful. "I do, indeed, maybe until they step on my boots or sh . . . um . . . there's no better word . . . well, do that all over my hands when I'm trying to deprive them of their manly parts. It's our life, Julia."

Julia nodded, grateful. She insisted on staying until the calf figured out how to rise, the rump end going up first, and after several attempts, the front legs rising too. She laughed out loud as he tottered on uncertain legs, falling down a few times, but making his way purposefully to his mama's engorged udder. In a moment, he was tugging on a teat and nursing. To her delight, the cow made a sound remarkably close to a purr, low and deep in her throat.

"One more baby for the Double Tipi," Paul said. He washed his hands in cold water, dried them with another piece of burlap bag, and held out his arm formally. "Your turn now, Julia. Let's go home."

Peter Jedediah Otto joined the Double Tipi cow-punching corporation before the sun was up, two mornings later. A blizzard raged outside as, red-faced and straining, Julia clutched her best guy's hand and delivered a squalling son. What a long night it had been, with Paul going outside a few times to break off an icicle from the house and bring it in for her to chomp on between labor pains. He wiped the sweat from her face and sang all the verses to "Redeemer of Israel" over and over because it calmed her. Without Doc asking, Paul climbed behind her into the bed and held her in his arms as she pushed, and cried, and finally sagged against him in relief as their son was born.

"Darling, you do beat all," he said when Doc plopped their son on her chest, and she reached for the slimy, noisy baby. "Quite a set of lungs." Paul kissed her sweaty head, then gently lowered her to her pillow as he got up and went around to cut the cord.

She protested when Elinore reached for her son to clean him up. Paul kissed Julia's forehead. "He's only across the room. Elinore, can you just move over that table so Julia can see him? That's better."

Doc and Elinore worked quickly and efficiently. Julia watched them, interested now that the pain was gone. *Elinore's a good nurse,* Julia thought. *I wonder what will happen to these two?*

Julia put her arms around Paul's neck when he picked her up from the bed so Elinore could change the sheets. She started to shake when Paul put her back in bed, but Doc had a hot water bottle for her feet.

"That's a common reaction, Julia," he told her. "If you get really cold, you could probably convince Dad here to get in bed and keep you warm. In fact, why not? Elinore, hand over the baby and let's leave these three alone for a while."

Elinore did as Dr. McKeel asked. "He's beautiful, my dear," she whispered as she handed Julia her son. "All red faced and wrinkled like Paul."

With a sigh, Paul got in bed, after the door closed. When she asked, he raised her carefully onto the second pillow, then helped her settle their son in the crook of her arm. Gently he pulled back her nightgown as she pressed her nipple between two fingers and teased Peter's cheek with it. The baby turned toward her and latched on, his small hand flexing on her scar. Julia leaned back and closed her eyes as her son nursed for the first time and a blizzard roared outside.

"We ought to convene the Double Tipi corporation, and officially welcome the newest voting member," she murmured. She glanced at Paul, loving him with a ferocity that startled her. "Are we the luckiest people ever?" she asked.

"Quite possibly. Another tender mercy, sport." Paul

kissed their son's still-damp black hair, then leaned over and kissed her.

In a few minutes, Peter started moving restlessly. "I think he needs a burp," she told his father. "I'm so tired. Put him on your shoulder, Paul."

He took Peter and nestled him against his shoulder, rubbing his back, then nodding at the soft burp. "He's asleep. I'll keep him for a while. Quite a night, eh, partner?"

Julia leaned against his shoulder, listening as her best guy hummed "Dear Evalina." "It's been quite a *year*," she murmured, drowsy now and completely content. "We've been pummeled, but we're still here."

"More storms to come, I imagine," he told her. "You're good for it, sport, and so am I." He looked sideways at their sleeping baby. "You too, Pete?"

The answer was the smallest sigh from the newest member of the corporation, curled into a tidy package on his father's chest. Paul just looked at Julia. He didn't say anything; he didn't need to.

# Selected Recipes

## from *Borrowed Light* and *Enduring Light*

## Sonofagun Stew or
## The Gentleman from Cheyenne

2 lbs. lean beef
Calf heart, liver, sweetbreads (throat, stomach, thymus gland)
Brains
Marrow gut
Salt and pepper
One bay leaf (Julia's version)

Cut the beef, heart, liver, and sweetbreads into one-inch cubes. Slice marrow gut into thin rings. Place in Dutch oven and cover with water. If you're Julia Otto, add one bay leaf, and remove it before serving, of course. Let simmer 2–3 hours. Add salt and pepper. Squish brains into small lumps and add to stew. Simmer another hour.

# Rocky Mountain Oysters
## (calf fries, cowboy caviar)

2 lbs. calf oysters, cut into ½-inch thick ovals
Vinegar water
2 eggs, beaten
1½ cups flour
¼ cup cornmeal
Salt and pepper to taste
Hot oil

After oysters are cut into ovals, soak for two hours in vinegar water. In shallow bowl, combine eggs, flour, cornmeal, salt, and pepper. Drain oysters and dredge thoroughly in flour mixture. Deep fry three minutes or until golden brown (will rise to surface when done). Drain. Serve as is, or with ketchup or hot sauce.

# Bear Sign

1 cup buttermilk
2 eggs, beaten
1 cup sugar
1/3 cup butter, melted
2 Tbsp. baking powder
½ tsp. salt
½ tsp. cinnamon
4 cups flour

In one bowl, mix buttermilk, eggs, sugar, and melted butter. In second bowl, combine baking powder, salt, cinnamon, and flour. Slowly add the dry ingredients to first bowl and stir together. This mixture should be stiff enough to hold spoon upright; if not, mix in more flour. Knead together lightly for a minute, then turn onto floured board. Pinch off dough in egg-sized balls, then roll into little logs about 1-inch high. Deep fry until golden. Drain and coat with sugar and cinnamon mixture or powdered sugar.

*Carla Kelly:* Julia preferred powdered sugar, but Mr. Otto's sweethearts didn't care.

## Cecils with Tomato Sauce

1 cup cold roast beef or rare steak finely chopped
Salt and pepper
Onion juice
Worcestershire sauce
¼ cup flour
2 Tbsp. bread crumbs
1 Tbsp. melted butter
1 egg yolk, slightly beaten

Season beef with salt, pepper, onion juice and Worcestershire sauce; add remaining ingredients, shape after the form of small croquettes, pointed at ends. Roll in flour, egg, and crumbs, fry in deep fat, drain, and serve with Tomato Sauce. If you're on the Double Tipi and cook for cowboys, substitute ketchup.

# Cream of Watercress Soup

2 cups white stock
2 bunches watercress
3 Tbsp. butter
2 Tbsp. flour
½ cup milk
1 egg yolk
Salt and pepper

Finely cut leaves of watercress; cook five minutes in 2 tablespoons butter, add stock, and boil five minutes. Thicken with remaining butter and flour cooked together. Add salt and pepper. Just before serving, add milk and egg yolk, slightly beaten. Serve with slices of French bread, browned in oven.

# White Stock

4 lbs. knuckle of veal
2 quarts boiling water
1 Tbsp. salt
½ tsp. peppercorns
1 onion
2 stalks celery
Blade of mace

Wipe meat, remove from bone, and cut in small pieces. Put meat, bone, water, and remaining ingredients in kettle. Heat gradually to boiling point, skimming frequently. Simmer four or five hours and strain. If scum has been carefully removed and soup is strained through a double thickness of cheese cloth, stock will be quite clear.

# Potato Croquettes

2 cups hot riced or mashed potatoes
2 Tbsp. butter
½ tsp. salt
1/8 tsp. pepper
¼ tsp. celery salt
Few drops onion juice
Yolk 1 egg
1 tsp. finely chopped parsley

Mix ingredients in order given, and beat thoroughly. Shape and dip in crumbs, egg and crumbs again, fry one minute in deep fat and drain on brown paper.

*Carla Kelly:* Miss Farmer does not say what kind of crumbs, but I suggest fine bread crumbs. The egg mentioned would be in addition to the yolk of one egg mentioned in the recipe.

# Potatoes en Surprise

Make Potato Croquette mixture, omitting parsley. Shape in small nests and fill with creamed chicken, shrimp, or peas. Cover nests with Croquette mixture, then roll in form of croquettes. Dip in crumbs, egg, and crumbs again; fry in deep fat, and drain on brown paper.

# Duchess Potatoes

To two cups hot riced potatoes, add two tablespoons butter, ½ teaspoon salt, and yolks of three eggs slightly beaten. Shape, using a pastry bag and tube, in form of baskets, pyramids, crowns, leaves, roses, and so on. Brush with beaten egg diluted with one teaspoon water and brown in a hot oven.

*Carla Kelly:* Most cooks then understood a hot oven to be around 400°. Miss Farmer also does not indicate a specific time, so watch them.

# Warm Liver Salad

    6 rashers of bacon, in ½-inch pieces
    12 oz. chicken livers
    3 slices white bread, cut into ½-inch cubes
    1 Tbsp. garlic, wine, or perry vinegar (vinegar made
with pears)
    3 Tbsp. olive oil
    2 tsp. sugar
    1 head lettuce, torn into bite-sized pieces
    ½ lb. spinach leaves, torn in bite-sized pieces
    1 Tbsp. chives, finely chopped

Fry bacon until crisp. Drain. Fry the chicken livers in bacon fat for about five minutes or until firm and well browned on the outside, but pink in middle. Drain and keep warm. Fry bread cubes in garlic and oil until golden and crisp. Drain and keep warm. Heat bacon fat and add sugar and vinegar. Cook gently until sugar dissolves. Arrange chicken livers and bacon on top of lettuce and spinach. Pour warm dressing on this, top with croutons and chives. Serve immediately.

# String Bean Salad

Marinate two cups cold string beans with French Dressing. Add one teaspoon finely cut chives. Pile in center of salad dish and arrange around base thin slices of radishes, overlapping one another. Garnish top with radish cut to represent a tulip.

# Tomatoes in Aspic

Peel six small, firm tomatoes and remove pulp. Have opening in tops as small as possible. Sprinkle insides with salt, invert, and let stand thirty minutes. Fill with vegetable or chicken salad. Cover tops with mayonnaise to which has been added a small quantity of dissolved gelatin, and garnish with capers and sliced pickles. Place a pan in ice water, cover bottom with aspic jelly mixture, and let stand until jelly is firm. Arrange tomatoes on jelly garnished side down. Add more aspic jelly mixture, let stand until firm, and so continue until all is used. Chill thoroughly, turn onto a serving dish, and garnish around base with parsley.

## Cheese Straws

Roll puff or plain paste ¼-inch thick, sprinkle one-half with grated cheese to which has been added a few grains of salt and cayenne. Fold, press edges firmly together, fold again, pat, and roll out ¼-inch thick. Sprinkle with cheese and proceed as before; repeat twice. Cut in strips 5 inches long and ¼-inch wide. Bake eight minutes in hot oven. Parmesan cheese or equal parts of Parmesan and Edam cheese may be used. Cheese straws are piled log cabin fashion and served with cheese or salad courses.

## Boiled Onions

Put onions in cold water and remove skins while under water. Drain and put in a saucepan, and cover with boiling salted water; boil five minutes, drain, and again cover with boiling salted water. Cook one hour or until soft but not broken. Drain and add a small quantity of milk. Cook five minutes, and season with butter, salt, and pepper.

## Onions in Cream

Prepare and cook as Boiled Onions, changing the water twice during the boiling; drain, and cover with Cream or Thin White Sauce.

# Welsh Rarebit or Rabbit

1 Tbsp. butter
1 tsp. cornstarch
½ cup thin cream
½ lb. mild soft cheese cut in small pieces
¼ tsp. salt
¼ tsp. mustard
Few grains cayenne
Toast

Melt butter, add cornstarch, and stir until well mixed. Then add cream gradually and cook two minutes. Add cheese, and stir until cheese is melted. Season, and serve on bread toasted on one side, rarebit being poured over untoasted side.

# Beefsteak with Oyster Blanket

Wipe a sirloin steak, cut 1½ inches thick, and broil 5 minutes, and then remove to platter. Spread with butter and sprinkle with salt and pepper. Clean one pint oysters, cover steak with same, sprinkle oysters with salt and pepper, and dot with butter. Place on grate in hot oven, and cook until oysters are plump.

*Julia's variation:* Make a Yorkshire pudding, and add oysters as above. Cover finished roast with this blanket and bake an additional twenty minutes in hot oven.

## Snow Cake

¼ cup butter
1 cup sugar
½ cup milk
1 ⅔ cups flour
2½ teaspoons baking powder
2 eggs whites
½ teaspoon vanilla or ¼ teaspoon almond extract

Follow recipe for mixing butter cakes. Bake 45 minutes in a deep, narrow pan.

## Lemon Queens

¼ lb. butter
½ lb. sugar
Grated rind one lemon
⅔ tsp. lemon juice
4 eggs yolks
5 oz. flour
¼ tsp. soda
¼ tsp. salt
½ tsp. baking powder
egg whites of the four eggs

Cream the butter, add sugar gradually, and continue beating. Then add grated rind, lemon juice, and yolks of eggs, beaten until thick and lemon colored. Mix and sift flour, soda, salt, and baking powder; add to first mixture and beat thoroughly. Add whites of eggs, beaten stiff. Bake from twenty to twenty-five minutes in small tins.

# Currant Cake

½ cup butter
1 cup sugar
2 eggs
1 egg yolk
½ cup milk
2 cups flour
3 tsp. baking powder
1 cup currants mixed with 1 Tbsp. flour

Cream the butter, add sugar gradually, and eggs and egg yolk, well beaten. Then add milk, flour mixed and sifted with baking powder, and currants. Bake forty minutes in a buttered and floured cake pan.

# Imperial Cake

½ lb. butter
½ lb. sugar
5 egg yolks
5 egg whites
Grated rind of ½ lemon
2 tsp. lemon juice
½ lb. raisins, seeded and cut in pieces
½ cup walnut meat, broken in pieces
½ lb. flour
¼ tsp. soda

Mix same as pound cake, creaming the butter, adding sugar gradually. Add egg yolks and continue beating. Beat egg whites until they are stiff and dry, then fold those in. Combine flour and soda in a separate bowl and then add gradually to the creamed mixture, along with lemon rind and lemon juice. Add raisins dredged with flour and nuts at the last. Bake in a deep pan 1¼ hours in a slow oven; or if to be used for fancy ornamental cakes, bake 30–35 minutes in a dripping pan.

## Queen Cake

⅔ cup butter
2 cups flour (scant)
¼ tsp. soda
6 egg whites
1¼ cups powdered sugar
1½ tsp. lemon juice

Cream the butter, add flour gradually, mixed and sifted with soda, and then add lemon juice. Beat whites of eggs until stiff; add sugar gradually, and combine the mixtures. Bake fifty minutes in a long shallow pan. Cover with Opera Caramel Frosting.

## Opera Caramel Frosting

1½ cups brown sugar
½ Tbsp. butter
¾ cup thin cream

Boil ingredients together until a ball can be formed when mixture is tried in cold water. It takes about forty minutes for boiling. Beat until of right consistency to spread.

# Ornamental Frosting

2 cups sugar
1 cup water
3 egg whites
¼ tsp. tartaric acid

Boil sugar and water until syrup, when dropped from tip of spoon it forms a long thread. Pour syrup gradually on beaten whites of eggs, beating constantly; then add acid and continue beating. When stiff enough to spread, put on a thin coating over cake. Beat remaining frosting until cold and stiff enough to keep in shape after being forced through a pastry tube. After first coating on cake has hardened, cover with a thicker layer, and crease for cutting. If frosting is too stiff to spread smoothly, thin with a few drops of water. With a pastry bag and variety of tubes, cake may be ornamented as desired.

With the exception of Sonofagun Stew, Bear Sign, and Rocky Mountain Oysters—range classics—these recipes appeared in Fannie Merritt Farmer's 1896 cook book. *The Boston Cooking-School Cook Book* was the first such book to use actual graduated measurements: scientific cooking.

Photo by Marie Bryner-Bowles,
Bryner Photography

*A*newcomer to Cedar Fort, Inc., Carla Kelly is a veteran of the New York and international publishing world. The author of more than thirty novels and novellas for Donald I. Fine Co., Signet, and Harlequin, Carla is the recipient of two Rita Awards (think Oscars for romance writing) from Romance Writers of America and two Spur Awards (think Oscars for western fiction) from Western Writers of America.

Recently, she's been writing Regency romances (think *Pride and Prejudice*) set in the Royal Navy's Channel Fleet during the Napoleonic Wars between England and France. She comes by her love of the ocean from her childhood as a Navy brat.

Carla's history background makes her no stranger to footnote work, either. During her National Park Service days at the Fort Union Trading Post National Historic

Site, Carla edited Friedrich Kurz's fur trade journal. She recently completed a short history of Fort Buford, where Sitting Bull surrendered in 1881.

Following the "dumb luck" principle that has guided their lives, the Kellys recently moved to Wellington, Utah, from North Dakota and couldn't be happier in their new location. In her spare time, Carla volunteers at the Railroad and Mining Museum in Helper, Utah. She likes to visit her five children, who live here and there around the United States. Her favorite place in Utah is Manti, located after a drive on the scenic byway through Huntington Canyon.

And why is she so happy these days? Carla looks forward to writing for an LDS audience now, where she feels most at home.